Surviving
JUSTICE

Surviving
JUSTICE

Philip R. Hirsh

MARINER
PUBLISHING

1 3 5 7 9 10 8 6 4 2

Library of Congress Control Number: 2017960792

Surviving Justice
Philip Hirsh

p. cm.
1. Fiction: Crime
2. Fiction: Thrillers - Crime
3. Fiction: Mystery & Detective - Amateur Sleuth

I. Hirsh, Philip, 1938– II. Title.
ISBN 13: 978-0-9992885-0-4 (softcover : alk. paper)
ISBN 13: 978-0-9992885-2-8 (ebook)

Edited by Judy Rogers
Design and Layout by Karen Bowen

Mariner Publishing
An imprint of
Mariner Media, Inc.
131 West 21st Street
Buena Vista, VA 24416
Tel: 540-264-0021
www.marinermedia.com

Printed in the United States of America

This book is printed on acid-free paper meeting the requirements of the American Standard for Permanence of Paper for Printed Library Materials.

Dedicated to SKW

Chapter 1

SAN QUENTIN INMATES SAY THE only place worse than death row is the prison laundry. It's true that more inmates die in the showers and dining hall, but the laundry's ear-shattering noise, sweltering heat, and mindless repetition can unhinge the toughest convict. Accidents are commonplace, and its many hidden corners are ideal for settling grudges.

Still, it's a distraction from existing in a vacuum devoid of time, hope, and any sense that life may have value. And then there is the generous pay, currently somewhere between eight and thirty-seven cents an hour.

George Laine had been working in the laundry for forty-one of the fifty-two years he had been in San Quentin. He started in 1969, two years after his unexpected transfer from death row, the result of a 1967 California Supreme Court ruling that held that being slowly smothered to death in the prison gas chamber was cruel and unusual punishment. Within six months, he became the laundry's overnight supervisor working the 10:00 p.m. to 7:00 a.m. shift.

"Give me the wrench, Martinez."

"Fuck you, Laine! I'm gunna kill that *pendejo*! If you don't get out of my way, I'll kill you, too!"

"LAINE! Where the hell are you?! There's a wrench missing!"

"Officer Smith is coming, Martinez. You've only got a few seconds to make a good decision. Give me the wrench."

"I can kill you both!"

"Of course you can, Antonio. Now give me the wrench."

First names are rarely used in prison. Hearing it, Martinez hesitated. Laine took advantage of the brief thought flicker to grab the wrench just as the guard rounded the corner.

"What's going on here, Laine?" growled the guard, holding his nightstick cocked at shoulder level.

"Nothing, Mr. Smith. I was just showing Martinez how to get more steam up in Number Nine."

"Bullshit, Laine! Get back out front, Martinez!" the guard said shoving his nightstick back in its holster. Martinez mumbled something and walked away, followed closely by Officer Smith.

"Get out here, Homan," Laine said to the prisoner crouched under the skirt of the enormous washing machine. The man emerged dripping sweat, the combined effect of heat and fear.

"Jesus! That was crazy. Thank you…"

"Shut up, Homan, and listen to me. You've got the same short time as Martinez to get this, so be quiet and listen."

Feeling safer, Homan glanced around the corner, wiped his face on his sleeve, and said, "That fucker coulda killed us both and…"

"Okay, Homan, have it your way." Laine turned and started to walk away. Homan grabbed the older man's arm.

"Hey, man, I'm just trying to thank you."

"Take your hand off my arm, Homan. Never touch another inmate. It's just one more thing you've got to learn about surviving in prison. You may be new, but in here you don't get a second chance. By the way, Martinez *is* going to kill you."

"What the hell did I do to his ass? That fucker got no reason to mess with me—I ain't in no Spic gang, and I done nothin' to him."

"Yes, you did. He was very pissed off, so if you're not in a gang, it means you disrespected him."

"Bullshit, man, I didn't do nothing to that sucker."

"Yes, you did. You looked at him wrong or maybe you didn't get out of his way fast enough. Or you stayed in your seat when he went by. You disrespected him."

"That's fucking crazy, man. I don't get out of nobody's way. And if I do, then I'm just a pussy, nothin' but a pussy. You're too old to understand that shit."

"This is prison, Homan, not the street. The rule here is you don't look at another inmate until you're accepted. If he wants your seat or your dinner, he gets it. You stay clear. Do it long enough and you get accepted, then you can defend your dinner."

"Yeah, and if he wants my asshole, he gets that, too?"

"Yeah, but he doesn't want it. But piss him off enough and he'll send someone who does. You've got to be invisible until you're accepted. But I don't think you'll make it that long."

A whistle sounded over the din.

"Shift change, Homan. Get going."

Homan started to speak, but Laine was already gone. At the gate, guards were cuffing prisoners, necessary because they had to pass another group assembled to start the morning shift. Laine locked the wrench into its position on the tool board and handed the key to Officer Smith who said, "You know you're going to get yourself killed one day, don't you, Laine?"

"Maybe. But do I let these kids get their heads bashed in just so I can have another day of life in San Quentin?" He turned around without waiting for an answer, put his arms behind his back, and listened for the familiar eight clicks that said he could follow the others to the mess hall for breakfast.

After eating, he was returned to his cell, empty because his cellmate was out on kitchen duty. He washed up, read for a while, and fell asleep. Night shift workers got to sleep until two in the afternoon, have lunch, then blow off steam in the modest freedom of the exercise yard. Most used the time to strut, pose, threaten, and fight, all over turf and status within the social fabric of the prison.

For Laine, it was his chance to detach. Over the years, he had learned to let his mind float out of the dusty yard, over the massive prison walls, razor wire, and guard towers, out to the bay where the air is always fresh, moist, and smells of freedom. He could linger there until the yard whistle jerked him back.

The older inmates had their own corner of the yard next to the Mexicans' makeshift handball court, a couple of benches against the wall, but no exercise equipment. Gangs and groups arranged by race dominated the exercise areas. The dominant members of each clique spent most of their yard time doing strengthening exercises, surrounded by a protective phalanx of younger wannabes on guard for attack from rival groups. Having a perfectly chiseled body covered with menacing tattoos was the prison way of maintaining dominance, a visible warning to others who might dare cross an invisible boundary line.

Laine liked to prop himself against the wall and close his eyes, provided the yard was calm and there was no indication of an imminent explosion. The others in the oldsters' group were more wary, largely because they were not as physically able to defend themselves as Laine. He was just under six feet tall, slender edging on thin, strong, his muscles taut from years of hard work in the laundry. His close-cut white hair was the only visible indication of his age. His movements were minimal, and while modestly friendly when approached, he tended to be reserved, even disengaged. He looked more like a retired math teacher than a convicted murderer. But he was quietly alert, agile when he had to be, and generally respected by other inmates. To them, he was not a threat, just another cautious old con finishing out a wasted life, the same fate they saw coming for themselves. In time, he would be moved to the geriatric wing, and no one would ever hear about him again.

Just before one o'clock, the door of his cell banged open. "Hey, Laine, get up or you'll be late."

"Late?" said Laine tossing back the thin blanket. "Late for what?"

"Jesus H. Christ, Laine, you're the only con I ever met who doesn't seem to give a shit about parole. You've got a hearing at one thirty, remember?"

"Oh, yeah, sorry, Mr. Solas. I forgot. I'll get ready." He put on a shirt while Solas put ankle chains on him. He cuffed Laine's hands in front of his body, a slight courtesy afforded some prisoners considered to be a minimal risk. It also allowed the inmate a small degree of dignity at the hearing.

It took nearly twenty minutes to make it through all of the locked doors and safety portals to reach the hearing room in the administration building. Fifteen other inmates were already sitting in the hall, each secured to his seat by a chain anchored to the wall. They sat in silence—talking was not permitted—watched by two guards who paced back and forth, breaking the routine only to escort an inmate in or out of the hearing room. One by one, they went in, made their case, then returned to the hall to sweat it out until being called back to hear the verdict. A short hearing and equally short wait in the hall was usually bad news. Sorry, try again next year.

About one in thirty eligible for parole gets a favorable ruling. Most took the bad news in sullen silence, doing their best to look indifferent, but occasionally an inmate erupted. The guards knew who to watch and quickly subdued the offender. Laine didn't seem to notice or care that even though his was the first hearing on the schedule, one after another went before him. Finally, at four thirty, after all the others had left, he was called into the room.

Inside, two more guards flanked the door watching the proceedings in silence. The room itself was small, its only furnishings a table and five chairs: three chairs behind the table for the parole committee, one with the ever-present lap chain facing the table, and one—the witness chair—at one end of the table. All were bolted to the floor. Late afternoon light from a heavily-screened window high on the wall behind the officials' table was losing out to the blue-green illumination of the ceiling lights.

Laine sat down and waited while the three officials shuffled files and spoke in whispers to each other. The only sound was the hum of a faltering fluorescent light ballast. Finally, the presiding officer started the recorder, cleared her throat, and spoke.

"Good afternoon, Laine. I am Patricia Longrette, Presiding Officer representing the State of California. We met at your last parole hearing. You know Warden Thompson," she said nodding to the man sitting to her left. "And you've also met Mr. Dalton—

several times, I believe—here to represent the Victims of Crime Project."

Dalton appeared to be studying a file and didn't look up.

"Yes, ma'am."

"You know the procedure, Laine: you will have a chance to present your case for parole, we will ask questions, you'll be escorted back to the hall while we discuss your case, then you will be given our recommendation. Our decision is final, there is no appeal, nor will there be any discussion of our decision. Do you have any questions before we begin?"

"Yes, ma'am. I don't see the witness, Mr. Carter. He always attends. Shouldn't we wait for him?"

"Took the words right out of my mouth!" injected Dalton, suddenly animated. "Probably the only sensible thing we'll hear from this man today."

"No, he is not here, Laine," Longrette said, ignoring Dalton's jab. "It's the reason your hearing has been delayed all afternoon. We held off at Mr. Dalton's request. However, the witness has had ample time to show up or contact us. It's getting late, and we are not going to delay…"

"I must object, Mrs. Longrette. Mr. Carter's presence…"

"Please don't interrupt me, Mr. Dalton. And 'objections' are for courtrooms. This is a hearing, and I'm in charge. Mr. Carter was duly notified, he signed the post office notice—you have it in front of you as I have already pointed out several times—and that is the end of it."

Dalton shook his head and mumbled, "We'll see."

"Laine, you were convicted of rape and murder in 1958. You were given a death sentence, your appeals were rejected, and it's only because of a legal fluke that you were not executed. We realize you have spent fifty-two years in prison, but is that really enough punishment for your crime?"

Laine hesitated, then spoke, his tone even, resigned. "I don't think about my punishment in terms of what might be 'enough.' I don't understand how a life can be matched against a certain punishment, then said to be over because one has outlasted the sentence. It can't be over. It's unimaginable to think that having served a sentence—no matter the length—somehow 'pays' for that life."

"But surely you would like to be released from prison, right? So, it follows that you must think you've been punished enough. That takes us back to my original question."

"Quite frankly, beyond wondering at times what life has become on the outside, I have not pictured ever leaving prison. As you said, I'm alive only because of a legal event that had nothing to do with me or my crime. My life is here."

"It's hard to imagine that perspective."

"I'm sure it is. Working in the criminal justice system, you've known thousands of offenders, but even so, it must still be nearly impossible to imagine the mindset of an inmate, especially one who has spent virtually all of his adult life in prison. To you, freedom is a given; you cringe at the thought of giving it up. More to the point, you think that inmates must have the same drive to be free as you do, especially after serving a really long sentence. But savvy inmates know the truth: you never really leave prison, your punishment goes with you. The comforts you imagine to be out there are an illusion. They can never be yours. No, even if it looks like 'enough' has happened, it never really is."

"But what if you are released into the 'illusion,' as you put it, what would you do? Don't you think you could find some way to use whatever time you have left to do some good? Maybe help others who may be struggling with the same demons you have? You seem to have done that on the inside, Laine, why not out there?"

"I have no idea, Mrs. Longrette. You're talking about a world I simply don't know."

"Lovely speech, Laine," said Dalton, clapping his hands in slow, mocking cadence. "But we've heard it before. You really ought to work on a new approach."

"Mr. Dalton! You are out of line. You'll have a chance to voice your opinion when we talk."

Dalton made a dismissive gesture with his hand but remained silent.

"I'm sorry for the interruption, Laine. Please go on."

"I'm finished, Mrs. Longrette."

"Very well. Mr. Dalton, it's your turn."

"I'm not sure why I bother with this, but I'll ask anyway: do you still think about killing Julia Penthoser? Or has that little fact faded from view like your images of ice cream and 3-D movies?"

"I do think about Julia Penthoser, her death, and the horrible pain that I have brought to so many people."

"Terrific. But tell me: why did you do it, Laine? Eh? If Mr. Carter was here, what would you say to him about his sister-in-law's death?"

"I'd say what I've said before: I regret every bit of the pain her death has brought to so many people."

"I should have known better. Platitudes. Nice-sounding but completely empty. I'm done."

"Very well." Turning toward the warden, Longrette asked if he had any questions.

"No," he said.

Laine was escorted out by the two guards. The door closed.

"Well! That certainly wasn't our proudest moment," Longrette said glaring at Dalton. "But since you obviously have a lot to say, I'll let you begin."

"Look, I'm sorry, Mrs. Longrette, but that guy is a stone-cold killer, and fifty-two years haven't put a dent in his armor. Did he say how sorry he was for brutalizing that girl? No! Did he apologize or even acknowledge his guilt? No! He doesn't even try to sound repentant. He just gets all holy about the pain the crime caused everyone else. Even if the victim's brother-in-law *had* been here, he would have said the same tiresome stuff.

"Speaking of Mr. Carter, do you know how frightened he and his family are of this man? Letting him out is unthinkable. Laine is a silver-tongued devil, and he must *never* see the light of day again."

"Warden?"

"Just for the record, Mrs. Longrette, Mr. Carter is the only remaining member of the family we know of. If there are others, they haven't come forward."

"Fair enough, Warden. Your comments?"

"Yes. Mr. Dalton has addressed the nature of the crime, as well as what he sees as Laine's lack of remorse, two of the major issues we are mandated to consider in deciding if parole is appropriate. Though I certainly respect Mr. Dalton's passion for the Victims project, and agree the crime was 'heinous,' other secondary criteria normally supporting the concept of 'heinous' are strangely absent. Laine has no prior criminal history, no juvenile record, no history of mental instability, and no history of violence.

"On the question of remorse, I believe Laine meant everything he just said. I think you can't accept it, Mr. Dalton, because what Laine is talking about goes beyond the drama of self-reproach and promises of repentance we usually see in here. He isn't defensive, nor does he offer himself as a born-again saint; far from it, he has shown his worth in the way he has quietly lived out his sentence. We've all read his file, you know what I'm talking about. He's helped a lot of inmates stay out of trouble, leave, and not come back. He teaches in the school, helps inmates decipher legal documents, and he's worked tirelessly in the laundry for many years. He's been an exceptional inmate. In the entire time he's been incarcerated, he has never had a single disciplinary action, not one."

Dalton pounced. "No, Warden, not 'one,' let's make that *three*. Are you forgetting the fights? How about the two people he put in the hospital some years ago?"

"That was over thirty years ago, and each time the evidence showed he acted in self-defense. He received no disciplinary action. The inmates who attacked him got what they deserved."

"Mr. Dalton!" injected Mrs. Longrette. "You've had your say! Please go on, Warden."

"Thank you. There are just two more quick points I want to make. First, remember the two most important questions we're mandated to answer today: *Would releasing the prisoner pose a threat to society?* And, *Does the prisoner's institutional behavior indicate he can function within the law?*

"Laine is not seeking parole; in fact, releasing him would be more a curse than a favor. Think about it: he's been living here for over a half century, doesn't have any family on the outside, is way too old to find a job, has no money, and no idea about life on the outside.

"Still, that's not a reason to deny him parole. I have voted 'No' at previous hearings, but I've changed my mind. My vote is to grant him parole."

Dalton twisted his face in disbelief, mouthed the word "bullshit," but remained silent.

"Okay, it's my turn," said Longrette. "This is the second time I've met Laine—both of you know him better than I. But I have reviewed everything in his record very carefully. I know about the crime, his time on death row, the circumstances that spared his life, and all the details of his behavior since he was moved to general population. I've seen many younger men with similar crime histories get parole. He's seventy-five years old, a burden on the state, certainly no threat to the community, and I see no reason to keep him in prison any longer. I vote to parole the prisoner."

"Jesus! Mrs. Longrette! This is crazy! You can't let him out!"

"We just did, Mr. Dalton. Call the prisoner back."

Laine was brought back and stood in front of the panel.

"Congratulations, Mr. Laine, you have been granted parole."

Laine said nothing; he simply stood, a look of confusion slowly inching across his face. "I'm sorry? You said…"

"You heard me; you have been granted parole. Please sign and date this acknowledgment on the bottom line. Use this pen."

"But Mr. Carter…"

"The pen, Mr. Laine. Take it. Sign your name and date."

Laine slowly took the pen, and signed, "Laine 325674." While he was signing, Dalton jammed papers into his briefcase and left the room.

"I'm sorry, I don't know the date."

"September 13, 2010."

Warden Thompson came around the table and shook Laine's hand, rattling the cuffs and chain.

"Thank you, Warden."

"You're welcome, and congratulations. I'll walk out with you."

Laine looked completely lost, disconnected, almost unable to move. The warden led him out of the room. The two guards fought back smiles.

"What am I going to do, Warden? I don't understand this."

"You'll have dinner and breakfast in your cell. Tomorrow morning, you'll be moved to Stonebridge House, you know the place. You'll meet their staff and a social worker who will help you start preparing for life outside. It's up to the Division of Parole to decide where you'll live, what's best for you and the community. Now go back to your cell and get your stuff together. I'll come and see you at Stonebridge, okay?"

"But why do I have to go so fast? I need to wrap up my work and say…"

"You know why, Laine. Not everyone in here feels good about guys who get parole. We have to minimize your contact with the other inmates."

Word of Laine's parole had already reached D Block when the guards led him back. Along the way inmates cheered, booed, or simply stared as Laine shuffled by still burdened by his chains. His cellmate, Leroy Fortune, greeted him with a hug but waited for Laine to speak.

"I feel sick, Leroy. This can't be happening to me, can it? I have a reason to be here. I never thought about the outside. Everyone I know is here; I have a job. It doesn't make sense." Laine sank down on the lower bunk and dropped his head into his hands.

"You're right, man, it don't make no sense, but it happened. Who knows why? Don't matter. I know you don't believe it, but just maybe the Lord has other plans for you. You're always saying

11

to get more out of doin' time we gotta accept what we can't change. So, Brother, time you took your own advice."

Laine clenched his eyes shut, shook his head in disbelief, but didn't speak. Leroy waited.

"What am I going to do out there? I don't know anybody anymore. I don't even know where they're sending me. It's crazy."

"Okay, then," said Leroy. "How about what that dude Marcus you're always talking about said: You have power over your mind, not outside events...?"

The words seemed to pull Laine back. He hesitated then said, "...and if you realize this, you will find strength."

"That's it, man. It's like in AA when we say the Serenity Prayer, askin' God to help us with stuff we can't change. Don't matter, it's all the same. We use what we got 'cause, in the end, it's all we got. That's it, right, George? You got take your own medicine, man. You ain't the preacher no more; you're in the congregation. Crack open the hymnal—you got some singin' to do."

Chapter 2

"It's about time you called, Dalton. How did it go?"

"Not so good."

"What do you mean, 'not so good'?"

"Carter didn't show up."

"What!? Didn't you send people to get him?"

"They couldn't find him. We shouldn't have paid him ahead. For sure he went on a bender. He's probably passed out in his cab somewhere."

"Shit! That's the last time we do that. So the rest of it was okay, right? You put it to them, right?"

"Yeah, but both of them turned on me. It was two to one. They paroled him."

"THEY WHAT?! Are you fucking crazy?! They paroled him?! How could you let that happen?! All the freaking money I pay you and this is what I get?"

"Look, Judge, I did my best. But don't worry, he won't make it five minutes on the outside."

"You're damn right he won't make it on the outside, starting with an appeal. Find Carter, get your victim's group to start a lawsuit, and tie this up in court as long as it takes."

"Hey, Judge, you know better than anyone there's no appeal for this. And who knows if we can find Carter? Even if we do find him, what standing would he have to sue, especially if he tells the court we've been writing his letters for him and paying him to go to the hearings? How long do you think that suit would last? "

"Listen to me, Dalton. I don't care what you have to do or what it costs, but you see to it that bastard never gets out of that jail!"

Click.

Chapter 3

LAINE AND LEROY TALKED LONG into the night. Leroy was asleep well before Laine fell into a mumbling slumber. At five thirty, they hugged for the last time before Leroy left for the kitchen. At six thirty, an inmate delivered breakfast in a Styrofoam box. Laine didn't touch it. He sat on his bunk staring at his hands, trying to make sense out of the confusion in his brain. At seven, a guard appeared and handed him a plastic box just big enough for all of his possessions: toiletries, a dictionary, several paperback books, an envelope containing a sealed notebook left from his time on death row, pencils, statement of wages with attached waiver of federal and state taxes, and two tattered photographs. One was a picture of Constance, holding their newborn daughter, Rebecca; the other, his parents standing in front of their 1948 Plymouth Deluxe.

He was cuffed with his hands in front, but leg chains were omitted as a nod to safety because carrying the box was awkward, and it wouldn't do to have a prisoner trip on the way out the door. He was led to the administration building where he was given a document to sign acknowledging that because he was originally admitted to death row, he had no clothing or personal property to recover. From there, he passed through several doors and down the steps to the delivery area where a minimum security bus sat idling. Just before he got on the bus, the escorting guard handed him a folded envelope.

"Listen, Laine, when you leave Stonebridge, they'll give you gate money, two hundred dollars. It won't last five minutes out there. Some of the guys got up a collection. Here's two hundred and twenty bucks—maybe it'll help a little."

"Oh, no, Mr. Solas, I can't take that. It's kind of you, but I don't deserve..."

"You got to take it, Laine. It came twenty here, ten there. No way to give it back. Just take the frigging money. And good luck."

Solas shoved the envelope into Laine's shirt pocket and literally pushed him onto the bus. The door closed, Laine sat down, and the driver removed his cuffs.

"No need for these anymore, buddy."

Laine looked at his hands, spread them apart like a fledgling trying its wings for the first time, but quickly folded them back into his lap.

"But you gotta wear a seat belt. Put it on."

Again, Laine was confused, but seeing the driver belt himself in, he followed suit. The bus moved out, the first time Laine had been in a vehicle since an armored bus delivered him to death row fifty-two years before.

The ride to Stonebridge House was short—only fifteen minutes—but Laine was immediately lost in the images flashing past the windows. Every turn, sign, tree, and billboard was new. Each flew by in a meaningless blur. Cars streaming past the lumbering bus seemed too big for the road. He couldn't put a brand name on any of them. *And why are there so many pickup trucks? This isn't farming country.*

A uniformed DOC guard waved the bus through the chain-link fence gate in front of Stonebridge House. The bus inched up the short crescent driveway, stopping in front of an enormous three-story Victorian house on the edge of a wooded hillside. Except for the surrounding chain fence, it could have been the home of a large and wealthy family, or perhaps an upscale rooming house.

In spite of its name, there was no bridge in evidence and the only stone was a large chunk of granite by the gate in front of a sign reading, "Stonebridge House." A smaller sign just below said, "Department of Corrections. No Entry Without Permission." The stone itself was taller than wide and flat on the front, suggestive of a gravestone.

Accompanied by two guards, Laine and four other prisoners were herded up six wooden steps, across a wide porch, and into the house. The guards wore sneakers, khaki pants, and shirts, not the crisp military uniforms and steel-toed boots Laine was used to. But a badge on the shirt and a small sap poking out of a back pocket made it clear Stonebridge House was still part of the prison.

The front door opened into the library, a large space empty in the middle, surrounded by a roughly circular arrangement of couches and chairs. A dozen large bookcases lined the walls, all stuffed with weathered paperbacks and coverless magazines. Large framed posters filled the gaps between bookcases, each with either a warning or a message, including The Twelve Steps of AA and The Ten Commandments. Opposite the front door, a wide staircase led up to inmates' rooms. Beyond the stairs to the right, Laine could see a cafeteria; beyond that, another porch looking over an empty space, presumably the exercise yard. There was a hallway to the left of the stairs, guarded by a sign on a post reading, "Administration Offices, Do Not Enter."

The group was led into the library and told to sit. Laine put his basket of possessions on the floor and sat down on a couch, momentarily startled by the give in the cushions. The guards stood quietly by the door. No one spoke. After several minutes, two women appeared from the forbidden hallway, announced by the synchronized click of their shoes on the hardwood floor, their pace more march than walk. They wore near-identical dark pantsuits and low-heeled black shoes, their austere clothing a match to their paired look of disapproval.

"Gentlemen! I am Mrs. Lender, Superintendent of Stonebridge House, and this is Mrs. Burton, my assistant. Stonebridge is a transitional place, not a halfway house or dormitory. This will be your home only as long as it takes to issue identity cards and sort out your next step. Those of you who are leaving because you have completed your sentence but are awaiting pickup, or still require travel arrangements, will be here for a shorter time, hopefully only a day or two. Those who received parole will be here until your parole officer notifies us where you go next and arrangements have been made to get you there, a process that can take a week or more. No visitors are allowed, and there are no pay phones or computers. Calls can be made from our office but only to arrange transportation, call your lawyer, or speak to your PO. Because we expect you to maintain good hygiene, we will provide basics like soap and toothpaste. We don't have washing machines here, so take care of laundry just like you've been doing it—in your sink. For those of you who did not recover clothing when you were discharged, we can provide you with the basics when you leave. Don't worry: we won't send you out wearing prison clothing.

"We urge all of you to take advantage of the group meetings we have designed to help start your reintegration into society. Even just a few meetings can prove helpful, so listen and participate. We know you are excited to be going home, but release or parole can be tougher than you might think, so slow down, be smart, and you'll have a better chance of making it on the outside."

She paused, scanned the group, then continued. "Just because you have left San Quentin proper, don't think for a moment that you are free or that there are no rules here. Technically, you are still in prison. Don't try to test us—we have no give. Each of you will receive a package containing information about Stonebridge House, our rules, and a schedule of activities. Attendance is mandatory at all meetings. I urge you to read this material carefully and obey all of the regulations. Failure to adhere to our rules of conduct will get you sent right back to prison, no second chances. Do you understand?"

Everyone mumbled something amounting to "yes" in the real world.

"There are two dormitories for direct release inmates. Parolees have individual rooms as they are usually here longer. Keep your room or bed area tidy, bed made every morning, and no—absolutely NO—visiting other rooms at any time, day or night. You can meet here, in the cafeteria, on the exercise yard, but NEVER in your room, got it?"

Mrs. Lender droned on about the rules, meeting other residents, exercise hours, and lights out, but Laine only heard it in disconnected fragments. It was like being drunk the first time when he was a teenager. The room was spinning; nothing made sense; he felt vaguely nauseated, enveloped in a terrible sense of impending doom.

When the meeting was over, Laine went upstairs, found his room, and sat down on the bed, the first time in a half a century he felt the softness of a mattress more than two inches thick. It all seemed completely unreal, like visiting an alien world. He drifted into the supposition that maybe he had died and this was a transitional place, a temporary hold just before being dropped into the void. The spell was broken when another inmate banged on his door, the call to lunch.

He found his way to the dining room, took a tray, and sat down at a round table with two other inmates, older men he knew fairly well. More to the point, they knew Laine and out of respect didn't try to engage him in conversation.

There were twenty-eight men at Stonebridge, each in a different phase of triage back to various communities, most in California. It was a mixed group of offenders, some released straight out after completing their sentence, some—mostly older men—paroled. Laine was the oldest of the group. The prevailing mood among the younger offenders was one of hyperactive euphoria, translating into a lot of horseplay, bragging, and swagger. In a typical month, several would tempt the system by getting outsiders to sneak cell phones, cigarettes, or alcohol through the exercise yard fence. The ones who got caught were immediately sent to the local jail to be processed for committing a crime on state property.

One of the men Laine knew, Brownie Parker, finally broke the silence. "Really weird, isn't it, Laine?"

"Yeah, I can't figure out what happened, why I'm suddenly here. For the first time since I can remember, I don't know what's next."

"If it helps any, none of us has any real idea. You got family to go to?"

"No, no family."

"Well, knowing you, you'll make it work somehow."

Again the group was silent.

"How about you, Bill?" Brownie asked. "You got a place to go?"

"Yeah, I do. I've got a sister down in Phoenix. She's always said I'll have a place with her and her family when I got out. I wrote to her, but she hasn't had a chance to write back yet, but I'm sure it'll work out."

"You going to call her?" asked Brownie. "That director lady, Mrs. whatever-the-fuck her name is, said you could call from her office to make arrangements, remember? Better call before she throws you out in the street."

"Yeah. Sure. I need to do that. How about you, Brownie?"

"I think my brother may have something. I'm waiting to hear."

After lunch, there was a long meeting run by Lender's assistant, Mrs. Burton, spelling out the grim statistics facing inmates newly released from prison. "Most of you will be back. That's the simple fact of the matter," she said repeatedly.

Laine was beginning to be able to focus better, but even so, the only part of her talk that was the least bit helpful was a promise to help older parolees connect to Social Security to see if they might be eligible for some limited benefits, perhaps a way to get started wherever they ended up.

Next, leadership switched to an outside psychologist, Dr. Alan Something, a bearded man who spoke slowly in a low funereal voice. He used the words "challenge" and "temptation" in every other sentence. No one seemed to be listening. The younger ones squirmed, flashed hand signals, and occasionally yawned loudly to let the others know they weren't giving in to the system.

Laine tried to listen, but nothing seemed to stick. There was talk about resisting drugs, gangs, and the temptations of the street. Talk about jobs programs, AA meetings. Talk about how to handle confrontations with family and people in the community who might be hostile to their return. But nothing about what an empty man who hadn't made a personal choice in half a century might do to survive. *And maybe that's it,* he thought. *Maybe hollow men aren't supposed to survive. Perhaps in some purposeful cosmic twist, this is the death sentence that was supposed to have been carried out long ago.* Maybe the system was getting impatient for its revenge. Letting him drift slowly into a cognitive wasteland in the prison geriatric wing simply wasn't harsh enough. The process needed to be accelerated, with some uncertainty and outright pain thrown in for good measure.

After the meeting, Laine went to the exercise yard, a fenced area as wide as the house and three times as deep. Just outside the fence, a thick hedge about four feet high crowded the perimeter, its leaves pushing through the links, unaware they were going in the wrong direction. Across the back, above the hedge and fence, eucalyptus trees shaded the far end of the yard. Beyond the trees, the woods extended several hundred yards up a hill, ending on the edge of a small canyon.

Laine stood on the porch stunned by the view—leaves, limbs, and grass—all growing, all alive and free. Aside from an occasional glimpse of a few stunted dwarf oaks near the warden's house, the only images of nature inmates knew were long-distance views through wire-laced smoky glass windows in the mess hall at San Quentin.

"Amazing, isn't it, Laine?" said Brownie. "And can you smell those trees?" Not waiting for an answer, he added, "You know, if I die today, just seeing this would make it okay."

Three steps led down into the yard. The two men found a bench against the rear wall of the house, next to the steps. They sat in silence until the next group session was announced.

The first night was not as difficult as Laine had expected. He missed Leroy and their whispered chats after the lights were turned off, but sleep came quickly, dreams tumbled by, and morning light pouring through the window pulled him to his feet. He dressed, cursed himself for forgetting to wash his underwear before going to bed, and stood looking out the window at the eucalyptus trees until breakfast was announced.

The second day was a repeat of the first except there was a new crop of prisoners coming in and an equal number leaving. Laine was summoned to the administration wing to have his picture taken for an official California identity card. His old prison card went into the grinder.

He was next taken to see Mrs. Burton who began by telling him she had heard from DAPO—the Division of Adult Parole Operations—about his post incarceration placement and status.

"What I know at this point is you'll be placed somewhere in San Francisco. Your probation officer is Aella Tomaras, and as soon as she gets all your records and finds a placement for you, she'll let us know, and we'll release you. That's all I know now, so don't ask me anything else."

Laine nodded.

"Okay, let's talk about Social Security. You don't seem to have any other possible source of income, so it's vital you contact them as soon as you get to the city. Got that?" Mrs. Burton didn't pause for an answer. "At your age, to get Social Security benefits, you need to have worked ten years, paid social security taxes, and earned forty credits. I assume you worked before college? Maybe even in college?"

"Both," Laine said in a near whisper.

"Good. That, plus your earnings in the prison laundry over the past forty-one years, will certainly qualify you for at least minimum benefits. When you sign up for your benefits, be sure to include Medicare. If your check isn't enough to cover Medicare, you may qualify for Medicaid. They'll explain all of that to you." She handed Laine a two-page Social Security application, told him to fill it out before his appointment, using the address of his placement once his PO decided where he would be living. She provided another form, this one from the State of California Department of Corrections, Inmate Employment Division.

Sensing the puzzled look on Laine's face could turn into a question, her tone changed from didactic to impatient.

"Same deal, Laine: once you have an address, send this in, and they'll send you any back wages owed, plus a statement for your income tax to show that all withholding taxes have been paid."

End of meeting. Mrs. Burton's Social Security tutorial lasted about one minute.

Laine thanked Mrs. Burton for her help and headed for the exercise yard. In spite of the relatively relaxed atmosphere in Stonebridge House, he approached the yard carefully, an automatic caution learned from being caught in countless explosions erupting from seemingly benign situations. The danger was particularly acute in the exercise yard, the one place where prisoners were relatively free to move around out of the immediate control of guards. The signs were subtle: a prisoner in the wrong place, a group making too much noise—any small signal that something was out of place could mean trouble.

He scanned the yard quickly before walking down the steps. *Something isn't right,* he thought. There was one lone inmate in the corner to his left, two more at the far end of the yard against the fence by the woods, and a group of ten or twelve milling loudly in the middle, partly obscuring the back of the yard. *Why is the group that was seemingly so tight at breakfast suddenly separated? The lone prisoner is clearly watching the door to the cafeteria. Is the group in the middle screening the two in back? Didn't we hear that contraband can find its way in through the fence?*

Time to go.

Laine turned and walked casually back to the library as if he had forgotten something. He slowly browsed the bookshelves looking like anyone in a library searching for a title. But he was also studying the room, listening for signals that would direct his next move.

Suddenly, the two guards materialized rushing through the cafeteria into the yard. More yelling. Then three local police officers burst through the front door; one remained in the library while the other two went straight back to the yard. It happened quickly as if they had done this many times before.

The cop eyed Laine suspiciously, but Laine smiled, kept his back to the wall, and waited as the police and guards returned hauling three inmates, already in cuffs. There was a lot of yelling, but as quickly as it started, the cops and inmates disappeared out the front door into waiting cars.

Laine selected a book and started toward his room.

"Well, Laine, looks like you missed all the fun." The voice belonged to Mrs. Burton.

"Ma'am?"

"The fracas in the yard, Laine. Did you have anything to do with that?"

"I'm not sure what happened, Mrs. Burton, but whatever it was, it didn't concern me."

"Looks like you were headed that way. What changed your mind?"

"Forgot my book, that's all." Laine turned and walked up the stairs, but he could feel Mrs. Burton's eyes on his back.

Chapter 4

"It's about time you called, Dalton! What the hell is going on?"

"Jesus! It's only been two days, Judge. I can't be calling you every five minutes. I know this is important to you, but you need to back off and let this play out."

"Don't tell me what to do, Dalton. And you're damn right this is important to me. You know what that prick did. I don't need this shit storm in my life. Now, what the hell is going on?"

"Nothing so far, but I've got eyes on him. Any mistake at all and he'll be back on the bus. He's only been there for a day, let this play out—he'll slip up. Don't worry. He's not going anywhere; besides, he's assigned to the Bitch."

"What 'Bitch,' Dalton? Don't jerk me around!"

"His PO, Aella Tomaras. I've also arranged for Laine to be put on Restricted Status, meaning he'll stay right here in San Francisco, confined to a small area, probably in Hunter's Point or the Tenderloin with all the other junkies and drifters in her stable. She won't cut him an inch of slack. Relax, let this play out. He'll hang himself without even knowing it."

"Are you crazy?! San Francisco?! In case you forgot, that's where you live and work. Do you want to run into him on the street some evening? Really, Dalton! Do you think he'll forget you're the one who kept him from getting parole for the last six years? Why couldn't you have him sent to some mountain town in the north?"

"Because they don't have Tomaras and all the muscle she has here. She'll feed him to the local cops, and that'll be the end of it. There's no way either one of us will ever see him. I doubt he'll be on the streets a week before he trips up or some wino cracks his skull. I'm not worried."

"Make it happen, Dalton."

Click.

Chapter 5

BILL WAS LATE GETTING TO breakfast the next morning. He sat down at the table and stared at his food without speaking.

"Did you make the call, Bill?" Laine asked.

"Yeah," he mumbled.

"What happened?" asked Brownie.

"Nothing," said Bill. "My sister can't...like...take me right now. Maybe later. She's got a lot going on. Kids and all, you know." He sipped his coffee, then looked up and said, "Truth is, I think her husband doesn't want a con in his house. All these years she said he was good with it, but..."

"Now what?" asked Brownie. "You've got to come up with a plan or one of the ladies will be happy to throw you out in the street."

"I don't care, Brownie. I'll take my two hundred bucks, catch a bus, go as far as I can, then get out and walk."

"You need a plan, Bill," said Laine. "Do you have any other relatives or friends you could call?"

Bill shook his head.

"Okay, you're a veteran, right? Vietnam, right? So tell Mrs. Burton you need a ride to the VA hospital here in San Francisco. Don't look so skeptical; this is something I know about from a lot of guys I've worked with in the school.

"If you can't take the prison bus, call the VA from here; they'll pick you up. Like I said, I know because I've heard back from a lot of guys who have done exactly that. They used to hate Vietnam vets, now they can't do enough for them. And I hear they have volunteers who love to give people rides. When you get there, they'll start the registration process. It takes time—they look up your service records, but once you're in, you can get help at any VA in the country.

"After you get that part going, go to the bus station and get a ticket to Phoenix…"

"Phoenix! Are you crazy?"

"No. Your gate money ought to get you there with a few bucks left over. It's a big city, so there will be plenty of missions and soup kitchens. They're always near the bus terminal, too. Get a Social Security form from Mrs. Burton, fill it out, take it to the Social Security office in Phoenix, check on your status at the VA, and look for work."

"And my sister? Are you saying I should just show up and say, 'Hi, Sis! I'm here! Your convict criminal brother is here. Where are the boys? I'll show 'em how to rob a grocery store.'"

"No, forget your sister for now. That comes later when you're more on your feet."

Brownie agreed; it was a plan.

Right after breakfast, Laine was called in to see Mrs. Burton, only it was the warden who opened the door.

"Warden Thompson!"

"I told you I'd come over to see you, didn't I?"

"Yes, sir, you did. Thank you."

"You're welcome. Look, I can't stay here long, and you don't need to be seen with me, so I'll get straight to the point. I came for two reasons, Laine. First, to give you a warning. There are people out there who seem to be very upset with your parole, people who would be a lot happier if you screw up and get revoked. I don't have any idea why anyone would care about an old con who's done so much hard time, but you'd better watch your step.

"The other thing is this," he said, handing Laine a manila envelope. "I found your death row file and made copies of a few of the documents. Reading it will be hard, and I sure don't want to stir up a lot of bad memories, but I can't shake the idea that what's in here might have something to do with the uproar over your release."

"Why, Warden? Why are you helping me like this?"

"I have my reasons."

"Could I ask what you're thinking?"

"Yeah, well, okay, but I've got to be quick." Thompson hesitated, looked at his watch, the door, the envelope, then at Laine. "Okay. Look, I think I know you pretty well, Laine, probably better than I know most inmates, but I never felt I had a grip on what makes you tick. On one hand, you're a convicted rapist and murderer—the worst of the worst. On the other hand, you're a seemingly benign inmate with a strangely positive effect on other prisoners.

"So, which is it? Are you a decent man in an indecent place, the ultimate con artist, or that rare bird who really changes in prison? I've seen 'em all. I can tell them apart, Laine. Decent people are rare, con men are obvious, but the ones who change over time are tougher to figure out, especially when they claim some sort of divine salvation. For a long time, I couldn't decide where you fit on that spectrum—or if it applied to you at all. Not that it mattered; after all, you weren't going anywhere. When you came up for your first parole hearing six years ago, knowing you didn't stand a chance, I didn't dig very far into your record. But every time you came up after that, I looked a little harder, starting with your time on death row.

"It seemed strange there was really no fight over your execution. You had a really powerful San Francisco lawyer, but his defense looked feeble."

"I was lucky to have any lawyer at all, Warden. Mr. Preston's son, Alfred, and I were both in graduate programs at UC Berkeley. I was in electrical engineering; he was in law school. We were both just starting the second year when it happened. I was totally lost, didn't have any money or any idea where to turn. He arranged for his father to represent me—pro bono. At the time, it seemed like a miracle."

"Miracle or not, when the court brushed off your appeal, he bailed out. And where was the public defender? When outside lawyers quit, they always connect their client to the PD service. From what I see here, the public defender didn't get involved until the last minute. By then you had basically given up. That's very strange, especially for a guy who continued to protest his innocence. Without the PD and a lot of luck, you would have been executed the first time you were scheduled.

"That got me curious, so I tried to dig into your life before the crime and during the trial. It was a long time ago, but there are some newspaper articles on the internet, enough to see that nothing added up.

"You had a wife, a kid, an academic career, no history of anything approaching a violent background. You were always a great student, class president—literally a Boy Scout. Your parents were obviously hardworking middle-class people. Nothing out of line. Absolutely nothing.

"From the time you were arrested, your wife was with you the whole way, as awful as it was."

"That's true, Warden. Why does that stand out? Of course, she was with me."

"So why did her visits stop three months before your execution date? That doesn't happen unless the family decides they don't want to have anything more to do with the inmate. When it does happen, it's always early in the game—never at the end. Most families visit right up to the hours before execution. It's excruciating, but they do it. It may help the condemned, especially those who are resigned to it, but the effect on the family is monstrous. They are *never* comforted. They're devastated. They can barely stagger out of there after the last visit. The inmate dies within hours, but the family relives those hours forever.

"But you and your wife seem to have come to some other kind of understanding, maybe figured out a really out-of-the-box way to deal with your impending death. That really pulled me in, made me dig deeper.

"Before your hearing this time, I went back and read everything in our records again, especially reports from the two assistant wardens who saw you before your first scheduled execution. You'll see what I mean if you can bring yourself to read their notes. That's when I began to understand what went on. I think you and your wife decided that with no real possibility of reprieve or even a delay, somehow it was better to stop visiting *before* those horrible last moments, spare both of you that additional agony. Am I guessing right?"

Laine sat quietly staring at his hands. "Yes, that's right," he said without looking up. "Is that it? Is that why you want me to have the records?"

"No. There's more. There are a couple of documents in there that make no sense. They simply don't fit in with what you and your wife seem to have been thinking and doing. One is a court order issued right before your first execution date."

"Oh, God! The court order!"

"You remember it? Did you see it?"

"I never saw it. Most of that time is foggy, but I sure remember being told about it. About two weeks before the execution, the deputy warden…can't remember his name…"

"Dunn?"

"Yes! Dunn. He came to my cell with his assistant. All the other inmates in our section were sent off to exercise. When they were gone, he sat down on a little stool in front of the cell to tell me about what to expect when I was taken downstairs, what time they would do it—all of the details of killing someone. I remember him starting off saying he hated that part of his job; I believed him, too. He even said I shouldn't eat much ahead of it, and once I was strapped down, to wait until I smelled gas, then hold my breath, count to ten, breathe—and it would be over. Can you believe I still remember that?"

"I can believe it. But what about the court order?"

"Two days later he was back with a document of some sort, told me he didn't really know why, but there was a court order prohibiting further communication with my wife! I wasn't allowed to write to her, or to anyone else who might contact her. He said any mail—going or coming—would be screened for compliance. I was stunned! I couldn't understand it. I remember he said that all prison communications had to go to someone I never heard of, but not to my wife.

"I remember Dunn telling me that maybe it was a way to avoid having my wife receive the death certificate, that maybe it was a well-intended idea that went too far. He didn't know.

"Up to that point, I thought I had been living in the deepest despair a human being could imagine. But when he walked away from my cell that morning, I found another level of pain, like I'd already been executed, but I wasn't allowed to die. I had to keep on dying over and over for two more weeks until they finally let me go.

"There was nothing—absolutely nothing—I could do about it. I had no right to make a phone call, send a letter, or make any contact with anyone. I was cut off, isolated, and utterly alone. I was so agitated I couldn't do anything but pace, trying to get some kind of grip on what was happening. Nothing worked, nothing made sense. I couldn't meditate or do even the simplest exercise without falling apart.

"The next time I saw Dunn was two days before the end. He told me he had some good news, that my public defender had won a stay to allow me time to prepare another appeal. The only thought I had was to let my wife know. He said I couldn't write or call her, but the prison would immediately contact the person on the court order; presumably, my wife would be notified and quite possibly the order would be lifted.

"When July twentieth came and went, I had no idea if she knew I was still alive. There's a lot more—that was only the start of the legal craziness."

"Well, Laine, that's exactly why I want you to have the records. I think there's a whole lot more to this than the records show. I know you'll have trouble remembering this stuff, so I put it all in chronological order—that might help. Some of the documents are so faded they didn't reproduce very well, but most of it's legible. I have no idea how to sort this out, but I feel I owe you the chance to look at it. You can either accept what has been, or maybe—even after all this time—find something in there that helps you."

"Thank you, Warden."

They shook hands, and the warden left through a side door. Laine tucked the envelope into his shirt, returned to the library in the middle of a speech being given by a former inmate on the dangers of pride. He didn't hear a word of it.

Before lunch, he retreated to his room, sat on the bed, and stared at the envelope until the meal-call knock on his door jolted him out of his reverie. He emptied the Stonebridge information folder, pushed the unopened envelope inside, tucked it under his arm, and closed his door. Sometimes the best hiding place is right out in the open. As he turned the key in the lock, he tucked a tiny ball of tissue into the crack between the door and its frame.

The rest of the day was a blur, but he did his best to look calm and pretend interest in what the various speakers had to say. He went from the last meeting to dinner, again trying to seem connected to what conversation there was. Bill was quiet but Brownie took up the slack with talk about his brother, excited to have a plan to get on his feet and stay out of trouble. Laine was glad he didn't have to get into the conversation. As quickly as he could without seeming to be in a hurry, he said he was going up to his room to read.

As he put the key in the lock, he noticed the tiny white speck on the floor.

Again, he sat on his bed holding the unopened envelope. Inside his head, a ragged voice warned that opening it would be a huge mistake, a reversal of all the years of mental discipline he had used to avoid reigniting exiled memories and emotion. *Is it worth it? What difference could it possibly make? Why relive all those horrible days waiting to be killed without the slightest possibility of recovering any fragment of what was lost?*

He picked up the envelope and put it down a dozen times. He washed his underwear and socks. He tried to read, but couldn't concentrate. Finally, he took a deep breath and opened the envelope.

The first document was titled "Intake Assessment," dated December 15, 1958.

Name: George H. Laine
S.Q. Prisoner number: 325674
D.O.B.: 1-18-35
Marital Status/Next of kin: Married,
    Constance Marie (Wilton) Laine
    One child, Rebecca, b. 7-14-58
Social Security Number: 104-77-1243
Attorney of Record: Edward R. Preston, Esq.
    235 Montgomery Street
    San Francisco, CA 94104
Crime: First Degree Rape and First Degree
    Murder
Victim(s): Miss Julia Penthoser, Oakland,
    CA
Prior Convictions: none
Prior arrests: none
Date of Crime: September 6, 1958
Date of Arrest: September 17, 1958
Date of Trial: December 2, 1958
Date of Conviction: December 5, 1958;
    petition for new trial denied at hearing
    December 10, 1958
Date of Sentencing: December 11, 1958
Intake: The prisoner was transported
    by DOC bus to San Quentin Prison on
    Monday, December 15, received at 10:35
    a.m., admitted directly to the Reception
    Center. Prisoner had no personal
    property. Legal papers were removed to
    be searched and returned to the prisoner
    after his placement was completed. He
    was body/cavity searched, showered, and
    his clothing changed to S.Q. prison
    suit. He was interviewed by Mrs. Hazel
    Anderson, given standard written Rules
    of Conduct booklet, photographed,

and sent to the prison hospital for intake physical examination. Following completion of physical, he was transferred back to the Reception Center to be held under Close Observation Status until staff determines it is safe to transfer him to East Block. He is tentatively scheduled to be housed in cell 449.

SPECIAL NOTE: Prisoner is known to be a martial arts expert. Staff is urged to use EXTRA CAUTION when transporting the prisoner.

Physical Examination: George H. Laine 325674 was examined by Rose Zelp, R.N. at 3:45 p.m. on 12-15-1958.

Height: 6'1"

Weight: 142 lbs.

Pulse: 54

Blood pressure: 108/58

Current medications: none

Nutritional status: Nurse noted the prisoner is markedly underweight, appears dehydrated, probably accounting for low pulse and B.P.

Family History: Father died of Myocardial Infarction approximately 8 years ago; mother's health fragile b/o diabetes mellitus, cardiovascular disease (type unknown). Sister said to be healthy.

Immunization History: smallpox vaccination in childhood; usual childhood vaccinations and diseases; unsure of tetanus status; given tetanus booster.

R.O.S.: No specific system issues.

The rest of the physical examination was

Within Normal Limits. Prisoner does
not wear glasses. Appendectomy and
Tonsillectomy both noted. Dental status
unremarkable; no dental prosthesis
in evidence. No birthmarks or tattoos
noted. Appendectomy scar lower right
abdomen.

Mental Status: The prisoner was cooperative
with the evaluation but significantly
distracted. Frequently had to repeat
questions to elicit a response. Answers
appropriate but monosyllabic. Affect was
despondent, tearful at times. Prisoner
was lethargic, sat slumped in chair,
frequently shook his head mumbling
inaudibly while staring at the floor.

Impression: Undernourished, depressed
male prisoner with no specific medical
condition except dehydration with
secondary hypovolemic low pulse and
hypotension. Suggest he be encouraged to
drink fluids, pressed to eat his meals,
and watched closely for any indication
of suicidal thinking or behavior.

Recommendations: The prisoner has
completed the intake process. Because of
indications of depression and possible
suicidal behavior, prisoner will be held
in a safe cell in the Reception Center
under close observation for three days
before transfer to East Block.

> Harold Clemmons
> Supt. Reception Center

Laine put the report back in the envelope, laid back on his
bed, and closed his eyes. Though he had no specific memory

of his first days in San Quentin, he did recall the long early morning bus ride around the San Francisco area collecting prisoners on the one-way trip to San Quentin. Because of his death sentence, Laine was isolated in a cage just behind the driver's seat. The other prisoners were cuffed to their seats by leg chains, but their hands—though still locked together—were released from their waist belt. Laine's chains remained in place making it impossible to find any way to get comfortable or even doze off for more than a few minutes.

Two guards sat across from his cage facing the other prisoners through a wire mesh screen. Talking was allowed, and it didn't take long for taunting to begin. At first, it was loud whispers; things like, "Hey, Chain Boy! I hear the food's great on death row." Then some started coughing and making choking sounds: "How long can you hold your breath?" Finally, the guards told everyone to shut up. He remembered trying to use his tai chi training to block out the noise and discomfort of the bus, focusing instead on images of his wife and Rebecca's happy baby sounds. He was well practiced: when reading and meditation failed to dampen the combination of boredom and nonstop yelling in the city jail, he could often soften it with images of his family.

The only part of the report he really noticed was the warning to staff about his martial arts skill, the second time his training had been misinterpreted. He could never get anyone to accept that tai chi was about self-awareness, not aggression, a way to use relaxation and controlled breathing to maintain energy balance, softening one's muscles to allow the mind do what the body could not.

But the prosecutor had a different interpretation. He hammered the jury with the idea Laine was a trained killing machine, splendidly equipped to make quick work of his helpless victim, then walk away with the pretended innocence of a schoolboy. Every time his lawyer had a chance to highlight his pristine record, the prosecutor counter-punched with the idea his record was meaningless, asking rhetorically, "What possible use does an engineering student have for killer training?" Or,

"Stealth and deception are his trademarks!" And, "Who knows how many crimes has he already gotten away with?" Each time his attorney successfully objected, but the damage was already done—he could see it on the faces in the jury box.

No matter how many character witnesses testified for him, the prosecutor compelled each to acknowledge a lack of knowledge of the dark world of martial arts. Most didn't even know Laine had any such training at all.

At his sentencing, the prosecutor paced in front of the jury box waving Julia Penthoser's panties, reminding jurors that George Laine had coldly hidden his "trophy" in his basement, sealing the case for the death penalty. "Death is the only way to honor Julia Penthoser and protect society from this brutal killer."

Laine rested a while trying to force those words out of his head. *Keep going,* he told himself. *The warden said there could be something helpful. Don't stop now.*

The next four pages were clipped together, each titled "Writ of Execution," followed by several paragraphs of convoluted legal jargon leading up to the final sentence setting an execution date. The date on the first writ was July 20, 1960. The first three were voided at the bottom. The last, dated September 8, 1967, simply said, "Transfer to General Population."

The next several reports were written by Special Operations Assistant Warden, Paul Dunn. Everyone knew that "Special Operations" was the euphemistic title for "Executioner." Inmates and prison personnel alike dodged words like "execution" and "death house." It was a strange dance around the morbid business of killing people.

Laine remembered Dunn as a stern, sparse man who insisted everyone—inmates and guards alike—follow rules and procedures exactly. Food had to be delivered on time, cells kept clean, even library books were offered only at certain times. Privileges like books, exercise time, and the most precious of all—visits—could be lost for even a minor infraction. His system extended to the way guards dressed and related to inmates, always calm, focused, pseudo-polite, and above all: inflexible.

East Block Reception Report
Name: George H. Laine, 325674
December 19, 1958, 7:30 a.m.
Scheduled execution date: July 20, 1960
      The prisoner was transferred from
the Reception Center, accompanied by an
extra R.C. guard as a precaution because
of the prisoner's knowledge of martial
arts. He was taken directly to cell 449
where he was interviewed by the writer
and Chief Security Officer Lloyd James.
The Rules of Conduct were reviewed.
The prisoner offered no resistance and
appeared to understand the rules as
explained. His only question was when he
would be allowed a visit with his wife.
He was told that information is covered
in the written material he had been
provided. The interview was terminated
at 7:52 a.m.
      My impression is that inmate Laine
is in a mentally disrupted state, not
unusual for newly admitted condemned
prisoners. His continued placement
in East Block is contingent on good
behavior. If there is any violation of
the rules or if the staff feels he may
become either suicidal or aggressive, he
will be transferred to North-Seg.
                              Paul Dunn
    Assistant Warden for Special Operations

Six Month Review, East Block
Name: George H. Laine, 325674
June 29, 1959

Scheduled execution date: July 20, 1960
(Unchanged)

The prisoner remains in East Block,
cell 449. His behavior since admission
has been cooperative though his
interaction with staff and other inmates
remains minimal. He spends his time
either reading or doing some sort of
slow-motion exercises; fortunately, none
appear to be of a martial arts variety.
When not reading or exercising, he sits
for long periods of time with his eyes
closed without speaking or appearing
to recite prayers or the like. When
asked about it, Laine said he is simply
removing himself from his cell for a
while.

The prisoner's mother died one month
ago. He took the news calmly, said
she had been in declining health. He
said it was actually a relief to know
she wouldn't have to live through his
execution. His only stated concerns
involve two issues: visits with his wife,
and the expectation an appeal of his
conviction will be successful. Following
the required six-month probation period,
the prisoner was given monthly visiting
privileges. His first visit took place
on 6-22-59 with his wife. The visit
lasted the allowed one hour. No physical
contact was permitted. The visit was
quiet. They spoke in whispers. His wife
showed him family pictures. He was not
allowed to keep any of them at this
point. The prisoner was tearful as he

was returned to his cell. He did not
want to eat, but when reminded that
voluntary starvation is a violation of
the rules, his eating resumed a normal
pattern.

   There have been no health issues;
current weight is 152 lbs.

Six Month Review, East Block
Name: George H. Laine, 325674
12-11-59
Scheduled execution date: July 20, 1960
   (Unchanged)
   There has been little change in
the prisoner's behavior over the last
six months. No rule infractions. The
prisoner continues to isolate from
staff and other inmates, though not in
a hostile manner. No change in legal
status. Inmate apprehensive over time
required to learn results of appeal.
Quite aware that his execution still
scheduled for July 20, but hopeful his
appeal will be successful. Monthly
visits with wife continue. Inmate's
health stable. Weight 154 lbs.

Laine put the other papers back in the envelope, washed, and
went to bed. He tried to read but couldn't escape the memories of
visits with Constance. Finally, he put aside his book and stopped
fighting to forget. *Go ahead, remember it. For whatever crazy
reason, you're out now—temporarily, maybe—but you're out. So go
ahead, break the rules. Let it come back.*

   The first visit was the worst. They had waited so long for it,
tried to make it last, but it seemed to vanish in seconds leaving

only visceral emptiness for both. It was the same every month. Over time, Laine came to feel increasingly ambivalent about the visits. In the beginning, being so close to Constance—even for a few minutes—gave him a fragment of hope, a reason to stay fastened on living, a defense against the crushing despair of the death house.

But as time dragged them both closer to the seeming inevitability of execution, Laine began to dread the visits, knowing that whatever benefit there was for him, it was far outweighed by the unbearable pain it caused Constance. After his conviction, Constance lost their student housing, forcing her to move all the way to the outskirts of Clayton, California, to find an affordable apartment. Their meager savings were nearly exhausted; her only income was from a part-time editing job for a botanical journal. Laine suspected she had to borrow money to make the long, multi-change bus trip to and from the prison, as well as pay for a room overnight in a fleabag motel, necessary in order to arrive early enough to navigate her way through the visiting process, starting with a long line at the visitor's gate. Once inside, she had to endure protracted waits in noisy, stuffy waiting rooms packed with crying children.

Death house visitors were separated and subjected to a humiliating body search, then sent on a seemingly endless trek through gates, portals, and convoluted echo chamber hallways ending in a windowless room with a series of glassed-in booths at one end for difficult inmates, and a long metal table and chairs for the rest. Small partitions offered some slight sense of privacy, but not enough to prevent guards from observing everyone's movements. One by one, prisoners were paraded in and chained to one side of the table; once they were all secured, visitors were allowed to enter. Guards constantly patrolled back and forth, watching, warning. First-time visitors were not allowed to touch an inmate across the table. "Regulars" were allowed to reach across to hold hands. Most spoke in whispers just loud enough to overcome the constant rattle of handcuff chains on the metal table. At the end of the allotted hour, prisoners and visitors marched out, the table was wiped clean, and the next group came in. The process started at 10:00 a.m. and continued until 4:00 p.m.

Constance didn't complain or even mention the harrowing process, but he could see and feel it in her face and body movements. She had lost an alarming amount of weight, her clothes didn't fit, her complexion was gray, and she started wearing makeup—something she had never done before—though the camouflage didn't work. Instead of hiding her distress, it seemed to highlight it. He knew how alone she was in her tiny apartment in Clayton, her every minute devoted to Rebecca, letter writing, her job, and affording occasional day care. Even her parents were unable to help. They lived in Indiana in difficult circumstances of their own: her mother had advanced MS. Her father had to quit his job to provide her care, leaving them entirely dependent on a meager disability payment from Social Security. To them, the catastrophe playing itself out in California was just another ineffable betrayal of the promise that hard work and faith will always see you through to something better.

Enough, he thought. *Let it go. Maybe this will make more sense in the morning. I hope Leroy is okay.*

Laine woke up feeling he might still be trapped in his cell. The bed was soft, light coming through the window was real, but were those palpable comforts just illusions? Was Stonebridge House simply a taunting fantasy? Any second, the sounds and smell of death row would assault him again, laughing at his grasp of reality. It took several minutes to convince himself he really wasn't in cell 449 in the warren of death. As he dressed, he kept an eye on the package, asking himself if he should risk looking at the remaining documents.

Breakfast was still an hour away, no excuse to hesitate there. He paced back and forth, alternately cursing himself for his curiosity and lack of courage. Finally, he sat down on the bed and opened the envelope.

The next document was a copy of a letter from his lawyer, Edward R. Preston, written to the court saying that with the failure of two appeals, he was officially and "by mutual consent" discontinuing legal services for George H. Laine. *"Mutual consent?" When did that happen?* There was nothing in the letter about a referral to the Public Defender's service. The date on the letter was January 14, 1960, but the San Quentin stamp was dated March 18, 1960. A handwritten note in the margin said, "File, inmate Laine 325674."

Two appeals? A mistake?! I don't remember getting that letter from Preston! How could that be?! If he wrote to the court, why not to me? Not even a copy of the letter? There was still going to be another appeal, right? Isn't that what he said in his last letter? Or was it the public defender who was doing that? How could the second appeal have already been filed and turned down? Memory! Where are you?! How am I ever going to make sense of this if I can't remember those months?!

What he did remember was his constant struggle to accept the inevitability of being executed. The outside world had completely vanished from his thinking. Thoughts of Constance and Rebecca seemed to have been absorbed in the prison swamp. The legal system had ceased to offer anything hopeful. Even pictures of Rebecca seemed remote, like looking at someone else's child. No one offered a sliver of encouragement that some unforeseen development would even delay—much less stop—his execution.

True, he had seen other prisoners get delays, though never a reprieve. Delays were always the product of enormous pressure on the justice system brought by teams of lawyers, celebrities, community leaders, and death penalty opponents. None of those forces were at work on his behalf.

Twenty-nine men were executed while Laine was on death row. Even Caryl Chessman, who had famously been granted multiple delays—eight in all—over many years, finally ran out of time. He was executed only weeks before Laine's appointment with the same gas chamber. Like Laine, the majority of the condemned had no way to get even a brief delay. The few who did win a delay were all eventually put to death. Once sealed in death row, no matter how long it took, execution was inevitable.

By the time of his last visit with Constance at the end of April 1960, it was clear there was simply nothing left that could derail the execution. Even Constance tearfully admitted that his lawyer said he had done all he could and had no strategy left to reignite the case, much less find a way to secure clemency. Any thought the police might stumble over some exonerating evidence had completely faded away. The killer himself was only a few short months away from never again having the slightest concern of being discovered.

Laine remembered how hard it was for them to conceal their pain from each other. For Constance, her struggle wasn't making it through the visiting labyrinth; rather, it was a battle to present herself in a way that would give some tangible support to her husband. Each lived through the excruciating pain for the other, neither daring to say anything about it. But increasingly, Constance realized she was losing him, watching helplessly as he slowly drifted away from her into the hellish darkness of death row.

Until that last visit. It was not planned; it just happened. Constance asked if there was something else she could say that would possibly give him any comfort, some unspoken thought he might have. He answered that there was, but it was too painful to say. She said she couldn't imagine anything more painful than what they had already been through. That gave him the courage to surface the forbidden thought, something that could possibly mitigate at least some particle of their mutual distress. He began, saying, "I have a proposal—"

"I accept!" she said cutting him off.

They both burst out laughing. *Laughing!*

"You'd marry me again?"

"In a heartbeat."

Then the words tumbled out. He confessed that he worried so much about the distress their visits caused that he couldn't think of anything else. Constance said that she feared the same, that she wasn't masking her ordeal enough to protect him from seeing through her disguise.

The proposal was to end their visits in the best way possible: not at the final hour, but right there as they shared the first laugh either had had with the other for over two years. If by some miracle the execution was delayed, then they could resume visiting. In the meantime, they could continue to talk through a steady flow of letters. It seemed so right, so natural. No one else could possibly understand it.

But to Constance and George, it made perfect sense. Reason and emotion joined, taking both into a place where each could give the other freedom to cope with the crush of an immutable reality. They hardly had to explain it to each other; it was simply clear this was the best way forward. It would be infinitely easier to talk through their letters than in a few stifling moments in the visitors' room. They would write and touch each other with words that could never be heard over the distracting cacophony in the lobby of death.

Constance also accepted the idea that toward the end, George would signal the need to stop writing. Having seen so many become unmoored in their final days, he feared the same might happen to him, that he wouldn't be able to write a coherent final goodbye.

His apprehension about not being able to hold up at the end was well founded. He had seen seemingly resigned inmates suddenly become psychotic, combative, or catatonically dissociated from their surroundings. Laine was determined to bend all of his energy into staying in control, letting go of outrage and grief to focus instead on something better just ahead.

Constance was the last visitor to leave at the end of their final visit. She asked the guard if it would be all right if she gave her husband a hug as this would be their last visit. He looked at the other two guards and mumbled something about not telling Mr. Dunn. They nodded agreement. They hugged. It was brief, a violation of the rules, but no one objected.

Laine watched his wife walk away, freeze-shot pictures embedded in his memory. Turning back to wave goodbye, she nearly ran into the doorjamb. She made a "clumsy me" face, and they both laughed. There was the last frame: her face, smiling—then she was gone.

He repacked all of the documents, went down to breakfast, struggling to at least appear to be engaged with the people and conversations swirling around him. The names and dates on the documents kept rummaging through his mind, refusing to line up in an orderly way. He didn't hear a word at the morning meetings.

At lunch, Laine got his tray and sat down next to Brownie.

"Seen Bill yet?"

"Nope. Looks like it's just you and me, Laine. He went out the door with two hundred bucks and not much else. I'll bet he never makes it to Phoenix."

"I hope you're wrong, Brownie."

"You look like shit, Laine, if you don't mind me saying so. What's eatin' you?"

"Old memories, new enemies. It was easy to hide from both of them back there," he said, tilting his head in the direction of the prison. "Out here, there's no one to get my back, and everything around us says, 'Watch Out, Remember Me?'"

"Too deep for me, Laine. But I'm out of here this afternoon. My nephew is picking me up, taking me to Lakewood, up north. My brother found a place for me to stay, plus a bussing job in a local restaurant. The manager owes him a favor."

"Sounds great, Brownie. Good luck." They shook hands and Brownie went to sit by the front door to wait for his ride. Laine started to follow but was intercepted by Mrs. Lender.

"You can join the AA meeting later, Laine. I need to see you in my office." On the way down the hallway she pointed to a closet and said over her shoulder, "After we meet, you can look in there for some clothing. You're allowed a shirt, pants, a t-shirt, a pair of socks, a sweatshirt and a pair of shoes. Hopefully, you can find stuff that fits you. You can also take a gym bag to hold your belongings.

"Okay, Laine," she said, closing her office door. "I have information about where you will be placed. It's too late to move you now, so you'll be here over the weekend. On Monday morning, I'll give you your gate money and a map, along with instructions to get you from here to your hotel. We don't want you getting lost in your first ten minutes of freedom. You'll take the prison bus back to San Quentin. You'll be dropped off at the city bus stop near the gate. The bus will take you downtown, pretty close to your new home: the Madrid Hotel in the Tenderloin. Your PO has made the arrangements, and once you've checked in, you're on your own. But hear this: you've been put on Restricted Status, and that means under no circumstances are you to put your foot over the city line. Tomaras will explain everything when you see her on Tuesday. Your appointment is at three thirty; again, all of this will be spelled out in your instructions.

"Do you know anything about the city? You lived at UC, right?"

Laine looked puzzled, mumbled something about not remembering.

"Yeah, well, it's been a long time, I know. And like you've heard us say over and over, freedom is something you have to manage very carefully. Especially in your case."

"My case?"

"I just mean it's been a long time. Nothing will look familiar, and I don't think you'll find very many people out there who are eager to help."

"I'm sorry?"

"Nothing, Laine, I just mean you need to very careful. Now, we're done. Get back to the AA meeting, and I'll see you Monday morning to go over this in more detail. And be sure to go shopping after the meeting," she said pointing toward the hallway, "The store closes at five o'clock."

Laine struggled through the AA meeting, unable to keep his focus. *What the hell is happening to me? I thought I knew what inmates go through when they get out. You fool! You don't know anything!*

After the meeting, he collected his clothing allotment and retreated to his room to continue looking at his file. First, he laid the clothing on his bed, trying to absorb the strange idea that he would soon give up his prison blues for 'real' clothing, the kind that said—at least outwardly—*Hey! I'm not a prisoner. I have a first name, and a pair of nice sneakers, just like you. But how long will it last? Who's going to put a pin in the balloon?* He folded the clothing and turned back to the records. This time he didn't hesitate to continue. *Maybe there's something here to make sense of the court order. Wouldn't it be amazing if I could resolve that issue after all these years?*

```
MEMO TO FILE:
PRE-EXECUTION EVALUATION
April 15, 1960
Laine, George H., 325674
East Block, Cell 449
        The reader is referred to Mr. Dunn's
    previous reports.
        Met with inmate Laine to ascertain
    his mental state and clarify his
    intention concerning further legal
    action. Inmate in despairing state
    b/o recent visit with spouse, reported
    by the inmate to be their last visit.
    When reminded further visits were
    still possible, even up to the eve of
    execution, he replied they had decided it
    is better to stop now, spare each other
    the agony of that last goodbye. Also,
    the inmate is clear in saying he does
    not want the support of clergy. Asked if
    he isn't concerned about the afterlife,
    he said he has a better idea.
On appeals: inmate seems to think the
    Public Defender's Office is involved,
    referred by his lawyer. Seemed
    indifferent when told that may not be
    the case. Strange man.
```

Will call both his former lawyer and
P.D.'s office to find out more. Wouldn't
want implied indifference on our part to
become the basis of another appeal.

Jack Eppes
Asst. Warden

MEMO TO FILE:
April 22, 1960
Laine, George H., 325674
East Block, Cell 449
Met with inmate again to review
results of recent phone calls to his
former attorney, Edward R. Preston Esq.,
and the Office of the Public Defender.
Inmate was told his attorney refused
the call, but an assistant told me Laine
had been advised in January to apply for
a public defender. She believes Laine
was given an application and told the
wait could be six months or more. The
inmate does not remember getting any
such material in January. I brought a
completed application for the services
of a public defender, recommend he sign
immediately. He seemed indifferent,
said he wants to die before the library
runs out of books. Finally signed after
I told him it was probably too late
anyway. I am not sure where his mind
is, but in a curious way, he is totally
rational. Doubt he will be difficult at
execution. Should go easily.

Jack Eppes
Asst. Warden

Laine struggled to push through the cobwebs. He remembered at least one meeting with Eppes, but he couldn't remember the sequence of events, or even when he first met with the public defender. *What was her name? Cushman? Cashman? Can't remember.* He did recall how bluntly pessimistic she was about the possibility of derailing his execution even briefly. His only hope, she said, would be to write a statement of regret for his crime and beg for clemency. It was a long shot but could possibly win him a life sentence. He flatly refused, saying he would rather die telling the truth than be punished a lifetime for lying. She didn't understand his logic but said she was obliged to accept his decision, perhaps come up with a strategy that would give them more time for further maneuvering.

He remembered that at the same time Dunn told him about his stay, he received a letter from her saying she would meet with him again in a month or so to begin preparing an appeal. There was no mention of the court order. He was allowed a phone call to her. He described the court order, asked her to let his wife know about the stay, as well as look into the court order. Her formal tone made it clear she was disappointed he didn't seem to be grateful she had won the near-miraculous stay of execution. She also said she knew nothing about the court order beyond the fact it was in place, making it impossible for her to have any contact with his wife. She reminded him that her services were strictly related to his death penalty. She advised him to hire an independent attorney to look into any other matters. She also cautioned him not to try to find a way around the court order. Such a move would surely torpedo any chance of a successful appeal. That was the end of the call.

The court order itself was almost impossible to read. The date was obliterated, the margins were frayed; discoloration ran into the text; even the title was barely legible. The body of the text was, however, fairly clear: George H. Laine was

```
Prohibited from any contact—written,
verbal, direct or indirect—with
```

Constance W. Laine, their child, Rebecca
Laine, his former attorney, Edward R.
Preston, members of the victim's family,
or any other person who might act as an
intermediary between George H. Laine and
his wife, Constance W. Laine or other
listed persons.

There also seemed to be a list of other names on the left side of the page—perhaps ten in all—but he couldn't make out more than a few letters.

It ended with instructions, apparently directed to San Quentin officials, that all correspondence and official documents be directed to someone named Alice Abramowitz, but the address was almost totally obliterated. Only one number in the address was visible at all: either a "1" or a "4," seemingly at the end of the address, probably the last digit of a zip code, no help to Laine; the only zip code he knew ending in 4 was San Quentin's own zip code, 94974.

Who was Alice Abramowitz? Why was there a court order in the first place?

"Here I am looking at the damn thing," he said out loud, "And I still don't know why it's there!" But no matter what the explanation, just as he told himself fifty years before: Constance certainly didn't have anything to do with it. Someone else was pulling the strings.

Next, there was a copy of his Last Will and Testament, a one-paragraph document dated July 15, 1960. The image slowly returned. Because it was prison policy for all condemned prisoners to complete a will, a prison official had visited his cell to complete the form just before his execution. He remembered saying he had nothing, owned nothing, and didn't see the sense of rubbing it in with a meaningless will. The official said that even so, he would have a theoretical estate. If some long-forgotten uncle left him something, the estate would have to be settled or it would go to probate.

"The state doesn't want to get mired in that kind of mess. Obviously, you need a will."

He remembered saying something about not wanting to inconvenience the state. When pressed about a beneficiary, he said he would name his daughter, Rebecca.

"You can't name her, Laine."

"Why not?"

"Because there is a court order forbidding any contact of any sort with your wife and daughter, that's why. And a bequest is seen by the law as a form of contact. You'll have to name someone else."

He remembers staring at the man for several minutes before saying, "But I'll be dead. How is that 'contact'?"

"Look, Laine, I don't make the law; I just know it won't fly. Think of someone else."

"In that case, I'll leave everything to you. Maybe you'll get lucky."

That, too, was illegal, so Laine left his "bounty" to Mr. Harvey T. Trenton, Barton Road in Loma Linda, California. The official seemed happy to leave, and Laine was glad to see him go. In another world, it would have been funny to have satisfied the law with a completely imaginary name. The address was real, though, a sewer plant he drove by every day on the way to school when he was a kid.

The next document was a copy of a letter to Mr. Dunn from Naomi Keshet, Public Defender, asking permission to visit George H, Laine, SQ#325674, between September 19–21, 1960. *That's right,* he thought. "Keshet." He said it out loud.

He remembered the meeting because he had prepared for it by rehearsing a careful "Thank you" to make up for his ingratitude on the phone. She excused him, said she understood, and was herself apologetic for being so rigid. She surprised him by saying she had—quite off the record and on her own time—looked into the court order enough to know it was filed in San Francisco, and had not been revoked following his stay.

She agreed that his wife very likely did not initiate the order and quite possibly didn't know anything about it. It could have been done for her by someone with a simple power of attorney. Such maneuvers were common. Family members of condemned prisoners are often confused or too distraught to examine every document they are asked to sign. She also said it was almost certain Constance did not know he was alive. If she knew, she could have acted to at least have her name removed from the order.

Then came the part of the conversation he remembered with complete clarity: "She thinks you're dead, George. Realistically, it's only a matter of time until you *are* executed. In all the years I've been doing this, I've won a lot of stays, but never a reversal. Do you want her to find out you're alive only to have to go through the whole thing again? Leave it alone."

There was no argument—Keshet was right. With outright dismissal beyond impossible, his only outside shot would be winning a new trial. But with no new evidence, the chance of a favorable ruling from a higher court was well beyond remote.

It was time to let go. Get a new book, let Mrs. Keshet do her work, and see where fate took him next.

There were two more documents. One, a short memo to his prison file, dated November 10, 1960. A single line: "Change inmate's marital status to Divorced."

Divorced! How in the world did that happen? And why? If Constance thought I was dead, why the divorce? Once again— after he calmed down—the conclusion was obvious: she had nothing to do with it. *Never! Maybe the power of attorney again? Can someone who knows the system use it to get a divorce without the person even knowing it? Crazy!*

And finally, a copy of a one-paragraph amendment to the original court order, dated February 15, 1961. It was faded, but legible. Another name had been added to the list of people on the forbidden list. Henceforth he was forbidden to contact with either Mrs. Constance W. Preston or her husband, Alfred P. Preston. *Her husband?! Constance married my lawyer's son, Alfred?! That bastard! No! That entitled prick? My God! How could that have happened? Why? He was around a lot during the trial, he did offer a lot of support—I'll give him that. But marry him?*

"I always had my doubts about you, Alfred," he mumbled loudly. "But maybe the warden is right, no matter how wrenching, this could make some sense out of how all of this happened." He made a note on the back of the copy of the court order: *Check the address.*

Laine paced the floor until the call to dinner, his mind jammed with astonishment, despair, and anger—the forbidden emotion pushing its way through his finely honed defenses. Slow down! Eat your dinner, sit out in the yard until you get back in control.

Most of the inmates had been sent on their way, leaving just a dozen or so over the weekend. The exercise yard was quiet and safe. Laine closed his eyes and tried to empty his mind. He was only partially successful. He decided to spend the rest of the evening reading, recalibrating. *Pace yourself, there will be plenty of time for this over the weekend.* He went to the library and selected a book, Fodor's *Guide to San Francisco.*

May as well start getting acquainted with my new home. God! That sounds weird!

Laine was up early Saturday morning, read more of the Fodor book, then went down to breakfast. Knowing there would be no afternoon meetings, he planned to eat first, get through whatever was planned for the morning, then spend the rest of the day studying the documents, reading Fodor, and trying to prepare for the Monday free fall into the unknown. *It's like teaching a kid to swim by throwing him in the river,* he thought. *Sink or swim, good luck, kid.*

After a fairly short Narcotics Anonymous meeting, and an hour pacing the exercise yard, Laine returned to his room. He reopened the package of documents, turning again to the last page. He stared at the phrase, "...or her husband, Alfred P. Preston..." Her *husband!*

Then he saw his note: "Check the address." The amended notice was sent to the prison by Alice Abramowitz, the same name on the original court order. The address on the original order was almost totally obliterated, but the address on the amended version was clear: 235 Montgomery Street, San Francisco, CA 90048.

Montgomery Street…holy shit! That's my lawyer's address! How many hours did I spend in that damned office? So it was Edward Preston—Alfred's father—who was behind all of this! He dumped me, promised the public defender was on tap, coached my wife in the hopelessness of my appeals, and finished off by severing any possible communication with her—just in case there was a slight delay in the plan. Meanwhile, his son moved in, ingratiated himself, and somehow convinced Constance to marry him. What a fool I was! I never even imagined such a thing!

And now I have to live with this. It would have been so much easier to simply fade away on the porch of the geriatric wing in San Quentin. Now what? Do I open the notebook I sealed up fifty-some years ago to reread my detective work about who might have killed Julia? For what?!

It was important fifty years ago when figuring it out could have saved his life. Plus, writing gave him a way to fight back, to convert some of his despair into a quest, one with a tangible goal. It was like trying to convert a forest fire into a pocket warmer, but gradually his writing became more detached and detailed, a minute examination of everything he could think of related to the crime, all of it focused on just two words: "Who?" and "Why?"

Over time, he had revised and condensed his notes, ending up with just five pages of tightly constructed conjectures he called "models." He reasoned the "Who?" part came down to six or seven other graduate students—including Alfred, Ken Buck, a maintenance man at Julia's apartment, one of her ex-boyfriends (previously arrested on a "Peeping Tom" charge), and her brother-in-law. There was one other "suspect," a totally unknowable random killer who somehow knew enough about George to frame him for the crime. At best, it was a far-fetched idea.

Alfred was on the list because, along with Laine and Buck, he was the last person to see Julia. The other grad students were there, too, but Alfred seemed more interested in Julia than the others. Still, of all of his suspects, Alfred had seemed the least likely candidate.

In spite of all his hours of memory and calculation, he could never decisively conclude who had raped and murdered Julia Penthoser, hid her underwear in a box of old books in the basement storage area of his apartment house, and shoved him off the edge of the earth.

Three weeks from his first execution date, with death a virtual certainty, he decided to give up the journal. He wrapped tape around the pages, put them in the back of his notebook, and never opened it again. Would opening it now change anything, or make any more sense out of all these goddamn reports?

No, he thought. *I've had enough remembering. And maybe the slant I'm putting on what my lawyer did is all wrong. Possibly—in spite of how it looks—he really was trying to protect Constance and Rebecca. Maybe by the time I was transferred to a life sentence— assuming he knew it—he saw no reason to change anything. Maybe he reasoned if I did somehow resurface, it would do irreparable harm to everyone involved, especially Constance and Rebecca.*

Remember what Mrs. Keshet said, her advice still holds. Let it go. You've learned enough—put away the documents and the notebook. Pushing it any harder would be like opening a grave to stare down at your own decayed corpse.

Laine went to the library to wait for the call to dinner. Mrs. Burton appeared, tugging on her jacket, clearly on the way out. When she saw Laine, she veered off course, stood in front of him, and spoke, her tone taunting.

"I have some bad news for you, Laine. Your buddy Bill didn't get very far. He took a cab from here to Chinatown, apparently had a big lunch, left a hundred-and-fifty dollar tip, walked down to the wharf and straight off the end of a pier."

"Oh, no! That's awful!"

Mrs. Burton shrugged. "Some people simply can't handle freedom. They don't know what to do if someone isn't there giving instructions. It happens."

"Some, perhaps, but not Bill. It wasn't at all about freedom."

"Oh, yeah? Twenty years in the slammer and it wasn't about freedom? If it wasn't freedom, what was it?"

"Dignity, Mrs. Burton."

"Dignity? Are you joking?"

"Not at all. You lose everything in prison, but hanging onto a shred of pride can keep you going, something that's still yours. He also had a lot of hope, but it turned out to be an illusion. Some people kill themselves because they're depressed. I think Bill did it to preserve what little dignity he had left."

"Yeah, well, that's too bad. By the way, Laine, you think too much, and it won't help you a bit when you hit the streets." She turned and walked away without waiting for a reply.

Laine struggled through dinner, went to his room, washed his clothing, and went to bed. He didn't look at any of the documents or even try to meditate.

On Sunday morning, a service was held by a local minister. He went on about sin and retribution, living the sinless life, and being on constant lookout for the Devil.

"Old Satan can sneak up on you in broad daylight, Brothers, sneak up and jump on your sin-filled soul. Renounce the Devil! Confess your sins and get with Jesus, the only hope for sinners!"

After a final prayer, Laine said, "One question, Reverend."

"Yes, Brother, what is it?"

"What happens to those who sin against sinners?"

"What kind of question is that?!" boomed the reverend. "You'll never feel the comforting hands of God asking questions like that!"

The others in the group echoed their disapproval with scowls and a near synchronous "Amen!"

Laine regretted not showing better control and retreated to his room.

Chapter 6

AFTER BREAKFAST ON MONDAY MORNING, Laine was invited into Mrs. Lender's office.

"You look pretty good in your new clothes, Laine. Did you leave your prison suit in your room?"

Laine nodded.

"Good. I have several things for you, starting with your gate money, two hundred dollars. Here are the directions to get you from here to your hotel. Follow them precisely and you won't have any trouble. Your gate money is all in twenties, and the bus driver won't take that, so here's a pass that will get you to within a few blocks from the Madrid. The only tricky part is changing buses at the San Rafael Transit Center. Read the instructions: the Forty bus from Morphew to San Rafael, then the 101 to Geary Street. They call out the stops—just listen for Geary. The rest is easy, just follow what I've written.

"When you get to the Madrid, ask for Mr. Zwick. Your PO told him you'll be there around noon. Should be easy. I marked the Madrid on your map, as well as some other important places like the parole office, DAPO; remember, your appointment with your PO is Tuesday afternoon at three thirty. Do NOT be late. I also marked the Social Security office, and three missions in the Tenderloin where you can get meals. Zwick will tell you where everything is.

"There are a couple of things for you to sign, starting with acknowledgement that you received your gate money, then one saying you turned in your uniform, and most important of all: the one that formalizes the start of your parole. Initial the boxes saying you have read all the rules, you promise to attend all required probation meetings, and you pledge to abstain from drugs, alcohol, and unlawful behavior. That last one includes any other legal restrictions that may apply currently or in the future. Sign it and you're a free man." After signing, Laine was given a copy of each document.

"That's it. Just wait in the library until the bus comes." Laine put the papers in a manila envelope, stood up, thanked Mrs. Lender, and turned to leave the office.

"One more thing, Laine," Mrs. Lender added. "None of this is going to be easy. Uh...some people have a really tough time out there...especially if their release is...well...maybe, controversial."

"Controversial?"

"Yeah. You know that some crimes stir up more feelings than others, and some people see parole as a mistake. Put it this way: the parole people play strictly by the book. But others..."

"And *others*? What?"

"Others could have different ideas. That's all I can say, Laine. Better get going. Good luck."

On the way back to the library, Laine passed Mrs. Burton in the hallway.

"I see you've got your gate money, Laine. Maybe you could stop off in Chinatown for lunch. Be sure to leave a big tip."

Laine choked on an automatic "Thank you," struggling to suppress the forbidden tinges of rage trying to invade his mind. He recovered and hurried to the library to wait for the bus—and whatever else lay ahead.

The bus only had three inmates. Once they were inside, Laine was allowed to board. He immediately reached for his belt.

"This is the big day, right, buddy?"

"Yeah."

"You don't seem very excited."

"I'm grateful, of course, but the truth is, I don't have any idea what I'm doing. Crazy as it sounds, where I've been is less scary than where I'm going."

"I get it. But I'll tell you: that's a good sign. The ones like you, the careful ones, they don't come back. The ones who are all excited about having a drink and getting laid don't last five minutes out here."

The bus pulled up to a small shelter on the edge of a sidewalk. The driver pointed straight ahead and said, "It's easy. Get on the Forty bus going that way, get off at the first stop, follow the signs that say, 'Downtown.' Get on the One-O-One and listen for your stop."

Laine thanked the driver, got off and took a seat next to a woman holding an infant. The child stared at Laine over her shoulder, expressionless, its head bobbing, but its eyes stayed fastened on Laine's face. *What do I do? Stare back? Make a face? Look away? Please don't cry, kid. What do I do if the kid cries? This is crazy. Where's the damn bus?*

The bus came, Laine made the transfer at San Rafael, and a few minutes later they were on the highway, the Golden Gate Bridge dead ahead. Laine's apprehension eased slightly, displaced by the rapidly shifting images flashing by. There it was: the Bay, just as he had imagined it while pressed against the exercise yard wall all those years, lost in reverie, floating out over the walls. Suddenly, he really was floating high over the water. And when they left the bridge, he was on his way into San Francisco, not back to his cell.

The bus wound through the lush green of the Presidio, past the Palace of Fine Arts, down into the city. Laine traced their path with his finger on Mrs. Lender's map, grateful the Van Ness stretch was so slow. More time to prepare. *Maybe I'm getting the hang of this,* he let himself think.

"Geary! Next stop, Geary!"

Laine got off, the gym bag holding his documents and few possessions clamped tightly under his arm. He crossed the street and headed into the Tenderloin, trying to look like this was something he did every day. *Keep moving! Don't stop. Just pay attention to the map.* Seeing Jones Street gave him a feeling of elation. It was where it was supposed to be! *How stupid!* he thought. *Of course, it's where it's was supposed to be. You can still trust a map.*

Several blocks later, where Jones crosses Caliente, he saw the Madrid Hotel marquee. He slowed his pace as inconspicuously as he could, finally coming to a complete stop just short of the entrance. He looked up at the five-story building, its walls made of grey cement block textured to look like quarried stone. Over the entrance, an ironwork marquee held up by metal rods anchored in the wall above hosted a perimeter of stained glass panels, all but a few broken or simply missing. Two department store-sized windows flanked the entrance; a third window around the corner looked out onto Caliente Street.

A tired neon sign hung over the marquee doing its neon best to look optimistic.

MADRID HOTEL
OVERNIGHT ROOMS
LUXURY APARTMENTS

Most of the apartment windows were covered with laundry sagging on invisible cords, or simply covered with yellowed sheets or limp blankets. There was an empty lot next to the hotel on its north side, its walls covered with graffiti; above, a fire escape zigzagged down the side of the building from the top floor.

Laine stepped through the double doors into the lobby, a large room perhaps a hundred feet square filled with an assortment of chairs and old couches, no two alike, all arranged randomly except for a row lined up to the left in front of the large window facing Caliente Street. A pathway through the lobby furniture followed a more or less straight line from the front doors to the desk in the center of the back wall. To the right of the desk, an elevator, and to its right, a wide staircase disappeared into the gloom above. There were perhaps twenty men and several women scattered around the lobby, some talking, some watching a game show going full tilt on a television set in the far left corner. In spite of several No Smoking signs, the air was heavy with tobacco smoke.

No one appeared to notice Laine when he walked in. Several men sitting near the front door glanced up, but just as quickly returned to their cigarettes and conversation. The man sitting behind the desk didn't look up from his newspaper. Laine walked up to the desk and paused, waiting for the man to react.

After a painful ten seconds, the man—without looking up—said, "Yeah?"

Okay, Laine thought, *first Madrid challenge.* "Are you Mr. Zwick?"

"Yep, and you're…" he paused to look at a scrap of paper, "…George Laine, fresh out of San Quentin, right?" he said, slowly lifting his gaze. "You're one of Aella Tomaras's lepers, right?"

"I haven't met her yet, Mr. Zwick. I take it you don't think much of parolees."

"As long as they pay their rent, I'm okay with 'em. You'll get Social Security, right?" Laine nodded. "Good, that's half the battle."

John Zwick was a short, bald, modestly overweight man who presided over the lobby from a barstool perch behind the desk. His scraggly whiskers suggested either shaving neglect, or more charitably, an early attempt at a beard. His torpid looks were, however, deceiving. With an uncluttered view of the lobby, and through its enormous windows, the street beyond, he was acutely aware of what was going on in his fiefdom. When provoked, he could lash out with the speed of a viper. He maintained snarling control of the mailboxes and key rack on the back wall. As the Madrid's self-appointed postmaster and mail snoop, it was his job to inspect every envelope, his vigilance sharpening toward the end of the month when the checks started rolling in. The price of missing one was severe. Given the chance to grab a check ahead of Zwick, many of Madrid's patrons would head for the nearest check cashing store, gladly fork over the fifteen to twenty percent cashing fee, take the money, turn it into cigarettes and maybe a big meal, then take the rest back to an infuriated Zwick. He would scream like a wounded eagle, add the unpaid balance to the tab—with interest—and wring every penny out of the next check, applying any overage to the tab. That balance, not surprisingly, was as unchanging as a face of Mount Rushmore.

He studied Laine over reading glasses threatening to fall off the end of his Falstaffian nose. Finally, he slid a pen and piece of paper across the desk.

"Put your name and social on top, and sign on the bottom."

"What's this?" asked Laine as he picked up the document.

"It's your tenant's agreement, Laine. Sign it."

"I have to read it first. Perhaps you could summarize it for me."

"What?! Look, mister, it's a standard contract. You agree to pay four hundred bucks a month starting when your first Social Security check arrives. You agree to keep your room clean, we can inspect any time we want, you won't smoke in your room, and if you make too much noise or piss me off, you're out. So sign it or go sleep in the freaking street."

"Tell me more about the check. It's likely to be more than four hundred dollars. What happens to the rest?"

"Jesus Christ, Laine! Were you in jail on Mars? Look: your check gets sent here, you endorse it to the Madrid, and if there's any change, you get it back. Don't try my patience with this; believe me, you won't do any better on your own. So sign it."

Laine signed the contract and handed it back. Zwick scribbled his signature, held out his hand, and said, "And I'll take the two hundred, too."

"No," said Laine calmly.

"What did you say?" Zwick said, leaning toward Laine.

"I said, 'No.' I won't give you the two hundred. We made a deal; we both signed. There is nothing in there about giving you the money."

"Look, asshole, I make the rules here…"

"That's not a rule—it's a robbery. If there's one thing I know about, it's extortion."

Zwick glared at Laine for a full ten seconds. "Fine, Perry Mason, go find some gutter to sleep in. I guarantee your two hundred will be gone when you wake up. If you wake up."

"According to this," Laine said calmly looking at his map, "there are three missions within as many blocks. I'm sure they'll put me up until I can find something else. Someone out there wants my guaranteed rent money." He turned to leave.

"Okay, okay. I'm in no mood for this. Let's see, the key, the key. Oh, dear, I don't see that second-floor room I promised Tomaras—you know, the one reserved for older tenants—seems that room got taken. The only one I have left is on the fifth floor, 560, in the back." He slid a key across the desk. "Oh, and sorry, but the elevator is out of order. They're going to send someone out next week to fix it." He grinned, shrugged his shoulders, and went back to his newspaper.

Laine picked up his key and started toward the stairs. As he started up toward the first floor landing, he heard a male voice command, "Zwick!"

Not the tone of a Madrid resident, Laine thought. In prison, it pays to be able to keep an eye on what's behind you without being obvious. Just a slight drop of the chin and ever-so-quick turn of the head is all that is needed. Laine could only see the lower half of the two men approaching the desk, but it was enough: cheap suits and black shoes—cops. *Shit,* he thought, *here comes my prison paranoia. Cops...so what? How could it have anything to do with me? Still...*

Laine hesitated, took a chance, and leaned over just enough to see the top of Zwick's desk. He couldn't hear what they were saying over the TV game show, but he could plainly see they were looking at his tenant's form. He quickly pulled back and went up to the landing between the first and second floors.

There was a bathroom and trash can on the left, and on the right, several vending machines, a pay phone with no receiver, and a dust-covered ice machine long a stranger to anything colder than a dead mouse. A small window at the end of the alcove provided the only light. Laine looked out the window onto the empty lot and Jones Street. There was a black sedan parked across the street in a fire lane. A few minutes later the two men emerged, walked across the street, got in their car, and drove away.

Cops! How in the word could they know I'm here? And why bother with me in the first place? It makes no sense! He remembered Mrs. Lender's caution about unnamed people who might be upset over parolees convicted of…what did she call it? "Controversial" crimes. He continued up to the fifth floor.

There were twelve rooms on each side of the fifth-floor hall. Number 560 was the last one on the right. *At least it's quiet,* Laine thought as he twisted the key in the lock. His room was a twelve by twelve box with a closet and small bathroom on the right, blank wall with a bureau and bed on the left. There were two windows opposite the door, a desk with a lamp, and chair in between. The only other light came from a bare bulb in the center of the ceiling. Over the left-hand window, a sign read "Fire Escape." A helpful arrow pointed to a metal platform structure and a narrow ladder outside the window. The bathroom was small, just big enough for a toilet, sink, and three-quarter sized bathtub with shower head. There was no shower curtain or toilet paper. The window was small, its glass either smoky or simply dirty. Either way, it was opaque.

There was no door on the closet; inside, just a shelf, two wooden hangers, and a toilet bowl plunger. The bed was made up with a pillow, two sheets, and a green wool blanket. On top, two bath towels and a washcloth with a small printed notice saying sheets and towels could be exchanged every Thursday before noon at the housekeeper's office on the third floor. In smaller print, it warned that lost or damaged sheets and towels would only be replaced at the tenant's expense.

Laine sat down on the armless wooden chair, surveyed the room, and wished Leroy was there to talk about the stuff racing through his head. Leroy could always cut through the static when his thinking became too jumbled. A knock on the door jolted him back to the Madrid.

"Cops or robbers?" Laine asked as he opened the door.

"Howdy! They call me Cowboy. I'm your neighbor across the hall. What did you do to piss Zwick off so fast? It took me nearly a month to get sent up here."

Cowboy really did have a "rangy" look, tall, skinny—almost emaciated, cowboy boots, blue jeans, and a faded shirt with snap buttons.

"Where's your horse, Cowboy?" Laine asked extending his hand.

"Left her down at the corral, mister," he answered, shaking Laine's hand. "Jesus! You've got one hell of a handshake."

"Sorry, Cowboy. The name's Laine, George Laine. Come on in, tell me about life in the Madrid Hotel."

Chapter 7

"WHAT THE HELL IS GOING on, Dalton? Why has it taken you so damn long to call me?"

"Jesus, Judge, give me a break. I can't tell you every time he takes a shit. But I can tell you Tomaras has sent him to a dump in the Tenderloin—the Madrid Hotel—last stop on the road to hell. I've already got Metzi and Carlos on the job. We'll have him back in the can soon enough."

"No, it's not soon enough, Dalton. You said he wouldn't get this far, remember? I thought Tomaras was going to chew him up, not see to his frigging comfort in our backyard."

"She hasn't even met him yet. But she's a real hard-ass, and she knows how important this is. She'll trip him up. She hates cons and junkies—in that order. If he so much as sneezes in the wrong direction, he'll be back in custody. So relax; it's all under control. Her boyfriend, by the way, is a detective; it's all one big, happy family."

"I don't care who she fucks; what I want is results."

"I get it. But listen, there's one other thing, maybe it doesn't mean anything, but I thought I'd mention it."

"Yeah? What other surprise do you have for me?"

"The Warden visited Laine a few days ago."

"Thompson? He visited Laine in that halfway house? What for?!"

"Don't know. He only stayed fifteen minutes, but we think he gave Laine papers of some sort. One of my people searched his room but she didn't find anything. Looks like he carried the stuff around with him. A lot of the inmates do that with important documents like discharge orders."

"Why didn't they search him?"

"On what pretext? I don't have any influence with the head monkey. She wouldn't go for a search without a reason, and having papers the warden gave him certainly wouldn't qualify."

"Shit! I don't like this."

"Relax, Judge, we don't..."

"Don't tell me to relax. If this had been under control, he wouldn't have gotten out in the first place."

"Yeah, that's true. Carter not showing screwed us. Oh, and by the way, they found Carter. He was dead in his cab, just like I predicted."

"Dead!? Dead or dead drunk?"

"Dead. The kind with a bullet in his mouth. Looks like he got way too drunk and decided he didn't want the hangover."

"Fuck him. Just make sure we never have to go to another hearing, have you got that?"

"When he goes back, even if it's just on a technicality, he'll never have another shot at parole. Then you can rest easy, he'll be where he belongs."

"Maybe. It would be even better if he goes out in a body bag."

"Jesus Christ! You really hate this guy. I've got to ask—I've always wondered—what is it about Laine that makes him so special? You never really told me. I always assumed you knew the victim, right?"

"It's my business, Dalton, but since you bring it up, I'll tell you. But this is strictly between us, got it? For your ears only, not the cops, not Tomaras, not anyone. Agreed?"

"Of course."

"Okay. Well, the truth is my father represented Laine at his trial, a pro bono case he did to be sure he got a fair trial even though it was obvious he was guilty. When he was convicted, Laine swore he'd get back at Dad for not getting him off. Crazy as it sounds, we were convinced he really meant it. We all hoped he would be executed, but like a lot of other killers, he slipped the knot. There's more to it than that, but I'm not going into it now. Suffice it to say, he's a dangerous man, a threat to me and my family—and you."

"No wonder you're so concerned! It all makes sense now. The 1967 ruling, the transfer to general population, the hearings—and now this mess. Thank you for explaining it. I'm truly sorry you have to go through this, Judge. But don't worry, I'll do everything I can to put him away again. Count on me!"

Chapter 8

COWBOY CONFIRMED MOST OF WHAT Laine had already figured out: that Zwick was a dangerous prick, that Tomaras owned half the people in the place, and that the police had a different set of rules when it came to dealing with folks in the Tenderloin in general—and the Madrid in particular. He also warned that the door lock did little more than keep out most of the other tenants. To protect anything like money or important papers, one would do well to find a really good hiding place somewhere else.

What Laine didn't know was that the Madrid stood at the confluence of Harlot and Hooker, or that Zwick's real income came from extremely short-term rentals—in the region of one hour. The action started around eight o'clock every night of the week, the reason there were two rows of couches lined up facing Caliente Street. Sitting face out to the street provided an aquarium-like view of the always interesting and sometimes violent world of lowlife prostitution. It also suited Zwick, who insisted that tenants remain quiet and well clear of the door and desk during evening business hours. Customers didn't like to feel anyone was observing their coming and going—so to speak—especially when escorting male prostitutes.

The third floor was strictly for quickie rentals, off limits to tenants at all times except Thursday mornings when new linens were handed out. A bouncer, acting as fee collector, and three maids worked the third floor from 8:00 p.m. until 3:00 a.m. closing time. The elevator, usually out of service, magically worked during those business hours.

Zwick always had a bouncer at the ready in case of trouble, either from a tenant who might have forgotten his or her evening manners, or to quell an outburst on the third floor. Keeping strict control was part of the reason the police turned a blind eye to Zwick's enterprise. The other part was regular payments made to key members of the constabulary, men (and women) who regarded the remuneration as just compensation for maintaining order in an otherwise unruly part of town.

Cowboy's take on the other residents was somewhere between cautious and sparse. "No one *chooses* to live at the Madrid. It might be a step up if you're coming out of prison, but more likely you're here because you got nowhere else to go. You'll see that except for a couple of old married folks on the second floor, everyone here is alone. This is where you go when the only thing you got left is you, and even that's running out of time. The last thing they want to talk about is how they got here, so you'll find yourself in a lot of empty conversations about hookers or what they're serving at which mission. People out there," he said pointing across the fire escape, "want to learn history, tell you about a famous battle or who was president when Christ was a corporal. In here, it's the opposite: everyone wants to forget history. And some are very touchy about it. You've got to be careful what you ask people.

"We got some here that lived in big houses and took trips to Hawaii every winter. Now, the only trip they take is to Social Services or maybe the public health clinic. But no one really talks about it anymore. It's too depressing.

"Most of the people here are okay, but like any place, there are rules hidden behind the rules. At the Madrid, that means first off, don't piss off Zwick or get in the way of evening business; beyond that, don't steal or get caught smoking reefer in your room. If you're careful, it's an okay place to be miserable.

"Just watch out for Zwick—he has a really bad temper. Another one you want to avoid is a dude named Elton. He came out of jail about a year ago, went to a mission, but got tossed out for getting in too many fights, especially when he was drunk. There's a kid named Tommy, lives down on the second floor. He got to know Elton, and when he got booted out of the mission, Tommy let him move in with him."

"Why? What's in it for Tommy?"

"Protection. Tommy isn't all there, if you know what I mean. On top of that, he's small and was getting beat up in the streets all the time. Elton about killed a guy who robbed Tommy down in Bayview, got his money back and then some. After that, Tommy didn't go nowhere without Elton."

"How do they get around Zwick? Certainly, he knows Elton lives with Tommy, right?"

"No, what happened is, Tommy's parents put him here because they just don't want to mess with him back home—wherever that is. So they set him up with a room and some allowance. Tommy had enough to get Elton his own room, and they live on the rest of it plus what they can scrounge. Everybody's happy, especially Tommy who has his own bodyguard."

"You say Elton came out of jail a while ago. Any idea where he was or is that just part of a conversation that never happens?"

"San Quentin, I think. That's the rumor."

"I might know him. Big guy, heavyset, never has anything to say that doesn't start with a cuss word or a threat?"

"That's him. Not to be nosy, but is that where you came from?"

"Yes, I was just paroled."

"Wow. Well, congratulations. How long were you in? I mean, if it's okay to ask. Here I am telling you not to get pushy about people and ten minutes after I meet you I'm asking questions."

"Hey, it's okay. I don't mind. I was there fifty-two years."

Cowboy shook his head. "Holy shit, man, I can't imagine it! But if it's the same guy, do you think he'll come after you?"

"Not by the front door. Really, he's more noise than substance, but I'll watch myself." Laine remembered Elton, a classic jailhouse bully, lazy, always looking for the easy way out. *Looks like Tommy is it for now.*

Cowboy didn't have much to say about his own history, just that he had grown tired of Arizona and came to the coast a few years ago, "for a change of pace." Since then, life had been bearable. He quickly changed the subject, turning instead to what he called "survival training."

Laine learned where the missions were, when they served meals, where he could find a Goodwill store for clothing and other essentials, what stores ripped off down-and-outers, especially parolees who weren't likely to make a fuss when they were cheated—all essential information for people living in the suburbs of hell.

"Most of all, Laine, don't go roaming around in places you don't know, especially after dark. People out there will kill you just for the fun of it. If you hear gunshots, beat feet back here as fast as your little *zapatas* will carry you. And never, NEVER ask a cop for help or expect one to stop and help you, even if someone is ripping your heart out. It won't happen, and you're the one likely to get arrested."

Laine thanked Cowboy, promised to be careful, and eased his neighbor out of the room. Time to address the problem of security, and that required a few basic tools and some ingenuity. *At least now I won't have to make tools out of mattress wire,* he thought.

Looking around the room, Laine only saw three possible keeps: under a floorboard, in the hollow tubing of his metal bed frame, or by hollowing out a narrow pocket in the back of the closet shelf. Also, he'd need some kind of window shade or makeshift curtains.

Time to get out of the Madrid for some careful exploration—ever mindful of Cowboy's street rules:

Rule One: Always look like you know exactly where you're going. Don't make eye contact with anyone and stay well away from buildings—walk near the street.

Rule Two: Move a touch faster than everyone else to give panhandlers and pickpockets less time to size you up and make a move.

Rule Three: If someone steps in front of you to block your path, make your move at the last second, always toward the street, even if you have to step off the curb. Get right back on track, and don't look back.

Laine stepped out onto the corner, got his bearings, and headed north on Jones toward Geary Street, destination Goodwill, a scant (and hopefully safe) five blocks away. He didn't sense anyone watching him, so he relaxed slightly, enjoying the feeling of being able to walk in a continuous straight line uncontained by walls or a barbed wire fence. He watched the traffic signals ahead, regulating his pace to hit the next intersection without having to stop.

It only took a few minutes to reach the Goodwill store. The store was enormous and seemed to have everything Laine needed. He quickly found new underwear, a pair of pants, two T-shirts, denim work shirt, and three large bath towels—all in good shape. At a table filled with literally hundreds of used tools, he found a small screwdriver, chisel, pair of pliers, hammer with a cracked handle, and a small bag of mixed nails. Total cost: forty-eight dollars even. He wrapped it all in a tight bundle, declining a shopping bag; again, one of Cowboy's rules:

"Avoid bags, they're easy to snatch. No one will rob you if they see you carrying something that looks like your laundry. Put it in a bag, and they'll think you've got something worth stealing."

On the way back, Laine stopped in a Vietnamese convenience store (one of the "honest ones," according to Cowboy) for soap, toilet paper, and dental floss.

Back in his room, Laine nailed two of the towels over the windows. When he wanted sunlight, he could tie them back with dental floss. Then he went to work on the bed.

Four hollow metal posts supported the bed frame, each topped with a decorative finial held in place with two small screws. He undid the screws on the post next to the wall farthest from the door and twisted off the finial. He rolled his release document and Last Will and Testament together and slid them down the tube. Next, he tied two five-dollar bills together with floss, lowered them down the tube, ran the end of the floss out and down the outside of the tube, and replaced the finial. Finally, he cut the dangling floss off just below the lower edge of the finial, taking care to leave just enough to be seen by someone standing at the foot of the bed. He didn't replace either screw.

Next he removed the finial from the post at the foot of the bed nearest the door, stuffed a wad of paper about two feet down the tube using the shaft of the toilet plunger, tied all but ten dollars of the rest of his money in a tight wad using floss, left a tail about three feet long, and dropped it all down the tube. Unless one shone a light straight down the tube, the cache was invisible. He practiced retrieval using his toothbrush tied on a length of floss—it easily grabbed the floss tangle at the bottom of the tube. He replaced the finial and secured it tightly with the two screws, making sure the screw slots both pointed in exactly the same direction.

He sat on the edge of the desk to evaluate his progress. *So far so good. I still need a really secure keep. I have time to figure that one out, but right now I need another good decoy.* He pulled the bureau away from the wall, tapped a small nail into the back, hung the Stonebridge information package on the nail, and replaced the bureau.

Good, time for dinner. He put a tiny ball of paper in the doorjamb before heading downstairs to the lobby where Cowboy and two other regulars—Louis and Kitty—were waiting. After a brief introduction, the group set out for the Second Chance Baptist Mission soup kitchen. The "Second BM," as it was called, was a popular place with the homeless or those whose resources were almost entirely drained by housing and cigarettes. Alcohol, Laine found to his surprise, did not figure significantly in the lives of the Madrid crowd. They couldn't afford even the cheapest wine, and if Zwick caught them boozed up in his lobby, he didn't hesitate to toss them out. Again, it wasn't a moral thing, just one more example of principled business behavior.

Before dinner, Reverend Sully offered prayers and a short sermon in the chapel. At exactly six o'clock, the doors to the dining hall were opened. The food was basic, filling, and the crowd was surprisingly orderly. Most of the regulars formed small groups, talking quietly. Some of the loners were too busy having animated conversations with invisible companions to even notice anyone else. Others assumed paranoid postures, either crouched over their food like a wolf defending a dead rabbit, or fixing a curled-lip glare at anyone coming too close. Others were simply left alone because of hygiene issues.

After dinner, Laine drifted back to the Madrid with the others, thanked the group for their hospitality, and headed for the stairs.

"Aren't you staying for the show, Laine?" asked Cowboy. "It starts in an hour. Come early; get a good seat."

"Not tonight, Cowboy. I'm shot. I need to be up early to go to Social Security, and I meet my PO for the first time in the afternoon. If I screw up any of it, well…"

"Social Security ain't far, George, but it's a real zoo in there. If you don't mind the walk, there's a branch over on Valencia. It's a lot less crowded."

"Thanks, but my PO's office is in that direction. I thought it would be smart to see how much of a walk it is. It'd be a shame to get violated just because I was late for my first appointment. There's another reason to go that way: the main library is on the way. That's one place I really do want to see. Besides, taking a long walk is an experience I haven't had for a long time."

"For someone who's been away for so long, you seem to know an awful lot about the city, George."

"I've been reading, plus they gave me a map. At least a map is something I still know how to use. And doing my homework prevents surprises."

Laine went upstairs to his room, checked the paper wad (it was just where he left it), washed up, studied the map for over an hour, and turned out the light.

"God, I miss Leroy," he mumbled and fell asleep.

Learning one's way around San Francisco isn't easy. The city is a patchwork of roughly two dozen districts, each with its own character and rules. Their names are often ethnic: Japantown, Chinatown, and Little Russia, for example. Others are geographic: Pacific Heights, Fisherman's Wharf, and Presidio. Some seem to make no sense at all, names like Polk Gulch, Cow Hollow, and Dogpatch. The original Tenderloin was in New

York City, a red light area of west central Manhattan known for crime, corruption, and crooked cops. The name first appeared in 1887, a reference to cops living high on bribes, dining on only the finest cuts of beef. The term came to San Francisco in the 1930s when the area was a hotbed of wild nightlife, gambling, and prostitution. The Tenderloin is a fifty square block district located in the heart of the city. It is bounded on the west side by Route 101 (Van Ness Avenue), on the north by Geary Boulevard, on the east side by Union Square with its major shopping and tourist hangouts, and to the south, it merges with the city's civic buildings lined up on Market Street, an area of open plazas, the main library, art museum, and City Hall. Ironically, of the group, the California Supreme Court, the court that saved Laine from the gas chamber, is closest to the Tenderloin. In Laine's time—and today—the Tenderloin is a gloomy and often dangerous place, even in the daytime. Homeless people, drug addicts, drifters, and the mentally ill live in and around the area's many missions. The more fortunate find some degree of safety in places like the Madrid. The Tenderloin is more an infection than a neighborhood.

Chapter 9

IN THE MORNING, LAINE WAITED until 9:00 a.m. to give the streets and stores time to come to life. He checked to be sure he had his identity card and completed Social Security application form, then went over the map one more time to be certain he had the route to DAPO and the Social Security Building imprinted in his head. It wouldn't do to be seen carrying a map, or worse: getting lost.

With Cowboy's advice about street safety in mind, Laine stepped out onto Jones, casually examining the intersection before turning onto Caliente. He stopped at Dusty's Deli, got a cup of coffee and an egg sandwich, then turned down Polk toward Mission Street, past City Hall and the Civic Center. He knew the main library was just another block east, but he was determined to maintain his focus on first locating the parole office, then the Social Security building.

The transition from the Tenderloin to the area surrounding the Civic Center was startling. The streets of the Tenderloin were sullen and bleak, many shops empty, their windows cracked or covered with plywood. People on the street moved slowly, some simply leaning against a wall or doorway, smoking or perhaps holding out a cupped hand hoping a passerby would drop a few coins. *Hope lives in some other neighborhood,* Laine thought as he moved along, maintaining a steady, deliberate pace.

Fifteen minutes later, he reached the parole office on Market Street. He observed the building for a while before entering the lobby. A receptionist asked if she could help. He thanked her but said he had an appointment soon and just wanted to be sure he was in the right place. Scanning the large directory next to the elevators he saw "Tomaras, Aella" listed in bold letters, third floor, office 340, just as it said on her card.

Also on the third floor, rooms 356–360, the offices of Edward Dalton, Director of the Victims of Crime Project. He nodded to the receptionist on the way out and started walking toward the Social Security building only a few blocks away.

But the pull of the streets was too strong. *What the heck, he thought. I'm being too rigid, too much like I'm still in prison, every minute accounted for. No, I need to let myself go a little, perhaps walk down Market Street toward Union Square. It's a big street, busy, and probably a safe way to start exploring.*

The transformation from the brooding streets of the Tenderloin to the heart of San Francisco was dazzling. In spite of the early hour, the streets were alive with noise, traffic, lights, color, and people—lots of people. Tourists were everywhere, snapping pictures, babbling excitedly in a dozen different languages. There were sidewalk vendors hawking books, souvenir pictures of the city, and what looked to Laine like fancy handbags and watches, the stuff he imagined in pricey department stores. It was like a circus parade: dogs on leashes, strangely costumed people with green hair, artists ready to sketch your portrait in colorful caricature, even a man towing a goat. Store windows were jammed with every gadget, computer, camera, video game, movie, souvenir, toy, and confection imaginable. Clothes were particularly vexing for Laine. Dress shops featured what looked like men's suits, and the manikins in men's shops had pocketbooks slung over a shoulder.

The unbridled excitement of the streets swamped Laine's finely honed caution against allowing forbidden feelings to worm their way into his brain. Everything around him defied the rules. Don't-You-Dare was replaced with the temptation to open up, let his feelings take the wheel for once. *Go ahead! Celebrate just how far your imagination can go.*

All of it slammed into Laine's rigid control system, dangerous places to go. *It will only make you want more. Nothing good can come of it—just more loss, more grief.*

Standing in front of a toy store window filled with a childhood full of Christmas gifts, Laine fought back against the pain good memories from childhood always brought. He was immediately reminded of a cautionary story he once read about a blind man who had lived his life having no vision at all, save a faint, unchanging light immune to movement or even the closing of his eyelids. When he was nearly fifty, he was offered the chance to undergo experimental surgery, a procedure that might give him vision. He was cautioned that if it failed, he would risk losing even the faint light. But if successful, he would see a glorious world of color and opportunity beyond anything he could have imagined. Still, there was the danger he would be overwhelmed, struggle to sort out shapes that made no sense, a confusion of sounds and meaningless images. He wouldn't know a Dalmatian from a barking lampshade. He opted for the surgery, it worked, but the only way he could make his way around was to close his eyes and feel with his hands. Eventually, he committed suicide.

Laine tried to force himself to press on, keep sight of his purpose, shut out the fireworks going off in the stores and on the streets. *No, this is too much, too soon. Time to reverse course, get back on task.*

He found the Social Security office and took his place in a long line of grumbling people, slowly snaking its way around the halls until finally reaching a window. The clerk barely looked up.

"Do you have an appointment?"

"No, ma'am, I didn't realize I needed one. I just have this application...and here's my identity card." He pushed them through the semicircular opening in the clerk's window.

She picked them up as if handling a soiled diaper.

"I don't know what rock you've been living under, Mr....er... Laine...but no one waltzes in here without..." She paused. "Oh, I see. Sorry. You just got out last week. San Quentin, right?"

"Yes, that's right. How did you know?"

"Your identity card. It's dated last week, and see these letters down in the corner? They tell where the card was issued. Yours says 'DOC,' so it was issued at a Department of Corrections facility. For an older man in this area, that usually means San Quentin. It also means you're on parole because if you were released straight out you would have gotten a card where you live. Simple."

"I didn't realize that. So anyone looking at the card immediately knows my story."

"Basically, though not everyone will read the fine print or know what it means." She turned to her computer, and added, "Judging from your employment record, it looks like you were away for a very long time."

"Yes, that's true."

"Hey, don't feel bad. It doesn't mean I think any less of you, or that you won't get every benefit you're entitled to. I know, because," she said dropping her voice slightly, "my brother was in San Quentin for fifteen years. I know all about what it's like there," she said. "He went through hell, but thanks to the Lord, he's doing pretty good now."

"That's wonderful. What's his name, if you don't mind?"

"Harvey. Harvey Douglass."

"I knew him, not well, but we talked. He used to say he wanted to go back to school, but he was afraid he'd fail. I rode him pretty hard, and he finally started. Did he continue outside?"

"Yes! Are you the one who taught literature?"

"Yes."

"Damn! I'd jump over there and kiss you if it wouldn't get me fired. Thank you, Mr. Laine! He did go on, got an associate's degree, and he's working for a computer company. Now, let's just see what we can do about this application, maybe we can work something out." She excused herself and disappeared with Laine's documents, reappearing ten minutes later.

"Looks like we can work you in. Third floor, desk thirty-one," she said pushing his documents through the window. "And good luck!"

Laine thanked her, went upstairs to a room that seemed the size of the San Quentin mess hall, found desk thirty-one, and was invited to sit down. The clerk had already found his records on her computer and calculated his benefit to be $422 a month.

She apologized about the amount but said it was all she could squeeze out of the system.

"I'm putting an 'Expedite' on this, Mr. Laine. You should get your first check in about a month." They talked about the system at the Madrid, how he'd have to sign it over to the hotel the instant the check hit the desk. He asked if there was a way to have it sent to a bank instead. He intended to open an account and hoped he could even find some work.

"Well, yes, you could get direct deposit if you have an account, but I hate to tell you, Mr. Laine, there ain't a bank in San Francisco that will have you as a customer. When you show them this card, it will be over. All over. I'm really sorry, but being poor makes it tough. Being poor and an ex-convict makes it impossible."

"But isn't that against the law? Don't they have to accept me if I have income?"

"In another universe, Mr. Laine. And last time I looked there's no Martin Luther King out there fighting for convict rights. Accept it—it's the system."

"Martin Luther King didn't accept it."

"Amen. And good luck."

Laine left the office, walked two blocks up to the Civic Center, and stood in front of the main library, an immense six-story structure decorated with flags, trees, grass, ornate sculptures, and quite a few homeless people. Laine moved briskly through the courtyard and up the steps into an enormous internal space reaching all the way up to the glass roof. Another breathtaking moment.

A guard, perhaps sensing a loiterer, asked in a barely polite tone if he could be of help.

"Yes, thank you," Laine said. "This is my first time here. It's an amazing sight. But what I really want is information about applying for a library card."

The guard melted slightly, pointed over the railing to an information kiosk below and said in an are-you-blind tone, "Down there, sir."

The kiosk lady was considerably more upbeat. She handed Laine an application and booklet for newly minted card holders explaining the library's many features, including a lecture series and an invitation to become a contributing member of the *Friends of the San Francisco Library*, starting with a minimum donation of only $100. Before releasing her captive, she recommended a tour of the Bingham Wing to enjoy the Diversity Celebration Display.

"The *what*?" asked Laine, not sure what the celebration might be about, but also sensing it would be unwise to be dismissive.

"*Diversity!*" she exclaimed, almost spelling the word. "Surely you know what that is?"

"Well, you see, I've been out of circulation for quite a while, still getting my feet under me, so to speak."

"Well, we are celebrating the liberating realization that being different brings us all together."

"Ah! So we're all in it together, right?" The kiosk lady nodded approvingly. A little voice was urging him to shut up.

"I've been...away...for quite a while. It's good to be back and feel included. Thank you." Kiosk Lady pulled back, mumbled something, leaned to one side, and invited the next in line to step up.

Laine found a table, filled out the application, gave it to a clerk at the main desk along with his identity card. She didn't seem to notice the "DOC" and issued a temporary card, promising his permanent card would arrive shortly in the mail. Looking around, Laine asked where he could find the card catalog. Another disapproving look. "Sir, we use computers for book searches; the Dewey decimal system went out with pet rocks." Laine had no idea what she meant, but it was clear he wasn't doing too well and needed to retreat to the Madrid before he got in any more trouble.

The walk back was uneventful. He was beginning to get used to the sidewalk carnival displays, ceaseless traffic noise, and the black car that showed up behind him every few blocks.

Chapter 10

"THIS IS FUCKING NUTS, METZI. It's like watching paint dry. Are we going to spend every day trailing one old con around the city? And then what? Arrest him for jaywalking?"

"Shut up, Carlos, this won't last long. Quit complaining and remember how come you get to go Baja every year."

"Yeah? Well, try this one on: I think he knows we're here. No one, I mean fucking *no one* walks like this guy. People walk in a straight line. Not this guy. Look at him: speeds up, slows down, steps into a store, out again, never looks back. How many times has he forced us to pass him and circle the block? Every con is paranoid—I got that part. Every con thinks someone's watching them—I got that part. But they're always looking around. Not this guy, Metzi. It don't feel right."

"The only thing that ever feels right to you is pussy. So shut the fuck up."

Chapter 11

SAFELY BACK AT THE MADRID, Laine retreated to his room to put his emotions back where they belonged, under control, and focused only on what was right in front him. *No memory disruptions. It's hard enough out here without that. Work on a safe place to keep your money and documents. Clearly, it's not just some random petty thief who might want to see what I'm hiding. Get to work, prepare to meet Tomaras.*

He checked the paper wad—still in place—closed and locked his door, and gathered his tools to start the painstaking job of hollowing out a pocket in the narrow back of his closet shelf.

The shelf was held in place by two nails, easily overcome simply by putting a hand on each side under the shelf and pushing up. The shelf wood was ¾" thick and bone dry. He split off a narrow piece of the entire back edge by putting the shelf on his desktop with a couple of inches hanging out over the edge, leaning heavily on the wide part, then pushing down sharply on the overhang. It only took a slight pressure to knit the fractured part seamlessly back in place.

Using the chisel, he carefully nibbled out small pieces of wood from the body of the shelf. An hour into the project he had it half done, but it was time to go to DAPO to meet his probation officer. At the last minute, he decided to take a copy of his release paper, just in case that was a hidden requirement. He folded it into his copy of *The Brothers Karamazov*, locked his door, reset the paper fragment, and walked down to the lobby. Happily, Zwick was too engaged in berating another resident to say anything provocative to Laine. The walk to the DAPO office only took twenty minutes, leaving a half hour to kill. He didn't want to remain exposed and aimless on the street, so he went straight to Tomaras's office.

I wonder if I'll run into Mr. Dalton! Wouldn't he be thrilled to see me! "Good afternoon, Mr. Dalton! Great to see you. Have a nice day." *No, George, just keep moving. Room 340. Stay focused.*

Laine apologized to the receptionist for being so early. She seemed indifferent, handed him a plastic cup, and pointed to a screening booth just off the reception area.

"Pee in the cup, put the top on securely, and put the cup on the shelf with the little door. Then have a seat." She returned to her computer.

The booth was just big enough for a toilet and small sink. Over the toilet, there was a sign he had seen hundreds of times prison:

NOTICE

Diluting or altering urine samples is a felony offense
and will be fully prosecuted under California law.

At least in here there isn't a guard staring at me, he thought as he filled the cup. He put the cup on the shelf, washed his hands, and returned to the waiting room to read. He quickly fell back into the meeting between the Grand Inquisitor and Jesus.

He was jolted back to reality by the receptionist. "This way, Laine," she said leading him down a short hall to Tomaras' office.

Tomaras was seated at her desk leaning on her elbows, looking at a large file open in front of her. She glanced up, studied him for several seconds, pointed to a chair, and said, "Come in, Laine, have a seat. I'm Aella Tomaras, your probation officer." Her tone and facial expression were both neutral, bordering on cross. Her gaze shifted back to the documents. She appeared to be on the short side of medium height with a tight, athletic crispness to her face, neck and hands. Her blue striped shirt was buttoned almost to her neck, sleeves rolled up to her elbows. She wore large hoop earrings, a simple silver bracelet on her right wrist and a watch with a large face on the left. A blue business jacket was draped over the back of her chair. Her olive skin, dark eyebrows, and long black hair twisted in a bun at the back of her head gave her a Mediterranean look. In another setting, she could have been a seasoned businesswoman preparing to meet a disappointing employee.

"It's nice to meet you, Mrs. Tomaras," Laine said as he sat down.

"It's 'Miss' Tomaras, and we'll see if you still feel that way after you get to know me."

"Yes, ma'am."

"My jurisdiction here at DAPO is San Francisco, meaning the entire city down to the Mateo County line. Do you know the city, Laine?"

"No, ma'am, it's been a while. But Mrs. Lender gave me a map. I've been studying it. I even managed to get to the Social Security office and back this morning."

"Good. Well, the reason it's so important is because you've been placed on Restricted Status, meaning that under no circumstances are you allowed to leave the city or cross the boundary into the county. The county line is invisible, so be damn careful you don't cross it by mistake. The only exception is if you have written permission from me, and you're accompanied by an officer from my office. I assume you've heard of Restricted Status before?"

"Yes, ma'am."

"Any questions so far?"

"No, ma'am."

"No questions? Aren't you curious to know why you've been put on Restricted Status, or why you're in my jurisdiction?"

"I assume it's a combination of my crime and the feeling that releasing a man who should have been executed is wrong." He added, "And perhaps you've also talked to Mr. Dalton."

"You're right about why you're on RD, but who I talk to is my business."

"Yes, ma'am."

There was a knock on the door. The receptionist poked her head in, mouthed the word "No," and closed the door.

"Okay. You seem to understand the situation. You also need to know that it's my job to see to it you adhere to those restrictions. There is no wiggle room here, Laine. No, 'Oh, gosh, I forgot my mittens' bullshit. In this ball game, you get one at bat, one pitch, and one swing at the ball. Miss it and you're out. Got it?"

"Yes, ma'am."

"You were placed in the Tenderloin, did you wonder why?"

"Not really."

"Don't fuck with me, Laine!" exclaimed Tomaras, suddenly on her feet. "This 'Yes, ma'am,' 'No, ma'am,' 'Not really' shit is pissing me off."

"I'm sorry, ma'...ma'am, but I'm not sure what you want?"

"What I want?! No questions? No comments? No anything?!"

"Sorry, but this is all new to me. A week ago I was doing life with no thought of ever leaving prison, and suddenly I'm here is this crazy bus station where nothing makes sense. On top of that, you're telling me I'm somehow manipulating you by trying to accept your help. Maybe you should just cut to the chase, ship me back now, and send some other yahoo to the Madrid."

Tomaras slowly sank back into her seat and stared at Laine who had resumed the posture of a man folded into his chair, held by invisible chains.

After a long silence, Tomaras spoke. "Okay, look, I'm sorry. I guess I'm too used to cons immediately trying to work me. So let's start over."

She took out a pack of cigarettes, hesitated, then put them back in her jacket pocket.

"Okay, here's the deal. Let's start with the Madrid. You've obviously met Zwick. How did that go?"

"Not very well. It probably would have gone better if I had let him steal my gate money."

"That's a first. How did you get away with that?"

"I told him no and said I'd walk if he pushed it. Go live in mission until I could find something else. That wouldn't have been a violation of my probation. Really, I think he didn't want to lose the easy rent."

"Agreed. And you were able to sign up for Social Security this morning?"

"Yes."

"Another miracle. I assume you've also found the local missions?"

"Yes. Plenty of others at the Madrid are in the same boat, they've been really helpful."

"Well, that only leaves a couple of other things to go over. You are free to go anywhere you want within the city, but I strongly advise you to stay close to home and resist the urge to go exploring until you have a better feel for the area. It can be dangerous, especially for older people who might have a few bucks in their pocket. Got it?"

Laine nodded.

"You'll meet with me every week for the first few months, then monthly as long as you're on Restricted Status. I doubt that will change in the foreseeable future. You'll also have a drug test every time you come here, and you're subject to random tests any time I feel like it."

"Yes, I understand."

"One more thing, and this may be a bit painful, but there is a court order in place that prohibits you from any sort of contact with your former wife and daughter. Are you aware of that?"

Laine looked down and nodded.

"Are you sure?"

"Yes. I have no plan to make contact or even look into their whereabouts."

"Really? I find that hard to believe. It's old, but maybe tempting to try to overturn it, find your family?"

"It may sound strange to you, but I detached from that part of my life fifty years ago. I'm certain they don't know I'm alive. It would be unthinkable for me to bring that devastation to them now. I gave them up when I was on death row, the only way I could accept being condemned. It's not a court order that keeps me away; it's whatever tiny scrap of self-respect I still have left."

Tomaras stared at Laine for a long minute.

"All right. One more thing, it might also be painful, but do you have any other relatives you know of? I think you have a sister, right?"

"Yes, I may have a sister somewhere, but I haven't heard from her since the trial ended. My wife wrote that she, her husband, and kids moved east after I was sentenced, and that's the last I heard about her. Before you ask, I have no interest in trying to contact her. She, too, would assume either I was executed or died in prison. That's all best left alone."

"No other relatives?"

"None I know of. I used to have some aunts and uncles in Finland. They had families, but I never met any of them."

"Finland? That explains the odd spelling of your name."

"Yes, 'Laine' is Finnish for 'wave.' My parents came here after the Great War, settled in a Finnish community in Loma Linda. That's where Katie and I were raised. Dad died when I was fifteen. Mom died just after I went to death row."

"Thanks for those details, Laine. You're an unusual man, I can't quite put you in some neat category like I can with most of the parolees I work with. I'm sorry if I seemed abrasive."

"I understand. Thanks for your help."

An appointment was made for the following Monday. Tomaras shook Laine's hand and said, "I have to tell you, Laine. Not everyone expects you to last out here."

"I've already figured that out. Can you tell me who 'everyone' is?"

"I've already said enough, Laine. Just be careful, and I'll see you next week."

Laine walked back to the Madrid using Leavenworth and Caliente streets so he could walk against one-way street traffic. No point making it any easier to tail him.

A few minutes after Laine left the DAPO building, Edward Dalton opened Tomaras's door.

"Most people knock, Mr. Dalton. I assume your curiosity overcame your manners, right?"

"Cut the crap, Aella. How did it go with your newest client? Pretty clever, isn't he?"

"Clever and smart—both. Most of the cons in my stable don't read Dostoyevsky. He's certainly not what I expected. So exactly why do you have such a hard-on about this guy? And don't go into a swoon over his crime and the poor, long-dead victim."

"Oh, my! Has Laine gotten to the Bitch?"

"Don't call me that, Dalton! I hate that. I'm tough when I have to be, but unlike some people, I can think for myself. So back to the question: what's the big deal with George Laine?"

"He's manipulative, smart and dangerous, that's what so special. Just because he's been locked up for a long time doesn't change someone like that."

"Really? A seventy-five-year-old man who hasn't been in a car for fifty years, hasn't got any money, and will be damn lucky if he gets two meals a day is *dangerous*? In the Tenderloin? It's bullshit. I can do a lot better job if you're straight with me, Dalton."

"Do your job, Aella: send that bastard back where he belongs. You've got a community to protect. And a career, too. Think about it."

Back at the Madrid, as Laine passed Zwick's desk he glanced at his mailbox, top right, easily seen at a glance, but a glance was all Zwick needed.

"Nothing yet, Laine. From what I hear, the Parole Board might be sending you a notice they fucked up, and you gotta go back."

Too much, simply too much. The little cautioning voice didn't have a chance. Laine turned, walked back, stood in front of the desk, folded his arms across his chest, cocked his head slightly, and leveled his eyes at Zwick.

"Tell me, Zwick: when you were a kid, did your parents fill your sandbox with rocks? Or did you grow up pissed off for some other reason?"

"Very funny, asshole," Zwick growled leaning forward, resting his chin on his fist. "You'd be smart to remember you're in my sandbox now."

Message received, Laine thought on his way up the stairs. He met Cowboy on the landing.

"We're all going over to the Second BM in an hour, George. Join us and stick around for the evening show." He promised to join the group, and went up to his room to continue hollowing out the shelf pocket. When he finished, he put the most important documents inside, reattached the back piece, and replaced the shelf using two nails slightly larger than the originals. The fit was tight and the seam invisible. Satisfied, he flushed the remaining chips down the toilet, wrapped the chisel in a wad of paper, and on his way to the lobby, pushed it under the trash in the can next to the vending machines on the first floor landing.

After dinner, Cowboy, George, Louis, and Kitty took their seats in front of the window. "Got your seat, George," Cowboy said pointing to a couch. "But don't sit on the end—that's Kitty's seat." There was some small talk about who was likely to show up on the street that night, who'd been busted recently, and most importantly, if there would be any newcomers trying out the corner. Laine was puzzled about the newcomer issue.

"It's because the pimps who think they own the corner go nuts if someone new shows up. There'll be a balls-on fight for sure," said Kitty taking her designated seat. "Usually, no one gets really hurt, but once in a while someone flashes a knife. Then it can get really messy."

Kitty was tall—maybe five-ten—and painfully thin. She wore no makeup, and her short hair, husky voice, and tan work shirt gave her a slightly masculine look.

"You know a lot about this, Kitty," Laine observed.

"Yep, that's because I used to be one of those poor bitches out there hookin' and cookin'."

"Cooking?"

"Yeah, George, that's street for using Vitamin H, smack, Mr. Magic, heroin, whatever you want to call it. You gotta cook it in a spoon to shoot it. Most of your money goes to your pimp, the rest into the spoon. Are you shocked, George?"

"Not really. There was heroin in prison. I saw a lot of deals made, a lot of overdoses. One difference is, up there the dealer often wore a uniform. Same result."

"Yeah, keeps you numb, dumb, and broke. But I was one of the lucky ones. I got out. Wasn't easy, but I got out."

"How did you do it, if you don't mind me asking?"

"Shit, no, I don't mind. One of the few things I ever did that worked out for me. It was my pimp who got me out."

"Tell him how!" injected Louis.

"Yeah, well, I told him I wanted out, so he beat the shit out of me. I still wanted out, so he beat me up again. The third time, he put me in a coma. When I woke up, I was in a body cast. When I left the hospital six weeks later, I had a glass eye, one arm that still can't salute the flag, my pimp was in jail for attempted murder, and I was stone sober. Best way in the world to kick the monkey: a coma and a body cast. Works every time."

Everyone liked Kitty's story. Cowboy and Louis remembered when she was on the other side of the glass.

The show did start pretty much on time, and Laine had to admit, as sad as it was, it certainly didn't lack excitement. There were a couple of fights, plus a flap caused by a john who claimed he had been ripped off by a hooker. After the cops talked it over with the girl's pimp, the customer was arrested for soliciting sex, or some such, and hauled away.

"It's all about keeping order, George," Kitty explained. "When you go to Walmart to buy underwear, you know you're getting ripped off, but you don't start screaming, 'This is cheap-shit Chinese cloth!' Same thing: they'll haul you away. Gotta have order in the underwear department, got it?"

"Yeah, I'm starting to get it, Kitty."

The next morning Laine ran into Kitty in the lobby and asked her if she wanted to go get some coffee. She accepted, and they walked up to Dusty's.

"I feel safer walking around with someone, even at this hour," Kitty said. "You'll find out, if you haven't already, this is a dangerous neighborhood. Women are particularly vulnerable, especially if they're alone, or even worse, out at night. That's why I dress to be invisible. Loose clothing, sneakers, hair tucked into my cap. I never let my guard down."

"I'm catching on, Kitty. Cowboy gave me an earful about street safety."

"He does it for everybody. But, really, what he says is true, especially for newcomers. They're forever wandering around where they don't belong. The worst is cons coming out after being locked up a long time. They can't get enough of the street and find themselves in Bayview or Hunters Point. Bad idea, especially if they've been drinking."

They talked about the streets, life in the Madrid, but Kitty was discreet in avoiding any questions about Laine's past. Eventually, the conversation turned back to Kitty's former life as a hooker. Without any prodding from Laine, she told him about coming to California from New Jersey thinking she might be able to get into acting.

"I used to be in every school play. And I could sing pretty well, too." But like so many sucked in by the same fantasy, she found she couldn't make it on her own, hooked up with a guy who said he had connections, and gradually found herself on arranged "dates" with men who supposedly just wanted a dinner companion. Her boyfriend told her it was how deals are made, the way attractive girls get attention from people connected to the movie business. But instead of auditions, she got pregnant. When she refused to have an abortion, her boyfriend threw her out. She held on doing motel cleaning, had the child, and in desperation moved in with two other women, both "escorts." Their apartment was raided, Kitty was arrested with the women, the court declared her an unfit mother, and put her daughter in foster care.

"I kept trying to see her, but the foster mother got a court order to keep me away. She moved out of town, and I haven't seen my daughter since. At that point, I said, 'Fuck it,' and went back to New Jersey. I worked a bunch of jobs, got married and divorced twice—thank God I didn't have any more children—and when the second one fell through, I came back here and started turning tricks again. You know the rest. And don't tell me how badly you feel for me. I don't let that feeling past the front door."

"I know exactly what you mean, Kitty. You won't hear it from me. I know all about managing those feelings, especially out here."

"I'd say you have a pretty good grip on it, George. Not like a lot of the people who come here all pissed off or full of self-pity. Either way, they don't make it. They can't support themselves and go back to whatever they did before. Or they OD. Don't matter. You've got to have your wits about you to make it in the Tenderloin."

"So how do you make it, Kitty? You're not old enough for Social Security, you're not a vet. What's the trick? Oops, sorry, didn't mean that the way it sounded."

"No offense, George," she said with a chuckle. "It's easy: you get disability income, basically early Social Security."

"For your glass eye and a stiff shoulder?"

"Nope. Here's how it works. And by the way, half the people you see in the Madrid have the same condition. There's a medical clinic down on Valencia Street. You go in and tell them you have terrible pain all over, especially in your back and neck. They diagnose something called 'fiber myalgia,' give you pain pills, and handle the paperwork to apply for disability. You get turned down a couple of times, then they send you to a disabilities lawyer who files an appeal. When that doesn't do it, you go to a hearing. The lawyer wears them down. It can take two years but you eventually get it. Meantime you sell the pills on the street and hang on until you're approved."

"What's in it for the clinic and the lawyer?"

"The clinic gets Medicaid money every time you put your foot in the door, even if you just pick up a prescription. The lawyer claims your problem started years ago, so they pay you a lump sum for the time between then and now. He keeps the lump sum for his trouble, you get the payments every month— plus all the pills. I gave that part up, though. There are enough junkies out there without adding more. And if you get caught selling the pills, you do time and lose the benefits. Ain't worth it.

"If you're a vet, you work the same thing at the VA, only there it's about nightmares and staying pissed off at everyone all the time. There are so many fucked-up vets, they can't tell the difference between drama and the real thing. If they won't help, you sound off to the complaints specialist, and it goes through. Better yet, you can add on other shit as you go along. It's done on a percentage of your base pay. Bad ankle—ten percent, bad back—twenty percent, can't hear—thirty percent. Keep going as long as you can, each one adds another chunk, and get this: it doesn't stop at one hundred percent! On top of that, they mail you the pills, and you don't have to monkey around with a lawyer."

As they walked back to the Madrid, Laine asked if she knew who was sitting in the car on the other side of the street. Without seeming to look, she said, "Yeah, cops, Metzi and Carlos. Two of the worst creeps in the world. Metzi is a schemer, has his hand in every scam around. Carlos is just a flat-out sadist, especially when it comes to hookers. The worst thing that can happen to you is getting stuck in a meat wagon with Carlos. Those two are around here a lot. Are they watching you?"

"Yeah, I think so."

"That ain't good, George. You better be careful."

Later that morning, Laine walked slowly down to Mission Street, but not seeing the familiar black car, he relaxed a little, picked up his pace, and passed DAPO, stopping three blocks beyond in front of the San Francisco Community Bank and Trust, a four-story brick and glass office building. The bank took up half of the first floor. Several large posters in the windows announced Free Checking for new customers. He entered the building lobby and scanned the directory while simultaneously sizing up the bank, particularly where the Customer Service offices were located. He noted that the law firm of Wallace and Dilworth occupied the top two floors. The rest of the building belonged to mortgage companies, engineers, appraisers, and quite a few computer-related businesses.

Inside the bank, he went straight to the Customer Service desk to say he would like to open an account. He was promptly taken to a small office where Mrs. Winslow greeted him warmly.

"Welcome to SFCBT, Mr....er..."

"Laine, George Laine. I'd like to open a checking account, and make arrangements for direct deposit of my Social Security check."

Yes, indeed, that could be arranged. Could she please see some ID and know how much he would like to deposit "to get the ball rolling"? Laine put five twenty-dollar bills on the table along with his identity card.

Mrs. Winslow's cheery mood vaporized when she saw the card. She excused herself, took the card into another office, and closed the door. A few minutes later she returned, handed Laine the card, and told him she was terribly sorry, but the bank wouldn't be able to open an account for him. When Laine asked why, given the fact there would be a regular monthly deposit, she replied it was out of her hands, "Bank policy, you see." She stood up and tossed a small bone his way: "But if your...ah... 'circumstances' improve, we can take another look."

"Isn't it unlawful to refuse service to a qualified applicant?"

"I'm sorry, Mr. Laine, but I'm sure it is perfectly legal. Now, please, I have other customers."

Laine pocketed his card and cash, thanked her for her time, and said he would work on his "circumstances."

Out on the sidewalk, he remembered the law offices of Wallace and Dilworth, turned around, and took the elevator to the fifth floor. He paused in front of a pair of large glass doors embossed with the names of at least twenty-five lawyers, noting the location of the large display of business cards in the center of the reception desk.

"May I help you, sir?" asked one of the three receptionists.

"No, thank you, I just need this," he said plucking John P. Dilworth's card out of the display. "Silly of me not to have asked him for one when I was here. Thanks."

From there he walked back to the library, past the guard, kiosk, and front desk straight into the reference room. It didn't take long to locate the California law section; specifically, texts dealing with public accommodation. He was familiar with law texts after years of experience in the prison library helping inmates understand sentencing, appeals, and their rights as prisoners.

He jotted a note on the back of Dilworth's card:

George,
Applicable statutes SOC 916:32, 576:45.
Stiff penalties. Any problem let me know.
Bill

He walked back to the bank for another round with Mrs. Winslow. The receptionist immediately recognized him, stood up ready to pounce, but before she could speak, Laine handed her Dilworth's card. "Mrs. Winslow told me to return when my circumstances changed. Would please give her this card? I'll wait out here."

He only had to wait five minutes before he was taken back to Mrs. Winslow's office.

"That was quick, Mr. Laine."

"Yes, pure luck, really. Mr. Dilworth is representing me in a lawsuit and was willing to see me for a few minutes. Of course, I had to wait a while, but he knew exactly what my concerns are."

"Yes, I see. Well, given the fact you are using direct deposit, I think we can let you, that is, *welcome* you to SFCBT."

She took his cash, the account was opened, and a few generic checks were quickly printed. Laine thanked her and returned to the Madrid.

Chapter 12

"ALL RIGHT, DALTON, GIVE ME some good news."

"Look, from your perspective, there isn't much good news beyond the fact we've been watching him carefully. But so far, he doesn't seem the least inclined to cause trouble. His only major move was to get a library card."

"A library card, Dalton? At the main library?"

"Yeah."

"Great! Just great! Have you noticed the library is next to the opera, the law library, and the freaking Civic Center? That's my stomping ground! Don't you remember what I told you? He threatened my father—do you think he doesn't feel the same way about me? I guess that just didn't occur to you."

"I had nothing to do with it. Be realistic, Judge."

"So far, Dalton, all I've got is a bunch of empty promises. So when, exactly, do you think your flunkies are going to throw him back in jail where he belongs? And wasn't he given the most toxic PO ever? And wasn't she guaranteed to violate his ass the minute she met him?"

"Look, Judge, it's not that easy. Yes, I thought he'd trip up the minute he smelled fresh air, but he's cautious to a fault, a whole lot smarter than any of us anticipated. The job will get done; you're just going to have to be patient, that's all.

"I met with Tomaras after she saw him yesterday. He was his charming self, but she won't buy it. When he trips, she won't hesitate to revoke him, but she'll protect herself—she won't break the rules."

"I'm running out of patience, Dalton. I understand he's no pushover—I could have told you that, but he's dangerous, remember? I still can't see why with all your resources he can't be nailed right out of the box, one way or the other."

"Look, Judge, far be it from me to tell you how to run your affairs, but I think you need to be careful not to rush this and make mistakes. Look, I know his history, but maybe all those years put out his fire. I saw him at the hearings. He was always the same: subdued, not the least touchy, and certainly not menacing. I've seen hundreds of killers over the last twenty-five years, some just as clever as Laine. But there's always something that gives them away. It can be as small as the way they sit, how they look at you, or the way guards treat them.

"But not Laine. He's the picture of consistency; the guards don't tense up around him. Nothing. So I have to ask: is it really worth all the risks, all the expense when if you left this guy alone he might be no more of a threat than if he was still across the Bay?"

"That's the difference between us, Dalton: I don't operate on what 'might' be. The stakes are way too high to rely on wishful thinking. That gets people killed. Laine is an actor—smart, devious, and seductive. You saw him on his best behavior, working the con. He only had to hold it together for what? Twenty minutes?

"No, when that prick feels the fresh air on his back again, that 'fire' you talk about will ignite. Don't forget: I knew his victim, I saw what he did to her, how he went from choir boy to savage and back again. He's a chameleon. He might fool you, but he didn't fool the jury.

"So, no, I won't let up until he's either dead or back in prison. Now, get to work!"

Click.

Chapter 13

THE ARGUMENT SPILLING DOWN FROM the second floor got louder as Elton and Tommy made their way down the stairs to the lobby. They were on their way out for breakfast, but judging from their squabbling, it wasn't clear if it would be the "freaking Vietnamese place" or the "lousy cafeteria."

"Hey! Elton! Come here. I've got a surprise for you."

"What kind of surprise, Zwick? I hate surprises."

"Come over here; I want to tell you in private."

"Private? In this dump?"

Zwick shrugged and went back to the newspaper spread out in front of him.

"Okay. Wait here, Tommy," Elton said. He walked over to the desk, put both elbows on the desktop, dropped his chin into his hands in an Edvard Munch posture, and slid forward on his elbows crumpling Zwick's paper.

"Here I am, asshole. What's the news?"

"We got a new guest, fresh out of Quentin, maybe someone you knew."

"How would I know anything about that place?"

"Cut the shit, Elton. Maybe Tommy doesn't know it, but everyone else knows you did time over there."

"All right, so why should I care about one more jerkoff con?"

"Just thought you might know him, that's all. His name is Laine."

"Naaah. Only Laine I knew was an old guy doing life for murder. No way they paroled his ass." He straightened up and turned to walk away.

"I'll bet that's him," Zwick said.

Elton turned back. "It can't be! They almost executed him. They're not going to let someone like that out. But if it is him, maybe I'll just have to finish off what the frigging prison should have done in the first place. He's a real prick. I don't want him around Tommy, either."

"No one will cry if you cancel his ticket. Fact is, word is already out that his parole pissed off a lot of people, people who are watching, people who can be grateful, understand? But be careful, he's no dummy."

"He thinks he's real smart. The only reason he survived in there is because he sucked up to the guards, acted like he was one of them, not one of us."

"Sounds like you had personal experience with him."

"Yeah, I did. I got a job in the laundry, really great job because I could work at night, sleep in the day, and eat when the mess hall was pretty quiet. But Laine didn't like me, kept bustin' my ass for nothing until he finally got me dumped. I had to go back to playing cards all day and fighting to hang onto my food."

"Why didn't someone take care of him? No one in prison puts up with a snitch."

"He was lucky, that's all. But out here there ain't no guards to hide behind, know what I mean?"

Zwick shrugged and went back to unfolding his paper.

"Come on, Tommy, I'm getting an appetite. The Vietnamese place, right?"

"Okay, but what was that about, Elton?"

"It's about a slimeball nobody I knew in prison. His name is Laine, and I don't want you getting anywhere near him, got that?"

"Why? I don't have any grudge with him."

"Well, I do. And that means you do, too. He's bad news, kind of like a hooker who looks all sweet and nice, but if you get anywhere near her you'll have lice crawling up your ass. But don't worry, I'll deal with him."

Chapter 14

LAINE'S THIRD NIGHT OF FREEDOM was fretful, his thoughts too crowded to allow escape into sustained sleep. In the morning, he decided to return to Dusty's, indulge himself with an egg sandwich, and think about his next steps. He turned onto the sidewalk, pausing briefly to see who might be watching. Everything seemed quiet, so he turned the corner toward Dusty's. Once off the street in the back of the shop with a large cup of hot coffee, Laine unfolded the map Tomaras had given him, looking for more streets and places to explore. It was Thursday morning, and the streets were comfortably busy, the perfect time to blend invisibly into the crowds.

But then there was the recurring image of Zwick, his sneer, and the warnings from Cowboy and Kitty. *No, don't get ahead of yourself. You're not a free man yet.* Exploring could be dangerous. Far better to learn the immediate neighborhood first, get a feeling for the streets around the Tenderloin, a sense of why people and traffic choose one route over another. Find the drug corners, the alleys, and vacant lots. Be aware of places people collect for no apparent reason. It's like the exercise yard, only here there are plenty of places to hide and the guards seem to be on the side of the bad guys.

For two days, Laine quietly probed the districts around the Tenderloin, careful to blend in, always with the air of someone going somewhere specific, never looking like he was studying the place, or worse, the people. The black sedan showed up in a random way. If they were trailing him, they were getting better at masking their surveillance.

Making his rounds on Friday morning, he passed the Second BM Mission. A large delivery van was parked in front, rear doors open. The minister, Reverend Sully, and another man Laine recognized from the previous night's dinner were unloading boxes of canned food and crates stuffed with various vegetables. The driver sat in the cab on the passenger's side, feet hanging out the open door, smoking a cigarette, entirely disengaged from the unloading process.

"Can I give you a hand, Reverend?"

"Sure, Mr., ah…can't remember…"

Laine reintroduced himself, picked up a crate, and followed the other two into the kitchen. It took just under thirty minutes to complete the job.

"Thank you, George. You were a big help. The driver is union. He wouldn't lift a finger if it took us all afternoon to unload. By the way, Tolbert and I are really impressed by how easily you handled those crates. They're heavy."

Laine didn't waste time dodging the observation. He told the men about his recent release from prison including the fact he had worked in the prison laundry for over forty years. "It keeps you in shape."

Laine was invited to join them for lunch. It didn't take Reverend Sully long to get around to questions about Laine's spiritual life; in particular, he wanted to know if Laine was a Christian.

"My family was Lutheran," Laine said, hoping the conversation wouldn't go any further.

But Sully went straight for the carotid: "Tell me, George, have you accepted Jesus Christ as your personal savior?"

"Put it this way, Reverend: I respect all beliefs, but I tend to hold mine close to the vest. I found it made life inside a lot easier when I didn't get into religious discussions."

"But you're out now, thanks to the Lord. You need to give Him joyous thanks, get on your knees and pray for forgiveness for your crime, and live a sinless life. Otherwise, you may fall back onto the dark path."

Laine stood up to leave. "Well, I certainly appreciate your enthusiasm for my soul, Reverend. The lunch was an added bonus. But the rest of it is far too complicated to get into right now. Let's just say that living a responsible life should be a goal for all of us, don't you think?"

Sully wasn't convinced but decided to hold back. They shook hands at the kitchen door. Watching him leave, Sully decided it would be wise to keep an eye on this man, give him a chance to adjust to life outside San Quentin, see if he began to lose some of his prison defensiveness. Then maybe he could bring him around to the righteous path. But if he was of the Devil, it would be a different matter.

On the way back to the Madrid, Laine was again overtaken with thoughts about Leroy. He was just as passionate about his commitment to God as Reverend Sully, but Leroy didn't push it. To him, there was nothing to be judged or argued about the difference between his and Laine's views of what may lie on the other side of the invisible horizon. Leroy knew in his heart he had the answer, that holding to his belief would one day bring him peace, but in the meantime, he enjoyed exploring other ideas. Leroy had a way of summing it up: "If you take the bus and I take the train, it don't matter. We're both just tryin' to get home."

That night at dinner, Sully greeted Laine by name, thanked him again for his help, and offered lunch anytime Laine might feel like doing some work around the mission. He also offered him a paperback book, *Move That Mountain*, explaining it might be "helpful."

"Perhaps we could discuss it next time you feel like dropping by."

Laine accepted the book, thanked the Reverend, and finished his dinner.

By Saturday, Laine felt confident enough to try going further afield. *How about Dolores Park? It's on the edge of the mission neighborhood, should be safe enough, plus there will be lots of people around. Who knows? Maybe I can find a place to sit in the sun and look out over the city and the bay.* He walked at a steady gait down Market to Dolores Street, then straight down into the park.

The park itself was a large open rectangle on a steep grassy hillside, once the site of a Jewish cemetery, according to the brochure Laine picked up at the gate. From the top, one had a commanding view of the city and the San Francisco Bay beyond. The brochure also explained that touching the replica of the Mexican Liberty Bell at the entrance is known to bring good luck.

"Can't pass that up," Laine said out loud as he rested his hand on the bell's smooth surface.

But again the voice, always the voice: Caution! Don't get too used to this; remember, bell or no bell, you don't belong here. The more you come to like it, the worse it will feel when you wake up back in one of those cells. Maybe it will be in the building with "CONDEMNED" written over the entrance. Or maybe the one you had before the laundry and Leroy, alone, one book a week, a few hours in the yard, then back on the mattress trying to meditate, block out the yelling, the smell, exiled from any possible use of your mind except to find a way to stop thinking anything.

The park was green, alive with families and children. It suddenly hit Laine that this was his first exposure to children since…since when? True, he saw a few at the Goodwill store and on the street, but there weren't any kids around the Madrid, at the mission, or at Dusty's. But there were plenty in the park. Their energy, excitement, and voices all tried to make him remember Rebecca, the forbidden image of his daughter, long banished, the anguish controlled. Now the pain was creeping back.

Get out. Go home to the Madrid. Maybe you can handle this another day. Walk, get back on the vigil, focus your mind on what's around you.

And suddenly, there it was, the black car, just a glimpse, a reflection in a store window. Then a few blocks with no image. *Where are they? Was I just so screwed up from the park that I'm starting to hallucinate? Is this all just prison paranoia?*

Passing McAllister, almost back. Then the black car screeched to a halt next to him, the passenger out and on top of him in an instant. Laine's instincts kicked in, and he tightened his muscles just enough to protect himself from getting hurt as he was slammed into the wall, but not enough to be interpreted as resisting.

"Okay, tough guy, up against the wall, feet apart, just like always." Metzi joined Carlos in time to kick the inside of Laine's ankles to widen his stance. Laine remained silent as Carlos frisked him, roughly squeezing his pockets against his thighs and buttocks, driving his thumbs into his armpits before sliding his hands down over his sides and legs, all the way to his feet. Metzi then spun him around, grabbed his chin, and pushed his head against the brick wall.

"Out for a little stroll, buddy? Maybe pick up some drugs?"

"Is there a problem?"

"Oh, yeah. We got a call. Seems someone has been harassing people down in Dolores Park. We're looking into it."

"Well, thanks for the warning. I'll be careful."

"We got us a fucking comedian here, don't we, Carlos?"

Carlos agreed. Laine decided to stay quiet, listen to the voice, wait this one out. Perhaps they hoped he would try to defend himself, so they could arrest him for resisting, or better yet, maybe he would throw a punch. But he remained passive.

"Why don't you assholes pick on someone who's actually doing something wrong?" a passerby yelled. He got an earful from Carlos, prompting several others to stop and watch, clearly disapproving, on the edge of hostility.

Metzi looked back and forth between Laine and the gathering crowd. "A warning, buddy: Stay in your own neighborhood. It's too dangerous out there for an old con like you. Next time we won't be so gentle, got it?"

They pushed through the bystanders, got in their car, and roared off.

"You okay, mister?"

"Yeah, I'm fine. Thanks for your help. It was brave of you to speak up. Those two are really dangerous."

"Except to criminals. Everyone around here knows them."

Back in the Madrid on his way up the stairs, Zwick called out, "Have a good walk, Laine?"

"Yeah, terrific. Your brother Carlos said hello."

"Fuck you, Laine."

He met Cowboy on the stairs, promised he'd join the group for the evening trip to the mission, went back to his room, and locked the door.

"Shit!" he said out loud, angry that he let his emotions overrule caution: he forgot to look for the paper ball. He checked his keeps—nothing out of place. He pulled back the towel curtain to look down on the street. That, too, seemed normal. No need to watch him now—the message had been delivered.

The sermon that night was mercifully short, the meal surprisingly good. Laine's encounter with Metzi and Carlos was the focus of the conversation. Everyone had a theory. They do that just to let you know who's in charge. It was because Zwick was pissed and called a favor. They did it because Tomaras is eager to revoke him and wants to speed up the process.

Laine was silent throughout the discussion. Finally, Kitty asked him straight up, "Come on, George, tell us, why you think they did it?"

"Delivering a message, I guess. Seems like everyone in the neighborhood knows those two. I'm the newcomer; they're letting me know who's in charge." That was the end of it.

Back at the Madrid, Laine reluctantly decided to join the show.

"Hang out with us," Kitty urged. "We ain't much, but we all know how it feels to get jumped like that."

"Thanks, Kitty, but it's not getting hassled that's got me. It's hard to explain. Best I can do with it is to say it's too much too soon. I've got to slow down, let my thinking catch up with where I am. Things that worked in the old prison don't seem to work in the new one. I keep making mistakes. It's not like me."

"I sorta get it, George. I was in a different kind of jail, but I think the same shit happened to me. What's crazy is that we seem to gravitate—is that the word?—back to being locked up, like, it's awful but it's the awful we know how to manage. But I know—listen to me, George—I know that if you can keep your head on straight for a while, they'll lose interest, and you can become as invisible as the rest of us."

"And get a load of Johnny Jump-Up's new rubber skirt! Ooo-eee!" crowed Louis. "Price just went up ten bucks, for sure!"

Attention shifted to the street. There was immediate agreement: at least ten dollars extra for the rubber. Even Laine had to admit it was quite a sight.

Heading out for coffee the next morning, Laine nearly bumped into Tommy at the front door.

"Sorry, mister," Tommy said holding the door for Laine.

"Sorry my ass, Tommy! This is someone you don't want to know. Get out of our way, Laine, or I'll use you to mop the floor."

"My goodness! Elton! I heard you were here. As far as mopping the floor with me goes, I bet it's just your way of saying, 'Good to see you again.'"

"Fuck off, Laine. And remember: there ain't no guards out here to hide behind."

"I'll watch myself, Elton. I appreciate the warning."

"It's a promise, not a warning. Come on, Tommy," Elton said pushing Tommy ahead of him into the lobby. "You see how slick he thinks he is? I gotta tell you something you need to know about that prick: he's a murderer. And if he doesn't like you, he'll either kill you, or get someone to screw you over while he's off somewhere else. That's what he did in prison."

"I'll be careful, Elton, I promise. But did you mean it that you'd...you know..."

"Kill his ass? Sure, but I'd do it so no one knows it was me. I don't want to get sent back to jail on account of that miserable bastard."

"You never told me about him before."

"I wouldn't give him the pleasure."

"So, what will you do?"

"I'm working on it, Tommy"

After his encounter with Elton and Tommy at the hotel, Laine turned onto Caliente on what was quickly becoming his routine morning walk to Dusty's. Happily, it was a short, minimum risk walk with the rising sun at his back. But countless sudden assaults in prison made him wary of even the most innocent-looking situations.

Halfway up the block, Kitty called out for him to wait for her.

"What's up with those two?" she asked.

"It's about Elton. I knew him in prison, not well, thank goodness. He's was always hostile, ready to fight, but a lot of it was a bluff. He was so crazy looking that everyone just stayed out of his way if they could; if not, they usually gave in ahead of any real fight. People rarely called his bluff.

"For a long time, the only place I saw him was on the exercise yard. But then for some crazy reason, they decided to put him in the laundry on my shift. He wouldn't do anything right. I tried him in several places, but he was always yelling at someone or complaining. Finally, I put him on 'sorting.' All he had to do was empty hampers and put sheets and towels on one line, clothes on the other. Simple. Then I caught him sleeping in a hamper and warned him I'd write him up if he did it again. A couple of weeks later—same deal, sound asleep. That time I did write him up. The third time, a guard caught him sniffing cleaning solvent, threw him out on the spot. Elton blamed me and said he was going to kill me.

"He's a lot of talk, Kitty, but still a dangerous man. I'll watch myself."

"That's pretty much the way he is at the Madrid: everyone but Zwick avoids him. But I do worry about Tommy; he's really vulnerable, and Elton seems to have some strange hold on him. I don't think it's a sex thing, either. Every time I get anywhere near him, Elton barges in like I'm trying to do something awful to Tommy. So I just leave 'em both alone.

"But I didn't come to talk about them. I'm concerned about you, thought maybe you could use some company after that non-conversation last night. Tell me if I'm out of line, George. I'll go back."

"No, Kitty, glad to have the company. And, yeah, you're right, I just didn't want to go into any of it, too close to the bone, if you understand what I mean."

"I think I do." They walked in silence all the way to Dusty's. Kitty bought the coffee, and they took a table in the back of the shop, the one with the best view of the door.

"Do you open up to anyone, George? I mean, you're obviously sitting on a ton of stuff. You can't keep it in forever."

"True, but I've been holding it in for a long time. I wasn't that way at first, but it finally dawned on me I was literally at a dead end. Everything I had worked for was gone, everyone I loved was taken away, and there was absolutely no chance in the world I could ever recover any of it. The only way to deal with it was to make myself quit thinking about anything, figure out a way to keep my mind in prison, never let it out. That's the key: always focus on what's in front of you; never let your mind wander back. So I made a decision to put it all in some faraway mental vault, close the door, spin the lock, walk away, and stay focused on just what I'm doing at any given moment.

"And, yes, I did have a friend I could talk to—my cellmate, Leroy. We talked every day, and we knew each other so well we never stepped into some place that would cause the other one pain. We were really quite dependent on each other, something most inmates avoid like the plague. And suddenly I'm here in a coffee shop, and Leroy is alone in a cell in that hellhole on the other side of the bay.

"I feel like I've betrayed him by coming here. He's the one who should be out. He got life for defending himself in a fight with two guys, a fight he didn't even start. They called it murder, he had a record, a drug history, was black, and the prosecutor needed a conviction. He was expendable, end of story. I'm sure everyone congratulated the prosecutor for sanitizing streets none of them would ever visit."

"That's awful. But hopefully, he'll get out someday, too. Meantime, maybe he'll get another cellmate like you. But I'll bet he's glad for you."

"Yeah, that would be Leroy. Still, the unfairness of it all keeps screaming at me. I can't shove it down out here like I did in there. In prison, it's all about routine—mind-numbing repetition. Every minute of every day it's the same: you do your work and protect yourself until that becomes your world. Everything else disappears.

"But out here, every day there's something else, another curveball you didn't see coming. I used to think nothing was crazier than prison, but now that I'm out I see how wrong I was."

"Can I ask, George: what was your crime? Or is that off limits?"

"No, you can ask. I was convicted of rape and murder in 1958, sentenced to death, and only avoided execution when the court voided everyone's death sentence in 1967. It converted me to life and made me eligible for parole. I never imagined or even thought that could actually happen."

"Did you do it, George?"

"No."

"I didn't think so. Is it something you can talk about, or should I just shut up and drink my coffee?"

"It's okay. The minute I stepped out of San Quentin the past started hitting me again. I dread it, but I've got to allow that stuff back into my head. Call it self-defense, but if—big 'if'—I'm going to stay out here, I'll have to deal with it. I'm a sitting duck if I don't."

"What about your family? That has to be tearing you apart."

"Yes, that's the most painful part. I was on death row the last time I had any contact with my wife, Constance. My daughter was only two months old the last time I saw her. I just found out a few days ago that Constance remarried, but I have no plan to try to find out about her, or even worse, try to make contact. I'm sure they—I'm talking about my wife and daughter here—think I'm dead. Can you imagine how awful it would be to suddenly find out I'm not only alive, but I could be right around any corner? And what if I showed up? That must never happen.

"And how about you, Kitty? How do you deal with knowing you have a daughter out there somewhere who may not even know you exist?"

"It's like you said, George, you can't allow yourself to dwell on it. And I sure as hell can't try to find her, show up, and say, 'Hi! I'm your mom!' That would be crazy.

"To be truthful, it's why I stick close to the Madrid. Out there I'd be looking at every teenage girl wondering, are you my Angie? Do they even call you Angie anymore? That girl over there looks a little like me, could that be Angie? I know I'd recognize Foster Bitch if I saw her again. But then what? And if I ever did meet Angie in some chance way, what would I say to her? That her mom was a whore? Would she believe I had nothing to do with getting her taken away?

"No, I gotta leave it all alone. But there is one positive thing I do tell myself: I quit drugs, I quit hooking, and no one controls me anymore. Oh, and I quit smoking, too! So even though I'll never see my daughter, at least I can say I did all of that for her. Without her, I'd be dead by now. It's crazy, but every time I thought about giving up, pulling the plug, I thought of her. I love her for what she has given me, even if it's all just a fantasy.

"But I'll tell you, George, there were times I was this close," she said, pinching her thumb and index finger together. "You wouldn't believe the stuff I did just trying to get to the next day. Like, sometimes when I was working, I'd fantasize that the guy was a prince who had come to rescue me. And when that didn't work, I'd say, no, not him, it's the next guy. And an hour later, I'd be so full of hate, I'd lie there thinking of all the ways I could kill the guy. Totally nuts, but that was the way it was."

"There's nothing crazy about it. You pulled the energy out of the outrage and made it work for you. Survival doesn't come with an instruction manual: you figure it out as you go along—or it destroys you.

"It happened over and over in prison. I remember once when I got thrown in solitary after being in a fight—standard procedure while they sort out what happened. Suddenly, I was alone in a tiny cell with absolutely nothing. The bed was just a concrete slab, the toilet was backed up, there was no toilet paper, no conversation, just insane, random noise ricocheting off the walls all day and night."

"How did you turn the energy on that one?"

"At first, I relied on meditation and exercise…"

"Exercise? You don't look like a push-ups guy to me."

"I'm not. My exercise comes from tai chi. When I was an undergraduate, I minored in philosophy, imagining that by absorbing the ideas of Plato and Locke I could transform my own thinking, open my mind to a new level of knowledge. It didn't work the way I had hoped.

"Then by pure chance, I went to a demonstration by a dancer named Sophia Delza—and found the answer. She'd spent several years working in a Shanghai ghetto after World War II, got interested in Chinese philosophy, and began to see ways the mind could accomplish what the body could not. She used a form of dance to bring it to life by coordinating balance, breathing, and relaxation. It changed my life.

"Obviously, there's a whole lot more to it, but I was gradually able to grasp the paradox of using focused energy to relax my body, open it and my mind to reach a meditative state. You never stop learning how far you can take it, but along the way, it saved me from going completely mad."

"But George, I thought tai chi was about fighting. You know, jumping around kicking people's teeth out. Wouldn't you be a sitting duck standing there all relaxed in some sort of trance?"

"No trance. And it isn't about fighting—it's about *not* fighting. Too many people think it's all about aggression. I've paid dearly for that misconception. No, it's the opposite of fighting. However, if as a last resort you have to defend yourself, having concentrated all of your energy and focused your mind, you are prepared to make a sudden explosive move. No fight. One strike and it's over."

"Did it work when you were in solitary? I can't imagine spending hour after hour like that."

"No, it didn't. Sometimes I just couldn't get away from that stinking cell. The craziness kept pulling me back, but I used other tricks. I remembered reading about a guy in solitary who had no light, no bed, and just a bucket for a toilet. It was pitch black and dead quiet. He was going nuts trying to live meal to meal, not because he was hungry, but to catch just a glimpse of light that showed when they dropped the grub down the food shoot.

"He thought of trying to kill himself, but he figured that was what they wanted; if he did it, they'd win. So he invented a game to deal with the time and the dark. He pulled a button off his shirt, threw it, and spent hours crawling around the floor trying to find it. Then he'd throw it again. At first, he searched at random, then he figured out how to start in one corner and work around the cell in a pattern. When he mastered that, he changed the rules and followed the sound the button made rattling around the floor. Then he moved to the sound to see how fast he could put his hand on it. He became totally obsessed with the button, but it got him through three months in there.

"I did the button game, too. It helped, especially at night when it was dark. But during the day, I had to close my eyes to do it. I just couldn't keep that up for hours at a time.

"Another trick was reciting every line of poetry, every Bible verse, the words to every song, and every joke I ever heard—all out loud like I was giving a performance. I'd stand on the bed slab and announce the next act. I can still do 'Casey at the Bat' start to finish, all fifty-two lines. But Casey won't help me out here.

"I never gave freedom more than a passing glance, especially as I got older. To the extent I thought about it at all, I imagined it would be quiet, no one would even notice me. Now I'm suddenly there, and I can't find the button. I just want to be left alone, but it's clear others don't see it that way."

"Others? So who would bother with you, George? Why not leave you alone? You're always going to be in jail; the only difference is the coffee's better in this one. But you'll never have anything else, just a bunch of has-beens for friends, and whatever change you can pry out of Zwick's grubby fingers once in a while for a clean pair of socks.

"And one more thing, then I'll shut up. But I have to ask: do you know who committed the crime?"

"No, not really. When I was on death row I spent hours and hours obsessing every tiny detail thinking I could solve the crime, finger the real culprit, and reverse the whole insane process. I narrowed it down to five or six people, but the one I knew the most about didn't seem to have a motive. That's as far as I got. Finally, I just gave up.

"If you're wondering if that person could have anything to do with what's happening now, I simply can't make the connection. It doesn't make sense. Fact is, it's far more likely coming from someone I offended in prison. There were a lot of well-connected inmates in there, and I didn't bow down to any of them. Cons have long memories and thrive on revenge, especially when someone they don't like gets out. It's far more likely this is some sort of payback than anything connected to a crime that happened half a century ago."

"But you don't believe that, do you?" Before Laine could answer, Kitty looked at the wall clock and said, "Gotta get back soon, a few of us go to the noon mass at St. Timothy's. It's Saint Eusebiass Day. But you can pick any saint and say a prayer."

"Who's your favorite?"

"Saint Margaret of Cortona. She's the Patron Saint for Reformed Prostitutes. When you're hooking, you pray to her to get you out. When you're free, you thank her for delivering on the promise. Doesn't hurt to add a few coins to the poor box, either."

"Pretty good deal. Did you ever hear of Saint Nonnatus?"

"Nope. Is this a joke?"

"No joke. I heard about him from a priest who used to make the rounds of solitary on Sunday, see the guys who couldn't attend church. I was there doing the button game. He stopped by and asked if I was Catholic. I said I wasn't. He said it didn't really make any difference and offered to say a prayer for forgiveness of my sins. I asked if that included my crime. He said yes, it did. So I asked him, what if I didn't do it? Did he have a prayer for that? And quick as that," Laine said, snapping his fingers, "he said I needed to connect with Saint Nonnatus, the Patron Saint of the Falsely Accused. I gotta tell you, that one took me by surprise."

"Well, I'll slip in a good word for you with Saint Nonnatus."

On the way back to the Madrid, Laine was thinking about joining the others for Sunday lunch at the mission. It meant a longer sermon, but they didn't serve dinner on Sunday night, so there really wasn't any other choice.

"Don't turn, don't look at me, Laine," a man walking beside him said. "Tony Concano sent me to invite you to lunch. He figured it wouldn't be smart to be seen walking with you."

"Tony! You're kidding!"

"No joke. Walk over to Van Ness, take any bus north, get off at Bay Street, go east four blocks, you'll see the Napoli Restaurant. Be sure you're not followed. You got bus fare?"

"How much is it?"

"A buck."

"I can handle it." The man accelerated, turned left at the corner, and disappeared. Laine followed his instructions, pausing briefly a few times to see if he was being trailed. He caught the bus, got off at Bay, and walked east. The man who had given him his instructions was sitting on a bench outside the restaurant smoking a cigarette. He didn't speak or seem to notice Laine.

Inside, a waiter wearing a wraparound, full-length apron greeted him by name and pointed toward a room at the rear of the restaurant.

"George! How good to see you, my friend!"

"I don't believe it! Tony! Finally, a friend!"

The two men hugged.

"Back here, George, a private room. We won't be disturbed."

"How did you know I got out, Tony? And how is your dad? And how the hell are you?"

"Slow down, George, we got all afternoon to catch up. But first I gotta tell you: since I got out I have been completely out of the life, totally legit, George. I run a warehouse business for the Old Man, and if I smell anything that ain't right, I shut the fucking door on it. But there's more: I got Claire back! Can you believe it?"

"Yeah, I can believe it. Fantastic, Tony. How's your dad with the change?"

"Totally cool. And when he found out I was back with Claire, he cried. He actually cried. He thinks you hung the moon, man. He's retired and lives in Florida now, but he told me to tell you that if you ever, I mean ever, need anything, you call me and we'll take care of it. I may be out of the business, but I got cousins and uncles, you know, and I still know how to get shit done… well…in case of emergency, you know.

"But now we eat. Business later. When's the last time you had a good meal, George? Don't tell me. But one thing I remember you told me once when I asked you what your favorite food was, you said, 'clams in white sauce on linguine.' Right?"

They ate and talked about Tony's family, the kids and two grandchildren, the books he had been reading, Claire and her cooking class, and his plans for retirement. Over espresso the subject changed to Laine's parole, the shock of it happening at all, the crazy confusion of Stonebridge House, his PO, the Madrid, even the hooker shows at night.

"You're not telling me the whole thing, George. Fact is, I heard you were out from a guy I used to know in the police department. He called me up to ask if I knew you. I asked him why, and he said there was talk around the Tenderloin station about a guy someone up the line wants to get busted, a guy just out of San Quentin. He wanted to know what was so special about this guy—he never heard of him. I told him I sorta remembered you and tried to find out who was putting on the pressure. He clammed up, and that was it.

"So I asked around and found out a couple of cops have been tailing you off and on, looking for some reason to arrest you, get you sent back. So I sent Robert, and here you are. Have I got this right?"

Laine confirmed what Tony had heard. "It may sound weird, but it's a relief to know I'm not crazy or being paranoid. But I'm like you, I have no idea who could possibly want to go to so much trouble."

They talked about inmates they had known who might have a grudge, but none of them were connected or powerful enough to command this kind of play. And the ones who were capable weren't the sort to go after someone as non-threatening as Laine. Dead end.

"How about someone from a long time ago, someone related to the crime you got sent up for? Incidentally, George, even though we never talked about the details of your crime, I never bought the idea you did it. I never asked you, but am I right?"

Laine stared at his cup for a long minute. He was about to go into forbidden territory again.

"Yes," he said in a near whisper.

"I thought so. So maybe it's the girl's family, or maybe even the guy himself. I mean, if he's still alive and you're out, he could worry, you know, maybe you'd come after him."

"I doubt it. That was a long time ago. Really, Tony, I don't know who did it. There were several I thought might have done it. But we were graduate students, any number of them knew where I lived, and conceivably could have framed me.

"There was one guy who did stand out, but not for any really solid reason. He was with a group of us—including the victim—at a party the night she was killed. I thought he might have shown some interest in the girl. Who knows? But if it was him, I can't imagine he—or any of the others—would have the power or the resources for this. If he's alive, he's a retired lawyer.

"Of course, if he really is the one who did it, he certainly has a lot to fear with me being out, but the probability is he doesn't even know it. And he sure as hell couldn't come after me with cops and a toxic probation officer looking for an excuse to send me back to prison.

"The irony is, I have no interest in having anything to do with him—or his family. That's the last thing on my mind."

"Why? I mean, why wouldn't you want to at least let him know you're out, make him sweat even if you don't do anything else?"

"It's more personal than that."

"Personal? What's more personal than mailing you off to the freaking gas chamber? Maybe you mean he was a friend—is that it?"

"We were friends, but not too close. No, it's more personal than that."

"Jesus, George, is this Twenty Questions? Just friggin' tell me! It won't go anywhere—you know me and my word."

"It's because he married my wife and raised my daughter, that's why! Even if they're not still together, my wife certainly thinks I'm dead. I doubt my daughter has ever heard my name. It would destroy my wife to find out the truth, to say nothing of what it might do to my daughter. I could never do that to them.

"There you have it, Tony. Do you see why I won't do anything about him? Why it's actually a relief to know whoever is behind all this couldn't be him?"

"Yeah, got it. By the way, what's this guy's name?"

"Preston."

"What's his first name?"

"Alfred."

"Holy Mother of God!" Tony said making the sign of the cross. "*Judge* Alfred Preston?"

"No, Tony, he is a lawyer, smart enough to get by, but way too lazy and entitled to be a judge. I was a graduate student in electrical engineering, he was in law school. He helped me apply for a patent the summer before the murder. His father was a hotshot lawyer, and when I was arrested, his dad offered to defend me at no cost. We didn't have any money, so of course, I accepted his help. It went downhill from there.

"Jesus! That's cold. Well, if it is the same guy, he puts on a good show, but he's crooked as a dog's hind leg. He's the guy you want to hear your shady zoning case or the lawsuit you probably should lose. Big society dude in Burlingame. His wife does a lot of charity work."

"By the way, Tony, do you know her name?"

"Sure, they're in the news all the time. It's Constance."

Laine closed his eyes and dropped his head to his chest. He remained frozen in that position for several minutes. Tony waited in silence.

"I feel awful, George. I mean…I don't know what to say."

Laine collected himself, said he was bound to find out sooner or later, and that knowing who your enemies are makes it a fair fight. "Besides, I'm still not convinced it's him. How in the world could he go from a lazy, patent-geek lawyer to a judge? He wasn't a scholar; he was a rich kid looking for something to do. True, he was quite social, talked a good line, but a judge? The only part that rings true is the idea he would always be looking for the shortcut."

"So what's your next step, George?"

"No next step, Tony. No change of plan. I'll keep going until either they decide I'm harmless and leave me alone, or they get me in some way and send me back."

"That would be awful, George. It's unthinkable."

"It's the reality, Tony. If they decide to do something more than push me around once in a while, I'm cooked. Be honest about it, what chance is there I won't get revoked if they really want it?"

"It would make me crazy just thinking about it."

"No, Tony, it's the opposite. You've made it easier for me. Think about it: when I get sent back, they have to decide what to do with me. I'm already too old to keep running the laundry; they just let me stay because I kept the inmates in line. Back in general population, I'd be a target. That happens when you lose status, and getting revoked would be just that. The warden would do me a favor and send me to the geriatric wing. It's an open door area, no cuffing up every five minutes, no fights. I know most of the old cons, the ones who can still think and talk; best of all, there's a big porch up there—only one in the whole place—with a view of the hills. They push the nearly dead out there in wheelchairs to let 'em feel the sun one last time. I can sit out there and read myself into oblivion.

"And if you think Alfred gets off, you'd be wrong. The story would be out. Heaven knows what Constance would do, but it wouldn't be good for him. No, his life would be miserable, and mine would be a hell of a lot better than it has been for fifty-plus years. So either way, it's okay. If you want justice, there it is. If it's a little peace in the time I have left, there it is. If this short time outside prison was designed to give me a modicum of peace, there it is."

"Same old George. You're the kid who finds a pile of shit under the Christmas tree and looks around for his new pony. But in the meantime, can I give you some money?"

"No, thank you, Tony."

"Didn't think so. Okay, but here," he said handing Laine a slip of paper. "It's my personal phone number. Memorize it or make up a code, so if someone finds it, there's no way to tie it to me; you know, associating with known criminals would be grounds for revocation. I'm dead serious about this, George. Call anytime, day or night, if I can help you."

Laine thanked Tony for the meal, the companionship, and the chance to understand his circumstances better. He took the bus and went home.

Chapter 15

"WHAT DO YOU THINK, ELTON? We could walk up to that Chinese place on Taylor? All you can eat for five bucks. We haven't been there for a while."

"Long way to walk for noodles, if you ask me. But as long as Laine ain't there, I'm good with it."

"Holy cow, Elton, when are you going to stop talking about Laine?"

"When he's dead or back in the pen, that's when."

"You're not kiddin', are you?"

"Fuck, no, I ain't kiddin'. Remember that knife I lifted from the Vietnamese dump? I'm getting it real sharp. Then I'm going to stick that bastard and laugh."

"Don't do it, Elton. Please don't. You might get caught and sent off. I couldn't make it out here without you, man. Can't you just ignore him?"

"Ignore him!? Are you crazy? What do you think he's doing right now except planning some sneaky way to take me out? You don't get it, Tommy—this is self-defense, pure and simple. He won't quit just because we're out of prison. No, I've got to do it, Tommy—for both of us."

"Isn't there some other way? Can't you get someone else to do it?"

"Like who? Even if I knew someone, I haven't got the money. No, I have to do it myself."

"I know somebody who would do it for free."

"Yeah? Who?"

"Me! I'll do it. Give me the knife, tell me what to do. I'll do it!"

"No, Tommy, I couldn't let you do it. If something went wrong, I'd never forgive myself."

"What can go wrong? You said as long as no one saw it, there'd be no way the cops would even bother investigating. No one in the world would think I could do such a thing, and you could be elsewhere. And if we need it, Zwick will cover for us, right? Didn't you say he hates Laine, too? Let's just do it and get rid of the problem. The longer we wait, the longer he has to get you first."

Elton had his doubts about the plan, though he agreed that no one would suspect Tommy, including Laine. Tommy would have no trouble getting next to him. The bastard would never see it coming.

The big problem was the actual stick. Tommy wouldn't have a clue about how to handle a knife, but with a little practice, it could work. They talked about the plan and agreed on a strategy. Elton would get the knife razor sharp with plenty of tape wrapped around the handle for a good grip. Tommy could practice his moves, maybe get good enough for two or even three quick stabs. Elton would be close enough to intervene if Tommy only wounded Laine. Yes! Finish him off and celebrate with dinner at the steakhouse over on Van Ness.

Chapter 16

"ANOTHER BIG DAY, COWBOY," LAINE said as he walked out of the Madrid Monday morning. "My second meeting with my PO. Don't want to be late for that—she wouldn't hesitate to violate me. I can't tell yet if that's her nature or if there's more to it than just not liking convicts."

"From what I hear, it's both. She's a real hard-ass, but she seems to go after the easy ones, the drunks and junkies who can't stay out of trouble even when they're sober. My guess is she hates her job and wants to move up in the system. Busting people makes her look good, that's all."

"Maybe."

Laine left the Madrid an hour earlier than needed to make the twenty-minute walk to DAPO. He also varied his normal route, walking down Taylor Street so he could walk against one-way traffic. He arrived at DAPO well ahead of time, provided his urine sample, and settled down to read until it was time to see Miss Tomaras.

"Early again. You know, Laine, you don't have to camp out here all day just to see me."

"Just want to be sure I'm on time in case of an unexpected delay."

"Delay? Like what sort of delay?"

"Big city, lots of surprises. You never know."

The conversation drifted from there, covered some canned questions about drug and alcohol use, injuries, and any specific problems in the community. The receptionist stuck her head in the door, shook her head, and closed the door.

"I'm getting used to you, Laine: still no questions, no problems, no surprises, and no real information. All of it makes me suspicious. What's really going on in that head of yours?"

"I won't risk pissing you off by saying, 'Nothing,' and the truth—if you can accept it—is that I'm more aware than ever of what you said when we met last week: not everyone is thrilled to see me out of prison. And I don't think it's just the nature of my crime."

"Interesting. Care to go further?"

"No, just being honest. I think you want that."

"I do. But what gives you that impression, anything specific? Or just what I said? Isn't that the sort of thing I might say to anyone coming out of prison, a way of urging compliance?"

"It's partly a feeling, partly what you said, partly a carryover from half a century of being watched twenty-four hours a day. Oh, and partly getting roughed up by a couple of cops last week."

"What cops?"

"Now it's my turn to be doubtful. You really don't know that Metzi and Carlos put the wood on me?"

"I heard a rumor, put it that way."

"A 'rumor'..."

"They have a tendency to overreact to people they don't like. Let's be honest: paroled murderers aren't a welcome addition to the neighborhood."

"While we're being honest, that's not the story. Besides, from what I've seen, the addition of an old, burned-out murderer might do the neighborhood some good."

Tomaras abruptly ended the interview. She gave Laine another appointment for the same time each week for the next three weeks. She walked Laine to the door, opened it, and said, "Remember, Laine, it just takes one mistake to go from the Madrid back to San Quentin. Only one fuck-up and you'll never smell freedom again."

"I'm starting to have a problem telling the difference between a warning and a promise."

Tomaras closed the door.

Laine didn't bother to look around as he walked slowly back to the Madrid, trying to do what he used to do best: slow his thinking, control his emotions, and make a plan. But it wasn't working. He couldn't stop thinking about Constance, what she looked like, the sound of her voice. Would she still recognize him? Did she still have that silly laugh when she was nervous? And Alfred, that prick, what had he done to turn Constance away from him?

Yes, Alfred, you stole my wife. Did you also kill Julia? It's hard to imagine, but maybe you did. Planting the evidence would have been the easy part. The dates on the documents the warden gave me prove your father lied to me the whole way through. He literally fed me to the system for disposal. The only reason he would have done that is to protect his son. He set out to protect you, no matter the cost. He was behind the court order, and the damn divorce, too. Pure evil.

Filling in the blanks still didn't explain why Alfred would have killed Julia. There had to be a reason, something that pulled it all together. As he had done a million times before, George went over the details of the weeks before Julia Penthoser's death the night of September 6, 1958. George and Constance had moved into a new student housing apartment in Albany Village on the western side of the Berkeley campus in early summer, 1958, just before Rebecca was born. As he had the summer before, George had a job as a summer intern in William Shockley's semiconductor laboratory in Mountain View, soon to become the epicenter of Silicone Valley. Shockley and three others had invented the transistor in 1947.* In 1956, Shockley started a laboratory dedicated to research, especially on what would become silicone-based semiconductors. While he was working in the labs, George had developed a unique way to remove residue—mostly

---

* Shockley, along with co-inventers Walter Brattain and John Bardeen received the Nobel Prize for their invention in 1956. Explaining the transistor's function, Shockley described it as a way to dramatically amplify electrical signals. Imagine, he said, tying a bale of hay behind a mule, then lighting it on fire. A little energy on one side, a lot more coming out of the other.

flux—from circuit boards. Shockley encouraged George to patent his work. George went to the Berkeley Law School for advice and was partnered with Alfred Preston, a freshman law student interested in patent law. Alfred had plenty of time, no shortage of money, and they quickly applied for the patent.

The couple in the adjoining apartment had a friend, a graduate anthropology student, Julia Penthoser, transferring from an eastern school into the Berkeley program. George and Constance met Julia about a week before her death at a welcome mixer for graduate students, introduced by their neighbors, Ken and Lois Buck; Alfred was there, too. Together, they decided to have a fondue party at the Buck's the following Saturday night. The party spilled over into the Laine's apartment, ending in the Laine's kitchen. Constance, George, Julia, Ken Buck, and Alfred were all there. Julia didn't feel comfortable taking a bus home at such a late hour, so George volunteered to take her. He took her to her apartment, said goodnight, watched to be sure she got into her apartment, then drove home, stopping on the way at a 7-Eleven for a quart of milk. When he got home, he found Constance and Rebecca asleep in their bed, so George—not wanting to awaken Rebecca—spent the night on the couch.

Julia's body was found in the morning by her sister. Feelings of horror and disbelief rocked the graduate community. Police were everywhere, determined to find the killer quickly, make sense of the senseless, and calm the community. Everyone at the party was questioned repeatedly, especially George, Alfred, and Ken Buck. Then out of the blue, police arrived with a search warrant, the victim's panties were found hidden in a box of George's books in the basement, and he was arrested. At the trial, a witness testified she saw George in his car, perhaps spying on Julia's apartment. The 7-Eleven clerk thought he remembered George, but couldn't say when he was there. George hadn't kept the receipt. Even Constance couldn't say when George returned since he had slept on the couch and did not wake her up.

And now, so many years later, he was suddenly—and unbelievably—literally only miles away from the remaining players in that horrible drama. What should he do? How could he possibly push this to the periphery of his awareness, keep on with the same determination to leave it all alone? Leroy would have been able to help him puzzle it through.

Laine went through the motions of dinner at the mission with the Madrid group, begged off early, and spent the rest of the evening and most of the night trying to sort it out, make a plan. When he finally fell asleep, it was clear he had no choice: much as he hated it, he had to find out more, starting with knowing if Judge Alfred Preston really was the same Alfred Preston he knew. If so, how did he get to be where he was? And what did Julia Penthoser have to do with it?

Once he had all of that information in hand, he could decide what—if anything—to do next. Hopefully, just knowing the answers would help him get back on track, leave the past alone, and not explode the world his wife and daughter knew. He felt no need to bring justice to Preston. That would be taken care of in some other realm. In the meantime, doing the research would put energy into protecting his freedom long enough to finally resolve the nightmare. Then he could go back to prison and finish out his life in peace.

It all had to start in the library, and that meant learning to use a computer. In prison, library computers were all connected to law books and legal papers. The internet was strictly off limits. Laine had only the vaguest idea of what "Google" meant.

The next morning, Tuesday, he walked down to the main library at the Civic Center, again savoring the thrill of entering the vast lobby. All that space, all those books, documents, and knowledge were right at his fingertips. But to gain full and easy access, he had to master computer basics, the stuff most ten-year-olds did automatically.

He began with a quick tutorial, compliments of a volunteer at the help desk, a cheerful white-haired woman wearing sneakers and a blue smock festooned with tiny emblems, awards, and colorful state flags. She took him through the basics of finding and ordering books using the call system. Another surprise:

customers (as they were called) could no longer browse the stacks scanning titles.

"People pulled books out and left them all over the place. No respect anymore. We used to spend hours putting them all back. It's much better this way."

Laine's first book was one on basic computer skills, described as simple enough for "idiots" to follow. He settled into a chair in the main reading room and, over the next several hours, carefully read through the text trying to absorb the basics. It was a daunting task since he was really starting from the pre-idiot stage. He had done word processing in the prison library, but that was not much more than using a genius typewriter. Understanding computer function, language, and terms was another matter, especially for someone who had never used a cell phone or even an answering machine. Language, terms, symbols—it was all a new language. The part he did get was about the electrical input, the movement of signals through the CPU, the concept of binary function. But none of that would help him find a picture of Constance and Rebecca.

On the second day, well into his third book on basics, he sat down again with the ever-cheerful help lady, and together they practiced applying his nascent grasp of the system to do some basic maneuvers. But when he was again alone, he found himself suddenly tangled in screens he didn't want, unable to do more than start over and over.

On their way to the Second BM that night, Cowboy asked Laine where he'd been for the last two days. "You're not running around the city, are you, George?"

"No, I've been at the library trying to learn to use a computer. It's a lot harder than I thought. The books make it sound easy, but when I try it, all I get is dead ends."

"You need a tutor, George," said Louis. "I know my way around a computer. I'll show you, but not at the main library. That place makes me nervous. We'll go to the Bartlett branch tomorrow. You don't have to step over seventeen junkies to get in, it's quiet, and no one hassles you."

The Bartlett branch was just as advertised. Louis and George sat in a carrel working through the basics of internet search.

"What are looking for, George? If it's just general information, you have what you need to get started. But I sense there's something else going on. If you tell me, it might save you a ton of frustration. Especially if it's something really obscure."

George was silent for a while, wrestling with how much to tell Louis when he didn't even know himself how far he wanted to go.

"You're right, I do want to go further. Truth is, I'm afraid to go there. I have no idea what finding out things—personal stuff— would do to me. I've been living under a set of rules that made it possible for me to survive in prison. A major part of that has been banishing the past. Not just thoughts but the emotion that goes with them. What happens if I break the rules, just because I can? Suppose I find out I was just kidding myself and suddenly all the crazy rage I long ago drove out of my mind comes roaring back? What happens, then, Louis? What do I do with it? Does any of this make sense?"

"Look, George, I don't know exactly what you're talking about, but I gather you want to go back in time, maybe all the way back to whatever your crime was, back to the people you lost. Is that it? Are you saying you pushed all that aside and you're scared going back might destroy you? After all this time you're free, and ten minutes later you blow it?"

"Yes! Maybe it drives me to do something that would be even worse than anything I've already done."

"Like what? Go out and get revenge?"

"Not revenge: justice. I always told myself justice is out of my hands. My job was to accept what I couldn't change, overcome treachery by living above it, on another plane. I could make myself pull away from what had happened so those I loved would have a chance to live their lives. But that left me trapped in a living hell, and I wanted to somehow free myself enough to survive. Since it couldn't be in the real world, it had to be somewhere in my brain. I struggled to find a system that would take me there. There were too many gods fighting it out to make religion work. Philosophy failed—it was intellectually satisfying, but it didn't stop the pain. I came closest by combining physical and spiritual discipline. I can't explain it, but over time it stopped the pain and let me see myself in the mirror again."

"And you're scared that looking will take down your system, or philosophy, or whatever it is that drives you."

"Yes, that's it."

"I'm no Plato, George, but it strikes me that you don't have a choice. If what you believe really works, then finding out won't matter. Leave justice aside; maybe you'll find satisfaction in seeing your ideas really did work, people did rebuild. Maybe that's the element you were looking for, the thing that took you out of hell. The only thing I know is if you don't look, you'll never know. And if you really are that person you've tried to be, then you ought to have the courage to look. What's one more risk? You could find out your thinking was all chicken shit, or you could find out it worked. You want a guarantee, you buy a toaster. You want to put yourself to the test, you get to work."

"You're right, Louis. First, I need to tell you something about myself. I can trust you with this, right? Maybe you've gone through something like this."

"I'll tell you about it sometime, George. Meanwhile, where are we going?"

Laine told Louis about the crime, the fact he was convicted, sent off to death row, and by pure chance, moved to general population in 1967. He talked about Constance and Rebecca, and the crushing discovery that she had married the son of his crooked lawyer, that he was becoming increasingly convinced Alfred Preston could have killed Julia Penthoser, and now he was aware they were living just a stone's throw away.

Louis said they both needed to sleep on it, come back, and start a systematic search. "Nothing random, George. Let's go one step at a time, maybe start with looking for your wife and daughter, go from there. If it gets too weird we can slow down. But I don't think you can stop this."

Laine nodded in agreement.

That evening was a repeat of what was becoming a familiar—and reassuring—routine, starting with dinner at the mission, then idle chatter in the lobby followed by the evening street show.

The next day they were back at the Bartlett branch. Laine agreed there was no turning back, and he agreed with Louis that it only made sense to match his long-held beliefs against the emotional challenge of digging up suppressed memories.

It didn't take long to find pictures of Constance and Rebecca. When they did, Laine was surprised that instead of falling apart over the images, he was actually relieved—even happy. There they were, healthy and smiling. Constance was instantly recognizable. His first thought about Rebecca was that she looked exactly like her grandmother Laine.

Some of the images included Alfred, also easily recognized in spite of having gained a considerable amount of weight and losing most of his hair. His head seemed to have been sucked into his body, but the half-smirk, half-smile, pinched mouth, and arrogant tilt of the head were all still there. In one picture, he stood with both hands in his pockets, thumbs out grasping the front corner of the pockets like a 1910 politician delivering a stump speech. Yes, same Alfred, same self-important look. Physically, however, his was a clear case of reverse metamorphosis: he had regressed from the handsome butterfly to a bloated larva.

"All that bounty and you still can't shake that look of snotty entitlement," he mumbled loud enough to prompt a "Shhhh" from a neighboring carrel.

Surprisingly, the digression did not derail his search, it stimulated it. True, he returned to the pictures over and over, but each visit was easier than the last, every one reinforcing his determination to complete the task and, if possible, retire from the fray.

Louis said it was time for him to bow out, leave the rest to Laine. "I'll help you if you get stuck, George, but you need to handle this by yourself from here." Louis retreated to the reading room.

There was an abundance of material about Alfred Preston on the internet, mostly reports about chairing one group or another, giving a speech, cutting a ribbon, supporting a candidate, or giving his views on the California penal system. Historical information, however, was scant at best. He seems to have joined his father's law firm somewhere around 1968, and became a judge in 1982. There were fleeting references to his days with his father's law firm, but nothing before that. Even his appointment as a judge was barely noted. There was virtually nothing about his time before law school beyond some basics like receiving a B.S. degree in zoology from Pepperdine University in May 1957. He finished law school in 1961.

Nineteen sixty-one? Four years to finish law school? Why the detour, Alfred?

The September 1960 Berkeley Student Directory listed him as a third-year law student. What happened to 1959? Laine briefly thought of trying to track down and query others from the law program but quickly abandoned the idea. What lawyer would take a call from a murderer arriving from the grave and asking questions about a classmate?

Back to the internet.

Laine reasoned that Alfred, and presumably Constance, left Berkeley after graduation, around the end of 1961 or sometime in 1962. Where they went or what they would have been doing were both mysteries. He had money, that wouldn't have been a major issue, but Constance wouldn't hang around with someone who wasn't studying, working, or both. So the most likely track would have been to practice law, possibly patent law, far away from all the memories of Julia, the trial, and possible news of George's execution. But where?

Curiously, he didn't seem to be a member of any major lawyer organization, and wasn't licensed to practice law in California until 1968. Finally, after going through the lists of lawyers passing the bar in every state, Laine found that in 1964, Alfred passed the bar exam in Indiana. *Indiana! Holy shit! That's where Constance's parents lived! What was the name of that town?*

Brazil! That's it! Brazil. The home of Jimmy Hoffa. Who could forget that? But there was nothing to be found to put Alfred in Brazil. A search for journal articles written by or referenced to Alfred Preston was equally fruitless. A dead end.

By Friday night, Laine was exhausted, not physically, but the constant pursuit of information without rewarding answers was draining him. On Saturday, he, Kitty, Cowboy, and Louis went together to Dolores Park. Though Louis had been at the Madrid for almost five years, Laine got the feeling it took a while for him to become accepted, something he didn't understand until it came up that he was one of only a few residents allowed a small refrigerator and a hot plate in his room, perks that suggested he enjoyed some special favor with the otherwise poisonous John Zwick.

Kitty and Cowboy went off to get hot dogs. Laine tipped back against a tree and closed his eyes.

"I want to thank you again for helping me with the internet stuff, Louis. Without you, I'd still be in the main library going nowhere."

"It's nice of you to say it, but really, it's me who should thank you. I don't really get a chance to do anything that useful very often. The closest I get is some work I do for Zwick."

"That can't be easy. Sounds like sharing a lollypop with a sting ray. How does that work, if you don't mind me asking?"

"You do get right to the point, don't you, George? Well, you're right, I do get along with him. It's tricky, and for a long time people stayed away from me thinking I might spy on them for Zwick. But he doesn't own me. Pretty much everyone's figured that out."

"They thought you were a snitch?"

"For a while. But you've been in prison, George, you know what a snitch is. Ever see one operate right out in the open, go up to a guard and start talking?"

"No, I haven't. But I have seen what happens to snitches; worse, I've seen guys finger a perfectly innocent inmate just to get him out of the way."

"Well then, just so you know, I'll tell you about me and Zwick. I do some very low level accounting for him. Nothing official, but he's lazy and no good keeping track of his money, so once a week I go to his office in the back to add up receipts and expenses related to his business, you know the one I mean. I keep track of the money, sometimes make his deposits, but more to the point, I make sure no one has a hand in the till. He trusts me because I have so much to lose if I cross him, and in the highly unlikely chance he gets busted, I'm an invisible factor.

"Meantime, he gives me a big break on my rent, a couple of favors, and a few bucks for pocket money. Without it, I couldn't afford to stay. The only people I'd snitch on are the scumbags in his little enterprise, never on any of the residents. When it comes to friends, they're all I've got. Pretty bad when the best you can do is the Madrid, right, George?"

"I can think of a few places that are worse, like the one across the bay. The way you talk about snitches makes me think you've been inside, too."

"Yeah, I have. I pulled almost six years in Jackson State Prison in Michigan. It was hell, and you're right: even if I get tossed out of the Madrid and have to live in a mission or on the streets, it would still be better than that stinking jail. And the noise! The loudest traffic jam in the city is like music compared to that. The walls were all concrete, everything echoed. It was hard to read; sometimes, it was so loud you couldn't even hear a radio without putting it up to your ear.

"Of course, I've got no beef at all compared to what I hear you got. Sorry, I didn't mean to sound self-pitying."

"I understand. What was your crime, if you don't mind me asking?"

"Well, basically, accounting fraud. And make no mistake, it was my fault. It started out with an almost trivial move, but once it got going, I was on a slippery slope with no traction."

"Sounds familiar. There were quite a few business people in San Quentin, mostly guys who failed to get a federal conviction so they could do time in one of the government country clubs instead of a state prison."

"Yeah, in my case, I wasn't a big enough potato to interest the feds, but they still wanted to be sure I got the max in a state can."

"How did that happen?"

"Well, I was a business major in college, came out and worked for a local bakery as business manager. We were in a suburb of Ann Arbor, supplied a lot of supermarkets, but our markup was tight and my salary didn't change much over the ten years I was there. Then a guy I knew in high school approached me with an offer to work for him. Robert was the high school rich kid, football player, all of that. I was the nerdy guy who liked to play chess, so while we knew each other, we didn't travel in the same circles. He dropped out of college to work for the family business—they made metal shelving for warehouses. When his father died, he took over and reshuffled the organization. Basically, the people who worked for his father didn't like Robert, a lot of them left, and that's when he called me. He offered ten percent more than I was making at the bakery, a better pension plan, and the promise of a yearly bonus if I did well.

"I was married, had three kids, a mortgage, and not much to show for a decade of work. Even though I wasn't all that taken with Robert, it looked like a great deal, so I jumped at it. My job was to oversee the books, organize receipts and expenses, get it all tidied up for the accountant.

"It was fine for a couple of years, but then I began to notice charges coming from Robert labeled 'expenses,' but with little in the way of documentation. He was traveling a lot, always ate fifty-dollar dinners, and stayed in fancy hotels. When I asked for receipts and an accounting of the charges, he put me off, saying it was my job to make everything pretty, not to question him. On top of that, I got a huge Christmas bonus, so I decided that maybe I could make it all work.

"The accountants didn't bat an eye, and the IRS accepted everything without a whimper. So it went along like that, but the amounts got bigger. He was charging suits and watches off on the company, stuff that wasn't vaguely related to the business.

When I confronted him and said it had to stop, he threatened to fire me. I should have walked right out the door, but I didn't.

"Then the accountants questioned my numbers. They brought in a forensic accountant—I didn't know such a thing existed—and then the whole thing fell apart. I had the local tax people and the IRS up my ass, but Robert kept telling me it would all work out if I just played dumb. They kept threatening me, and finally I told the feds about Robert, thinking that would at least mitigate my burden. But he denied everything, saying I told him to do whatever he wanted in exchange for fat bonus checks. They saw the size of the bonuses, worked out a deal with him to testify against me in exchange for a fine and no conviction. He walked away, and I was fucked.

"I was facing trials and jail time from both the state and the feds, so my lawyer arranged a deal to get the feds off my back. In exchange for a guilty plea and acceptance of a three-year sentence, the feds would go away. When I went for sentencing, the judge gave me the max of eight years because he was pissed at the prosecutor for dropping a conspiracy charge to make the plea bargain work.

"You can guess the rest, George. My wife and kids were freaked out, all our money was used up, and I was in the slammer a hundred miles from home. She divorced me as soon as I was sent up. Worse than that, two of the three kids cut me off. They still won't have anything to do with me. My oldest son came to see me in prison maybe twice a year, a real lifeline for me; otherwise, I was alone. My mom had Alzheimer's. Dad tried to take care of her, but after my wife pulled out, he only lasted a few months. After he died, they sent Mom to a Medicaid nursing home, the first place I went after I got out. She didn't even know me.

"When I got home, no one would talk to me. I couldn't find work, so I started to drift. My son took me in for a while, but his wife didn't like the arrangement, so I finally decided to leave, come here to put some sort of life together. My son sent some money. I did dish washing and janitor work, but with my record, I couldn't get a job anywhere near a cash register or in an office.

"The Madrid was my last resort—no pun intended. My son got me started, paid a few month's rent, and between odd jobs, selling my plasma, and his help, I hung on. Then Zwick offered me the job.

"Funny, but you know more about me than anyone else. Are you sure you weren't a priest in a former life?"

"Absolutely certain, Louis. But I am good at keeping a confidence. Tell me, do you still get to see your son?"

"Yeah, my son comes out every year or so with his family. I put on my best clothes and go to his hotel for breakfast. In fact, they were here about two months ago."

"You're lucky to have that."

"Yes, but the other two kids won't budge. Still, I'll take what I've got and count myself fortunate. It's weird how something as small as a single meal with a few family members can mean so much. I don't think people who haven't been in a serious jail can begin to imagine that."

"You're right, Louis. It reminds me of a story I read years ago about a guy trapped in a Soviet labor camp. Talk about having nothing—he was on the edge of death from starvation and exposure every minute of every day. Then he found a small scrap of sausage, no more than one bite. He guarded it and waited until night when he was wrapped in his tattered blanket on the wooden shelf they called a bed. He slowly ate the scrap and smiled. I often thought about him when I was really down. He could find contentment where there was absolutely none. If he could under those circumstances, why couldn't I?"

"That's kind of how I feel, George. I've got more than a lot of people. If all I ever thought about is what I lost, I would have jumped off the bridge a long time ago. I think that maybe someday my other son and daughter will show up and say they forgive me. It's weird, but every time I walk into the lobby at the hotel, I automatically look around. I don't even think about it, but I keep hoping maybe I'll see my daughter or my son waiting for me. That would be a miracle day for me."

"It could happen, Louis."

"I know it, George. But, hey, I didn't mean to dump all this on you. From what I hear you've got plenty on your hands, but if I can help, let me know. Meantime, can we keep this between us? I don't need anyone to carry my water for me, know what I mean?"

Kitty and Cowboy returned with hot dogs and drinks. They all enjoyed the meal, then made their way back to the Madrid. They didn't seem to be followed, making Laine wonder if perhaps whoever was behind the pressure was losing interest.

Chapter 17

Elton used a sharpening stone "borrowed" from a hardware store to transform the Vietnamese dinner knife into a keen-edged stiletto. He embedded a pen barrel in the adhesive tape handle set perpendicular to the blade, a hilt to prevent Tommy's hand from sliding up the blade if he hit a bone while driving it home. A sliced hand is hard to explain when you're standing next to a dead man with a knife sticking out of his side.

"Remember, Tommy: stab, stab, release, and walk away. Leave the knife in him. That's important in case he doesn't go right down. If you pull the knife out of a guy, he'll run until he falls over. But if he sees a knife sticking out of his side, he'll go right down and won't move. He'll die watching the knife. They always do. You just walk away.

"If anything goes wrong, I'll be there to cover you."

Tommy practiced stabbing a cardboard box filled with wadded newspaper.

"Feels like the real thing," Elton assured him.

Tommy seemed fairly calm, both determined and proud to protect his friend from the vengeful George Laine.

"I'm ready, Elton. I've got the moves down. So when do we do it, and where?"

"The sooner the better. Like tomorrow morning, Sunday, when everyone sleeps late. And the best place is the landing by the vending machines. Laine always comes down early, so you wait on the landing like you're getting a drink or something out of one of the machines. You see him coming down the steps, you say hello in a friendly way, move like you're going upstairs, and just as you pass him, you strike. Pow! Pow!" he said making two quick stabbing motions. "If he goes down easy, you continue up to your room and wait for me. If he rolls around or makes noise, I'll come up from the lobby and finish the job.

"Total time is less than a minute even if I have to jump in. And if we miss him Sunday, we'll nail his stupid ass another day. Right, partner?"

"Right, Elton. I mean 'partner.'"

The next morning Elton and Tommy were up early. Elton stationed himself in the lobby near the stairs pretending to read an old newspaper. Tommy stood at the ready on the landing.

Laine got up, bathed, and prepared for an early morning walk up to Dusty's. He wondered if anyone else would be up for coffee at that early hour. As he came down the steps to the landing, Tommy gradually came into view standing in front of a vending machine.

Up mighty early, aren't you, Tommy? Laine thought. *And where's Elton?* He also noticed that Tommy was using just his left hand to insert money and operate the machine. The right hung at his side away from Laine. *You poor dumb kid,* he thought.

"Good morning, Tommy. Where's Elton?"

"Hello, Mr. Laine. He's not up yet." Tommy started toward the stairs just as Laine reached the bottom. "I just came down to get a drink."

"Are you going to take that knife upstairs with you?"

"What knife?" Tommy retorted. "Just getting a drink, that's all."

"Don't do it, Tommy. You're in way over your head. If you attack me, I'll have to defend myself, and that could be painful. Don't listen to Elton, Tommy. He's helped you in some ways, but not this time."

Tommy stood frozen for a few moments as tears filled his eyes and started to roll down his cheeks. "Damn you, Laine!" he said, running up the stairs still holding the knife. "Damn you!" he yelled from above.

As Laine walked down to the lobby, Elton jumped to his feet. "Tommy! Where's Tommy, you bastard?"

"He's not hurt. He ran upstairs. Listen, Elton, it's one thing to have crazy ideas about me, even to the point of trying to kill me. But bringing Tommy in is a different matter. You could have gotten him killed up there. So from now on, whatever beef you have with me, it's between us. And if you hurt that kid, you'll answer to me—and a lot of others as well."

Elton stood rooted to the spot, his eyes shifting between Laine and the stairs.

"You fucker!" he spat and raced for the stairs.

Laine thought about continuing on to Dusty's, but the image of the distraught boy with a wicked-looking knife made him change direction. He picked up his pace when he heard Elton pounding on a door yelling, "Tommy! Tommy!" Laine raced up the stairs.

"Open up, Tommy. It's me, Elton! Open up!"

"Break it down, Elton, or I will!"

Elton ignored Laine and kept banging. Other doors opened and residents poured into the hallway.

"Get out of the way!" yelled Laine as he charged past Elton, smashing into the door. The lock instantly shattered and the door flew open.

Tommy lay sprawled across the bathroom threshold in a rapidly expanding pool of blood. Too weak to continue stabbing his arm, he fell back onto the floor.

"I'm sorry, Elton...I...I let you down..."

Elton stood frozen in the doorway, but Laine rushed in, knelt in the blood, and locked both hands around Tommy's biceps trying to stop the blood coming from several deep gashes in his forearm. Laine yelled for someone to call an ambulance, yanked off his belt and wrapped it around the boy's arm. His call for help went unheeded as residents seemed to melt away leaving Elton and Laine alone with the Tommy.

"Elton! If you can't get in here then at least make sure someone calls for help! Move it, man! We're going to lose him!"

Elton slowly backed away, turned, and lunged toward the stairs.

"I can help," a woman with a thick Latin accent said as she, too, knelt in the blood. Laine recognized her as the maid who handed out clean sheets on Thursdays. Presumably, she also worked in Zwick's third-floor pleasure palace.

"Get a blanket, he's shivering," Laine said trying to tighten the belt. "Damn! I can't stop the bleeding!"

"No, sir, don't put a blanket on him. And take off that belt, put your fingers here and push. That will stop the artery." She pointed to a place on the inside of Tommy's arm just above his elbow. The flow slowed from gush to ooze.

"Thank you! But why no blanket? He's freezing!"

"He's shivering because he's losing his blood pressure. You want his blood vessels to get tight. Cold makes them tight. I'll lift his legs up, that will make blood go to his heart where he needs it."

"Where did you learn all this? Are you in school? And what's your name?"

"María. I'm not in school. I was a nurse at home before I came to the USA. I can't go to school or work here as a nurse without papers. Push harder on the artery!"

Elton reappeared. "Someone had a phone and called. Is he going to be all right? I mean, it's just a bad cut, right?"

"No, he's not going to be all right. So either get in here and help or find someone who can! Move it, Elton."

"I'll get help," he said weakly and left.

Louis and Kitty both showed up. At María's suggestion, Kitty put a cold wet towel on Tommy's head, Louis took over holding up his legs, and María replaced Laine whose fingers were numb from applying non-stop pressure.

"I can hardly feel the artery pulsing. They better hurry or he's going to die right here."

Tommy was dirty-sheet gray and barely conscious at that point, his eyeballs rolled up under fluttering lids, drool leaking from the corner of his mouth. He made random gurgling sounds as if trying to speak, but his movements slowed, and his breathing lapsed into a series of shallow gasps. The group continued in silence, each feeling the boy's life fading from their grip. When the blood stopped seeping, María suggested they release their grip on the flaccid artery and instead wrap his arm tightly in a towel and raise it straight up.

It was almost an hour before fire department medics arrived. Tommy's blood pressure was barely detectable, but he was still alive.

"You did good," one of the medics said as they bundled Tommy onto a gurney.

The group followed the stretcher on the bumpy ride down the stairs to the lobby—the elevator had been shut down after the last late-night customer left a few hours before, and the fireman's emergency key didn't fit the ancient override lock. The lobby was crowded with tenants awakened by the ruckus. Elton stood by the front door, sweaty, wide-eyed, and agitated.

"You need to go with him, Elton," Kitty said giving him a push in the back. "The hospital will need information. None of us has it. Go! Do something decent for once!"

Under any other circumstances, one would have expected Elton to lash out. Instead, he allowed himself to be pushed out the door to the ambulance. One of the attendants gave Kitty a card with the name of the hospital and the ER's direct phone number.

"Tell them your name, ask for the head nurse, and say Tim Budrow from Emergency Services authorized you to call for an update on the patient's condition. Otherwise, they won't tell you anything."

The ambulance doors closed and the huge box pulled away, its flashing lights and piercing siren assaulting the quiet Sunday streets.

Tenants filling the lobby parted and became silent as the group came back through the doors, their clothes covered with blood.

Hushed voices asked who it was, what happened, did someone kill the boy?

"How is he doing, Kitty?" Dokker asked.

Kitty grimaced and shook her head. "We better get out of these clothes," she said to Laine and Louis.

María met the group on the landing, told them to bring their clothes to her on the third floor. "I'll wash them in the laundry. And don't worry, I don't get in trouble. No one will know."

Laine asked the group if they wanted to go somewhere—maybe get coffee—to talk over what had happened and make some sort of plan to deal with Elton when he returned. "No matter what happens to Tommy, he's going to be a wild man."

Louis declined the invitation, saying he was too rattled to go out, but he promised to find Zwick and get him back to the hotel. "It's his job to deal with Elton, not ours."

Kitty said she was going to go to church. "I'm going to do some powerful praying. It might not help Tommy, but it will calm me down."

Cowboy was waiting in the hall when Laine emerged carrying his bloody clothing. He apologized for not helping. "I just couldn't do it, George. I feel terrible. I tried to make myself help, but I just couldn't. It was like getting back into a nightmare I'm always trying to forget. But I should have anyway. Maybe it would have been okay; maybe I could have done something."

Laine told him not to feel badly, there was nothing another person could have done to help. "What we really needed was the ambulance. I can't understand why it took so long to get here. But none of us could have made that happen, Cowboy. You're too hard on yourself. Come have coffee with me; we'll talk about it."

Cowboy looked at the bloody bundle but didn't answer.

"Don't worry, I won't carry this down the street."

Cowboy nodded, followed Laine downstairs, and waited on the third-floor landing while Laine looked for María.

"You were wonderful, María. If Tommy makes it, it's only because of you. If he doesn't, we can say we did our best."

María thanked him and took the bundle.

"María, you need to get back to nursing. What would it take to get your papers?"

"It's *muy complicado*, Mr. Laine. It takes money and a special kind of lawyer, you know? But I get there someday. I will do it for my children, you'll see."

"I believe you will, María." He leaned forward and kissed her lightly on the forehead. "I *know* you will."

Cowboy and Laine went to Dusty's, got coffee, and sat in Laine's favorite corner.

"No egg sandwich, George? Kitty says you always get an egg sandwich."

"No appetite, Cowboy. I've seen a lot of violence, some self-inflicted, some not. But no matter how many times it happens, it's always a shock, always leaves me a little shaky, if you know what I mean."

"Do I ever! I spend half my time trying to shut down those brain flicks, but no matter what I do, they just come back at me."

"What kind of images? And by the way, I never met anyone who could just pull the plug on bad memories."

"I always thought some could. I wanted to know their trick. There were guys in prison that had terrible stories, and they didn't seem all fetched up in reliving the crap that happened to them."

"Yeah, I know what you mean, but it always seemed to me that most of them were so antisocial they didn't give a damn in the first place. The rest of us either figured out how to bury it or, like you, suffer in silence. I mean, who would know you're hurtin' so bad, Cowboy? You always seem so calm and analytic."

"It's an act, George. I've learned to look okay, not be noticed, but when the door closes at night, that's when the craziness starts. What we see on the street every night is comedy compared to what's rattling around my head."

"Like what, Cowboy? Would it help to talk about it?"

"I never talk to anyone about it. Well, almost nobody. I used to talk to my brother, at least I did when we lived back in Arizona."

"At least you have a brother. Do you still talk to him?"

"No. He lives in Flagstaff, has a job, a wife, two kids, and a house with an aboveground swimming pool."

"Above ground? Sounds like magic. I never heard of that!"

"A big plastic tub right there at the back door. Can you imagine? He's got a good job in an auto parts store—been there fifteen years. We used to write sometimes. I still send him a card on his birthday and at Christmas. His wife writes a letter every Christmas about the family, what the kids are doing, that sort of stuff. And he always sends me a nice note on my birthday, invites me to visit. Maybe I will someday. I'm just not up for going back there yet."

"Sounds like your brother really cares. You're lucky to have that, Cowboy. Is he older or younger?"

"Older, thank goodness. I wouldn't be here today if it wasn't for him protecting me."

"Protecting you?"

"Yeah. It's complicated. Basically, my old man was like Elton: a big, nasty bastard who never drew a sober breath. We lived out in the desert with the rattlesnakes. But he was meaner than any snake I ever saw."

"Sounds awful. Where was this?"

"We lived way the hell out in the middle of nowhere, up a dirt road right on the border of an Indian reservation. My mother was part Navajo. She inherited a few acres with an old trailer, small barn, and a windmill over a well that was dry half the time. They called it their 'ranch.' Some ranch! But we did have some goats, a few chickens, and an old horse named Bones.

"My old man couldn't keep a job. Either the truck wouldn't run or more likely he was too drunk to drive it anywhere. Funny, but when he ran out of booze, he always seemed to make it to the liquor store about ten miles back toward town. It was against the law to have liquor on the reservation, and they always gave Indians a hard time about buying booze. That's where the old man came in: he'd go to the store, buy all the rotgut gin he could afford, put it in a sack, and ride the horse over into the reservation. When customers saw him coming over the hill, they'd rush up to buy the hooch. Of course, he charged twice what he paid, enough so he could hold back a couple of bottles for himself. Sometimes he'd get so drunk on the way back he'd pass out and fall off the horse. When Bones came back alone, that meant me and my brother had to go find him, drag his pissed off, sorry ass back home, then go hide, 'cause when he got sober enough to stand up, he'd come after us.

"Mom tried to protect us, so she usually got the worst of it. If he could, he'd chase us. We'd run out into the desert and hide in a secret cave we had. If he couldn't run, we'd just go out to the barn and listen to them fight and throw shit around until he passed out again.

"But every Sunday, we'd get dressed in our best clothes and go to town for church. Then everyone was all smiles like we were the perfect family. And if there was any money, we'd eat at a restaurant. Then we'd drive home and the whole thing would start over.

"But it wasn't all bad. One of the best times for us was when Mom would say, 'It's time you boys went to the store for groceries.' That meant we could take the twenty-two and go hunting for dinner. We could only take a few shells—they cost money—so we made every shot count, but boy, we had fun out there, just us, no screaming or ducking a fist.

"You'd be amazed how much there is out in what looks like an empty desert. Gambrel quail, rabbits, ground squirrels, prairie dogs, grouse, and every kind of snake you can think of. Of course, there were deer, antelope, and coyotes, too, but we didn't mess with them. The best were the quail and grouse, but we were careful not to take too many and wreck the coveys. We saved them for special times like Christmas or when we were really hungry and couldn't even get a snake.

"Most of the time we went for rabbits. Just one of those big jacks would feed all of us. 'Course you can't eat rabbit all the time. It would make you sick 'cause they got no fat on 'em. But mostly we ate rattlesnakes—diamondbacks, not those puny rock rattlers. Even better, with a snake, you didn't have to waste a bullet. Just hold him down with a stick and smack him in the head with a rock. That way, you don't mess up the meat.

"We nailed the head to the back of the barn, skinned and gutted 'em out in less than a minute. We had it down, I'm telling you. And they were good, 'specially when it's all you got to eat.

There must have been a hundred snake skeletons on that wall and more on the ground.

"We weren't crazy about school, but we went pretty much every day. Anything was better than staying home watchin' Mom cry or listening to the old man yelling. We walked about two miles down to the highway, last stop for the bus. That was fun even when the wind was up and you couldn't see for the sand in the air. At school, they had lunch for poor kids who couldn't bring their own. We ate everything we could, like a couple of ground squirrels in a bucket of oats. And we took our sweet time walking home, too. We saw all kinds of birds and creatures out there. We gave 'em names and made up a kind of family story out of it. We'd talk back and forth like we were the animals.

"Anyway, one day we went down to the bus stop and the bus didn't come. Must have been some sort of holiday, I don't know, but we waited an hour and walked back. While we was walking, a car went by, one we didn't know, and when we got home it was parked in front of the trailer.

"We were scared it was the sheriff or something, so we snuck down and looked in the door, but no one was there. We went around to the bedroom side, and my brother boosted me up to the window. I peeked inside, and there was Mom going at it with some guy. The bastard didn't even have his pants all the way off. My brother wanted to see, but I couldn't lift him, so we went in the barn and waited. That guy left, and a couple of hours later another one came.

"We were freaked out, but believe it or not, it wasn't so much what Mom was doing as it was being scared of what Dad would do if he came home and found her...you know...doing it. We decided the best plan was to go back down to the hardtop, so if the old man came home before the last guy left, we could pretend we were sent home, then try to distract him, hold him off until the car went by. But he didn't come, so we walked back to the trailer, and everyone acted like nothing ever happened.

"Well, not soon after that, we came home one afternoon, went in, and found Mom lying on the floor, blood all over the place. She was cut up and obviously dead—living out there you know what dead looks like.

"We freaked out. I mean, who wouldn't? We ran all the way back to the highway, flagged down a car, and tried to bum a ride to town. The guy wouldn't let us in the car but said he'd go to the sheriff's office, and sure enough, about half an hour later here come two cop cars. They put us in the back of one of the cars and went up the road sliding all over, lights and siren on like they were chasing Bonnie and Clyde down the freaking highway. We were scared shitless, I'll tell you.

"Anyway, we sat in the car, and every few minutes they'd ask us where the old man was. We didn't know, but they acted like we were covering for him. Then a social services lady in a van came and took us to town. We spent the night in some sort of shelter next to the sheriff's office. In the morning they picked us up and took us to court. The judge took about three minutes to say we couldn't go home. They dropped me off at a house in town, told me I was staying with this family until things got straightened out. Then they drove off with my brother! I cried and carried on, wouldn't go in the house. They finally dragged me in. They had three other kids there, all like me, sent there because of crazy shit like parents dying or getting arrested.

"I missed my brother so bad I couldn't sleep, I wouldn't eat, and I was like a frigging zombie in school.

"Well, the people were nice, there was plenty of food, and they kept tellin' me I'd be with my brother soon if I behaved. Then one day the social services lady came back. When I saw her, I got all excited, thinking she had my brother with her, but she didn't. She told me we were both in foster care until they found my father and cleared him of killing our mom, even though she said it didn't look good for him. I didn't have the courage to ask what happened to my mother.

"That was the start of the end for me. I was in so many foster homes I couldn't count 'em. A couple were pretty good, ones where people really did want to help. But most of the time the people just wanted the money, packed in as many as they could, and treated us all like garbage. Some of them were real nut cases, whuppin' us and screaming we were Satan's children, shit like that. I ran away from just about every one of 'em lookin' for my brother. You can imagine how well that turned out.

"Finally, I was back in court and got sent to 'juvie'—that's what we called the juvenile jail. Talk about being alone! I was fifty miles from home, scared shitless—the littlest one in the whole freaking place. I got beat up a lot, but after a year or so, I was tough enough to defend myself and the bigger kids found new ones to pick on.

"They let me out when I turned eighteen. I hitched back home, all the way to the reservation thinking I would find my brother at the trailer and we could get ourselves going again. When I got there, the trailer was all busted up, looted, had one end burned out, and the barn was on the ground. I went up to the cave to spend the night, but it was so full of snakes I had to spend the night on the ground out in the open. In the morning, I beat it back to the road.

"I hitched back to town thinkin' the whole time I had to get out of there, put as much distance between me and that place as I could. I didn't have fifty cents, so I stole a car and headed for Phoenix. Guys at juvie always talked about how easy it was to boost a car. None of that crossing wires shit you see in the movies. You just walk around a parking lot until you find a late model with the keys in the ignition or hanging off the sun visor. Then you take it to a chop shop in Phoenix. If you live in the city, chances are you're walking down the street with three or four hundred bucks in your pocket before the person even knows the car's gone.

"The problem for me was I got this car—easy enough, just like they said—but I was a long way from Phoenix. On top of that, I didn't have a clue exactly where I was goin'.

"I picked up a guy hitchin', thinkin' maybe he had some money. I told him I'd give him a ride if he'd buy the food and gas. We got pretty near Phoenix when the cops stopped us. They had me for stealing the car, but it turned out the guy was wanted for armed robbery. Even worse, he hid the gun in the car when we were stopped, so they figured I was in on it, too, and being right out of juvie, I was cooked meat.

"They gave me a lawyer, she got some of the charges dropped, but I still got twenty years for having the gun in a stolen car. I went in at eighteen, came out thirty-six. I've been here five years, and believe or not, these have been the most comfortable years I've ever had."

"Wow, Cowboy! That *is* a nightmare. But tell me, when did you reconnect with your brother?"

"In prison, maybe five years into my sentence. He tracked me down and came to see me out of the blue. One day they said I had a visitor. I had no idea who it was. I never had a visitor before. I figured maybe it was a prosecutor or something. I walked in the room and there he was! I couldn't frigging believe it! We hugged and cried the whole half hour they gave us. I don't think we said twenty words. Every time I tried to talk, I'd choke up.

"He came twice a year after that. It gave me something to look forward to. And it changed my behavior. I didn't do anything to mess up my visiting privileges."

"Did you ever find out what happened to your mother and father?"

"Nope, not really. One of the foster parents told me they buried Mom on the reservation. I don't know if she was shitting me or not. It don't matter, though. I just like the idea she was back home. The old man was a different story. Nobody ever heard a word about him. If they did, my brother would have known. After I got out, he let me stay at his place for a few months. We talked about maybe going back to the reservation, but we never did.

"I couldn't get any kind of job, and I felt bad about being a problem for my brother. His wife was real sweet, but you could tell she was going to be a lot happier when I moved on. That's when I came here."

"By the way, Cowboy, you didn't mention your brother's name."

"Yeah, I didn't. It's Tommy."

As they were finishing their coffee, Kitty and Louis came in the shop. "I called the hospital, guys. It's bad news. Tommy only lived an hour."

"I had a feeling he was too far gone to make it," said Laine. "But now we've got to deal with Elton. Any sign of Zwick yet, Louis?"

"We won't have to worry about Zwick or Elton," Kitty said. "The nurse said when they told Elton that Tommy had passed, he went nuts, started screaming, and pushed the nurse over a bench. Then he punched a security guard, ran out into the street screaming crazy stuff, knocking people down. The cops caught up with him and dragged him away."

"You're right, Kitty," Laine said. "That's the last we'll hear from Elton."

Chapter 18

LAINE STAYED AROUND THE MADRID on Sunday, finished *Notes from Underground*, and started a book on astronomy he picked up for a dime at a sidewalk book stall. *Move That Mountain* remained unmolested. On Monday, he paid his third visit to Tomaras. She seemed to be in a rush, Laine had nothing to report, and she didn't bring up anything about Elton or Tommy. After confirming a negative urine drug test, the meeting was over. See you next week.

Laine approached the Madrid from Van Ness, a major street defining the west side of both the Tenderloin and the small Vietnamese district known as Little Saigon. As he turned onto Caliente, he paused, not out of caution, but because of a familiar smell, one that was decidedly out of place on a San Francisco street. Looking around, he saw a Vietnamese laundry on the other side of the street, one he had passed several times before. He wondered why he hadn't smelled it on previous outings.

He hesitated but quickly gave in to his curiosity, crossed the street, and looked in the window of the little shop. An elderly Asian woman was folding shirts at the counter while talking to someone invisible on the other side of a cloth curtain.

The smell was stronger, no denying it. Laine pushed open the door and stepped in.

"May I help you, sir?" the woman asked.

"Well, no, but sort of. What I mean is, possibly I can help you. I know it might sound strange, but I noticed the odor. I know it seems strange, walking in like this, but I know a lot about laundry machines. They have a certain smell when they're old and starting to wear out. The old grease gets too hot and starts to smell."

The woman didn't speak, but the blank look on her face and a slight tilt of her head said she was somewhere between puzzled and skeptical.

"I'm sorry," Laine said backing through the door. "I never should have intruded. It's just, well, I thought I might be able to help. Please forgive me." *Boy, you're really in the soup now, George,* he thought. *Just get out before you make a bigger fool of yourself.*

"Wait, please," the woman said. "You talk to my husband, Mr. Chu, tell him. I get him." She pulled back the curtain and called out something over the racket of a spinning drum. An elderly man appeared, the couple exchanged words in what Laine assumed to be Vietnamese, though clearly, she was having trouble explaining Laine's message, and he was having none of it. But his wife persisted, brought him back, and tried again.

Finally, he said something fairly emphatic, turned, and disappeared through the curtain.

"My husband say that old machines are like old people, you can't expect them to climb mountains."

"Please tell your husband I respect his age and knowledge, but old people and machines do better when they take care of each other. But thank you for putting up with me. I didn't mean to cause any trouble."

He got about twenty paces down the sidewalk when Mrs. Chu called him back. "My husband say you can look at machines. But he have no money to pay you."

"Oh, no, I don't want money. I'm not interested in money. I know about laundry machines…oh, dear, this is terrible, I'm sorry."

"Wait!" the woman said. "Don't go. People not come in here to give help. Not this neighborhood."

They walked back to the shop where Mr. Chu was waiting. Without speaking, he led the way through the curtain to the back of the shop. The smell was quite strong.

Laine started with the washing machine. The acrid smell intensified as he lifted the skirt protecting the gear mechanism. "There it is," he said pointing to the gearbox. Mr. Chu stood behind him, arms folded, a slightly skeptical look on his face. Mrs. Chu went back to folding shirts.

"It's an antique, Mr. Chu, an old Walker-Kline. I'm amazed you've been able to keep it going this long."

Mrs. Chu translated from the front room. Mr. Chu nodded slightly without changing his expression.

"You've taken good care of it, I can see, but the grease buildup is starting to burn. That's what we smell. It won't catch fire, but it's letting the metal heat up so there's more friction slowing the drum down."

Clearly, this isn't working, Laine thought. *He doesn't understand a word of what I said.* But before he could rephrase it, Mrs. Chu said something through the curtain and her husband smiled. He understood.

A teapot appeared and the three sat down in the front of the shop to drink and talk. Occasionally a customer appeared, Mrs. Chu would respond, then the conversation resumed. Laine told them exactly why he knew so much about laundry machines, information that didn't seem to have any negative effect on the Chus.

Finally, Mr. Chu got around to asking what could best be done to help the situation. Laine said that if he would get him a few things—a spanner wrench, a couple of screwdrivers, naphtha, mineral spirits, a wire brush, and lots of clean rags— he would be glad to come in and refurbish the machines. And, please, do not think about money.

"We have to pay you something, Mr. Rain, please."

"I don't need money, Mrs. Chu, but if you could give me more of this good tea, I would be deeply grateful."

The deal was struck, the only snag being the work couldn't be done until the machines stopped at the end of the workday, at five thirty. Laine explained he would be happy to come at that time, but he would have to leave by seven o'clock for a regular evening appointment. He didn't feel like explaining his concern about walking quiet streets. The shorter work hours would mean it would take longer to do the job, but if they didn't mind that part, he was up for the task. Mr. Chu said he would have the material Laine needed by Thursday. Work would start that evening.

On the way through the Madrid lobby, Laine could see a letter of some sort in his mailbox. Zwick plucked it out and handed it to Laine.

"Well, aren't you the fancy one, Laine. A library card," he said, his words dripping sarcasm. "Next week it'll be membership in the yacht club."

"I already have that one. By the way, Zwick, I'm surprised you know what a library card is. Really, you ought to try reading something other than a newspaper sometime. Do you a world of good." He didn't wait for a response before heading up to his room. The paper ball was in place, Cowboy was in his room, door open, apparently taking a nap—boots and all.

Laine examined the card as if it was an award. Coated in plastic, the multicolored card proclaimed George H. Laine to be a member of the San Francisco Library System. The accompanying letter welcomed him, highlighting a number of membership benefits including free lectures, admission to library exhibits, and a discount at city museums.

He stared at the card for quite a while, turning it over and holding it out as if proffering an engraved invitation from the White House. He remembered the first time he got his own library card when he was twelve. His father congratulated him as if he'd won a track event. Katie cried because she didn't get one, too. She was only ten and wasn't consoled to hear she also would someday have her own card. Just be patient.

At dinner every night, someone would talk about a fact or idea learned from a book that day. It could be a new word, a piece of information, or something that didn't quite make sense. That was the best part, his parents explaining something unknown or mysterious, often illustrated with a story from the old country. Some of the stories were frightening, tales about people lost in the woods or caught in the horror of the Great War. Others were wistful tales of Finnish folklore, people living with vast reindeer herds, or spirits moving through long, dark winter nights.

A card, a simple library card, brought it all back. Suddenly, he once again had "rights and privileges"—it said so right on the card. What an amazing feeling. "I can't wait to use you," he said out loud.

And use it he did, moving back and forth between reading and continuing to probe the internet trying to fill in the gaps in Alfred's career path. He did find out that Alfred—and presumably Constance and Rebecca—lived in a suburb of Terre Haute, where Alfred was part of a three-member law firm. Why they chose to live in Terre Haute remained a mystery. Everything reported about them in any detail happened in California after 1968.

Every day's search began with a prolonged review of all the material he had about Constance and Rebecca, especially the pictures. Just as Tony had said, Constance was heavily involved in charity work, especially projects to preserve open spaces and encourage community gardens. Rebecca was harder to follow, but intermittently she showed up in one of her mother's projects. More importantly, he learned she had been married, divorced, and had a son, Erik, now fourteen.

"Nordic spelling! Is that you talking Constance? A subtle way of keeping me in your life? Does Rebecca know about me?" True or not, it brought a smile and moment of comfort.

His reaction to their pictures and stories gradually evolved from curiosity to pride. Realizing he was the grandfather of a handsome, happy-looking teenager added to Laine's gathering sense of having substance—even value. Inmates are weightless, like ghosts exiled to the moon. The slightest moon breeze can send them off into an infinite void, a piece of nothing floating forever through nothing at all, achingly aware of their unmoored state.

Funny how a library card and a few memories can change that.

By Thursday afternoon, Laine was happy to be able to shift his attention to something new. He ate his meal at the mission, excused himself, and walked quickly to the laundry. He didn't want to be late for his first day of work.

Mr. Chu had all the material Laine requested, the machines were stopped, and he and the Chus had a cup of tea while waiting for the washer gears and main shaft to cool down. Crawling under the machine, Laine saw the buildup of grease mixed with lint and dirt was not only thicker than he expected, but high heat had baked it to a rock-hard finish. He worked until nearly seven o'clock, managing to clear just a few inches from the main shaft.

Walking back to the Madrid, Laine was elated. Yes, he was careful to scan the area as he walked, but he was working again, focused on a problem he could actually solve. He could see it, touch it, smell it, feel it—and make it right. In a curious way, he felt some sense of gratitude for all of those years of hard work in the laundry, training he never imagined he would be allowed to use in the world outside of prison.

But these are alien feelings, potentially disruptive. Can they be enjoyed without wanting more, without making the inevitable fall even more painful? Or could the moment stay with him, the brass ring he could keep hidden under his thin pillow in the geriatric ward?

On the way through the lobby, he saw another piece of mail in his box.

"Christ, Laine," Zwick said as he pushed a small box across the desktop. "First a library card and now checks. No one in the Madrid has a checking account. No one! How the hell did you do that? And by the way, if you have a checking account, how about writing me a check?"

"I would if there was enough in the account, but don't worry, the Social Security check is on the way. And opening an account was simply a matter of asking politely."

"Bullshit, Laine. I knew you were trouble the day Tomaras sent you here. But like I said, don't get too comfortable, the Tenderloin is a tough place even for a wise-ass like you."

"I'm aware, Zwick, but thanks for the tip."

Before joining the others in the lobby for the evening's distraction, Laine removed ten checks and two deposit slips from the supply, tore the rest into fine pieces, and put them in the box. The checks and deposit slips went into the secure bedpost keep. After scratching off his name and address, he dropped the box and check scraps into the trash can by the vending machines on the second-floor landing.

Laine worked at the laundry again on Friday and promised to return Monday evening. He was beginning to settle into a routine of sorts, all anchored by his time in the two libraries. Both had reading rooms with comfortable chairs and good light. With an infinite supply of books coupled with a safe and friendly atmosphere, it was easy to drift into reading without the need to maintain vigil. It was a sensation he hadn't felt since his days in graduate school.

Reading in prison was a distraction, but only as pleasurable as the immediate circumstances allowed. Even the prison library was sometimes a perilous place to be. There were fewer guards there—an excellent place for a sudden attack. In the yard or dining hall, there was less time to inflict harm before guards could react. Those extra moments in the library made assaults more deadly.

The only comfortable place to read—if "comfortable" is even the right word—was in his cell with Leroy. No fear there, but the noise and limited light could suck the pleasure out of any passage.

Thinking about Leroy brought with it the depressing picture of his friend trapped in San Quentin while Laine walked free. He had tried several times to write to Leroy but hadn't gotten past the first sentence. It seemed impossible to tell him anything that would give him a lift, make him smile that wonderful smile he showed on rare occasions. "News" about his life at the Madrid didn't seem to offer much, same for any talk about what he was doing day-to-day on the streets. Telling Leroy about the libraries, the park, or even the evening entertainment, all seemed flat and forced. Describing discoveries about his family or the surveillance wouldn't work, either; far too risky in the likely case Leroy's mail was being read. Even if no one saw it, Leroy would worry—the last thing Laine wanted.

He tried talking about Bill's death, the harsh reality people in the Madrid live with every day, and the way the system seems rigged to make freedom turn into just another form of incarceration. But that was way too gloomy.

He finally decided to write just one short paragraph and stop trying to sound like he was saying life outside was no better than it was in prison. The truth is, no matter how perilous or difficult freedom might be, most inmates wanted desperately to take a crack at it. Besides, Leroy had family, they truly wanted him back, and in time it could happen. So he simply told Leroy how much he missed their talks, how he regretted being unable to visit him—it was outside his restricted zone—and how every day he thought about him, hoping someday they might both be free to take a long walk together.

He mailed it on Saturday morning on the way to Dolores Park with Kitty, Louis, and Cowboy. He had lunch at the mission on Sunday and spent the rest of the afternoon at the Bartlett branch library reading about the age of the universe.

On Monday morning, he and Kitty walked up to Dusty's for coffee. Kitty was on her way for an appointment at the health clinic. Laine planned to read in the main library until his three-thirty appointment with Tomaras.

"Have you noticed how different Louis has been since you guys talked in the park? He's more relaxed and didn't hesitate when we all went back there on Saturday. I don't know what you said, but I want some, too. I've been around him for several years, and I hardly know anything about the man."

"I didn't say anything special; I just listened. He's no different from any of us. We all got to the Madrid through failed lives. No one is proud to call the place home. But we're all still trying to survive, get past the pain, and find something to hang onto. Call it peace or pride or acceptance, doesn't matter, it's all the same. Even Zwick, nasty as he is, is probably in the same boat."

"You and Louis are more charitable toward Zwick than the rest of us. I can't get anywhere near the man without feeling he's ready to jump on me."

"You're reading too much into it, I think. Zwick's a bully, a little smarter and more civilized than Elton, but a one-pony show. He's lost when someone stands up to him."

"Maybe you're right. It's weird living in close quarters with people you know so little about. I guess I know more about you than anybody else—and I've known you the shortest time. Why is that? Is it because I'm female?"

"That could have something to do with it, I'm not sure. But remember, Kitty, you shared a lot with me, painful things we've both been through. Maybe that's why we trust each other. I don't know about the female thing. Maybe Freud could tell us. I wonder what he'd say about a man who hadn't had a conversation with a woman in half a century."

"Did you ever think about women when you were in prison? There are all sorts of stories about what men fantasize and do in prison."

"Most of it is nonsense. True, there are homosexual hookups, and occasionally someone is raped in the shower or his cell, but aside from a lot of bragging, most cons—especially the ones doing long sentences—keep that stuff to themselves. Leroy and I never talked about it beyond saying how much we missed companionship, being close, having someone you could tell anything and it would be okay. Your thinking evolves; it takes a lot of time.

"At first, I thought about Constance all the time, especially on death row, but it was always anguished and desperate. I couldn't get past it. What I was calling meditation wasn't that at all. It was concentrating my preoccupation with her, the opposite of training my mind to shift from seeing what appears to be barren emptiness into something entirely different—infinite fullness. It sounds strange, I know, but over time I learned how to find stillness in the chaos. That's when I was really able to convert painful thoughts of Constance and my life with her into energy that allowed me to keep going, find the good that was left for me. And when I got a cellmate and started working in the laundry, it all seemed to come together.

"That's too long an answer, Kitty. I should have said, I don't think about women in a sexual way."

"Do you think you could ever fall in love again, George?"

"No. It would mean I'd have to fall out of love first, and that won't happen."

"Have you looked her up, George? I mean, have you searched for your wife on the internet? You say you've learned to use a computer, seems natural you'd try to find out about her. I'm not trying to pry; I just know I tried it for a while and finally gave up. It was probably a bad idea in the first place, part of letting go. Maybe it's what I needed for that acceptance thing you were talking about."

"Yeah, I have looked her up. I've been trying to put together some pieces, stuff about the past, and I couldn't really avoid it. It was a shock at first, but I've gotten comfortable with it. Now I know she's out there, married, and our daughter has a son. They all seem to be okay—as much as you can tell from a few scraps of information."

"Does it make you want to see her, I mean *really* see her?"

"No, just knowing is fine. It wouldn't serve any purpose; besides, staying away is a condition of my parole. There was a lot of legal stuff going on just before my first execution date, maneuvers I'm certain she didn't know about—she would have simply assumed I was dead. Later on, she married my lawyer's son. That really rocked me, but it doesn't change anything. It was better not to try to contact her back then, and certainly better to leave it alone now. I'm guessing our daughter thinks her stepfather is her real dad, and Constance thinks I'm dead.

"In a way, I'm glad she thinks I died and never had to deal with the years of me being so close to execution. Then when I went to the general population, what would she have done? Visit me every month for the rest of her life, still married to me? And Rebecca? What kind of life would it have been for both of them?

"No, it was better to think I was gone. She could move on with her life, and I wouldn't have to feel so awful about my situation, especially after that first stay."

"I get it. She wouldn't have to go through thinking about your execution over and over."

"And more. If I *had* been executed while we were still married, she would have been given notice of the exact time of my execution, and the state would have expected her to deal with my body. Can you imagine how that would have felt?"

"Horrible thought. But wouldn't the state do it anyway? You might have decided to let it go, she might have thought you were dead, but the state wouldn't let it go, right? She would have gotten an even worse jolt."

"Part of the legal stuff I didn't tell you was a court order put in place by my lawyer—completely unknown to me—directing that all communication from the prison go to his office; presumably, he would have taken care of my body without her knowing. Then later, he arranged a divorce—certainly without her knowing it— and that would have sealed it completely."

"But wasn't there a will? After you didn't die, wouldn't she wonder about that?"

"I doubt it. The only thing I owned was a car, but I signed that over to her after the trial. The last thing on her mind would have been a will.

"But here's a twist: they made all condemned prisoners sign a will just before execution, but the court order considered even mentioning Constance and Rebecca a prohibited form of 'contact,' so I had to name someone else in case I had some unknown or future asset."

"What a weird thought: something you could have in the *future*! On death row? Are you kidding me?"

"Actually, now that I think about it, there could have been something. The summer before I was arrested I applied for a patent. If it was accepted and somehow turned into anything, I suppose theoretically that could have gone to her. It's a pretty farfetched idea."

"A patent? On what?"

"On a chemical mixture to clean circuit boards. Sounds weird, right? I was an electrical engineer—always fascinated by anything electrical. When I was a kid there was a company that made kits to build almost anything electrical you could buy in a store. A radio, a record player, testing equipment—even a TV—and if you did it right, they all worked perfectly. To do any of it, you had to be good at soldering. Soldering requires a paste called 'flux,' and flux is messy. Standard cleaning methods all had their drawbacks, and when I was working in a lab after college, I figured out a solution that cleaned well, dried fast, didn't degrade anything it touched, and was cheap. My boss encouraged me to apply for a patent. Simple."

"Simple for you. Greek for me. Did you ever get the patent?"

"I have no idea. I haven't thought about it in years."

"Holy shit! It's all crazy. You wife wouldn't have had a clue you were alive, there was no reason not to marry again, and no computers around to stumble over the divorce issue. Wow! I can see why you don't want her to know you're still alive. She'd be horrified!"

"Exactly."

"Call me morbid, but I'm curious: what would they have done with your body if the lawyer didn't want to bother with it?"

"Until the early fifties, they buried unclaimed bodies, executed or not, in a plot near the Richmond San Rafael bridge. Since then, if they can't get someone to take the remains, the state pays to have you cremated, and the mortician disposes of the ashes. Probably dumps them in the bay."

"Well, I'm damn glad they didn't kill you. I never would have gotten to know you."

Laine arrived at Tomaras's office well ahead of his three thirty appointment. Again, the meeting was short, the urine screen negative, and Laine's next meeting was already scheduled for the following Monday.

When he got back to the Madrid, he saw another letter in his box. As he approached the desk, Zwick took it out, leaned forward, right forearm on the desk, left hand holding the letter up, tauntingly just beyond Laine's grasp.

"Another piece of mail for you, Laine. Pretty soon you'll need your own post office. Meanwhile, looks like a check from the State of California Comptroller's Office. Let's see what we have here," he said.

"No, Zwick. Give me the envelope."

"You forget, Laine, you owe me money, so I think I'll have a look-see and find out just how quick I get paid."

Laine's left hand shot out, grabbed Zwick's right hand and in the same movement pulled his body down over the desk. The pain was instant and so severe Zwick couldn't speak. Still, he held onto the envelope.

"Hand it to me, Zwick, or I'll crush your hand. Your call."

Zwick dropped the check. Laine picked it up and released Zwick's hand.

"Jesus Christ, Laine! You goddamn near broke my freaking hand! Fuck! That hurts!"

"I'm sorry. It's a prison thing: when things go wrong in there, they go wrong fast. You learn to react quickly, no 'Pretty please,' no hesitation. And as far as what I owe you, you can be sure you will be paid. In the meantime, I'd advise you to soak your hand in ice water for a while to keep it from swelling."

In the forty-one years Laine had worked in the laundry, he earned just over $15,000. Typically, he took three-quarters of each month's earnings to buy books and snacks at the prison commissary, "deposited" the rest with the state, earning a fraction of a percent in interest. There was some withholding but never enough income to pay taxes. Added together, including interest, the total was $4,520.

The check went into the keep. Laine ate quickly at the mission, then went back to work on Mr. Chu's mountain.

Chapter 19

"I KNOW BETTER THAN TO ask if the job is done, right, Dalton?"

"No, it's not done. Worse, I'm getting a lot of heat from Metzi. We need a change in strategy, meaning I need to get your go-ahead for more direct action. I don't like it, but it looks like that's the best way to get this done."

"You've had my 'go-ahead' all along. What's different now?"

"Okay, as you well know, Laine has been quite slippery. We haven't been able to trip him up, force him to break a rule, or tangle with some crazy on the sidewalk. Tomaras won't revoke him for having dirty thoughts, and he's been amazingly adroit at keeping out of any situation he can't control. He's predictable, sticks to groups, and doesn't venture out after dark.

"The boys are getting really tired of trailing him around. They're pushing me to get this finished. On top of that, they're getting a lot of heat from their superiors who wonder why their arrest numbers have fallen off. They want a change in tactics."

"Yeah? What kind of change?"

"Something more 'confrontational,' you might say."

"So what's that mean, Dalton? Quit beating around the goddamn bush. What are they talking about?"

"I don't like saying it, but they're talking about getting a couple of guys to mess him up, not kill him—I couldn't be party to that—but put him so far out of action he'd cease to be on anybody's radar."

"So what's the problem? The more messed up the better. I don't understand why it hasn't already occurred to someone to do it."

"It's because he always goes out on the street when there are plenty of people around, never after dark. Even in the Tenderloin, you can't just jump on someone in broad daylight with witnesses all over the place."

"So I gather that's changed?"

"Yeah. He seems to have a job, one that takes him out in the evening when the streets are quieter."

"A job? He has a job? What the hell kind of a job does a seventy-five-year-old con get?"

"You're not going to believe it, Judge, but he's working in a Vietnamese laundry."

"You've got to be shitting me!"

"No, I'm not. It looks like he's helping them with their equipment, I don't know, but it puts him on the sidewalk after the stores around there are closed. The guys think this is the best shot we'll get."

"A frigging laundry. Too much. Okay, just get it done."

"I have to tell you, this makes me very nervous. I've been willing to lean on the boys and Tomaras to find a way to revoke him, a *legitimate* beef that would hold up in a revocation hearing. But this is way past what I had in mind. We're talking about the possibility of killing someone."

"Listen, Dalton, you're in this up to your eyeballs. Do I have to remind you of the many favors you've done in the past, or of the money you've been happy to take? Do I? So send a smoke signal to the boys and get this over with so we can all relax."

"Christ! I hate this. All right, but then there's the cost. Metzi and Carlos aren't doing this themselves; these guys expect serious money to get this done."

"Yeah, get to the point, the cost?"

"Twenty K for both."

"Cheap at the price."

Chapter 20

"Okay Metzi, green light for twenty K. But listen to me: don't let them kill him. We want him out of circulation, not dead. Make him a permanent resident in a nursing home—that would be perfect."

"Listen, Dalton, that's not the sort of thing you tell guys like this. You can't say, 'Work him over so he needs an appointment to cross the street—but don't kill him.' That's not how it works on the street. You tell them who you want worked over, where he'll be and when, give them half the money, and that's it. After the job is done, you pay the other half. Everyone is happy."

"Okay, just make sure they don't get caught."

"Caught? Who the hell is going to catch them? Part of the reason they're willing to do it is because they know there won't be any cops around when it goes down. You need to get out more, Dalton, find out how the city really works. Meanwhile, bring me the cash, usual place."

Chapter 21

LAINE DEPOSITED HIS CHECK ON Tuesday, was told a state check usually clears within a day, so he would be able to write a check within twenty-four hours. He withdrew $50 in cash, left the bank, and walked back to the Goodwill store.

The first time Laine went to Goodwill he promised himself he would buy a radio and a coffee maker when—and if—he felt there was a chance his freedom wasn't just temporary, a cruel illusion that would suddenly explode and send him back where he belonged.

Leroy had a radio and a small television set, but he liked gospel and contemporary music. While Laine enjoyed the music, his preference was the classical music he listened to while Leroy was on kitchen duty. The idea of owning a radio and being able to listen without prison noise was suddenly a reality, though dampened by a nagging sense of hubris. How strange, he thought, that something so ordinary could feel undeserved, another reminder that his freedom was suspended by a thin thread that could be snipped at any moment. It was an emotion living a level below guilt.

It may sound foolish for anyone to wrestle with the idea of buying a used radio, but for Laine, it required some mental gymnastics. It had to do with being conditioned over time to see almost any indulgence as forbidden.

In the world outside prison gates, "guilt" means feeling bad for a real or perceived wrong, anything ranging from wishing something bad would happen to your neighbor's yapping Pomeranian to stinging it with your kid's BB gun. You can get over the guilt caused by the fantasy part simply by thinking it through, rationalizing it: the dog is just doing what dogs do, don't worry about it. If more work is needed, try an act of attrition, hit the confessional booth, or slip a Gaines-Burgers through the neighbor's mail slot.

Guilt in prison is a different matter. It's either a fact—guilty or not—or an emotion associated with the consequences of your crime. Many inmates are psychopaths, by definition untroubled by the slightest twinge of guilt. This isn't about them. For those who do have a conscience, it's about pain and regret that never resolve. In prison, there are no Pomeranian equivalents, nothing easily excused or brushed aside. You can be momentarily distracted by a fight, chapel service, or TV show, but then it's back to the same thoughts in the unchanging repetition of every slow minute of every slow day.

And because you can't make it up to anyone, the guilt doesn't go away. You can try religion to see if God will help you out, or do something for other prisoners, though that one is tricky and can get your head cracked open if your intentions are misinterpreted. If you are only in for a few years, you have the chance to get out and do something tangible about the guilt. Many do, especially those who manage to hang onto some support at home. Those folks don't have any trouble buying a radio.

But for inmates serving a long sentence, it's a different matter. Over time, visits and letters become fewer and may stop altogether. Any sense of the outside world becomes fragmentary until the disconnect is finally complete. Over time, feelings of guilt fade, displaced by a more pernicious emotion seeping in from below, the one that made Laine hesitate the first time he bought an egg sandwich simply because he was hungry, and now challenged his right to buy a radio. He didn't have guilt over having committed a crime, but it amounted to the same thing: feeling that through some invisible twist of fate he had caused his family horrific suffering, and while he didn't begin to understand why it had happened, it did, and guilty or not, the crime and the misery trailing behind belonged to him.

The next step down from there is the feeling of worthlessness, the idea you have lost everything simply because you don't deserve anything. People on the outside, sensing the possibility of having low self-esteem, pay a therapist to boost them up, help them look on the bright side. Go ahead, treat yourself to a new pair of skis. Really, you deserve it.

But long-term prisoners don't think about having anything beyond what they can buy at the commissary. Apathy and mindless obedience do their best to stamp out any vestige of self-worth. Psychologists call it "institutionalization," meaning that over time inmates become unable to function in any other zone, conveniently explained as a product of the prisoner's defective personality, the logical outcome of entrenched maladaptive thinking and behavior.

That is why, they will say, prisoners released after lengthy confinement so often commit suicide or deliberately break the law to get sent back to the only place they are comfortable and can function. It's never a consequence of the system. No, it's just another example of what society is up against from the criminal mind.

Laine thought the matter through, pushed back against entrenched prohibitions, and bought a radio. He also decided he was entitled to know it really worked. The Goodwill clerk objected to Laine going behind the counter to plug it in. Laine said he was sorry and plugged in the radio anyway.

The clerk sealed his complaint with an emphatic, "This ain't Crutchfield's, mister!"

Laine had no idea what he was talking about, but it didn't matter—the radio worked. He paid $12 and went back to the Madrid with his prize.

Back in his room, Laine positioned the radio by the bed on the edge of the desk, found the classical music station on NPR just in time to hear the *Goldberg Variations* played by Angela Hewitt. *What amazing good luck to hear my favorite piece of classical music the minute I turn on the radio*, he thought. *Maybe one day they'll play Glenn Gould's version. I wonder if anyone remembers his recording from the mid-1950s. Sad, but probably not.*

After dinner at the mission and his work with Mr. Chu, Laine retreated to his room to listen to more music. He fell asleep listening to Dvorak. Once again he forgot to wash his underwear and socks.

Laine spent the next morning at the Bartlett Street library, his attention divided between reading, looking at pictures of Constance and Rebecca on the internet, and following the sputtering trail of clues about Alfred Preston.

On the way back to the Madrid, he caught himself wondering if, in spite of everything he knew to be true about Alfred, he might not be the one trying to disable him. *The pressure seemed to be decreasing, maybe it's finally obvious I just want to be left alone.*

"Who am I kidding?!" he yelled. No one seemed to notice the outburst. In this part of town, sudden oral ejaculations of every type imaginable are common. No one cares.

No, it has to be Alfred. He's positioned to know the instant I was paroled, he probably owns all the key players, and legally or otherwise, he has the resources to make terrible things happen to people. He can't get inside my mind, and that has to be driving him crazy. Will I simply fade away, or try to unmask him? He can't afford to take chances, and any apparent lull is just a timeout before the next play. There's just no way Alfred is going to give up. I've got to stay on my toes.

John Zwick didn't look well; Laine could see that from the front door. He was sitting at his guard post, elbows on the desk, fingers laced together on his forehead, thumbs on both temples, facing down at the desktop.

"Bad night, Mr. Zwick?"

"Fuck off, Laine," he said without looking up.

"I came to cheer you up. Here, I have something for you." He put a check on the desk and slid it under Zwick's nose.

Zwick stared at it without moving. "What's this?"

"It's a check, the four hundred dollars I owe you for the first month's rent."

Zwick sat up and examined the check. "Jesus, it *is* a check. But you know, Laine, I collect that first month's rent at the end, when you leave you pay an extra month. You didn't have to do this. Shit, I never would have known."

"But I would. Besides, the way things are going, I might be leaving, say, 'prematurely,' and then you wouldn't get your money. It's better this way."

"Maybe I misjudged you, Laine. You're not the usual boarder we get here."

"I'm no different from anyone else, just have a different story to tell, that's all. Hope you feel better."

"Yeah, thanks. Maybe I'll learn some day not to drink with Russians."

Work at Mr. Chu's laundry was nearly complete. Two more nights should do it. He was already starting to miss the work and thought about what he could do next to be useful. Reading and library time would always be a major part of his day, but following the trail leading to answers about Alfred and Constance had lost its sense of urgency. Though it distressed him to think of his wife living with the man who had destroyed so much, at least she didn't know it. If he was sent back to prison or lived out his life in the Madrid, it wouldn't make much difference to anyone except Alfred. And his hash would be settled soon enough. How and when didn't matter, but no one disrupts the forces of human harmony that much and gets off scot-free.

Doing some regular work at the mission was the obvious next step. He could repay Reverend Sully's generosity, and as long as he didn't get tangled up in contentious discussions about religion, he could do productive work in a safe place close to the hotel. There was also the added benefit of lunch on days that he worked.

But first, he had to finish cleaning up the Walker-Kline. Wednesday night went smoothly, and he told the Chus he would be finished the next night. The improvement was already dramatic. The machines ran cooler, more quietly, and put off far less heat. The Chus wanted to pay him, but he again refused. In the end, they negotiated an extension of the tea deal: Mr. "Rain" would be welcome for afternoon tea any time he was in the neighborhood.

On Thursday night, the job completed, Laine and the Chus had their last evening tea. As always, he paused as he stepped out onto the street, quickly scanning both sides as he prepared to turn left, walk against the traffic, and carefully make his way back to the Madrid. His internal alarm immediately sounded.

Across the street and slightly to his right, a man was leaning against a building, seemingly reading a folded newspaper. As Laine emerged, the man lowered the paper and pushed off from the wall. *Where's the other one?* he wondered, turning left, starting up the street. *Ah! There he is, walking slowly down the sidewalk, right hand in his coat pocket, left hanging free.*

In prison, it's called a "pinch," the most common prelude to a quick assault on an inmate in the exercise yard. Typically, the target is walking on the exercise track, staying alert for anyone moving up behind him, the surefire clue that someone will suddenly step in front, momentarily sandwiching the man in a deadly pinch. If the man behind moves in at an angle, he can remain invisible until the last instant when he closes the gap. Since shanks are few and hard to hide, only one of the two would do the stabbing. Typically, the man in front holds the victim just long enough for two or three quick thrusts from the man behind. The victim won't collapse for several more seconds, time enough to pass the knife to a third man while the other two go in opposite directions. By the time the victim hits the ground and the alarm sounds, the blade is on the other side of the yard under the leg of an exercise machine or covered with dirt in a crack between a wall and the yard.

At the first sign of trouble, there is only one question to be answered: Can I duck this? Is there running room? If the answer is no, then the question becomes, how do I keep from being killed? Duck it if you can, run if you have to, fight only as an absolute last resort.

Retreating to the laundry would have been useless, possibly dangerous to the Chus. Laine only had two options: pick a direction and run, or figure out how to turn the situation to his advantage. Running would have been a mistake. If he spun to the right, the guy across the street would be on him. Same if he cut across the street—they would simply change the point of convergence. And running takes away your edge. As long as they don't know you see what's coming, they'll follow their plan, unaware they're the ones falling into the trap. Their minds and muscles are fixed on a certain point. The man across the street will angle across the traffic to end up right behind Laine just as the man in front steps into his path. The probability was that both had weapons, hopefully knives because dealing with guns was far riskier. If that was the case, so be it. Laine's move was the same in either case.

As Laine neared the man walking toward him, he felt the other approaching his back. With only a few steps left before the blocker made his move, Laine suddenly accelerated, moving slightly to his right. That increased the gap behind, making the startled blocker turn to his left while bringing his right hand up into play. The sudden turn and awkward hand movement changed the man's momentum, making it relatively easy to grab the rising hand, pivot, and using the man's momentum, pull him into the middle of the pinch. Laine's sudden move forward put him just out of stabbing range from the man behind, giving him the split second he needed to get behind the blocker. The man behind drove his knife forward in an attempt to hit Laine, but unfortunately for his partner, the knife went straight into his right kidney.

At exactly the same moment, still controlling the knife hand with his left hand, Laine drove the heel of his right hand straight up into the man's chin, shattering his jaw and knocking out several teeth. The force of the blow caused his head to snap back straight into the second man's face, breaking his nose, splitting his upper lip, and causing an instant gush of blood.

The two men were momentarily joined together, holding each other up before both slowly sank onto the sidewalk. By then, Laine was already crossing the street. The few bystanders who saw it said that it looked like one man was trying to rob the other. Only one even mentioned seeing a third person, describing him as "lucky" he didn't get caught up in the encounter.

Back at the Madrid, the evening group was forming. Laine excused himself, said he might be back later but he had to clean up after his work at the laundry.

"Better get that blood off your sleeve while you're at it," said Kitty. "Did you cut yourself or did someone just get in your way?"

"Just a little sidewalk misunderstanding," Laine said looking at his sleeve. "I'd better take care of this before I have to do any explaining. Thanks for pointing it out." He glanced back at the lobby door and started up the stairs, his thoughts focused on what he would do when the cops came to arrest him.

In his room, he quickly removed the shirt, scrubbed out the blood and blotted it dry. He turned on the radio and sat down at the desk to think.

Whatever foolish ideas he may have had about decreased surveillance went out the window. No, there was a clear change in tactics.

You're getting desperate, Alfred, and when you hear about the debacle in the street, it'll only make you crazier. So what's next? A bullet from a passing car? Another innocent bystander killed in the ongoing tragedy of gang warfare? A repeat of tonight with more people or a better ambush? I was lucky tonight, but there's no way to handle it if they send real pros, not street bozos.

No matter what, time is getting short. I don't care about going back, but maybe it's time to rethink the notion of going quietly. You had your chance, Alfred. You could have left it alone, but you're too dangerous to ignore. But how do I deal with you without bringing some really severe pain to Constance and Rebecca?

The answer, if that's even the right word, would be to let someone know that Alfred Preston killed Julia Penthoser. There is no real proof, certainly nothing that would stand up in court, but just raising doubt might stir things up enough to knock Alfred off his perch, force him to do some serious explaining. In all likelihood, he would be able to crush it, maybe even keep Constance from finding out about it. But even so, it would certainly shatter his confidence. Worse, word would be out in the law enforcement world, maybe scare one of his lackeys enough to start singing. And sing they will if they sense someone higher up is about to dump them.

But who do I tell? Who would even listen to such a far-fetched idea, much less initiate some sort of action against such a powerful public servant?

Tomaras, that's who. She's being used, and when she sees it, she'll strike back, no matter the consequences. How do I get her attention, make sure she takes the story seriously, and doesn't dismiss it as the raving of an unrepentant murderer?

God, I hate this. I'm becoming just like them: plotting, scheming, looking for revenge, figuring out how to trip someone up, manipulate circumstances to turn out in a certain way. That's the shit I spent fifty-two years getting away from. Here I am, a month into so-called "freedom," and I'm turning my back on what I believe. I've got to get back on track.

He finally fell asleep.

In the morning, he went to the lobby, again half expecting Tomaras, Metzi, or some other grim-faced cop to be waiting to haul him away. But there was no one. *Time for coffee and a sandwich,* he thought. *I wonder how the sidewalk boys are doing this morning.*

In fact, they weren't doing well at all. The back man had managed to get up and stagger away, but there was so much blood on his face and shirt that calls started to come into the 911 center about a bloody monster terrifying people on Caliente Street. The other man was down for the count, delirious from his facial injuries and weak from the blood slowly leaking out of his kidney. Both men were treated at San Francisco General, but only the man with the nasal fracture was able to talk to police; the other was immediately taken to surgery, and when he returned, his jaw was wired shut. The witness accounts and story from the man who could talk made no sense, so in the end, no charges were lodged. Metzi visited both men, hinted that the second half of their money still might be paid provided they both stayed quiet and out of sight during their convalescence.

Laine enjoyed an egg sandwich at Dusty's, already wondering if this might be his last breakfast or at least his last one as a free man, given the events of last evening. But the walk up to Dusty's and back was uneventful. When he got back, the only person in the lobby was Cowboy—no cops. It was still too early for Zwick, even without the Russians.

"Look what I have here, George!" Cowboy crowed. Before Laine could say, "A new coffee maker" (there was a picture on the box), Cowboy said, "A new coffee maker! I got just enough money to get one. It's a Mr. Coffee, see?"

"It's beautiful, Cowboy, but don't you already have one?"

"Yup, but this one is better. Brand new, too. I'm giving my old one to you, George. That way you can have coffee in the morning before you even get dressed."

"That's very kind of you. I accept, but…"

"But what?"

"But if something happens to me, please take it back and give it to someone else, okay?"

"So what's going to happen to you? Okay, okay, talk is someone jumped you last night. How come you didn't say nothing about it?"

"No big deal, just a couple of street goons thinking I might have a few bucks. I dodged them."

"That's not what I hear. But, okay, something happens, I'll deal with it."

They made the deal, though Laine immediately felt he had been a little too quick to accept Cowboy's gift. Still, the idea of early morning coffee—even for a few days—was too appealing to resist. Laine reversed course back to the Vietnamese market, bought coffee, sugar, and powdered creamer. He and Cowboy enjoyed a cup of fresh coffee in his room.

"It's probably none of my business, George, but if I was you, I'd be scared shitless if someone was trying to put me back in the slammer."

"You'd worry about that more than getting killed?"

"Yup. Dead is dead. Slammer is dead on dead."

"No argument on that point, Cowboy."

"Yeah. Eighteen years, four months, and six days in Arizona State taught me all I'll ever need to know about dead. I was alive and dead at the same time when I finally crawled out of that sewer. Never again, that's what I said when I stood in the street and looked back at that evil place. I'd kill myself first."

"I get you, and I certainly don't want to go back, either. Still, I'd be in the geriatric unit, and my guess is I wouldn't last too long. That's a whole lot better than life in general population."

As he stepped into the lobby, Zwick called out, "Hey, Laine, I need to talk to you." Stepping off his stool, he motioned toward a door behind the desk marked EXIT. He used a key to open it.

"Some exit, Mr. Zwick. Do you hand out keys during a fire? Bet the fire marshal loves that arrangement."

"He's on the take just like everyone else. He deals with the invisible people who own the stores and hotels around the Tenderloin. He gets paid from above, not below. He'll bust our balls just for fun, but when it comes time for an inspection, I get a call—I turn on the elevator and open the exits. Easy."

There was a huge open area on the other side of the door, a restaurant in the hotel's better days. The remnants of a kitchen could be seen through a large opening in the back wall that used to support a pair of swinging doors. Zwick had fashioned an office of sorts in one corner using two old tables and a few chairs.

"I give up—where's the so-called exit? Or does it really matter?"

"In the kitchen. It's got a fire ax stuck through the handles. All I do is pull it out, and I'm in compliance."

Before they sat down, Zwick checked the lobby through a crack in the exit door, then poured a generous aliquot of vodka into a drinking glass. Laine declined the invitation to join in.

"Practicing for your next bout with the Russians?"

"I hate Russians. You can live with the mob but not with Russians. The mob is a business run by reasonable people, but the Russians are frigging crazy. They're starting to show up in the

Tenderloin—bad news for everyone. Those bastards don't follow any of the rules; they just move in and take over what they want. So far the people with money have been doing a pretty good job holding them back. They can't penetrate the payoff system, so the law is all over them, but it's getting harder. They don't mind killing cops or anyone else who gets in their way.

"But I didn't invite you back here to talk about Russians. Listen: you know you were one lucky bastard to get out of that hit last night. And before you ask, no, I didn't know it was going down. I would have warned you."

"Even after I messed up your hand?"

"Yeah, well, you didn't bust anything. I wouldn't admit it to anyone, but I had it coming on that one. But listen: what I want to tell you is, just because you ducked that hit on the sidewalk, don't think that's the end of it."

"I've already figured that out. What I want to know is how come everyone seems to know I've got a target on my back? And that begs the question about who's pulling the strings. Do you know?"

"First, the easy part. No, I don't know who is calling this one, just that someone with a lot of power wants you dead or back in San Quentin."

"Okay, what about the hard part?"

"It's about the street, Laine. A couple of easy shots and you start to think you can deal with it. You think you know the street because you've been locked up with street people and you know how the prison system works. News flash: the street doesn't operate like a prison. You've got a new set of rules to learn, Laine. The street has a force like gravity: you can't see it, but you feel it. If you try to fight it, you get knocked down.

"You've been lucky so far, but your prison smarts and fast reflexes won't protect you for long out here. You know how something like this works inside, but it's a totally different ball game out here. It's closer to a military system than anything in jail."

"Sounds like you've seen it all up close."

"Yeah, I have. Too close, really, starting when I was in high school, not getting along too well, in trouble a lot—petty shit and misdemeanors. Then one day I got arrested for stealing a car and my lawyer told me I could beat the rap by joining the Army. I was nineteen, figured a couple of years in the Army beat the hell out of jail, so off I went.

"I fucking hated it. Everybody yelling at you all the time, up in the middle of the night, lugging bricks around in a backpack. Crazy shit like that. But if I screwed up, I'd go to jail, so I stuck it out. Finally, they put me in the military police, a good gig, really, but I never made it past corporal. At least I got out with an honorable discharge, and my 'experience' in the MPs got me a job as a guard in a county jail in Crescent City. When a spot opened up in Corcoran,* I jumped into the state system.

"That was a whole different ballgame. In 'county,' everyone was well behaved, trying to look good and get out. Corcoran was the bottom of the barrel. Every one of the inmates lived to make our job miserable and dangerous. I started out on the admin side, kinda working into the system. The first day I was in the segregation unit, I ran into a guy I knew from high school. Man, when he saw me his face lit up like a friggin' Christmas tree. He got right in my face and said straight out, 'I'm going to love killing you.'

"See, it went all the way back to school when we were dating the same girl. She was fucking both of us, but when he found out about me, he beat her up and came after me with a knife. I got away from him, he went to jail, and I thought I'd never see him again.

"When he said he'd kill me, I freaking knew it was true. At the end of my shift, I walked out and never looked back. The only good news is he's doing two consecutive life terms. Otherwise, I'd move to Borneo."

"You were right to get out. But how is that different from what goes on in the street?"

---

* Corcoran is a maximum security prison in south-central California, home of Charles Manson, Sirhan Sirhan, and Juan Corona.

"It's all the difference in the world. In prison, you know who your enemy is, on the street you don't. In prison, you know who hangs with who, so you know who's a threat and who isn't. Not so in the street. In prison, people kill for vengeance or loyalty with no worry about adding on more time. On the street, people kill for money or to improve their image with someone, always operating in a way that won't get them caught. In prison, instructions come from one guy straight to you. In the street, the chain is long and invisible.

"Like I said, the street is more like what I saw in the military. If General Jones wants Private Laine screwed over for some reason, he tells the colonel who tells the major who tells the lieutenant who tells the sergeant, and he sees to it you get put out of business. There's no way to trace it back to General Jones. As to payment, it works the same way. Word will filter down that everyone in the chain is doing a good job, promotions and little perks will follow. Everyone is happy—except George Laine."

"So what you're saying, Mr. Zwick, is that word has filtered down to the street that I have a bounty on my head. Take me out and you magically get compensated, plus your status within the invisible network goes up."

"Exactly! The rule is: never do yourself what you can get someone else to do. And whatever you do, don't get caught, and if you do, don't talk. In prison, status and revenge outweigh worry over getting caught."

"Unless you're a snitch."

"Yeah, that part is the same."

"So what's your advice? And by the way, I appreciate your telling me all of this, but aren't you taking a risk yourself?"

"I'm doing it because you've had a good influence on the people here, and that works for me. I hate to admit it, but I owe you. On top of that, I'm dead certain you won't say a word to anyone. As far as advice goes, I'd say keep a low profile, don't go out alone when the streets are quiet, and next time you see Tomaras, smear butter all over her and lick it off. Your best shot is getting her to release you from restricted status, then get as far away from here as fast as you can. If you can leave California, so much the better."

Chapter 22

"You don't have to tell me, Dalton, I've already heard. Once again, same excuse: we didn't think he'd be able to fight back. But he did. Surprise! Surprise! A crafty man slips away from something he's seen countless times in prison."

"Yeah, that's about it. But he keeps popping up again and again; it's like he's daring us to take another shot."

"Oh, we will! He can't last. Can you believe it? Now *I'm* the one saying it can be done. And you know why? Because I put it on the line with Metzi: you either do it, or you'll be transferred to Bayview or even worse. It's been a game up to this point. Well, no more. That applies to you, too, Dalton."

"Look, that was Metzi's play, not..."

"Shut up, I don't want to hear it. But here is what *is* going to happen, and it starts with Tomaras. I want you to get to work on her, prime her to expect more violence from Laine. Tell her you may have to call on her suddenly if things fall apart. Get her ready to intervene."

"She'll want more than that."

"Tough. Tell her you don't know, just that there's talk about it among the street cops. Flatter her. Tell her you're letting her know ahead as a courtesy. You know how important it is for her to be on top of everything; you're just trying to help. That sort of shit. All women go for that crap. Makes them feel special. In the end, it's in her interest to be ready, and she'll always do what's in her interest."

"I'm not her favorite guy, but I'll try."

Chapter 23

LAINE THANKED ZWICK FOR HIS help, met up with Louis, and together they went to the mission to cut carrots and scrub pots. On the way in, they were greeted by Reverend Sully. He didn't waste any time on small talk.

"So, George, have you read the book yet? You're probably tired of me asking, but it meant so much to me when I was in seminary school that I just think everyone should read it."

"To tell you the truth, I've only gotten as far as the part where they're driving down a hill to a tent meeting when their trailer full of revival equipment passes them. That had to be a really bad moment. I can't imagine how they'll get out of that one."

"Yes, but that's the whole point—that's the mountain that has to be moved. And all it takes is faith, starting with the idea the accident wasn't an accident at all! It was the Lord telling them they needed to dig down, start that revival from the inside, see? It all makes sense. Nothing happens that doesn't have a reason."

The little voice inside was starting to stir. *Be polite, walk away, go chop onions.*

"It's hard to wrap my head around the idea God sent a trailer full of folding chairs down the road into traffic to get the message out they had to try harder. Why not just show up and tell them, or..." Here Laine sputtered, started to say, "...or drop them a postcard," but this time the voice won, "...or something less dangerous than a runaway trailer?"

"Ah! You *really* don't get it! It's about faith! If God were to show Himself, there would be no reason for faith. There is far more power in believing without knowing than knowing without believing. Get it?"

"I'm working on it, Reverend. Meanwhile, how can Louis and I be helpful?"

The next day, Saturday, Kitty, Laine, Louis, and Cowboy all went together to Dolores Park. While no one said it out loud, there was an understanding among the cognoscenti at the Madrid that it was a good idea to keep Laine from going out alone on the streets, even in broad daylight.

They parked under their favorite tree, each quietly absorbing the sunlight, air, and laughter of kids playing on the nearby jungle gym.

"I love it here," said Kitty. "It all looks so innocent, so safe. The craziness of the street seems a million miles away."

"Yeah, but even here there's a pervert somewhere watching the kids."

"Jesus, Cowboy, you're too cynical. Give it a rest," said Louis.

"Sad to say, he's right," said Kitty. "And there's no way to tell which one it is."

"You can if you wait and watch long enough, Kitty," Laine said. "Sooner or later he'll give himself away."

"How?" asked Cowboy.

"I hate to keep talking about prison, but it's what I know. I learned early in the game how to tell the dangerous ones from all the rest."

"What's the trick, George?" asked Louis. Then in a lower voice, "I was in prison once, too, if you didn't already know. I never did get the knack of telling who was trustworthy and who wasn't."

"I take your point, Louis. I struggled with it, too. It was like being dropped into a room full of snakes, a few of them deadly poisonous, but which ones? Is it this one? Is it that one? Then I realized I was using the wrong approach. Better to be invisible, calm down, hang back, and watch."

"Watch for what? The suspense is killing me," said Cowboy.

"Sooner or later even snakes yawn—just watch for the fangs."

"Clever," said Louis, "but I hate all snakes."

They ate hot dogs and enjoyed the fresh air and carefree atmosphere of the park until late afternoon. Walking back, they gradually bunched closer together, their sense of caution rising as they made their way back to the Madrid.

On Sunday morning, George set out for Dusty's alone. The streets were quiet, probably not the best time to be moving around, but the idea he would squander his freedom on the fear of what might happen to get a cup of coffee rankled him. Besides, he thought with a chuckle, it's too early for bad guys. They're all too hungover to care.

"George! George! Wait for me," yelled Kitty as she ran up the sidewalk. "Going to Dusty's?"

"Yeah. Slow down, I won't run off. Is it your turn to babysit me?"

"What do you mean?"

"You've all been hovering over me since that sidewalk thing."

"That 'thing' nearly got you killed, George. We're worried about you, that's all."

"And I appreciate it, but I worry about you. When something happens out here, I sure don't want my friends getting hurt."

"Got it. But tell me honestly: What is going on with you? Do you think the guy who sent you to prison is behind all this? The last time I asked, you still weren't convinced."

"I just wasn't ready to accept it. It seemed too bizarre. But, okay, here it is, total honesty: Yes, I think he is behind this. And that makes me worry about my friends suddenly getting caught in the middle. I guess what I'm saying is, while I appreciate your help, you need to stay back and watch your own backs. This is going to get a lot uglier—I'm sure of it."

"Can't you tell someone about it? Won't your PO help?"

"What would I say? More to the point, what proof do I have beyond a few old documents and a bunch of conjecture? No, I think the best course is to let this play out. He's got to be very worried, and that works to my advantage. The more worried he is, the more desperate he becomes. Then he'll make a mistake and trip himself up. I may not have to do a thing."

"I sure hope so. I have to tell you, George, even though I hardly know you, you can't imagine how much you've already helped me. I was in a real mood rut until you came along. Suddenly I felt like I could say painful things out loud and feel better, not worse. I even catch myself laughing out loud sometimes. The only bad part is you've made me addicted to fried egg sandwiches."

"There are worse addictions."

On Monday, Laine walked alone to the Bartlett Street library, read for several hours, then went to the DAPO office for his three-thirty appointment with Tomaras.

"Okay, Laine," she said closing her door. "No more dancing around, no bullshit. Just tell me what happened on Caliente Street. And don't worry, I'm not looking to bust you, believe me."

"I believe you. I also think you really didn't know anything about that before it went down."

"Of course I didn't know," she snapped. "I'd scream like a banshee if I heard something like that. I'm an officer of the court, not part of a lynch mob. Now tell me, what happened?"

"Two guys tried to kill me, simple as that. The people who have been watching me saw an opportunity, brought in the muscle. I was lucky enough to escape."

"Escape? From what I hear you damn near killed both of them."

"They damn near killed each other; I simply introduced them."

"Some introduction," Tomaras said rolling her eyes.

"When I first met you, you warned me that someone was very unhappy to see me out on the streets. It begs the question: Do you know who's behind this? If you didn't then, you've had time to think it over, any ideas now?"

"I didn't know then, and I still don't. It's not that unusual for a contested parole to stir up old feelings. Given your crime—rape and murder—it didn't seem far-fetched that someone could want you back in prison. And if it isn't coming from someone connected to your crime, then the next choice would be someone you pissed off in prison, maybe in the mob, who knows?"

"Not likely anyone from prison, and certainly not the mob."

"Then who do you think it is?"

"Look, I'm not being cute. Whatever my suspicions, I'm in no position to push this. Even if I was, I certainly can't prove anything. Worse, telling you could inadvertently have a lot of bad side effects. I really don't care to expose him at this point; again, all those bad consequences. Don't look so shocked. I just want it to end. Right now, there are only two possible outcomes. The best—and least likely—would be if he stops and goes back to whatever he was doing while I was locked up. That way, no one would ever hear about me again. I could live out the rest of my life in peace.

"But he can't depend on me to leave it alone, so the more likely outcome is he gets me killed or sent back to prison. He'll see that as his only way out."

Tomaras didn't tell Laine that earlier that day she had a visit from Dalton who told her there was reliable information that Laine was starting to come unglued, the incident on the sidewalk just a signal of more violence to come. "Be ready to move if you get a call about him."

"I'm sure you've been under pressure to revoke me, right?"

"I follow the rules. And no one tells me what to do."

"Fair enough, we'll leave it at that. Meanwhile, let me ask a favor."

"A favor?"

"Yes. I may want to send you some documents. If I do, I'll use this address, but the name on the return will be 'Leroy Fortune.' Please watch for it and open it when you're by yourself."

"Christ! Why all the spy stuff?"

"Because the vultures are on the power line watching everything that goes on below, always ready to pounce. They're a lot closer than you think. The more I learn about the street the more I realize how easy it is for information to get around; worse than that, how easily it translates into violence."

Laine's "evidence" was indeed pretty thin soup, lacking any credible evidence that Alfred Preston was guilty of a crime. In fact, one could see the judge as a hero, selflessly stepping in to offer support and protection to Laine's shattered spouse in her worst moments. What a guy! No, the documents idea was a card

Laine did not want to play—certainly not now. But if Alfred started hurting other players, there might not be a choice.

The meeting ended as it began, neither getting a good look at the other's hand, both apprehensive about what lay ahead. Their next appointment was set for one week, same time of day.

On the way back to the hotel, Laine wondered if he had just made a strategic mistake. *What if I misjudged her and she passes what she learned back to Dalton or someone else connected to Alfred? In that case, they'll come looking for the documents.*

No matter, he thought. The next step was to see what else could be done to shore up his circumstantial case. After that, get it to Tony to mail in case he couldn't.

Short of finding some other tidbit of incriminating information on the internet, there were only two places left to go to finish up: the law library, and the sealed up pages from his notebook, written just before his first scheduled execution, still unread in his closet shelf safe.

Back in his room, he removed the pages from the pouch, took a deep breath, and pulled away the remaining shreds of dried tape. Fifty years later and the moment came back in a flash. He was transported back to his cell, putting his few belongings in a cardboard box for disposal after he was executed. The last thing he did was seal up the papers knowing that like him, they would soon be nothing more than a heap of ashes.

On top was a two-page review of everything that happened, starting with the first time he met Julia Penthoser. The details were spelled out in microscopic lettering, a minute by minute chronicle of the time just before and immediately after the murder. Next, there was an outline listing the dates of key events starting with his arrest. "Transferred from jail to death row." "Appeal One turned down." And the final entry: "No more, just waiting to be moved downstairs."

There were two letters from Constance, one written just before their last visit at the end of March, the other just before the court order stopped all correspondence. He took a deep breath and started to read.

Suddenly, in the middle of the first paragraph, a sentence rocked him: "Alfred told me the Public Defender said he held little hope of a reprieve or significant delay."

Alfred!? Alfred told her, not his father!? So that bastard was telling my wife the PD was at work, something I think I also believed, to the extent I thought about it at all. How did I miss that before?!

Then there was the last letter from Constance, written in her careful hand, each letter beautifully formed, each unembellished sentence straight to the point. He closed his eyes as he started to read, its words flowing again through his memory. Most of the letter was about Rebecca, her newest words, her dolls with funny names, her toy piano, the fact Gramma Laine gave her the nickname "Chatty." Constance was giving him images to sustain him, to last forever. And they had.

He skipped dinner, remaining instead in his room listening to music, fighting back the anger and grief pushing through his eroded defenses.

In the morning, he reread everything, immediately realizing his circumstantial case could be strengthened if he could show convincingly that David Preston had lied to him about both the second appeal and the alleged role of the public defender. That would make his subsequent acts more incriminating. But he needed more. Maybe there was something to learn in the way he worded the appeals. It was time for a trip to the law library across the street from the main library.

He had a second cup of coffee in his room while listening to Schumann's Piano Concerto in A minor. The music helped focus his thinking while the city came to life. Then he walked straight to the law library paying scant attention to the streets, relying on sidewalk traffic for protection, focusing instead on the obstacles he might encounter at the library. *Surely, there are hundreds of paralegals, students, and law office servants who do research there on a routine basis, why not me? Hell, I've got an ID and a library card. Where are your records?*

Happily, his library card got him through the front door. The clerk at the main desk was glad to explain the microfiche system and assign a carrel. Because Laine could pinpoint the dates of his search so narrowly, the librarian was able to give him the exact rolls he needed. Within thirty minutes Laine was looking at his first appeal, dated February 4, 1959, denied a scant seven months later. And no wonder it was so easily dispatched: the entire document was only three pages, most of it boilerplate, signatures, and seals. The actual appeal was just one paragraph long! It alleged that the evidence against Laine was "entirely circumstantial," that the first-degree murder charge was wrong, that it should be set aside for one of second-degree murder, a charge that did not qualify for the death penalty.

"So, you prick," Laine mumbled, "the best outcome I could have imagined would have been life in prison. You weren't even trying to say I was innocent."

There was no second appeal. Laine scoured the appeals records but found no hint of a second appeal. The next documents were clemency appeals filed by Naomi Keshet, the public defender, starting in June 1960. Apparently it was too late to assert his innocence; instead, the focus was on setting aside his execution to give him time to argue in favor of "the more appropriate punishment" of life in prison.

He remembered arguing with the public defender over her insistence Laine write a letter to the court accepting responsibility for the crime and asking for leniency. The lawyer told him he wasn't being rational. If he was converted to life, perhaps "down the road" something would emerge that could get him a new trial.

The meeting ended with Laine saying that if he was guilty, then a life sentence might be an improvement. "But I'm not, so I'd rather get a head start on what's next while it still matters."

He had a copy made of the appeal, the court's rejection, and the index showing no second appeal before the PD took over.

He started to leave when it suddenly occurred to him it would be worth taking a few minutes to see if there were any other references to Alfred Preston, perhaps something predating his time at UC Berkeley. A clerk at the front desk told him how to use the library's search engine to sniff out even fleeting references to individuals who might have juvenile records. Even though California law allows juvenile records to be sealed or expunged after the age of eighteen, "expunged" doesn't mean "eliminated." Technically, *dismissal* is the process behind expunging a juvenile record. That means a person over eighteen seeking a record cleansing has to get a favorable ruling on dismissal from a court to make the record become invisible to the public. Without details, the record still retains note of arrests and dismissal hearings. Also, law enforcement, some insurance companies, and certain federal agencies can access the full record.

There were five references to offenses committed by Alfred Preston between the ages of fourteen and sixteen, though the record itself had been expunged, and no details were available. He found one other reference to Alfred Preston, this one while he was an undergraduate at Pepperdine when he was eighteen. He had been involved in an assault case involving a female undergraduate who was attacked by an unknown assailant. Alfred was questioned by police but denied any involvement in the attack. The victim was uncertain, and no arrest was made. A subsequent article noted that the student had withdrawn from Pepperdine, and the assault case was closed. There was, however, one line in the article that caught Laine's eye. "Police records show Preston has been arrested at least five times, twice for second degree assault." Obviously, the article was written before Daddy was able to engineer dismissals.

Okay, Laine thought, *I see it now. I just wish I could penetrate the expunged records. Forget it, they're off bounds. Is there anything else? Something that casts enough of a shadow to see what lies behind it? Time is short. One more run, one more search.*

On June 10, 1970, Alfred Preston petitioned the court to reinstate his right to own a firearm. Motion granted. No explanation, but none needed! There's the shadow, and what's behind it is one of the expunged records containing conviction of a crime serious enough to void his right to own a gun. A violent sexual crime wouldn't have been expunged, but a lesser assault might meet the criteria for later dismissal, but not before the gun prohibition went into effect. That's a different matter.

Laine was back at the hotel by four o'clock. He met Cowboy in the lobby.

"There you are! Jesus! I've been looking for you. There were a couple of dudes upstairs on our floor poking around. They said they were fire marshals doing a spot check of the alarm system. They told me to get the fuck out of their way, so I came back looking for you. You better check your room."

Laine took the steps three at a time. The cotton tuft was nowhere to be seen. Inside, Laine instantly spotted the extra length of dental floss hanging out of the easy keep. On the end of the tape, there was a roll of $20 bills. Laine removed all but one of the bills, went into the bathroom, flushed the toilet and just as the water started to be sucked out of the bowl, he pushed his arm as far as it would go into the drain, and released the wad of bills.

The real keep was unmolested. It was on tight with the screw slots both pointed in the right direction. He went to the closet and pushed up on the shelf. It was solid and didn't appear to have been disturbed. Stepping back, he heard a squeak, looked down, and saw what looked like a pry mark at the end of a short floorboard. Using his screwdriver, he pried up the board revealing a space below the size of a shoebox. In the center of the box sat a plastic bag the size of a peach filled with white powder.

He quickly poured the contents of the bag down the sink drain, then washed out and dried the bag, turned it inside out, filled it with coffee creamer, dropped it into the space, and replaced the floorboard. Suddenly, there was a lot of racket in the hallway.

Laine opened the door just as the first policeman was about to kick it open. Two uniformed cops burst in, grabbed Laine, and slammed him up against the wall next to the door. Another cop, this one in plain clothes, followed.

After frisking him, they put cuffs on his wrists behind his back and sat him down on the bed. Laine said nothing and did not resist.

"I'm Detective Butler from the Narcotics Strike Force, Laine, and we have a report that you've been dealing drugs out of your room. I have a search warrant, in case you want to get cute about this."

Laine remained silent. There was more noise in the hall as other residents came out of their rooms. Suddenly, Metzi and Carlos were at the door.

"Why the fuck didn't you wait for me, Butler? This is my arrest."

"Piss off, Metzi. Narcotics has this covered. And the search warrant is in my name. So take a seat and watch real cops at work." Without waiting for a reply, he told his two officers to "tear the fucking place apart."

The search quickly focused on the sacrificial keep. The top was removed and the money retrieved.

"What have you got there, Augustine? Drugs?"

"Money, sir. Money on a string. But no drugs," he said peering down the pipe with his flashlight.

"How much money?"

"Twenty bucks."

"What!" yelped Metzi. "Twenty bucks? Look again!"

"No, sir, nothing else, just some papers of some sort."

"Keep looking," said Butler. And the search went on. Drawers were dumped on the floor, the bed was tossed, toilet tank and fire escape scanned.

"What the hell is going on here?" demanded Aella Tomaras as she stepped into the room. Everything stopped for a moment.

"Where the hell have you been?" demanded Metzi.

"Shut up, Metzi. Tell me, Detective, what's this about?"

Before Butler could answer, Officer Augustine said, "Sir! Look at this, a loose floorboard. Who's got a knife?" The board was quickly pried up.

"My, my," said Butler leaning over the opening. "What have we got down there? Looks like cocaine or maybe heroin. Get it out of there and test it," he said handing a test kit to the cop.

"You're busted, Laine. Put him in *my* car," Butler said glaring at Metzi. Laine offered no resistance as one of the cops jerked him to his feet and started toward the door.

Metzi pounced. "What did I tell you, Tomaras? Your boy is dirty, simple as that. He's been playing you. And it looks like he's pretty good at it, too."

"Laine! I can't believe this. No one…"

"Sir!"

"…plays me and…"

"Sir!"

"What!?" said Butler.

"It ain't coke or H, either one."

"Bullshit," said Metzi. "What the hell else could it be? Test it again."

"I did. It's not coke, heroin, or meth."

Butler took the bag, looked at it closely, wet the tip of his right pinky finger, dipped it carefully into the bag, and touched his finger to his tongue. The room was silent, everyone but Laine looking at Butler.

"It's powdered milk."

"Uncuff him," demanded Tomaras

Butler nodded, and the handcuffs were removed. "Let's go. And Metzi, I need to talk to you." The group left, the sounds of their argument fading down the stairs.

"I don't know what to say, Laine. Either you're dirty and damn clever, or I just witnessed an elaborate attempt to frame you. Either way, you just dodged another bullet. So which is it?"

"What do you think?"

"I can't believe police officers could be manipulated into a scheme like this. But on the other hand, I have the same problem imagining a seventy-five-year-old man who spent most of his life in prison becoming a drug dealer the minute he hits the streets. None of it makes sense."

Tomaras stood in the door for a long moment looking back and forth between the room and the hallway, trying to decide if she should say something else or just leave.

"Rules, Laine. Rules. We used to live by rules. People who followed the rules were clearly the good guys. They got jobs, raised families, gave money to the church, and went out with a big funeral. The ones who didn't follow the rules were the bad guys. They couldn't keep a job, hold a family together, or stay out of jail. There was a clear line between the two. Simple as that.

"But the line's gone, good and bad have inbred. The rules don't mean shit anymore. It's been a bad day for both of us. Be careful," she said, closing the door.

Laine pulled the mattress back into position, threw on the blanket, turned on his radio, and closed his eyes.

Chapter 24

"DALTON?"

"Yeah, Judge. I saw Tomaras yesterday as I was leaving my office. She was crazy angry, looked at me like I was the freaking Devil. She didn't say a goddamn word, just went in her office and slammed the door. I take it your plan didn't work out very well."

"No, it didn't. Someone tipped him."

"Who? Zwick?"

"Who's Zwick?"

"The manager at the Madrid, runs a whorehouse there at night, has his fingers in every scam in the neighborhood. He's in Metzi's pocket."

"I doubt it, but it doesn't matter. What I want you to do is calm Tomaras down; we may still need her. She's pissed because her precious pride was bruised. That's your opening. Tell her how many times shit like that has happened to you. Buy her flowers or something. I don't care."

"She's smart, Judge, and not the type to go for flowers. My worry is she could start putting things together and make noises I can't control."

"All the more reason to wrap this up. Don't lose your nerve, Dalton. It's almost over; I can feel it."

Chapter 25

LAINE SLEPT THROUGH DINNER AND didn't wake up until early Wednesday morning. He made coffee, finished tidying up the room, then sat down at the desk to think.

Clearly, this is Alfred's work. He won't quit until he destroys me, and I can't depend on luck to save me again. But the worst part is being pushed to think and even act like him. Doing that makes it easier for him. I've got to get out of his world, back into mine. Get above this and let evil destroy itself.

That's better. The only thing left to do is get the documentation in a safe place with a built-in trigger: if something happens to me, the material is automatically sent to Tomaras.

Laine wrestled with the concern that he could be putting her in the crosshairs, but of all the players, she seemed the best equipped to handle it. There was no good second option.

Over the next two hours, Laine organized and wrote a concise case against Alfred Preston, each document referenced and indexed, the entire package then sealed in an envelope addressed to Aella Tomaras from Leroy Fortune. He put that envelope in another, addressed to Tony Concano.

Laine used the pay phone at the Vietnamese market to call Tony.

"Christ, George! What the hell are you doing over there? The cops are all buzzing about a guy making a monkey out of them in some sort of raid."

"That was just yesterday. News travels fast around here."

"It sure does."

Laine told Tony what he knew and asked if he could send him the package in case he was arrested or "taken out."

"Christ, George, you talk about it so casually." Tony argued it would be a lot safer if he took it to Tomaras immediately. "Don't mess with it, George. Put the bastard back on his heels before something happens you can't control."

"No, not yet. It would put Constance and Rebecca right in the middle of the chaos. Even with what I have, there's really no way short of a confession to overcome his advantages."

"Well, he sure isn't going to confess."

"Maybe not yet, but I'm working on it."

"Dangerous game, George. But, okay, send me the stuff, and I'll do as you say. Remember: you have my number. Anytime, call anytime."

Laine got the address, rang off, and headed for the post office. He took a circuitous route but didn't see anything that would suggest he was being tailed. He came out of the post office, stood on the steps, looked around, and took a deep breath.

"That feels a lot better," he said out loud. "Time to go earn my lunch."

Happily, Reverend Sully didn't try to revisit lessons from a runaway trailer, leaving Laine to work in the kitchen and enjoy lunch with several other mission volunteers. He was back in the Madrid by midafternoon.

There was a letter from Leroy in his box.

Hey George,

Thanks for the letter. It really cheered me up knowing you are out there and still thinking about me. Don't feel bad because I'm still in here. You make me think if you can do it, then I can too. I'll be up for my first shot in six years. I can do it, and then we can have a walk together and breathe the fresh air. There's nothing new here, just that a new guy got stabbed in the laundry. He bled out before they could do anything for him. Everybody knows it was Martinez. As usual, no one is talking, and they can't find the shank. They closed the laundry for two days and still can't find it.

Well, that's it from here. Stay strong and write when you have a chance.

Your friend, Leroy

They won't find it. By the time they started looking it was already broken into several pieces and sent down one of the big drains. Stupid kid.

Hearing from Leroy brought a mix of feelings, most importantly a sense of relief knowing his letter seemed to have given him a palpable feeling of hope. Laine thought the first thing he would do if he could make it long enough to get off restricted status would be to visit Leroy.

That evening, talk was all about the planted drugs, the raid, and what might be next. Cowboy was the hero of the moment, confirmation that by sticking together Laine's friends could protect him. There were a lot of questions about who might be behind this. The consensus (minus Kitty) was that someone from prison paid the cops to do an easy job, but when the first attempt didn't work, it became a matter of pride for Metzi and friends to finish it off. They couldn't let some geriatric San Quentin inmate make them look bad.

Laine agreed that was probably it and finally managed to shift everyone's attention to Wednesday night's Theater of the Street presentation.

Just before midnight, Laine excused himself and headed upstairs. Hearing drunken voices coming down the steps from the third floor, he stepped into the vending alcove on the first floor to avoid any possible trouble with either a john or a hooker. Funny thing about that third floor: on the way up they take the elevator, the hooker is all over her mark. It's all giggles and fun. Coming down, the hooker takes the stairs, acting like she can't wait to get away from the untouchable trailing behind her.

After hanging up his socks and underwear, Laine turned on his radio and laid down on the bed to ponder his next move. *How do I get ahead of Alfred? Can I really outfox him or is this just a fool's game?*

The answer, of course, was both. *Sometimes even fools get lucky, especially when they do the unexpected.*

By now he'll assume I'm on to him, so he can't afford to delay. At this point, just getting me revoked could be risky unless it's lightning fast—revocation and return to prison in one breath. That way, I could talk all I want about Alfred—no one would be listening. And once back in San Quentin, I could be permanently walled off from the outside world.

The better option would be to have me killed, stone dead and permanently quiet. Otherwise, there's a chance Constance will hear about it, and the castle walls will come tumbling down.

If I get killed, Tomaras won't be able to ignore the package. She'll go after him, and that means Constance will find out everything. Alfred will probably escape prosecution from the law, but not from Constance.

If I'm going to stay alive, I'll have to keep an eagle eye on the back door of the shooting gallery. From there, the best outcome would be to find some way to disappear and leave Alfred in a permanent state of fear. If that can't happen, then Alfred and I are going to have to meet.

But the meantime, there are some loose ends to tie up.

Chapter 26

THE BLACK SEDAN EASED TO a stop halfway down the block from the corner of Jerold and Quint, deep in the heart of Bayview.

"There she is, under the light at the corner," said Carlos. "Do you see Bingo anywhere?"

"Naah, but he can't be far away. When he sees you, he'll come out of his hole, don't worry."

Carlos eased out of the car, moving slowly toward the corner. Minouche saw him coming, dropped her cigarette, pushed out her chest, and tugged up her already short skirt. Bingo saw him as well, his fingers tightening their grip on the .25 caliber pistol in his jacket pocket as he sized up the man approaching his worker. Customer? Cop? Some crazy with a thing about hookers? No telling quite yet.

Carlos stopped just short of the circle of light. "Is that a skirt you're wearing or just a wide belt, Minouche?"

"Shit! It's you, Carlos. What the hell are you doing down here in hell's backyard? You going to bust me or just beat me up for something to do?"

Bingo was already halfway across the street. "Hey, man, what's up? She ain't doing nothin'."

"Shut up, Bingo. Get your hand out of your pocket and come back here by the fence—both of you—I got a little action for you. That is unless you want me to bust you for that heater in your pocket, Bingo."

"Chill, Carlos. It's cool. We'll talk, right, Minouche?"

She nodded but stayed back. *This could get really bad in a hurry,* she thought. *I need a clear road out of here if Carlos and Bingo get into it.*

"So, what's up, man?" Bingo said, slowly removing his hand from his pocket.

"I have a job for you, baby. It pays three large for an hour's work. She won't even mess up her lipstick. By the way, 'No' isn't an answer."

"What kind of job?" asked Bingo. "Three grand for what?"

"Minouche meets me across the street from the Madrid at exactly one a.m. Saturday morning. I'll tell you from there."

"Tell me what, Carlos? What do I have to do?" asked Minouche, her tone a mix of curiosity and fear.

"You're going to walk into the hotel with me, we're going upstairs, and then we're going to leave. Think you can handle that?"

"There's got to be more to it than that, man."

"Fuck off, Bingo. Just deliver your bitch to the corner and collect your money. I like the dress, too. Wear it. Don't be late, or I'll find both of you and turn you into dog food."

Carlos returned to the car.

"Everything okay?" Metzi asked.

"Yeah. She'll be there. Plan A and Plan B, all set. But, you know, Metzi? I'm hoping for Plan B. I never liked that Kitty bitch, anyway."

Chapter 27

"Alfred, we have to talk."

"What about?"

"Let's see: perhaps we should start with the fact Rebecca is getting married in less than two weeks…"

"You mean 'remarried,' I think."

"I mean 'married.' There's still a lot to be done, starting with dealing with that supercilious wedding planner at the club who keeps calling about the goddamn hors d'oeuvres. So much fuss about what to put on a piece of soggy toast. You said you'd deal with her, but judging from the number of messages she's left, I'd say it hasn't happened."

"I've got a lot on my plate right now, Connie. I'm not in the mood to deal with soggy toast. Why can't you do it?"

"Because I think the whole idea of a country club potlatch is an absurdity, that's why. On top of that, the lovely Miss Peegram doesn't seem to get all warm and fuzzy when I'm around."

"If you hadn't made that remark about burning blankets on the Pacific Terrace, she might have been more receptive. She just wants it to be a great party. The Northern Woods Club is known for great parties."

"All right, Alfred, I'll make a deal with you: I'll make nice with Miss Toast Tips if you tell me what's been bugging you lately. For the last month, you've been moody, preoccupied, and remote. You won't let me in, Alfred. How can I help if you won't tell me what has you so rattled?"

"Sorry, I didn't know it showed. It's a work thing, Connie. But I'll get it taken care of in a few days, I promise."

"You're retired, Alfred. What kind of 'work thing' could be bothering you at this point? You left the bench almost ten years ago."

"It's an old case. I really can't talk about it."

"That never stopped you before. What's so different this time? Spill it. What the hell is going on?"

"All right, all right, if you have to know. It's about a guy I sent to prison a long time ago. He got out because of an administrative mix-up, and he's causing a lot of trouble. Naturally, I feel partly to blame, so I'm trying to get him sent back where he belongs."

"What can a retired judge do that the police can't? It makes no sense, Alfred. There's more to this than some con causing a stink somewhere. Is this character threatening you? Is there any danger to us?"

"It's an old case, Connie. The police don't know anything about what he did or how he operates. I remember all of it. I'm helping, that's all. It's my duty. Maybe he'd like to get at me, but he's well contained, and there's no chance of that."

"So if you gave them the information and he's as 'well contained' as you say, why are you still so damned upset? I don't buy it. I know you, Alfred, you could laugh off typhoid fever. Tell me, what's his name?"

"I can't tell you that, Connie."

"Bullshit! If he's so high profile, it was in the papers. We certainly talked about it before. Don't give me that 'confidentiality' crap. What's his name?"

"I said I don't want to talk about it! That's it! Leave it alone! I'll tell you when it's over. In the meantime, let's get back to the wedding. I'll go to the club with you and Rebecca. We'll get that out of the way—no more worry about crab dip and canapés.

"The name, Alfred. Give me a name."

"Okay. If you insist—it's Miss Peegram."

"Not funny. And this conversation is *not* over."

Chapter 28

THURSDAY MORNING, AND A LOT to do, Laine thought as he lifted the remaining checks from the keep. *It's laundry day; they'll be getting ready to hand out clean linen.*

Laine took a forbidden turn off the stairs onto the third floor. The double doors protecting Paradise Hall were closed, a note on the door declared:

NO LINENS BEFORE 11:00

NO LOITERING ANYTIME

It took a while for someone to answer Laine's knocking. Finally, one of the maids ripped open the door, pointed to the sign, and practically shouted, "Can't you fucking read? Go away."

She tried to slam the door, but Laine grabbed it, said he needed to talk to María. Another maid joined the first one trying to shoo away the intruder, but Laine persisted. They finally went to get María.

"Mister Laine! Good to see you, but you shouldn't be here." Looking back over her shoulder, she lowered her voice. "I still feel bad about the boy. Are you all right?"

"Actually, yes, quite all right, but I need some quick information. What is your last name?"

"My last name? Why do you need to know? I'm not in trouble, am I?"

"No trouble, María. I have something I want to give you, and I need your last name. I promise it's a good thing. Please trust me on this."

"*Pues*, it's Santaella," she said almost in a whisper.

"And just one more thing: were your kids born in this country?"

"Yes, both. But why do you need to know?"

"I'll explain later, I promise. Would you save some linens for me if I come back later today?"

"Of course I will."

It was still too early to risk going beyond Dusty's, so Laine settled in with his coffee and egg sandwich to wait until the streets started to breathe. Just after nine, he went to the main library to figure out the quickest way to find a Hispanic-friendly immigration lawyer. There were a number of possibilities—far too many to check out in the time he had—so he turned instead to a list of Hispanic community centers. There was one on 24th Street in the Mission District, a bit of a walk but a straight shot down Van Ness.

Laine made his way to the center staying as close to groups of pedestrians as possible. The center was located in a defunct Latin grocery store, its lobby filled with notices about immigrant rights, health services, language classes, as well as several menacing ICE and IRS signs threatening dire consequences (in English) for those who failed to follow the fine print. After explaining he was trying to find an immigration lawyer for a friend, he was introduced to Señora Belmonte. She listened as Laine described María's situation, explaining he wanted to help her get a green card.

"I'll pay her legal expenses, provided the lawyer is trustworthy, not some *abogado* who would take advantage of a defenseless illegal."

Señora Belmonte said the fact María already had a valued profession, two children born in the US, had been paying taxes, and never been in trouble made hers an encouraging case.

"Like everything else, Mr. Laine, all it really takes is money."

Working through their agency, the attorney's discounted retainer was typically $2,500 with another $500 on top of that for application fees.

"It all has to be paid up front, a lot of money for our clients, as I'm sure you understand."

Laine gave Mrs. Belmonte María's name but avoided any mention of the Madrid Hotel. He promised to return later with the money.

"Can I ask why you are doing this, Mr. Laine? It is incredibly generous. I'm not sure what's in it for you?"

"Nothing and everything," he said as he stood up. "I'll be back."

His next stop was the San Francisco Bank and Trust Company. This time around, Mrs. Winslow greeted Laine warmly, happily noting that his first social security check had just landed. She was, however, less enthusiastic about handing him $4,000 in cash.

"Please be careful, Mr. Laine. That's a lot of money to be carrying around on these streets. There are people out there right now watching through the windows for tellers to count out large sums of money. They do the same thing with our ATM, just looking for people to rob. We point them out to the police, but they just shrug. It's crazy."

"That's why I asked you to get the cash and not a teller, Mrs. Winslow. But thanks for your concern."

Back on the street, Laine followed the same track back to the community center. Several times he had to step into stores when foot traffic thinned too much, or when he felt a car behind him was moving slower than surrounding traffic.

Mrs. Belmonte was reluctant to accept the cash, but Laine told her he had to leave town immediately, leaving no time to deal with cashier's checks and the like.

"You don't know me, Mr. Laine, yet you would trust me with this cash? Why? You don't look like a rich guy. This is a lot of money."

"Tell me, if it isn't too intrusive, how much do you earn working here?"

"What a question! Put it this way, it isn't a whole lot."

"Exactly. I would assume that three thousand dollars is more than, say, five, maybe close to ten percent of what you make in a year?"

"Yes, not far off. What does that have to do with trusting me?"

"Everything. It tells me you're not in this for the money. That means you'll do all you can to help María. Besides, I'll be back. I wouldn't want to miss it when she gets her green card."

Laine was back in the Madrid by early afternoon.

"I've got another check for you, Mr. Zwick."

"It's not like me to turn down money, Laine, but you're paid up. Hang onto it for a while."

"No, the first check covered me through the seventeenth. Really, I'm a week late."

"Okay, Laine. I ain't goin' to fight with you. But you sure are one strange criminal."

"I guess I never got the hang of it. See you later."

Laine went to his room, collected his dirty sheets, and walked back down to the third floor. This time he was greeted warmly. María came out with his linens, and when they were alone, Laine gave María Mrs. Belmonte's card, quickly explaining the arrangement he had made. María was instantly confused, almost frightened.

"But why, Mr. Laine? What do I have to do for you? People don't do these things. I don't understand. I can't take your money."

Laine held up his hand, told María she owed him nothing beyond making sure she didn't give up until she had her papers.

"Please, do it for you and your children. Do it for me, too. *Por favor!* I have to go now. We wouldn't want Mr. Zwick getting upset, right? But pretty soon you won't need him. We have a deal, right?"

"A 'deal'?"

"Un acuerdo."

"Yes, *un acuerdo*. But you talk like you won't be here. Are you going away? Please don't go away. How do I repay you?"

"I may have to leave for a little while. Don't worry about that. Just work on getting your papers. That's how you repay me."

Laine returned to his room, locked the door, and removed everything from his two bedpost keeps. All of the important documents were already with Tony. Except for the battered picture of his parents, what was left was unimportant. He put $800 of the cash from the bank in an envelope, sealed it, and wrote "Cowboy" on the front. He put $6 from the keeps in his pocket. The picture, the remaining $200 from the bank, and $60 from the keeps went into the bottom of his socks.

Almost there. Next a letter to Leroy, this one every bit as difficult as the first.

Dear Leroy,

Thanks for your letter. It made me feel really good to hear you being so hopeful. I know you will make it through and one day soon get back to your family. I am doing my best to use every minute out here to fit in and hopefully find a way to make sense of what freedom is all about. Remember how we used to hear the news and say it sounded as crazy out here as it is in there? Well, it is! But one thing is the same: with a good friend and, if you're lucky, some family, it can work.

Thank you for being the friend who has helped me so much.

George

Cowboy knocked just before it was time to head over to the mission for dinner.

"Perfect timing, Cowboy. I was about to come looking for you. Come in. I have a favor to ask."

"A favor? Sure enough, George. What can I do? Name it."

"Well, there are two things, actually. First, the easy part: I want you to take this envelope and hide it really well. I won't beat around the bush with this, either. There's eight hundred in cash there, money I want you to use to go to Flagstaff to see your brother. I looked up the bus fare—it's under two hundred round trip. The rest is for you to get a motel room, so you can feel you aren't putting any pressure on Tommy and his family. There ought to be enough left over to take them out for dinner a few times."

Cowboy shook his head in disbelief, confusion. He started to protest, but Laine stopped him. "Please, Cowboy, just take the money and make the trip. It will be good for you and Tommy. You can talk about the good times out in the desert, take a dip in his pool. When you come back, you'll know you're part of a family. You mean a lot to each other. This way you can concentrate on the good stuff." Before Cowboy could speak, Laine quickly added, "And here's the hard part."

"Hard part? Jesus, what could that be? You're not going to split, are you, George?"

"No, but I might have to make a quick exit at least for a little while. I'm feeling a lot of heat, Cowboy. I can't rely on good luck and a rabbit's foot anymore. That's why I wonder if you'd let me sleep on your floor for two or three nights until I see if I can get out of the way of what's coming? I still have some unfinished business, and I'm not about to let down my guard. So, is it okay? I don't snore."

"Sure it's okay, man! Christ, that's the least I can do. But look, all this money...you'll need it, and..."

"I never argue about money. Let's go get dinner; I'm famished. I forgot to eat lunch."

Reverend Sully was in high gear that evening. The sermon droned on twice as long as usual. As they were leaving the chapel, George handed *Move That Mountain* to the startled preacher.

"Thank you, Reverend, I enjoyed the book. It helped me understand what you were talking about tonight. By the way, I was relieved that no one was hurt in the trailer accident."

"Well, yes, thank you, Laine. The Lord protects the righteous! Amen!"

Happily, that was the end of it. Laine, Kitty, and several others from the Madrid enjoyed their dinner together. The walk back was uneventful. Laine checked his room, noting first that the tiny door marker was still in place. He joined the group for evening entertainment in the lobby, and at midnight, he and Cowboy retreated to the fifth floor. Laine put his blanket and pillow on the floor next to Cowboy's bed, invisible from the door.

"Christ! George, how the hell are you going to sleep down there?"

"Believe me, I've slept on worse. And being a little uncomfortable means shallow sleep. I'll have a better shot at hearing noise in the hall."

"Do you think someone will come up here in the middle of the night to whack you? That's some scary shit, man."

"I haven't any idea, really. I just know how desperate people operate. But don't worry, they're not going to come knocking on your door. Hell, Cowboy, I may be way overworking this. But if you don't mind, I'll do this a few nights—just in case."

It was a long and uncomfortable night, but Friday morning finally arrived. Laine bathed and dressed in his room, waited in the lobby for the streets to catch up, then he and Cowboy walked to Dusty's. From there, Laine went to the Bartlett Street library to read and search the internet for something he had previously said he would leave alone. But during the night, in moments flitting between sleep and vigil, images from the past flashed through his mind, pictures and memories he sensed he would shortly have to leave, perhaps for a short time, perhaps longer.

One of the recurring pictures was literally an old snapshot he kept on his bureau in college. It was taken on a trip to the San Diego Zoo, a family portrait in front of the monkey enclosure. Katie was making a chimp face and scratching her sides. On the back, his father had written, "The Simian Family visits their relatives."

Remembering Katie made Laine feel he had been wrong to avoid knowing what had happened to her. He blamed himself for being so absorbed in his defense that he had failed to try to reach out to her, use the words a sibling can to assure her of his innocence. Even more, he should have told her how sorry he was to have brought her such pain. It didn't happen, and by the time he tried, she was already gone. The door was closed forever.

He searched the internet using every name and idea he could come up with but found nothing. Finally, he gave up, satisfied that he had at least tried. And if he had found her, what then? Better to leave it alone. He spent the rest of the day finishing the astronomy book.

That evening was like any other: dinner at the mission, theater time with Kitty, Cowboy, and Louis, then off to "bed."

Laine hardly noticed the street scene, his mind continually searching for anything else he might do to prepare for whatever lay ahead. He and Cowboy talked for a while before both fell asleep.

At 1:00 a.m., Bingo and Minouche cautiously approached the corner across from the Madrid, stopping just short of the corner streetlight. Carlos had been following them for the last block, blending into the shadows in his dark jacket and wide-brimmed hat.

"Right on time," he said, slipping up from behind.

Minouche startled, instantly shrinking back against the building.

"Relax, Minouche. I told you this would be an easy gig. I'm giving you half the money now, the other half when we finish. If you don't do exactly what I tell you, you won't get the other half. Got it?

"We're going to walk in the lobby; you're going to be on my left so the goon at the desk can't get a good look at me. We'll take the elevator to the fifth floor. You'll wait by the elevator while I go down to a guy's room. If he's there, we'll talk, I'll be right back, and we get on the elevator and leave. When we get off, you'll be on my right. That's what I call Plan A. Simple.

"If the guy isn't there, we do Plan B. And here's where I need you to do what I say and nothing else. You let the elevator go, we walk down to the fourth floor and go to Kitty Marren's room. You know Kitty, and I want you to very quietly knock on her door. She'll ask who it is, you'll say 'Minouche,' and when she unlocks the door, I'll step in. You go stand by the stairs, and I'll be right back."

"I'm scared, Carlos. I don't want to hurt Kitty. Please, can't you do this by yourself? You don't need me, right?"

"Shut up. I can't just walk in there and waltz up the stairs. I need cover—you're it, and that's all there is to it. Now let's go. Take my arm and start acting like a good hooker."

"Please, Bingo, do something!"

"I'll do something, all right. I'll hold the damn money and kick your ass if you don't get moving! Now go, bitch!"

Minouche clutched Carlos' arm tightly, not as an act, but to deal with tremulousness and an overwhelming feeling of weakness. They walked across the street, into the hotel, across the lobby to the elevator. Zwick's desk man didn't even look up from his racing form. They took the elevator to the fifth floor. As the door opened, Carlos grabbed Minouche by her arms and pressed her back against the elevator doorframe.

"Don't let the elevator go." Even in a whisper, his voice was menacing, words spoken through a thick cloud of foul breath.

Minouche struggled to hold back waves of nausea as Carlos moved silently down the hall. He pulled a .22 revolver from his jacket, screwed on a three-inch silencer, and holding the gun in his right hand, silently twisted a plastic master key in the lock with his left. He eased the door open and stepped inside, the pistol aimed at the bed. The towel curtains were tied back letting soft street light fall on the empty bad.

Carlos withdrew, quietly locked the door, and moved back to the elevator. Minouche was struggling to hold the door open.

"Let it go," Carlos whispered. "Time for Plan B." He pulled Minouche out of the clutches of the elevator door, half carrying, half pushing her down the stairs to the fourth floor. Standing in front of Kitty's door, he whispered, "Nice and easy, tell her you gotta talk."

Minouche knocked.

"Who is it?"

"It's me, Minouche. I've got to talk to you. Please!"

The lock turned and the door opened a crack. Carlos stood back against the wall.

"Minouche! What's going..."

In that moment Carlos shoved Minouche away with one hand, grabbed the door with the other, pushing it straight into Kitty's face. He stepped through the door and had his hands around her neck before she could make a sound. He pinned her to the floor preventing any thrashing movements. In less than a minute, she was dead. He reached up under her nightgown and pulled off her panties, then backed out of the room, being careful to leave the door slightly ajar.

Minouche was not at the end of the hall. Carlos could hear sobs mixed with retching sounds coming from the stairwell. He caught up with her just below the first-floor landing trying to make her way down the stairs, staggering along the wall, the vomit on her hands making it impossible to grip the banister.

"I told you to wait, you stupid cow! Now straighten up and walk!"

Again, the night clerk didn't pay any attention to the hooker and her customer as they staggered across the lobby. A few moments after they left; however, the clerk was alerted by a pungent odor drifting through the lobby. Sniffing out the source, he saw the trail of yellow-green stomach juice smeared along the wall coming down from the first-floor landing.

"Shit! What's with these people? Can't they puke in a goddamn toilet like the rest of us?" He called the third floor to get the maids down to clean up the mess their customer had made. There was an argument, the maid saying no one from there had just left.

"Don't give me that shit; just get down here and clean it up."

Across the street, Carlos delivered Minouche to Bingo.

"What the fuck have you done to my bitch, Carlos? How am I going to sell her ass smelling like fish guts? And where's the rest of the money?"

"There ain't no rest of the money, Bingo. Your hooker screwed up, didn't do what she was told. She damn near got us caught over there. So take her sorry ass out of here and be damned glad I'm in too big a hurry to kill both of you. And don't come back here anytime soon."

A few hours later, just after six o'clock, someone on the fourth floor started screaming. Cowboy and Laine were instantly on their feet. Laine had slept in his clothing (including his shoes), so he was out the door in seconds. He immediately saw the little ball of paper lying on the floor. He unlocked the door, glanced around quickly, and relocked the door. Cowboy came out, and together they started down the stairs. Already a dozen or so people were clustered around Kitty's door. Laine instantly knew what to expect. Kitty was lying on the floor, her feet toward the door. Someone had already pulled her nightgown down.

Laine staggered back, overwhelmed with grief, anger, and a crushing feeling of guilt for allowing this obscene act of vengeance to have taken Kitty's life. But he also knew how this tragedy was meant to play itself out.

"I've got to get out of here, Cowboy. It's the last act. If I let myself get caught, no one will pay for what they did to Kitty."

Sirens could be heard above the yelling and chaos on the stairs. Cowboy and Laine worked their way down the stairs, but as the lobby came into view, they saw two cops at the lobby door preventing anyone from leaving. Laine caught a glimpse of Metzi and Carlos getting out of their car on the corner.

"We're trapped, George! That's the only way out. They'll see us if we use the fire escape."

"Stay here if you can," Laine said. Turning back against the tide of people, he worked his way back up through the crowd to the landing. He broke the glass on the fire alarm box with his elbow and yanked down the lever. As the alarm bells sounded, he pulled a fire ax out of its bracket, reached up, and using the ax handle, smashed an overhead sprinkler outlet, sending an instant deluge onto the people trying to move down the stairs. Screaming and shoving, the mass pressed down the stairs into the lobby. As they moved, Laine smashed two more sprinkler heads. The sudden drop in water pressure caused all the sprinklers in the lobby to go off, engulfing the room in an indoor thunderstorm.

Water continued to shoot out of the sprinklers. People pushed, slipped, and fell in puddles forming on the floor. The alarm bells rattled nonstop, competing with the rising chorus of screams from panicked residents. Even with the help of Carlos and Metzi, the two policemen were no match for the human tsunami pouring through the lobby doors.

Laine dropped the fire ax, pulled Cowboy to the right at the foot of the stairs, moving behind the front desk to the door to Zwick's private office. Two kicks shattered the lock, blasting the door open. Laine and Cowboy raced through the old restaurant into the kitchen. The exit doors were secured by a fire ax just as Zwick had described. Laine pulled the ax out and tested the door to be sure it would open.

"Open it, George!" Cowboy yelled. "Quick, let's go!"

"Not yet, Cowboy. Give it a minute."

"What for?! We gotta go now! What are you waiting for?!"

The sound of fire engines overwhelmed the bells and yelling. Seeing the exit by the desk was open, people from the lobby were starting to pour through heading for the back door.

"That's the cover we need, Cowboy," Laine said pushing the doors open. He and Cowboy were suddenly in a wad of at least a dozen drenched and frightened people spilling onto the sidewalk. Two fire trucks disgorged firefighters as other trucks jockeyed for position, completely blocking the sidewalk to the left of the door. The only open direction was to the right, up Caliente Street, away from the Madrid.

"Here's where I leave you, Cowboy. I've got some work to do. Make your way back when you can. If anybody asks about me, just tell the truth: you saw me running out of the building."

Before Cowboy could answer, Laine was off, moving up the street with other pedestrians, losing himself in the gathering crowd of onlookers. He worked his way along the street toward the Chu's laundry. As he anticipated, Mr. and Mrs. Chu were already at work. He waited until there was no sign of police or fire vehicles, darted across the street, and tapped on the glass door.

"Mr. Rain! You are all wet! What is happening? There is a big fire, I think. Were you there?"

"It's a false alarm, Mrs. Chu, but I did get wet. Would you mind if I used your phone? And could I please have a cup of your tea? It always makes me feel calm."

He called Tony to say he needed help, told him where he was, and that he would be safe until Tony could get there.

"Twenty minutes," was all Tony said.

Laine and the Chus drank tea, and exactly twenty-five minutes later, Robert pulled up in a black sedan. Laine thanked the Chus, checked the street, and stepped across the sidewalk into the back seat of the car.

"There's a blanket back there, Mr. Laine. Pull it over yourself and lie on the floor. Let's not talk. Just hang on, and I'll get us out of here."

Laine was glad to be able to wrap up in the blanket. Within fifteen minutes or so the shivering stopped, but the image of Kitty lying on the floor was unshakable. Finally, the car stopped. There was a grinding noise; the car moved briefly and stopped. The grinding noise repeated, and the car door opened. With Tony's help, Laine untangled himself from the soggy blanket and stepped out of the car.

They were in a large, empty warehouse, perhaps three tennis courts long and two wide. There were hundreds of rows of empty shelves reaching two stories up to the roof, each shelf tall and wide enough to hold several refrigerators. On the right-hand side, a flat-topped, shed-like structure made of plywood panels stood against the wall. Except for a door and one small window facing into the center of the building, it could easily have been mistaken for an enormous shipping container.

"In here, George," Tony said opening the door. "It may not look like much, but it's an apartment. I lived in here for two years after I came out—before Claire made up her mind to take me back. The warehouse is empty because I wanted to be alone. We still just use it for overflow. But don't worry, you'll be completely safe here. We're in an enclosed area between two other warehouses. I've got my office in one, and the whole place is guarded twenty-four hours a day."

The kitchen area was to the left of the door, complete with cabinets, a two-burner stove, sink, and small refrigerator. The bed, bureau, and pipe rack full of clothes were on the left end. Opposite the door, a few chairs, a desk, computer, and large bookcase.

"The only bad part is the bathroom. You have to walk around to the end to get there. The guy who built this place didn't think about a bathroom until the job was done. And, yeah, it was me that forgot.

"Oh, and it would be smart not to use the phone without checking with me first. You'd be amazed how easy it is for people to trace calls. But feel free to use the computer. The password is 'warehouseone.'"

"Tony, this is fantastic, but I'm worried about getting you involved in this…"

"Please, George. There's no way anyone will ever connect me to you, so stop worrying and tell me what happened."

"I'm sure you already know. I'll bet your connections are buzzing."

"Not this time. All I know is there was a false alarm at the hotel. No big deal, no chatter."

"Nothing about a murder?"

"A murder! Hell, no! Who was murdered?

"A friend of mine named Kitty Marren, an innocent woman snuffed out to get to me. You'll hear about it when they find evidence that says Killer Laine has struck again."

"That makes no sense, George. Look, let me make coffee while you find some dry clothes, then we'll talk."

Laine showered, washed his underwear and socks, and put on a warm shirt and a pair of denim work pants. The money and photo were damp but undamaged.

"I feel better, Tony. I'm starting to be able to think straight again. You know, if it weren't for you, I'd be headed back to San Quentin right now."

"You're safe here, but please tell me what's going on. While you were in the shower, I made a couple of calls. All I got was a police alert about guy fitting your description wanted for questioning about the false alarm at the Madrid Hotel. Nothing about a murder. Are you sure about that?"

"Absolutely, I saw her. But I think I can explain why no one is talking about it. I don't know exactly who killed Kitty, but

I'd put my money on one of two cops: either Metzi or Carlos. If it wasn't one of them, they certainly called in the hit. How else would they know to show up at the Madrid at six o'clock in the morning no more than fifteen minutes after Kitty was found, even before I pulled the fire alarm?"

"You pulled it?"

"Yeah, they had us bottled up, wouldn't let anyone out. Someone had been in my room earlier, too. Clearly, they were after me, and once they had me, I could be silenced or at least totally isolated. I wouldn't even have the right to make a call or get a lawyer. After my PO found out I was wanted for murder, flight, and turning in a false alarm, I would have been revoked on the spot. End of problem. Kitty was a nobody as far as the system is concerned. There would have been no mention of her death in the press or even the suggestion of an investigation. After a few weeks, she would have been cremated and dumped in the bay."

"But I would have sent Tomaras the package. Maybe she could stop it."

"Not a chance. By the time she got it, I would have been revoked and sent back to prison. Even if she thought I might be innocent of the original crime, there would be no denying the violation of my probation. She'd get nowhere, and probably lose her job for even trying."

"But why not call it a homicide, tell everyone to be looking for a murderer? No one cares about a false alarm."

"This is pure Alfred Preston. Use the murder to flush me out, have a heavy charge to show my PO, but don't run the risk of having my name show up in the papers. If Constance saw it or heard it on the news, that would be it for Alfred. This way, it's all quiet, low-risk, and I instantly disappear.

"Besides, how long would I have lasted on the streets looking like a drowned rat? How far could I get with no clothes and a few soggy dollars? No, without you and Robert, I was done for."

"But murder, did they have to go that far?"

"Yes. I'd bet anything that Kitty was strangled, and when they 'search' my room, they'll find something of hers—just like after the death of Julia Penthoser. This was designed for Miss Tomaras's benefit. I can hear that bastard, Dalton, spelling it out for her. 'I told you so! He's a killer! Struck again just like the first time!' There's no way she could resist that narrative. Kitty was a prop, a tool to make sure I was immediately and permanently silenced."

"It's too much to take in, George. I mean, sure, I saw some really bad shit back when I was, you know, 'involved,' but nothing as evil as this. At least the ones we dealt with weren't innocent bystanders.

"But what are you going to do now? You're welcome to stay here as long as you want, you know. Take your time, think it out like you always do. Meantime, I'll do a little shopping, get you some clothes, shoes, food, or anything else you want.

"And let me put another idea out there for you. Please consider it, okay? I know people who make documents, things like social security cards and driver's licenses, even a passport, all the stuff you need to move around safely and unnoticed. We can get you to the East Coast, find a place to live, even a job if you want it. You can leave Alfred to stew in his own rotten juices worrying if you'll ever show up again."

"I may take you up on the East Coast offer, Tony. But first I have to deal with Alfred. I can't walk away and forget Kitty. No, Alfred and I need to meet and have this out."

"You're nuts! He'll chew you up!"

"I don't think so. I'm working on it, Tony. Believe me, I won't do anything without having a clear plan. I think I can arrange this so Alfred doesn't really have a choice.

"But go home to your family. Leave me here—I'll be fine. I need to meditate for a while, get my brain and body playing in the same key. By the way," he said, pointing to the bookcase, "I'll have plenty to read. I already see some old friends."

"Yeah, your influence, George. But you've probably read them all."

"That's fine. Like Oscar Wilde said, 'If you can't enjoy reading a book over and over, there's no use reading at all.'"

Tony smiled, shrugged, promised to return later with supplies, and left. Laine laid down on the bed, pulled up the blanket, and was instantly asleep.

Chapter 29

"Judge? Listen, we have to talk. All hell broke loose at the Madrid. A woman was murdered there last night. Strangled, probably sexually abused! It's crazy! Metzi is convinced it's Laine, but why would he…"

"Slow down, Dalton! I told you again and again that Laine is a killer. Don't be so surprised. More important: has he been arrested? He's in custody, right?"

"No, he got away. People were going nuts over the dead girl. The cops tried to keep everyone from leaving, but apparently, Laine tripped the fire alarm and skipped out in the chaos. Several people saw him go."

"You're telling me he just walked out?! Where were Metzi and his people?! How the hell did they let this happen?!"

"I don't have any idea. It's all insane! Why would Laine, a known murderer, kill someone, go to bed, and wait until morning to skip out? It stinks to high heaven. How in the world could anyone—Metzi or God Himself—know this would happen? How could they know right away it was Laine?"

"Calm down, Dalton. We all knew this was coming. We warned everyone, but Mr. Slick put on his aw-shucks charm and this is the result.

"Hang on, Dalton, I've got another call. Stay on the line."

Five minutes later he was back. "That was a call from a friend downtown. They're handling this very carefully. But first, you should know that when they searched Laine's room, they found the woman's underwear. It's the same scenario as the first killing fifty years ago! Who knows what goes on in the mind of a killer like that? I'm no psychologist, but I know this: Laine has to be found and silenced for good before anything else happens. Right now the girl's death is being called a heart attack. They're not saying anything about a murder. No sense upsetting the entire community. And it's vital that the press not get involved. So far Laine is only wanted for questioning about the false alarm. If there's no mention of murder and no arrest warrant for Laine, the press won't get wind of it."

"What if Laine goes to the papers?"

"Think about it, Dalton: some guy convicted of rape and murder calls a reporter to say...what? That someone killed a woman in the Madrid and they're trying to pin it on him? They'd hang up on him. If someone did decide to check his story and called the precinct, guess what? There's no murder to report, just a plain old heart attack! And if a reporter goes snooping around the Madrid, who would be stupid enough to talk about any of it? Those people know perfectly well they'd be out on the street—or worse—in five minutes flat. No, they're handling this mess the best they can.

"Now, I'll call DAPO and talk to Captain Henderson, bring the boss up to speed on what you and the precinct people told me. You need to find Tomaras and let her know what her boy has done. If she gives you any shit, we'll just shift the whole thing to Henderson. He'll sign the revocation order on the spot, and this entire misadventure will be over. We can all rest easier."

"I don't know, Judge. It all seems too contrived. How do we know Metzi didn't off the girl to flush out Laine?"

"Who really cares as long as Laine is back in San Quentin in the next twenty-four hours? Sure, there may be some rough edges here, but the important thing is sewing this up quickly and quietly. Then we can all go on vacation."

"There's something missing here. This just doesn't hang together. I hope you won't mind me saying so, but it feels like this thing with Laine has completely taken over your thinking. You're a judge, not a cop. You're too personally involved. It may be putting you and even your family in danger. Wouldn't it be better to just let the whole thing come out, turn the state police loose on him, and solve the problem that way?"

After nearly a minute of silence, the judge spoke.

"All right, Dalton, it's time I let you in on another part of this. Remember when I told you there's more than I felt comfortable sharing? Well, there is.

"I am married to Laine's wife."

"What!"

"Yes. During the trial we—that is, Dad and I—gave Laine's wife all the support we could. As she came to see what kind of man her husband was, she distanced herself from him. At the same time, we became close. We assumed he would be executed the first time around, and Dad arranged to have his body cremated, so she wouldn't have to deal with it. Out of nowhere, he got a stay. I didn't tell her, so she assumed he was dead. We moved out of state and got married. She didn't know it, but Dad got a divorce, so if anyone ever looked into it, our marriage would be legal. His death was inevitable, but he kept getting stays. Then he got moved off death row after the sixty-seven Supreme Court ruling. I never told her because it would have been too upsetting. Dad had a court order in effect, so Laine couldn't contact her even after he got into the general population. I assumed the bastard would die in prison, but...well, you know the rest.

"For a long time, I handled it so she wouldn't have to deal with the fact he was alive. But now that he's out, she and I, you, and everyone else—we're all in danger. She still doesn't know he's alive, much less free in San Francisco. I'm trying to handle this in a way that protects my wife and daughter. If we can end it quickly, the danger will pass without scaring the life out of my family. I'm depending on you and others to do your job. Put a net over George Laine before someone else dies.

"It's very painful to say all of this, but you need to know."

"My, God! I had no idea. Even more reason to open it up if we can't get our hands on him quickly."

"Okay, but I feel we're close. Let's bring in everything we've got and end this. If that doesn't work, we'll go big. Fair?"

"Yes, that's fair. I'm sorry if I seemed like a doubting Thomas. Now I understand. I'll call Tomaras right away. I won't mention

Henderson, but we may need him soon if I can't budge her. Call me if you think of anything else."

"I will."

Chapter 30

Tony returned late in the afternoon with bags of groceries and clothing. He also had a little more information about how Kitty's death and Laine's flight were being handled.

"It's coming right from the top, George. The official line is the girl died of a heart attack, there was no murder, but you're wanted for questioning about the false alarm that trashed the Madrid Hotel. Your description is in every beat cop's pocket. Extra patrol cars have been brought in, and the search area has been extended over to the mission, down to Bayview and Hunters Point.

"So far they've kept it out of the press, and the Madrid is crawling with water damage restoration people. Give it a couple of days, and no one will remember anything about you or your friend. For the life of me, George, I can't see how you could even imagine getting near Alfred, much less actually talking to him. I hope you'll reconsider that part of your plan, give it a week to calm down, then let me get you out of here. Robert will drive you to New Jersey to start a new life. I'll have people lined up to give you a new identity.

"If you want, I can send your package to Tomaras after you've left. You said yourself that even if it came to nothing more than some questions, his happy life would come crashing down around his ears."

"I'm not ready for that play yet, Tony. Like you say, let's give this some time, see how it sorts out. Meantime, go home, we'll continue this conversation in the morning. By the way, thanks for all the stuff! Looks like I'm going to eat like a king tonight. Better yet, I won't even have to listen to a sermon."

Tony left, and Laine explored his new quarters. Climbing the shelves to the ceiling, he could look out the roof vents at the area around the warehouse. Tony's compound was part of a large industrial park on the edge of East Palo Alto. In the distance, he could see the San Francisco Bay and a small piece of the Dumbarton Bridge.

His first night in the warehouse apartment was restless at best. He got up several times, paced, tried reading, meditation, exercise, coffee—nothing slowed his brain down or released him from the images of Kitty and the sounds of panic at the Madrid. He tried to walk around the warehouse, but it was so dark he kept bumping into metal posts. That reminded him of being in solitary looking for a missing button in the dark. He retreated to his room, left the door open and the lights on. There was no radio, the TV was disconnected, and he couldn't figure out how to find classical music on the computer.

He finally decided to stop fighting with himself over images of Kitty lying on the floor. *Go ahead, look at her. Let it sharpen your thinking, not blur it. Sleep is secondary; plenty of time for that later.*

The sound of Tony opening the huge garage door woke him up. It was ten thirty in the morning.

"You look awful, George."

"I just woke up."

"Well, get yourself dressed, I'll make something to eat, and then we can talk."

"Something new?"

"Yeah, a couple of things. But you need to wake up first."

Laine took a shower, dressed, and sat down with a cup of coffee. "Okay, Tony, what is it? You look too serious for this to be good. Did something else happen at the Madrid?"

"No, not at the Madrid. I got a call this morning from one of my people still in the game. He wanted to know if I ever heard of a guy named George Laine."

"Ouch."

"Yeah, well, I told him 'no' and asked why he's asking. So he tells me the guy is loose somewhere in 'Frisco, he's pissed off some really big fish, plus there's a fat reward to make him disappear. He wants to know if we would want in on that or not? I ripped him a new asshole for even asking the question. I told him that's the sort of crap Russians do, and if the Old Man hears he's suggesting we start competing with the Russians, he'll be the one who disappears. He got the message."

"That's what I've been worried about, Tony, dragging you into this."

"Nah. This way I didn't have to say we're protecting you— that *would* be dangerous. As long as it's a business decision, he'll put out the word we don't want to be involved. That will be the end of it. I'm actually glad he called and gave me the opening."

"Okay, but that's not all you have. What's the rest?"

"I don't know if it's good or bad, but knowing you, it will be a game changer. Just remember: no matter what, I can get you out of here in short order. You don't need to stick around to cook Preston's goose."

"Fine, message received."

"Okay, so we're having breakfast. I'm reading about the Forty-Niners. Claire's reading the engagement and marriage section of the Sunday *Times*, going on about this one and that one. I'm eating my eggs, not listening. Then I look over and see this." He handed the paper to Laine already folded to the article.

Rebecca Squires to Wed Philip Upton

Burlingame. Rebecca Preston Squires and Philip Tims Upton will be married in a private ceremony on Saturday, October 30, 2010. Mrs. Squires is a graduate of the Northern Woods Preparatory School and a Cum Laude graduate of the University of California, Berkeley. She holds a Master's Degree in Middle Eastern Studies. She is currently working as an assistant to State Congresswoman Estelle Evans-Prince. She has a 13-year-old son from a previous marriage. Mr. Upton attended the New Trier School and the University of Chicago where he received a BS degree in Biology and a Ph.D. in Molecular Biology. He is currently working for the SynarvisTech Corporation in San Jose. Following a private ceremony, there will be a reception at the Northern Woods Club. After a honeymoon in Baja California, the couple will live in Hillsborough.

"Holy smokes! That really is a game changer! Looks like I may have to attend the reception. I just hope I can remember my party manners. What do you think, Tony? Father of the bride there to toast his daughter's happiness?"

"You're bone crazy, George. Aren't you the one who's always saying you don't want to mess up your family's life? If you walk in there, security people will land on you like stink on shit. It'll be played like you went there to kill someone. Everything you've tried to do will go up in smoke."

"I see your point. Still, it's hard to walk away without doing *something*. Just seeing them would be enough to let me leave it all in peace. But we agreed to take this one step at a time, no rush. Let me have some time to ponder this; meanwhile, go home to Claire and watch the Forty-Niners play. I'll see you in the morning, Tony. And thanks for showing me the notice. Just thinking I might see them makes me feel better."

What he didn't tell Tony was how Kitty's death had already changed his thinking. A glancing blow and speedy exit to New Jersey would not do. No matter how logical or tempting it might be, he simply could not walk away from Julia, Kitty, and every principle that had sustained him over the past fifty-two years. Just the thought of it filled him with feelings of betrayal and self-loathing. Seeing it through, no matter the consequences, immediately cleared his mind. He had this one chance left to catch up with the light farther up the road.

It was also clear he couldn't deal with Alfred without Constance finding out he was still alive. The only way to keep her from the painful discovery would be to leave without lifting the devil's mask. *Unthinkable!*

When he thought about it from her perspective, it was obvious she would want to know. In fact, she would be furious if he didn't trust her to be able to deal with the truth, no matter the outcome. *Let that worry go. The trailer is going by; let this be a redefining moment. Certainly, it will be a shattering moment for Constance—Rebecca, too—but beyond the anguish, it could actually free them. More to the point, it's exactly what she would want.*

Got it. I see exactly what to do next. Constance, you don't know it yet, but we're about to join forces to bring this to a conclusion.

Chapter 31

"WHAT'S THE MATTER WITH DAD? He's been really weird lately. Is he that upset that I'm marrying Philip? I know he isn't crazy about him, but…"

"It's not you or Philip. It's something else entirely, though I don't know what it is. When I asked him what was going on, he gave me a convoluted answer about an old case coming back to cause trouble. When I pushed him for details, he got really agitated. I have an ugly feeling about this, something I can't put my finger on. But I am certain it has nothing to do with your marriage."

"Is it something financial? One of his let's-not-talk-about-it deals?"

"No, I'd know about that. This one is different; something from the past has come back to haunt him. He says it's an old case; supposedly, someone he sent off to prison years ago has gotten out unexpectedly, stirring up trouble somewhere in San Francisco. It doesn't wash.

"But right now we need to focus on the wedding. And don't worry about Erik; he'll be safe with us. And if anything strange comes up, I'll take him to your house and leave Alfred to deal with his demons. Besides, that would make it easier to get Erik back and forth to school."

"It scares me to hear you talk like this, Mom."

"Don't worry, Rebecca, I've been through worse. Lots worse."

Chapter 32

LAINE SPENT MOST OF SUNDAY on the internet researching props for his next move. Continuing to comb through what he already knew about Alfred was pointless. The only nagging question was why Alfred and his new family moved to Indiana. And why they came back six or seven years later. *At this point it's useless,* he reasoned and went back to climbing the warehouse jungle gym. The more he climbed, the more energized he became.

Sunday night was considerably more restful than the night before. For the first time, Laine felt he had an understanding of all of the grotesque events that destroyed so many lives. He could finally stop bombarding himself with incessant demands to know who was behind it all. True, Alfred's motivation wasn't entirely clear, but when they met, perhaps that, too, could be resolved. Beyond that, perhaps he could regain the seemingly impossible sense of peace he thought would never be his again.

When Tony arrived in the morning, Laine was already up, dressed, and reading an Ambrose Bierce ghost story.

"Have you thought about my offer to get you out of here, George?"

"Yes, I'll gladly accept."

"When?"

"If it doesn't go well when I meet Alfred."

"I knew it! This is freaking insane, George. Just fucking *leave!* I'll mail the package, Alfred will get what he deserves, and everybody wins. It will be tough on Constance and Rebecca, but a damn sight better than if you get yourself shipped back to prison or killed!"

"And then there's this!" he said, shaking Laine's shopping list in the air. "I get the hair dye and black-rimmed glasses, and

I'm sure you'll explain 'Wedding Gift.' But what about all this spy shit? You aren't James Bond, George. The idea that you're going to wear a wire and trap Alfred Preston into confessing to two murders—assuming you could get anywhere near him—is totally nuts!"

"There's more to it than meets the eye, Tony. Trust me. I've thought this out carefully. I see a clear path through the minefield. And I promise to go to New Jersey the minute this is over, I really do. But if you don't want to mess with this anymore, let me borrow some money and I'll shop the stuff myself."

"Ow! You're twisting my arm. Okay, but explain it all to me, starting with the disguise. You'll let your beard grow out, dye your hair and beard, put on the windowpane glasses, and somehow manage to get into the wedding. Am I right so far?"

"No, not the wedding. The reception. But before you get any more upset, tell me something about the Northern Woods Club. Is it a union shop?"

"Ah! Now I get it. So the next question is who is doing the catering, and can I get you in with their staff?"

"Exactly."

"I'll have to check to be sure, but I'd guess they're all union, and that would mean any outside help would have to be union, too. I gather you want to slip in dressed as a waiter, right?"

"Right."

"Okay, maybe I can do it, but it calls for a favor that would come with a guarantee you won't draw attention to the caterer."

"That's a promise. I just need twenty minutes to deliver the wedding gift and slip out. Clean and simple. No explosions."

"And the gift?"

Laine explained he wanted a silver locket with a large "L" engraved on the cover. Inside, two pictures. He showed Tony the tattered photograph of his parents.

"Christ, George, you can hardly see their faces. Rebecca won't have any idea in the world who they are."

"And by the time…"

"I get it. By the time she shows it to Constance and she recognizes them, you'll be gone. But won't the shit hit the fan then? Constance will freak out."

"She will, but it'll be an underground explosion. She'll freak out on Alfred, to be sure, but not in the middle of the reception. I'm sure of it. She's not the screaming kind."

"Okay, then what? Assuming you're right—big 'if' on that one—when and how do you do your CIA thing?"

"Later. We'll have to see how it plays out. Hopefully, I can figure out how to isolate Alfred from Constance. I can't imagine her staying with him right after she hears I'm alive."

Tony took the picture and promised to get the locket made, as well as check on the feasibility of sneaking Laine into the club through the back door. Robert was given the job of visiting the spy-goods stores in San Francisco.

"You know, don't you, that Alfred will have some muscle around him after the Northern Woods Club fracas, assuming you get away with it at all."

"Just another problem to be solved. But, yes, I do know it. I'm counting on it."

Tony rolled his eyes, finished his coffee, and left Laine to his internet study and jungle gym games. Robert came by later to go over the spy gear list.

"It's about size and audio fidelity, Robert. I know this stuff is very expensive, and I feel bad about asking Tony to foot the bill, but this is the final play, the key to everything."

Robert assured him cost was not an issue. "I'll tell you something else, Mr. Laine. If this was anyone but you, Tony would have flat-out refused to have anything to do with it. Period. Way too dangerous. Even if he really loved the person, no argument on earth would make him change his mind. But the feeling he has for you exists in another place altogether. To Tony, that means affection and concern have to take a back seat to the respect he has for you. He says that you should never get in the way of someone who instinctively brings dignity to adversity no matter the pain it causes him. And that means even if what you're doing seems impossible, it's your play, and his job is to give you every chance to make it work.

"Okay, sermon's over. I've got errands to run." Robert left and Laine returned to his book.

By Friday morning, Robert had gathered all of the electronics together and helped Laine prepare the gear and test it out. It quickly became apparent that because the microphone had to be concealed under his shirt, even slight body movement caused clothing to rub the pickup producing a scratching noise that obliterated conversation.

"Either you have to sit zombie still or we have to figure out a way to protect the microphone." They finally settled on sticking a piece of thin transparent packing tape on the shirt over the mike. It reduced the shirt static significantly. Robert also helped him dye his white hair dark brown, but they wanted to give his beard another day to grow before completing the facial overhaul. Even without the dark beard, the hair and glasses drastically changed his look.

Tony was stunned when he saw the change. "You know, George, I'm beginning to think you might just be able to pull this off."

Tony had made the arrangement for George, dressed in caterer's garb, to make a brief, unobtrusive appearance at the reception. Alerted by a call from Robert, the caterer would meet George behind the food tent, guide him through the service area, and point out who was where in the crowd. It was then up to George to invisibly deliver the package, reverse course back to the car, and leave. Hopefully, the entire round trip from the warehouse to the club and back would take less than two hours.

Laine continued to alternately read and exercise through Friday afternoon. In the evening, while searching the internet for more pictures of Constance and Rebecca, he stumbled onto a newspaper article about a charity event sponsored by, among others: Judge Albert and Mrs. Constance Preston. Among the remarks about Constance was the passing mention she was "originally from Indiana," reminding Laine that even though he had declared his search into Albert's dark side to be over, there was still the unanswered curiosity of their leaving California sometime after Albert's graduation from law school.

Why leave Daddy's swimming pool and bocce court to go live in the barren Midwest? Maybe it had to do with Constance's parents. They were elderly and quite ill the last time Laine heard about them. Mrs. Wilton's name was Ida, but he only knew her husband as "Bud." Not much to go on. He started his search in Brazil, found nothing, tried Terre Haute and struck out again. Louis always said if you're not finding something, it's not because it isn't there, it's because you're looking in the wrong place. Change your key words. He went back to Brazil, this time searching death notices, and from there, the obituaries. Bingo!

> April 9, 1964. Brazil. Ida Wilton, 86, passed away at the Belle Haven Retirement Home in east Terre Haute after a long struggle with multiple sclerosis. She went to be with the Lord, surrounded by family and friends. The article concluded with: Mrs. Wilton is survived by her husband of sixty years, William "Bud" Wilton, her Daughter Constance, and one grandchild. After a Ceremony of Thanks at the Riverside Funeral Home, she will be buried in the First Congregational Church graveyard on Patterson Avenue.

It didn't take long to find Bud Wilton in the online records of the Congregational church. He was buried next to his wife on June 4, 1968.

One more piece of the puzzle filled in, Laine thought. By itself it didn't mean much, but it closed the time loop, and gave him a glimpse into part of Constance's life after Alfred and his father slammed the tomb door shut.

Tony and Robert arrived at noon to prepare and go over all the details of the Northern Woods Club riposte. They were convinced Laine's disguise would work, especially if all he did was walk in, deliver the box, and leave.

The drive to Northern Woods took forty-five minutes. Robert was at the wheel of the rented limousine dressed in chauffeur's livery. As they approached the club, he made the call to the caterer. They were waved through the gates at the club and quickly pulled up to the service entrance where a caterer dressed in a tuxedo opened the door of the car.

"Let's go. No talk, just follow me. I'll point out who's who. You do your thing and get back in the service tent quick. No fuss, no noise."

They wove through the organized chaos of the service area to the opening just behind the buffet table. There were easily two hundred guests swirling around, talking, drinking, and dancing. The band was playing, "That's Why the Lady is a Tramp."

"Funny song for a wedding, don't you think?"

"I make the food, not the music. Now look over there, the big round table. That's the bride and groom's table. His parents are the grumpy looking ones on the far side; the bride's mother is sitting closer to us."

"I see her," Laine said. His voice was steady, but he was suddenly light-headed. He took a deep breath trying to steady himself, maintain focus. Constance sat between two empty chairs, a vigilant look on her face. Her eyes didn't pause as her gaze swept past the two men standing in the tent opening.

"You're still so beautiful," Laine whispered under his breath.

"Hey! Are you listening, mister? I said that's the bride's mother sitting by herself. The bride is dancing. See her?"

"Yes, I do. She's lovely. Is that her husband she's dancing with?" He didn't hear the answer. "And where's the bride's father? I don't see him."

"I don't know. Last I saw him, he was at the bar."

Laine spotted a youngster standing alone on the edge of the dance floor listening to the music. Laine pushed off saying, "I'll be right back."

He walked through the tables toward the boy.

"Good music, isn't it?"

"Yes, it is. I really like the tenor sax. Great sound, sweet and mellow."

"Agreed. Do you play?"

"I'm learning. Practice, practice. I'll get there, though. Some of my friends say it's too hard an instrument, but I don't agree."

"'Hard' is just another word for 'lazy,' I think."

The boy turned and looked at Laine. "Wow! That's one of my grandmother's favorite sayings. I never heard anyone else use it before. My name's Erik, by the way. What's yours?"

"George."

"Just 'George'?"

"Yes, but Erik, I wonder if you could do me a favor."

"Of course, what is it?"

"One of the guests had to leave early and asked me to deliver this gift to the bride. Would you mind taking it to her? I have to get back to work."

"Sure, glad to." He held out his hand. "It's been nice to meet you, George."

"Same for me, Erik," Laine said shaking the boy's hand.

Laine walked quickly back to the tent, turned, and watched as Erik put the box on the table next to Constance.

"Come on, your cab's waiting," said the caterer, anxious to be free of the stranger. Laine took one last look back before retreating to the car.

"How did it go, Mr. Laine?" asked Robert as they moved down the driveway.

"Wonderful and painful, Robert. I just wanted to go over, scoop her up and get her out of there, but well…you know. But I did get to see her and my daughter. I even got to talk with my grandson. All those years I tried not to think about seeing them, but the idea always had a way of creeping back. Just those few minutes with them are more than I ever imagined being allowed to have.

"But while I'm sitting here feeling so complete, I know I've left behind a terrible amount of pain. But it had to be. There was no other way."

Back at the reception, Constance watched Erik approach with the little white box. "What's that, Erik?" she asked as he put it on the table.

"A wedding present, Grandma. One of the guests had to leave. He couldn't bring it over."

"Really? What guest?"

"I don't know. A waiter gave it to me."

"A waiter?" Constance said, her tone cautious. "Point him out, Erik. Where is he? What does he look like?"

"Gosh, Grandma, I don't know. He was over there, but I don't see him now. He was tall, had brown hair, a beard, and glasses."

"What's going on, Mom?" said Rebecca as she sat down. "You look funny. Are you okay? What's this box?"

"It's a wedding present, Mom," said Erik.

"Open it, Rebecca," Constance said.

"Why? It's a little weird. There's no card. I'll open it later."

"I said, open it now, Rebecca. Please. Humor me."

Rebecca untied the small white ribbon, opened the box, unfolded the tissue revealing a locket attached to a fine silver chain.

"A locket. What a strange wedding present. And the engraving...just one letter, an L."

"Dear God! It can't be..."

"Can't be what, Mom?" Rebecca said as she opened the cover. "They sure didn't waste any money on a photographer. Who are these people?"

Constance took the locket but seemed unable to look directly at the pictures. Finally, she glanced at them, gasped, and fell back in her chair. She tried to close the case, but her trembling fingers couldn't grasp the locket. Rebecca and Erik stared at her, not knowing what to say or do.

"Mom! What's wrong? Please! Who are those people? You know them, right?"

"Yes, I know who they are. It's a message for me from someone I knew a long time ago, someone I thought was dead. It has nothing to do with you.

"Erik, did the waiter who gave this to you say what his name was?"

"Yes, Grandma. He said it's 'George.'"

"Where is Alfred?" Constance whispered to no one in particular. "And, please, don't ask me to explain right now. You keep on with the party, and I'll be back. I promise. Just tell me where Alfred is."

She stood without waiting for a reply, wiping her eyes with her napkin as she set off through the crowd in the direction of the bar, the most likely place to find Alfred. He wasn't there, but someone said he had gone into the clubhouse, probably to the men's locker room on the lower level.

The sound of men laughing grew louder as she rushed down the hallway to the swinging door at the end marked, "Men Only." She barely slowed as she hit the door. It smashed into the inside wall with a loud bang.

A waiter started to protest her presence, but when he saw the look on her face, he backed up and let her pass. The ten or so men gathered around two tables fell silent.

"Connie! What the hell is wrong?" asked Alfred with an anxious laugh.

"I need to talk to you, Alfred. Now! And not here."

"Whoa! What's so important I can't finish my drink?"

"Now, Alfred, or you won't like the consequences."

"Okay. Sounds serious, guys. I'll be right back." He caught up with Constance halfway down the hallway. She was trying doors as she walked, looking for one that would open. Just past the stairs, the manager stepped out of his office, alerted by the noise made by the door to the men's bar.

"Is something wrong, Mrs. Preston? What can I do to help?"

"You can get out of your office and let us talk. We won't be long."

"Connie! That's no way to speak to Mr. Lincoln. We can find another…"

"Shut up, Alfred," she said, moving past the bewildered manager. "Get in here and close the door." Constance turned as he closed the door. "Now listen to me. I have one question to ask you. Don't even imagine lying to me. What is the name of the man who has had you so upset, the one you said was let out of prison and is causing trouble in San Francisco?"

"Connie, I told you, I can't…"

Constance fumbled the locket cover open, holding it just inches from Alfred's face. "Take a look! Do you know who those people are?"

"No," he said, shaking his head. "Should I?"

"How about the engraving? One letter, an L. Is this helping your memory?"

Alfred's bravado was starting to lose steam. "Honestly, Connie, I don't know anything about that thing. Where did it come from?"

"A waiter gave it to Erik to deliver to Rebecca. He told him his name is 'George.' Now, again: what is the name of the man who has you so terrified? SAY IT!"

"I have to go get security right now, Connie! Jesus Christ! He could still be here!"

Constance stepped between Alfred and the door. "Say the name, Alfred!"

Alfred's posture slumped. He sat down on the manager's couch. "George Laine. The name is George Laine."

"Right this second, Alfred Preston, every blood vessel in my head is about to burst. I want to scream, claw your eyes out, something, anything!! How can this be?! It means my husband wasn't executed, doesn't it? DOESN'T IT?!"

"Yes."

"And he's been in prison all his life?!"

Alfred nodded.

"And you knew it all this time, you rotten son-of-a-bitch!"

"Yes, but I did it to protect you! He was supposed to be executed that July, but the Public Defender somehow pulled off a last minute stay. I didn't know about it; no one saw it coming. When I found out, I didn't tell you because it was absolutely certain he *would* be executed; it was just a question of time. I couldn't let you go through that hell all over again.

"Jesus Christ! Connie, don't you remember that horrible night we thought George was being executed?! That was the worst night of our lives. God! We were a mess for days leading up to it. We couldn't eat, sleep, or do anything. You stayed at our house, so you wouldn't be alone, and my mother could help with Rebecca. You couldn't do anything but hold the baby and rock back and forth. Horrible! All day you cried; we cried."

"Yes, I remember that night! I remember it like it was yesterday! Tell me again you didn't know he had gotten a stay! Tell me!"

"Of course I didn't know, for God's sake. I didn't find out until the next day. But it was a 'stay,' Connie. It just meant a delay. Like I said, his execution was an absolute certainty. No matter how long it took, it would have happened. Who would have imagined the State Supreme Court would void all death sentences? Or he would be moved to general population to serve out a life sentence, much less get paroled."

"And when he wasn't executed that first time, you must have made it impossible for him to let me know he was still alive, right? RIGHT?!"

"There was a court order already in effect, yes. His mail was monitored. He wasn't allowed to use a telephone."

"A court order, you say. Whose idea was that? And what in the world reason could there be to cut him off so completely? George had to know about the court order, right? RIGHT?!"

"Yes, he knew. He never saw it, but he was told," Alfred said almost in a whisper.

"When?! When was he told, you bastard?! Was it before he was supposed to be executed in July? Was it?!"

"Yes, I think so."

"Oh, God! So he couldn't let me know he was still alive when he won a stay! Then you made him sit there waiting to die knowing I thought he was already dead! How could you do that?! ANSWER ME!"

"It wasn't my idea. Dad thought it would be best to put the order into effect before the execution. That way, all communications would go through him, so you wouldn't get the death certificate or have to deal with his body. It was to protect you, Connie.

"But when the execution was put off, he felt it was best to continue the order; after all, it was just a delay. There wasn't a chance in hell he wouldn't be executed after the stay ran out. That way, you were spared the pain."

"And his pain, Alfred, what about that? And then there's the little matter of our marriage! I was still married when we got our license! Or is that another detail your helpful father took care of?"

"You weren't married at that point. Dad had your power of attorney. He used it to get a divorce. Our marriage is totally legal."

"A DIVORCE! Dear God, when did he do that?! More to the point: did George know? Has he been sitting in a cell for fifty years thinking I cut him off *and* divorced him?!"

"No, he couldn't have known, Connie. Any notice from the state would have been diverted. He couldn't possibly have known. What difference does it make now, anyway? And before you ask: yes, the court order is still in effect. If he makes any attempt to contact any of us, he goes straight back to jail. His little stunt sealed that for him."

"'What difference,' you ask?! He was destroyed even before he was to be executed! Dear God! What did we do to the poor man?! How could he possibly come to grips with it? He couldn't even write or receive a letter or a call from me! Am I hearing you say he still can't even speak to me, and just coming here tonight sends him back again—forever?!

"Wait! In all these maneuvers, is there a chance—any chance—that while he was in prison, he found out I married you? Could he have known that, too? If he was told about the court order, if there was even a sliver of a chance he knew about the divorce, wasn't there also a chance he somehow found out about the marriage?! Oh, God! How could I have done this to him?!"

"Hold on, Connie! You didn't do anything to him. Remember: George Laine is a rapist and a murderer! No matter what he knew or didn't know, whether he was alive or dead, he was out of your life, out of Rebecca's life. It was a lot better to assume he was dead and never think about him again. Just remember what he did, why he was in prison. Murder, Connie, murder! You didn't betray him, he betrayed YOU!"

"So you say."

"What do you mean, 'So you say'? So said the trial court; so said the appeals court. My father knew it. He told me there wasn't a chance in the world he was innocent. Don't you remember how many times we talked about it? How painful it was to know what he did and what was going to happen to him? I took you away from all of that. I protected you, shielded you from that agony."

"You did not! You told me you had real doubts about his guilt in spite of what your father said. You were supportive of me. You said you were as helpless as everyone else. It was your father who was so adamant, remember? Now you sound just like your freaking father! Is that what you *really* thought when you were trying to soothe me?" Constance turned away, crying, shaking her head, then spun back around and spoke, her voice almost calm: "George Laine did not kill that girl."

"WHAT?! I can't believe you said that! Didn't you hear what I just said? I thought you accepted it when you married me. I told you all of this; you agreed to every word. I even remember when Dad told you that he hated to admit it, but he knew George was guilty."

"I never said I agreed George committed that crime. I said I accepted the inevitability of his death, that there was no possibility of a reversal, much less any chance of him regaining his freedom. And at the end, when I stopped hearing from him, your father told us he heard from the public defender that George just wanted to get it over with. Your father told us he knew at that point George was crushed with guilt over his crime and betrayal of me. I argued with your father, remember? I told him point blank he didn't understand George, that what he called 'grief' was really anguish over what his conviction was doing to me! Don't you remember that? Where is your memory, Alfred?!

"I never wavered in my support of George, but I was up against a completely solid wall. Everywhere I turned, everything I did took me back to knowing the man I loved was going to die for something he did not do, and there wasn't a goddamn thing I or anyone else could do to stop it!

"Apparently, you don't remember, Alfred, but you weren't yelling about him being a murderer and rapist—you were supportive. You told me over and over how unfair it was, how terrible you felt for George. And when I told you about George's idea of ending those awful visits, you told me how George was doing it for me, that I needed to let him have that time to deal with what lay ahead.

"I'll never forget how much you encouraged me to accept it. I would have gone on visiting right up to the end if George had given me the slightest encouragement. But you kept telling me that I had to make that sacrifice for George's sake. Remember?

"So it was all a big fake! You really *did* think George killed Julia! You were posturing just to manipulate me, a cynical scheme to pry us apart while you pretended to be so sympathetic, right?

"Don't just sit there staring at me! Answer me, you fucking dog!"

"Calm down, please. Listen: I did think George killed Julia. In fact, I knew it. But I couldn't tell you that or it would have destroyed you. I was loving and supportive to save you from the ugly reality of George's guilt. I didn't lie or manipulate at all. I simply offered you what you needed to get past that awful time, a chance to get your life going again, to focus on Rebecca, to feel affection that wouldn't again be yanked away.

"Did I soften my feelings about what George did? Yes! Guilty! But I did it for you and Rebecca. You've got to understand that. And frankly, I thought that at some level you realized the truth about George, too. To me, you were simply too irrational at the time to grasp what had really happened. 'Denial,' that's what they call it. Psychologically, your feelings wouldn't let you see the truth. It was time to let go of George, and I was there to support that decision because it was best for you and Rebecca."

"Bullshit, Alfred. That was not my mindset at all. George's letters were full of affection and concern for us. He desperately wanted to spare me the unthinkable pain of seeing him in that place, of having to say goodbye forever to the man I loved, the father of our child. That's how we made the decision to end our visits. Don't you remember? I made a pragmatic decision, Alfred. I realized there was absolutely nothing I or anyone else could do to save George. If he didn't want me to visit, it was for my sake and nothing else. There was nothing irrational about me or George. One of my many mistakes was imagining that you could understand that as strange as it might seem to most people, it really was both rational and loving. It took the blazing heat out of that injustice. You didn't understand it—you used it."

"Really? You didn't seem to fight the idea of marrying me. Where was all the heat when that happened?"

"I was completely shattered, penniless, a mother with zero family support, and I thought I had become a widow by execution. I couldn't think, sleep, or even talk with people without falling to pieces. Every time I picked up our daughter, I could see George, I could feel him through her. I felt guilty that I was somehow a bad mother for relying so much on her smile to give me what I needed to continue living.

"My life had gone from joy to horror overnight. But there was always one thought that never left my mind, never wavered:

George Laine was an innocent man. I had to live with that, so I made a decision. I would try somehow to manage my feelings and survive. You held out your hand, and I took it. I paid a price, but I took it. I did it with two absolute certainties in mind. First, that George was gone and could never know what I had done. And second, that I would never cave into the idea George Laine was guilty of anything.

"George Laine did not harm Julia Penthoser. Rapists and murderers are filled with rage. George was the exact opposite. I spent endless hours with him after his arrest; I saw and lived his anguish, first about Julia, and then about us. From the start of the nightmare, George's concern was about us. By the way, a stone-cold killer would *not* risk his life to bring his daughter a wedding present.

"No, Alfred. Someone else killed Julia, framed George, and destroyed our lives. I am as certain now as I was then."

"Fine, but what would you say if I told you that your oh-so-innocent man murdered another young woman just weeks after leaving San Quentin?"

"I don't believe it. I don't know what years and years of incarceration does to a person—I can only imagine—but I can't picture any force on earth evil enough to corrupt George Laine. And who was this person? How come I didn't see any of this in the *Examiner*? I read the paper every day. There was nothing about George Laine, nothing about a murder. Nothing! How do you explain that?!"

"I used my influence to keep it quiet. Again, I was trying to protect you, especially with the wedding coming up."

"The wedding! What does that have to do with anything? And how do you have so much power that you can control the news? This is getting crazier by the second! I'm seeing a side of you, an icy, calculating, scary side I always forced myself to ignore. But I can't pretend anymore, you son-of-a-bitch!"

"Fine. The truth is out. And what the hell difference does it make that he was alive all this time? You couldn't talk to him anyway. And what would you say if you could have?"

"If I had known, I would have found a way to talk to him, court order or not. I would have told him what has been burning in my soul ever since that last awful visit. I would apologize for abandoning him, for marrying you, for being so weak, so gutless, for allowing myself to be manipulated by you and your rotten father! I put my pain ahead of his agony. I failed him as I failed myself. If I had just been able to look at him once to say, 'I'm sorry.' Just once! I could have had that if it hadn't been for your misguided notions about protection! Can you even begin to understand what I just told you?!"

"Yeah, I hear you, but I can't believe all this crap about apologizing to him. You're a victim, too, you know."

"Whose victim, Alfred?! You're the liar! I think you're scared shitless of the truth. So tell me, how long has George been out of prison, and where has he been in the city?"

"He got out about six weeks ago. They placed him in a boarding house in the Tenderloin. Like I said, it was a fluke, a flaw in the system that he exploited. And, no, I didn't tell you. You call it misguided; I call it devotion."

"*Devotion!* You bastard! You could have told me and let me deal with it! And what right do you have to think for me?!"

There was a knock at the door, the manager saying through the closed door that the bride and groom were about to leave.

"Please tell them we'll be right there, Mr. Lincoln. Thank you." She paused, took a deep breath, and said, "We are going up there to see them off. I am going to use whatever it takes to keep myself under control. I expect you to do the same.

"After they leave, I am going to take Erik to the house, get his things, pack my bag, and go to Rebecca's house. I need time to deal with this. When I'm ready, I will call you and we can talk. I do have one request, though. I want you to use all your amazing clout to see to it no harm comes to George. If you are even remotely sincere about protecting me, you'll do that. Anything less will doom you."

Rebecca was at the door of the clubhouse when her parents came out. Constance took her daughter by the arm and led her behind a potted palm, a modest screen at best.

"Please, Mom! Tell me what's going on? I can't leave you like this!"

"You can and you will. The locket was a gift from someone dear to me long ago. I promise to tell you about it when you get home from your honeymoon. In the meantime, your job is to get your marriage off on the right foot. I will look out for Erik, but there is one change: if it's all right with you, I'll stay at your house with Erik until you get back. It'll be easier to get him to school, he'll be with friends, and I'll have time by myself to think."

"Of course you can stay at my place. Erik would prefer it, really. But what has you so upset? Please tell me."

"Listen to me, Rebecca, it's way too complicated for right now. But as upset as I am, I think, in the end, it will have been a gift for all of us."

"Even Dad?"

"Especially your father."

Chapter 33

"DALTON! WE NEED TO TALK."

"Christ, Judge, it's nearly midnight. I'm in bed. Give me five minutes and call me back." Dalton hurried to his den and closed the door. "Okay, I'm awake. Is this good news or bad?"

"Bad. Laine showed up at my daughter's wedding reception! Can you bloody believe that?! He gave her some sort of Laine family picture and got out before Connie realized what was going on. She went nuts, told me a whole lot of crazy shit about how she never thought he was guilty. She's twisted it all around so everything I've done to protect her is somehow an attack on her.

"She has it in her head that she should meet this monster, tell him how much she's missed him. I can't talk sense into her. She's taken the grandkid and gone to our daughter's house."

"Didn't you tell her he may have killed again? Didn't she realize she was in danger?"

"Didn't faze her. She was too whacked to put it all together. So the gloves are off. She now knows Laine is out, and I don't have to make nice about it anymore. But someone is helping him; even worse, he's mobile."

"Well, Judge, at least we can put out a warrant, involve the state police, get some publicity, and make it harder for him to move around. Maybe this was his big play. He got away with it, but he knows everyone will be after him, time to go. You may never hear about him again."

"No, I'm sure this wasn't his last move. In a weird way, it may make it easier to find him. He has one more visit to make: he'll want to see me—I can feel it. That stunt at Northern Woods was aimed at me. He's playing her to get to me."

"Christ! We'll get some state cops over there tonight!"

"No, that would scare him away. I'll bring in a couple of guys; maybe he'll see it and use the phone. If he's crazy enough to come here, we'll have him. What a goddamn irony, Dalton. What if after all these years it all ends right here?"

"Way too risky, Judge."

"No, it's the best way. I'll be ready for him. Then I can repair the damage with Connie. It'll cost me with Rebecca if Connie tells her I'm not her dad. Right now it looks like she will. But when they both realize Laine is like some sort of cicada who crawls out of his hole every fifty-two years to kill again, they'll change their tune. If Laine will just remain predictable a little longer, this will only be a bump in the road. An expensive bump, mind you. But what's money for if you can't make it work for you?"

"Okay, if you say so. I'll call out the cavalry, put on the pressure. But be careful."

"Always, Dalton."

Chapter 34

"I CAN'T BELIEVE YOU PULLED that off, George. But I have to ask: what was it like seeing Constance, Rebecca, and Alfred up close like that?"

"I didn't see Alfred, just Constance, Rebecca, and Erik. I told Robert on the way out, it was the fulfillment of something beyond a wish or a dream. It instantly filled the hollow deep inside, gave me an overwhelming feeling of intimacy I never imagined being allowed to feel again. At the same time, I know I caused a frightful disruption in their lives, but the rational part of my brain says it was not only necessary but actually the right thing, long overdue. No matter what happens from here, I have the satisfaction of knowing I've given what I can to dissolve illusion; after that, it's up to each one to come to grips with the truth."

"Even Alfred?"

"That's the hope, though chances are he'll double down on his bet. Still, it doesn't mean I won't take a shot at it."

"Let me remind you, George, you have already done everything possible to, as you say, 'dissolve the illusion.' It's time to withdraw from the field. How much longer do you think you can defend yourself? Your family now knows you're alive, Preston is on the ropes, the end of his happy life and the start of a new one for Constance.

"You've done it, George. Let your family struggle through in their own way. Isn't that what you always used to say? If you want to help someone solve a problem, start by giving them the information they need, then get out of the way? No one gets strong being told what to do—it only weakens them. Your words, George.

"Well, here are *my* words: it's time to retire to the Jersey shore."

"You're forgetting Alfred. Leaving now doesn't force him to do anything but continue to play the hero while he searches for me. He'll corrupt anything that Constance says or tries to do."

"I'm coming to that, George. All you have to do is let me mail the package to Tomaras. Like you said, she'll look into it. Even if it costs her job, Alfred will be exposed, and even if he isn't charged with anything, he'll never see Constance again. By the way, that would take all the urgency out of finding you, plus he'll go broke defending himself and dealing with Constance. Please, George, you don't need the last step. It's already done."

The discussion went on for several hours, but in the end, Tony agreed to see it through the last step, "Provided two things. First, you have to tell me you are not suicidal. Second, that if the various pieces of the last act don't line up exactly, you'll agree to leave for New Jersey and let me mail the package."

"Fair enough. I've never been suicidal, Tony. In my worst moments suicide never entered my mind. A lot of inmates on death row commit suicide, but I never came close to it. Not then, not now. True, I don't have any particular need to prolong my life, but that doesn't translate into tossing it away without a fight."

"Fair enough. Now, New Jersey?"

"Agreed. No argument, just gratitude. I owe you both."

"Okay, George, what's the plan?"

"It's two a.m., Tony. Go home and get some sleep. We'll see how this plays in the morning. Now that Constance knows I'm alive, Alfred won't have to hold back. He'll open the cage and put every hound he's got on my trail. All we'll need is a little misdirection to take advantage of the frenzy."

George Laine fought sleep, unwilling to let go of the images of his family, especially the magical moment when he shook hands with his grandson. He dreamed about his parents for the first time in years, peaceful fragments seen through a gauzy lens. He woke up early, grateful for the quiet hours to reflect on his good fortune and plan his next move.

Tony came by with lunch. "Claire made clams with white sauce for you. They're still warm. Let's enjoy the meal before we talk about Alfred."

When they finished, Tony reported that Alfred had been up early mobilizing his troops.

"Even though it's Sunday morning, the Tenderloin is cranking. Looks like Kitty's heart attack has suddenly become a homicide. No surprise: you've been promoted from fire department rule breaker to a full-on ax murderer. For sure, there will be a warrant, publicity, the whole enchilada. By tomorrow, DAPO will be leaning on all its parole officers to squeeze their clients for tips. It'll be a full court press: broadcast news tonight, newspapers tomorrow. The picture they have is the one from your identity card; that's the one you'll see in the news. So far, no one seems to know how radically your look has changed."

"Strange as it sounds, Tony, all of this can work for us, but it does narrow the window considerably. We need to catch Alfred while he's still shouting what *he* wants, forgetting it might be smarter to think about what *I* might be after. First, though, we have to know where Alfred is. Hopefully, he's at home in his fortress protected by some bodyguards or maybe state police. My guess is he'll feel better with his own people, not with state cops who would limit what he could do if I show up. We also need to know where Constance is. It won't work if she's there. Far too dangerous for her, plus it would sink any real chance to talk to Alfred."

"All right, George, I'll get Robert and a couple of other guys on it right away. I've already looked up Rebecca's address. If you're right about her getting away from Alfred, that's the logical place to go. It should be easy to tell if she's there and out of the way. Getting rid of cops or bodyguards will be another matter. I suppose you have an idea how to do it?"

"Yeah, I do. If Constance has left, and Alfred has bodyguards, not state police, we'll just need to make a call to one of Alfred's trolls and say I'm hiding in Bayview. That should light the fuse."

By late afternoon, Robert confirmed that Constance was at Rebecca's house, a half-hour drive from her home in Northern Woods. Alfred was at home with two bodyguards on duty, one in a car in his driveway, the other in the house. Laine gave Tomaras's card to Robert with the number for DAPO and Dalton's office. They decided to make the call to Dalton because he would immediately contact Alfred. If they let Metzi know, he might just go off on his own looking for glory, inadvertently ruining the whole plan.

In the morning, one of Tony's men was assigned to watch Rebecca's house, while another drove through Northern Woods to make sure Alfred and his goons were still in place. Robert was sent to the city to scout Bayview for the right location to plant Laine. Then he would call Dalton on a throw-away cell phone, one with the locator switched on in case Dalton had the call traced. If the call had the desired effect, everyone would pounce on Bayview. The big question was whether Alfred would send in his clowns or just sit tight.

After making the call, Robert would return to the warehouse, pick up Laine, and take him to Northern Woods.

"I promised Tony I would drop the whole thing if his bodyguards are still there. And I will. If they've gone, I'll need about twenty minutes. I'll come out, walk down the street. You pick me up, and it's over. If I'm not out in half an hour, leave. "

After Robert left, Laine made an egg sandwich and settled in with Tony's well-worn copy of *The Old Man and the Sea*.

Chapter 35

"DIVISION OF PAROLE AND PROBATION. How may I direct your call?"

"I want to talk to Mr. Dalton."

"Mr. Dalton is not available. Would you like to leave a message?

"No. I need to talk to him. It's urgent. Tell him I know where George Laine is."

"Just a minute, sir. I'll see if I can locate him."

The hold lasted less than thirty seconds. "This is Edward Dalton. Who is this?"

"No names, Mr. Dalton. I have information about this guy Laine everyone is talking about. Are you interested?"

"Of course, but why call me? Why not the police?"

"Because you can do me a favor, and they can't."

"What kind of favor? Are you looking for money or what?"

"No money. I got a friend in San Quentin comin' up for parole in six months. His name is Harold Touchman. If I give you Laine, you put in a good word for my friend. Simple."

"And if your information is bogus, what happens to Touchman?"

"He's fucked."

"Okay, let's have it. Where is Laine?"

"Did you write it down? Harold Touchman. Got it?"

"Yeah, all set. Now, where is Laine?"

"He's in Bayview."

"That's it? Somewhere in Bayview?"

"Shut up a minute and listen. Here's how it went down. I'm comin' out of the Rusty Nail on Revere Avenue Saturday night, maybe eleven o'clock. A car drives right by me, ten feet away. I see this guy I know in the front seat, a con who did time in San Quentin. They call him 'Spider.' Then I see a guy in the back seat. So who notices shit like that, right? Well, this dude in the back, he ain't looking right or left, he ain't smilin', he's staring straight ahead like some kind of zombie. I'm saying to myself that guy needs a drink."

"And you think that was Laine? A guy in a car? That's it?"

"Hang on, Dalton. So I see the car, and it's got one of those tires they use when you get a flat. You know, the kind that looks too small for the car. So, okay, the car goes by and turns right on Hawes Street. So that's all there was, a con and a zombie in a fucked-up car. But on Sunday, I'm waiting for the Nail to open, and I see the same freaking car go by and turn down Hawes, just like the night before. Only this time the guy in the back wasn't there, just the guy drivin' and Spider."

"Get to the point; I'm a busy man. So far you haven't told me shit. So what does the guy look like, can you describe him?"

"Yeah, taller than Spider, dark hair, dark beard, and glasses."

"That's not him, mister, you…"

"Hear me out, Dalton. So the news comes on, and there's a picture of Laine, right? That's when I figured out why I paid attention to the guy in the car. The cops down here have been showing that picture around, and when I seen it again on TV, I said, 'Holy Shit!' That's the guy. Give him a shave, lose the glasses, and it's him."

"Okay, maybe it is. So where in Bayview is he? It's a big place."

"Look, I got you within a few blocks of him, starting with Revere and Hawes. Find the car and you got him."

"What's the car look like? Did you get a license number?"

"It's black, small four-door, kinda banged up, and it's got that weird tire right front. The license plate is bent over; that's the best I can do."

"Okay, we'll look into it."

"Harold Touchman, got it?"

"Yeah, I got it."

Chapter 36

"JUDGE, I GOT A TIP a while ago from a guy who says he saw Laine in Bayview Saturday night around eleven. Supposedly, he was in a car with two guys, one he recognized as a former inmate from San Quentin. He saw the car again Sunday, but he didn't put it together until he saw Laine's picture on the news. Problem is, he says the guy has dark hair, a beard, and glasses, but he was sure it was him. I called Metzi, he put it out, and I just heard they located the car exactly where the guy said. They're staking it out while they run the plates."

"Finally! It all fits together! The disguise—no big trick—and a couple of his old buddies to drive him around. The timing is right, too. That's just when Laine would have arrived back from Northern Woods. Simple and crude, right under our noses. I'll call Metzi and let him know I'm sending in a couple of my boys to help out; strictly unofficial, of course. But it sure would be sweet if they could catch up with Laine first. Either way, I want this over with today.

"Good work, Dalton."

Chapter 37

LAINE PREPARED HIS RECORDING APPARATUS, drank a cup of coffee, and returned to his book.

"You're right, Hemingway: 'A man can be destroyed but not defeated,'" he said out loud as he closed the book.

Tony and Robert arrived just before ten o'clock.

"He took the bait, George. The bodyguards left fifteen minutes ago. It sounds like every cop in San Francisco is in Bayview right now."

"And Constance?"

"Took the kid to school and went to the grocery store."

"Excellent! It's time to visit Alfred Preston."

The three men drove in silence to Northern Woods, passing the house once to be as sure as possible the bodyguards were gone. Laine got out of the car well down the block from the house.

"Twenty minutes, maybe a little more. If I'm late, move on. See you in a little bit, then on to New Jersey."

George walked up the driveway and rang the doorbell. The door opened as far as the door chain would allow.

"Hello, George. I should have known you had one more trick up your sleeve."

"Hello, Alfred. May I come in? We need to talk."

A small semiautomatic pistol rose in the gap. "I could kill you right here."

"True, but then you wouldn't know what else to expect from me. It's better for both of us if we talk. Can I come in or are we doing this on the doorstep?"

"Yes, but first, lift up your jacket and turn around." Laine complied, followed by pulling his trouser legs up to his knees.

"I'm not armed, Alfred. I didn't come here to kill you."

The door closed, the chain rattled, and the door swung open. Preston was standing well back from the door, his pistol pointed at Laine's chest.

"Okay, George, let's do this again. Jacket up and turn slowly around."

"I told you I'm not armed, Alfred."

"Just a precaution, George. It's not a gun I worry about. It's that bulge just above your belt in the back. Pull up the shirt, George. Or die right here, right now."

Laine lifted his shirt revealing the small recorder and a wire running around his waist.

"My, my! How sophisticated! A wire. So that's what our talk was to be! Get Judge Preston to reveal all. Then what? Call the cops? Take that goddamn thing off. All of it!"

Laine removed the wire and, at Preston's direction, placed it on a side table.

"Good, now we can really talk. Have a seat in the living room, George."

They sat in two armchairs separated by about eight feet. Preston kept the pistol pointed at Laine.

"Okay, George, tell me why I shouldn't shoot you right this minute. I'd be a hero, and you'd be out of my hair."

"What's the hurry? Aren't you curious to know why I've come? The wire, by the way, was an afterthought, maybe useful if after we parted you decided to come after me again."

"Really? What makes you so sure you'll be able to walk out of here?"

"Because you have no reason to kill me. In fact, you're better off if you don't. Kill me, and you'll have a real mess on your hands, starting with Constance. Hear me out; you may change your mind."

"And the wire? Are you telling me you weren't counting on getting something embarrassing on that thing? That would have been a bigger mess, right?"

"Not really. Like I said, the wire was just insurance. But let's not waste time on the wire; let's talk about why I'm here and what I expect from you."

"I'm all ears. But I warn you, George, if I get bored, I'll put a hole in you. Now, tell me, why the hell are you sitting in my living room right now?"

"I've come to look you in the eye and say I know you killed Julia Penthoser, framed me, and with the help of your complicit father, sent me off to be executed."

"Bravo for you, George. But wouldn't it have been a lot safer to call me up or send a letter?"

"Safer? I'm not interested in safety. That's your mindset, not mine. You start with fear and end up with violence. Fear dulls your brain, Alfred. It takes you down convoluted trails to indecent places. There's no peace when all you think about is protecting yourself. You end up isolated and alone.

"I came here to reclaim the feeling of peace you ripped out of my heart so many years ago. I'm also here to speak for Julia Penthoser and Kitty Marren, to give them a voice to confront you as well."

"Who's Kitty Marren, by the way?"

"The woman you had murdered at the hotel, probably by Metzi or Carlos. Your boy Dalton certainly had a hand in it, too."

"Oh, yeah, the hooker. Whatever. And who cares who popped her? Go on, I didn't mean to interrupt. So far, all I hear you saying is you want some sort of revenge for yourself and the other two, right?"

"Wrong. That's your thinking again. Revenge is just another crime committed to make up for the last one. It's like biting down on a toothache thinking that'll make the pain go away."

"Okay, no revenge. How about justice? Back to the wire. Get the goods on me and bring me to justice. Sound closer to the mark?"

"No closer. I've been immersed in the consequences of justice every day for a half a century, Alfred, and I'm not impressed. Again, you're thinking about this strictly from your point of view. I'm only interested in delivering a message. It's for me, for us. What happens next is of no consequence. What you do with it is your business. I'd like to think there's something positive in it for you, but that's for you to figure out."

"Pardon me if I seem a little skeptical about you not wanting to bring some sort of misery down on my head. I can't quite wrap my brain around the idea you would be content to just deliver your message and walk out of here. Surely, you'd like to see me clapped in irons."

"No. In the near run, what happens to you is in your hands. Maybe you'll try to do the right thing, get a start on coming to grips with what you've done. But later, in some way I can't even imagine, you'll have to deal with your crimes."

"Sounds like you think God will have a special spot for me, George."

"I don't think about it that way."

"Well, that's lovely. Quite a lesson. But I'm still having trouble with the justice part. I've got a different theory. I think you haven't gone to the police with any of this because you can't prove a goddamn thing. You say you know I killed Julia, but there isn't a scrap of evidence of it. And good luck proving the other one, whatever her name was. By the way, a tape without anything to back it up would be useless. All I have to say is I was too frightened to disagree with you. I just wanted to get you out of here. Bang! End of case."

"You're right, I can't offer the kind of proof that would stand up in a court. But I can prove it to you. Part of coming here is to make that very point. I am certain you killed Julia because I know why. Until I understood that, I was still floundering."

"Very interesting. How, exactly, do you know I killed Julia? Or how I framed you and magically got the courts to go along? Except for the frigging Supreme Court, that is."

"You were always on my short list, Alfred, but I just couldn't picture you as a sex-crazed murderer. Every time I pondered it, I came back to the same thought: how could it be Alfred? He's lazy and entitled, to be sure, but a murderer? The day I left San Quentin, I still had no idea who did it. Even after I was moved into the Tenderloin, I was so confused and overwhelmed, the last thing on my mind was revisiting the horror of being condemned for Julia's death. When it became clear someone was trying to put me back in prison, I didn't think about you, at least not immediately. To me, you were probably a retired patent attorney, living in a nice house somewhere, maybe married with a family. Not the picture of a killer.

"My only wish was to be left alone, to find a good book, and someday take a peaceful walk with a friend of mine. Even when I found out you had married my wife, I still didn't see that as proof you killed Julia."

"So you didn't know I'd married Connie? Wow! I never thought of that. Somehow I assumed you'd know."

"No, it wasn't until I was given some old documents from my days on death row that I found out."

"Who gave you that stuff? I'll bet it was that frigging warden. What else did you find out?"

"That your father did not file a second appeal. But even then, I wasn't certain you killed her. Where was the motive? You had just met Julia—what could possibly turn 'lazy and entitled' into 'vicious murderer'? Still, I tried to leave it alone. But you kept pushing until I finally broke and started trying to figure out who was so desperate to destroy me. I went to the internet—it didn't take long to find you. There you were, a rich, retired judge. How in the world did that happen?"

"And when you saw Connie, I'll bet that was a startle! Is that when you made up your mind to come after me?"

"No, it wasn't. True, it was wrenching, but I had no desire to disrupt her life. Seeing her and knowing that she and Rebecca were healthy was good enough. But it did drive me to look even harder at you—and your father.

"I went to the law library and found the first appeal, the one your father told me he spent so much time preparing. It was three pages long, Alfred. Three pages! He couldn't have spent more than five minutes dictating it. And there was no second appeal. The message to the courts was clear: he's guilty, go ahead and execute him, please.

"I also found out you had a juvenile record—at least five arrests—and you were involved in an assault case in college. Clearly, your father got a dismissal and your records were expunged. But they didn't disappear. Then I found your 1970 application to restore your gun rights. It takes a serious charge to lose your gun rights, and ten years just to qualify for a review. I don't know what you did, but it had to be serious. But there was your father, well-practiced in getting you out of trouble. He got me sent to death row; in comparison, restoring your right to own the gun must have been child's play. Ironic, isn't it, Alfred? He made it possible for you to legally own the gun you're pointing at me now."

"And coming here makes it possible for me to legally kill you. Some irony! We can agree on that."

"Tell me, Alfred, did you and your father ever talk openly about the fact you killed Julia? Or was it more subtle than that?"

"He never said anything to me directly. I just remember one day he said he thought you were being framed. I said something like, who would do that? He got all weird on me. We never talked about it again. He didn't want to know."

"How touching. Anyway, the more I learned, the clearer it was you killed Julia, a jolt that made me realize continuing to hide the truth from Constance was not only impossible, but something she would reject on its face. I always thought there was some grand mystery behind Julia's death, some fact everyone was missing that would explain it. I couldn't see it because it was too obvious. It really was about pure, insane lust. I couldn't begin to imagine such a thing in someone who seemed so controlled—so normal. In the same way, it never occurred to me there were two killers: you and your father. You, the predator; your father, the protector. He was every bit as guilty as you are.

"You'd make a great detective, George. But I'm still mystified why you felt you had to come here and tell me all of this."

"It's simple, Alfred: I came here to confront you with the truth. I'm here for myself, Julia, Kitty, and everyone else whose lives you've destroyed. It brings my nightmare to a close. It's your nightmare now, Alfred."

"So that's it? All of this for some kind of corny symbolism? And you imagined making a deal with me after putting this together, fucking up my marriage, and costing me a frigging fortune? Why shouldn't I just shoot you?!"

"Because I'm no threat to you. Another irony! There's no case against you, Alfred, no proof of your crimes. I'm a wanted man on the run. If I'm caught, I go back to prison. Meanwhile, I'm out of your life. Hopefully, you'll do something positive with what we've talked about.

"That's all I have to say," Laine said standing up.

"Pretty stale bread, George," Alfred said bringing the gun up to eye level. "Did you expect me to get all weepy and turn myself in?"

"I don't know what you'll do, though letting go of this would go a long way toward relieving your conscience."

"My conscience isn't troubling me. You are."

"Then do it for your soul, Alfred."

"Soles are for shoes, George," Alfred said as he steadied the front sight over Laine's heart and pulled the trigger.

The .25 caliber pistol exploded, its 50-grain bullet striking the left side of Laine's chest. For an instant, Laine stood looking at Alfred through the small cloud of gray smoke enveloping him, his mouth dropped open, but he said nothing as he sank to his knees, toppled over backwards, his folded legs causing him to roll slightly onto his left side. His eyes closed, and blood began to saturate his shirt.

Alfred stepped forward pointing the gun at the motionless figure. He prodded Laine's leg with his foot, stepped back, and said, "Thanks for dropping by, George." He pocketed the gun, walked to the door, and peered through a glass panel at the street beyond. No movement. From the door, he went to his den across the front hall from the living room, opened a drawer under a bookcase, took out a bone-handled hunting knife, and using his handkerchief, wiped the blade and handle. He walked back across the hall, knelt next to Laine's body, and carefully folded both of Laine's limp hands several times around the knife's blade and grip. He then let it fall onto the rug next to his right hand.

"You're right-handed, aren't you, George? Probably so. But who's going to care, anyway?"

He went to the front door, opened it slightly, checking to see if anyone was rushing up the driveway. With the door open enough to reach around from the inside, he used the butt of his gun to break one of the glass panels, the one closest to the lock handle on the inside. He closed the door enough to slip the chain into its slot, and using both hands, yanked the door open, thinking it would snap the chain. But the chain held, instead ripping off a chunk of the doorjamb, leaving the wood swinging on the end of the chain.

"Even better," he said, stepping back to admire his work. He went back to the living room, sat down, and dialed 911.

Judge Preston's call was received at 11:14 a.m. The judge reported he had been attacked by a knife-wielding intruder, quickly reassuring the dispatcher he had been able to fight off the man and shoot him.

"We're sending help. Have you been wounded, sir?"

"No."

"Is the intruder wounded?"

"No, he's dead. I'm sure of it."

He hung up and called Dalton.

"Listen, Dalton, I've got to be quick—"

But Dalton interrupted saying breathlessly, "Judge, listen— that call about Bayview was a hoax..."

"Old news, Dalton. In fact, I'm sitting here looking at George Laine right now. He's lying on my living room floor, dead as a smelt. I knew the whole thing smelled bad. The bastard came roaring through my front door with a goddamn knife, but I was ready for him. So it's over, Dalton. Turns out *I* was one who had to do it. But, listen, that's not the point. I want you and your Keystone Cops to find out who was helping him. It has to be someone really well-connected, and for once, I haven't got any idea...oh, shit, here come the cops. Gotta go. Get on it, hear me?"

The police were the first to arrive, four patrolmen and two detectives, followed closely by firemen and EMTs. The two officers, Detective Thomas Orlando and Sergeant Bill Moses, immediately went into the living room, walked around the blood-soaked figure on the floor, kneeling several times for a closer look, carefully avoiding any contact with the body. While Sergeant Moses took pictures, Detective Orlando picked up the knife with his handkerchief, dropped it into a plastic bag, and suggested they all move across the hall to the den so they could talk out of the way of the EMTs swarming into the room. In just a few seconds, they straightened Laine's legs, rolled him onto his back, and ripped open his shirt. One EMT attached a blood pressure cuff to his right arm, another pressed a bandage onto the small, bloody hole oozing blood from his chest, and a third scanned his chest for movement while feeling for a carotid pulse.

"I think he's got a pulse. It's really weak, feels like a beat every two or three seconds."

He slipped a stethoscope into his ears and yelled, "SHUT UP!" as he pressed the bell end onto Laine's chest without even trying to wipe away the blood.

Everyone froze in place, even Alfred, already anxious to tell the story of his harrowing experience.

"Can't tell. You got any pressure?" he asked the man operating the cuff as it hissed down in search of a beat.

"He's alive. I've got a little pressure, thirty systolic! Oxygen! AED NOW!"

Another group of emergency workers rushed in pulling a wheeled stretcher. A loud "CLEAR!" was heard followed by the thump of the defibrillator. It was followed by two more thumps.

The detectives introduced themselves, and while Sergeant Moses started to write down the judge's statement, Orlando took Alfred's gun, inspected it quickly, removed the clip, and shucked the breech slide, throwing the chambered round onto the floor.

He picked up the bullet, looked at it for a moment, then dropped the gun, clip, and bullet into another bag.

Turning to Preston, he shook his head and said, "That was one really close call, Judge. You're damn lucky you had that gun." He went on to apologize for having to put His Honor through any more stress but said they had to get as much information as they could quickly, especially if the intruder had accomplices who might want to come back to "finish the job."

The judge thanked him for his understanding and promised to do his best with the detective's questions.

Orlando started by asking if he had any idea who the man on the floor was, or why he would target him for such a vicious attack. The judge seemed more concerned about the drama unfolding across the hall but answered in a distracted way that, yes, he did have a good idea of who the man was. He watched as Laine was lifted onto a stretcher and wheeled out the door to a waiting Advanced Life Support vehicle. In seconds it was gone, lights flashing and siren screaming. The officers waited for the judge to gather himself.

"Sorry," Alfred said. "It's just so crazy seeing that in my living room. I can't imagine how he could still be alive with a bullet in his heart."

"His heart? You had time to aim?"

"No, of course not. It was a reflex. But the blood...all over his chest..."

"Yes, sir, you're right. Well, hopefully they'll be able to save him, and we can find out what the hell made him do something as crazy as this."

Alfred explained they wouldn't need Laine to tell them. "Like I said, I know who that has to be." He explained he had been warned that a man named George Laine, a murderer recently paroled from San Quentin and already wanted for killing a woman in San Francisco, was almost certainly out to get him, too. He explained that he knew Laine many years ago when they were graduate students together in LA, before Laine was convicted of the rape and murder of another member of their group.

"My dad was a defense attorney. He represented Laine *pro bono* at his trial, but the evidence was clear. The jury convicted him and sentenced him to death. Even Dad said it was a good thing the jury saw through his story. Of course, Laine blamed Dad. He even threatened to kill him if he ever had the chance. Can you imagine? He blamed Dad for his conviction!"

"Whoa! What a story! For starters, how come he wasn't executed?"

"Freak accident of the legal system. The state Supreme Court voided the death penalty in sixty-seven, and he got life from there. And before you ask, the life sentence technically carried a chance for parole. He never should have gotten out, but he fooled a couple of sob sisters on the parole board into thinking he was reformed. Crazy, but they let him out. Even worse, they sent him to San Francisco, right into my backyard. Didn't take him long to revert, kill a girl in his boarding house, and come after me."

"Why you? You're not the one who put him there, right?"

"Yeah, but there's another twist here you need to know. We were friends, grad students. It's a tight community. After he got sent up, we—that is, me and my family—tried to help his wife. We got close, and eventually we married. You can see how that would look to him."

"Holy shit, Judge! If he wasn't crazy before, he sure would have been after he learned that! He had a long time to stew about it, too. No wonder he came after you. By the way, where is your wife? Good thing she wasn't here, right?"

"Our daughter just got married. My wife is at her house taking care of her kid while she's on her honeymoon. I'm not looking forward to that call. Is there much more? I really feel awful, and I do have to call her. She'll be scared shitless if she hears this on the radio and I haven't called."

"Sure, Judge, just a couple of questions while my guys get some more pictures. We can finish up the rest tomorrow if there are any loose ends to tie up—always are in these situations. By the way, I can come back here, or if you'd prefer—maybe to keep your wife out of this—we can meet at the station. Your call. But first, tell me exactly what happened from the instant you heard him break in. You say you were ready for him. Where were you, and did you have your gun?"

"Yeah, I had the gun. The place was locked up, and I was in the den, at my desk."

Orlando walked over to the window, looked outside, then back to the desk. "There's no curtain; you had a view of most of the yard. Did you see him coming?"

"No, like I said, I was at my desk. I didn't sit next to the freaking window, Lieutenant. The house was locked up; I had my gun. Why are you asking?"

"Just curious. So, the first thing you know, what—you heard him smash the door?"

"No, Lieutenant, the glass. I heard the glass break. I grabbed the gun, ran out in the hall just as he came through the door. He stumbled, then came at me with the knife like this," he said, raising his hand above his shoulder. "I backed into the living room, he kept coming at me, and I fired. He went down, and I called nine-one-one. You have a problem with that? Was I supposed to make nice with him, offer him coffee or something?"

"Take it easy, Judge, I'm just trying to see how it went down, how come he ended up on the living room floor. But it all makes sense." He paused. "Are you sure he was coming at you when you fired? He didn't stop or say something?"

"No, why?"

"I dunno, just seems like he would have fallen forward after you shot him. You know, momentum."

"Have you ever been hit in the chest with a bullet, Lieutenant? It will drop you on your ass."

"You're right, Judge. Happened to a friend of mine. He was wearing a bulletproof vest and it still broke three ribs."

"My point exactly."

Orlando's men found the spent shell casing, finished taking pictures, and prepared to leave. "We'll leave a car out front with a couple of cops just be sure no one tries again. Would you like us to go pick up your wife for you?"

"No, she probably can't leave the kid. I'll call her. That's my responsibility."

"Okay, then. You can go ahead and get someone to fix the door, we have what we need. Is there anything else we can do for you?"

Yes, there was. Alfred asked if his men could roll up the rug and put it in the garage. "I don't want my wife to come home and see all that blood."

The rug was removed, and the Lieutenant and his deputy got in their car.

"You thinking what I'm thinking, Lieutenant?"

"That it don't look right?"

"Yeah. For starters, did you see the glass? It was about a foot from the door sill. So the door had to be open when the glass was broken. And that knife—where did a down-and-outer like Laine get such a fancy blade? By the way, do you really have a friend who was shot in the vest and got three broken ribs?"

"Actually, yes, but the bullet was from a forty-five, not a puny twenty-five like that thing," he said pointing to the gun in a bag on the seat. "And look at the slug—it's jacketed. I don't think they even make a hollow point for a twenty-five, and even if they did, it wouldn't throw a raging bull on his ass. And take a look at the butt on that pistol. See anything?"

"Yeah, scratches." Looking at the knife handle through its plastic bag he added, "No scratches."

"Right. The judge isn't telling the whole story. And where was the wife? Babysitting while her husband is in mortal danger? I'm sure this guy Laine is a creep, but I don't buy the rest of it. We've got to talk to the captain about this."

When they shared their concern with the captain, they were reminded that Judge Preston was an important member of the law enforcement community, pillar of the community, and whatever "corrections" he may have made to his story were either understandable, given the terror he endured, or simply irrelevant.

"Save the Sherlock shit for the bad guys. Wrap this up."

Tony and Robert knew Laine's plan had gone horribly wrong even before the first police car came screaming down Pine Crest Road. They heard the 911 operator's call over their police radio scanner. Neither spoke until they were back on the highway.

"The way dispatcher sounded, George is dead. I'm numb."

"Me, too. I'm shocked but not surprised. He knew exactly what he was doing. I don't imagine he even thought about dying. And it certainly wasn't suicide—it was something else. I can't begin to get my head around it."

"It's out of our hands now, Tony."

"No, it's not, Robert. Get us back to the warehouse, I've got a job for you."

"That package George sent you?"

"Yeah. I want you to take it to his PO, Tomaras. You've got to go straight to her office, do what you have to, but get it into her hands. If she isn't there, find out where she is, or wait for her. And whatever you do, don't get detained or give it to anyone else.

"Another thing—I've got to get Constance's phone number."

"You're going to call her? That's pretty risky, isn't it? If anyone connects you to this...well, you'll be in a heap of trouble."

"True. But maybe the recorder worked. Or maybe he's alive and makes it. Maybe..."

"Too many 'maybes,' Boss."

"I owe it to George. Even if I get busted, I owe him."

They rode in silence back to the warehouse. Robert left for the city at 12:30.

Just after the police left, Alfred called the Simazen Rug Service to have his Persian rug picked up, explaining it was soaked with blood and he didn't want it to dry and leave a permanent stain. His next call went to Constance.

"What do you want?" she snapped in a flat, icy tone.

"Look, this isn't easy, but I have to tell you, George came to the house, attacked me! I had to defend myself..."

"You killed him?"

"No, I mean, I shot him, but..."

"He's still alive?"

"He was when they left…"

"Where did they take him?"

"San Mateo, I guess, but look, Connie, you need to come…"
The line was already dead.

His next call went to Dalton to report that Laine could still
be alive, barely, but "just in case," he wanted Captain Henderson
to immediately revoke Laine's parole, get word to the San Mateo
police that he wanted jurisdiction, and if Laine survived, he
wanted him moved to San Francisco Trauma while arrangements
were made for a speedy transfer back to the San Quentin prison
hospital.

"Make sure they know he's a prisoner, not a suspect. I want
him under twenty-four hour guard. No lawyers, no visitors,
nothing! I don't care if he's in a coma or not—no one, I mean *no
one*, gets anywhere near him. The San Mateo cops will love to
get this mess off their hands. I'll make a few calls just to make
sure it happens." He also instructed Dalton to see if the call
that sent the cops to Bayview could be traced. "Put Metzi and
Carlos on the people at the Madrid, especially that manager you
told me about. Oh, and nail the caterer who let Laine into the
Northern Woods Club. Pull out his frigging fingernails if you
have to, but find out who made that happen."

"What about your wife, Judge? Does she know about this
yet?"

"Yeah, I called her. She's really confused. Best thing I can
do is leave her alone. When she sees all of this stuff in the
news, she'll realize she's been wrong about him. It'll take a while,
but she'll come back. I'm counting on Rebecca to help me, too.
She doesn't have any reason to doubt me, even if Connie tells her
George is her father."

"I don't envy you, Judge. But I'll do my part. I'm on this,
starting with Henderson."

"I knew I could count on you. Thanks."

Chapter 38

As soon as she hung up on Alfred, Constance started pacing, her mind raging with confusion, fear, remorse, and above all—anger. Nothing fit together, nothing made sense. "Think!" she kept telling herself as she fought off the impulse to jump in her car and go to the hospital. But she knew it wouldn't do any good, especially showing up in her current state of agitation. *Besides,* she told herself, *George could already be dead. Then what?* And, if he was grievously wounded, she wouldn't have a prayer of getting near him, much less talking to him. No, the first thing to do was call Rebecca. That couldn't wait no matter what else was going on.

She dialed Rebecca's number, but got a recording saying that number could not be reached. *Of course,* she said to herself. *Stupid! They're in Baja.* She found the travel information Rebecca had left, switched to a landline, called, and immediately got through to the Playa Azul. She explained as calmly as she could that there was a family emergency, and their guest, Mrs. Upton, needed to call her mother immediately. "And tell her that her son is not involved."

She waited, paced, cried, cursed herself for being so disorganized, and tried to rehearse what she would say to Rebecca. Fifteen minutes later her phone rang.

"Mother! What's happening! Is Erik okay? Are you okay? Is Dad okay? What happened?!"

"Listen to me, please, Rebecca! Erik is fine, so am I, and so is…your father. But there's been an incident at the house…"

"It's that man from the wedding isn't it, Mom? That person from your past you told me not to worry about. Right?!"

"Yes, it is. But before you go any further, I need you to get home. Can you do that, please?"

"Yes, of course, I can."

"When can you get here? I mean, can you get here by tomorrow?"

"Tomorrow? Mom, this is Baja, not Baghdad. They have flights every hour. We'll get there today, I promise. Where are you now?"

"I'm at your house. Erik's in school. He has band practice today, so he won't get home until six. If you're not back, I promise to be here when he comes home. Call me the minute you get to the airport."

"Where's Dad? Why isn't he there with you?"

"Don't worry about your father. I just spoke with him—he's at the house and he's fine. Please, let's not waste time. I'll see you later."

Constance continued to pace, but slower, as her thinking began to overtake her agitation. As difficult as it would be, she dialed the San Mateo Hospital. She knew better than ask the operator—or even the ER—for information. Instead, she asked to be connected with the administrator. His secretary answered, said he was busy, and would have to call her back. Marshaling all the control she could manage, she told the secretary she was Judge Alfred Preston's wife, this was an emergency, and she would hold while Mr. Martello was located.

"Mrs. Preston, this is Arthur Martello. You must be calling about the situation at your house...The intruder is here in our ER."

"I know that, Mr. Martello. I just spoke with my husband. I'm calling to find out about the man who was shot. His name is George Laine. Is he alive?"

"George Laine? I didn't know the name. But, you see, I am not allowed to say anything about the man at this point."

"You can damn well tell me if he's alive or not, Mr. Martello. By the way, didn't we meet at the sponsor's party for the Eye Ball last April?"

"Ah, yes, I do recall that. Look, Mrs. Preston, I only know that the man is in the ER—he's alive but too critical to be moved to a Class One trauma center. They're working on him now. That's all I know. And before you ask, please do not come here right now. The police won't let anybody near the ER. Please, I have to go now."

Constance said she understood, thanked Mr. Martello, hung up, and dropped into a chair, sobbing, but still trying to think what she would say to Rebecca when she came home.

About twenty minutes later her phone rang.

"Constance?"

"Who is this?" she asked cautiously.

"My name is Tony. I am the man who has been helping George. We need to talk."

Chapter 39

THE AMBULANCE CARRYING GEORGE LAINE arrived at the San Mateo Hospital emergency room at 11:55 a.m. The stretcher was rushed into the room reserved for emergency surgery. The ER physician and a general surgeon were already in place along with a "crash team" of nurses and x-ray and lab technicians. A unit of type O negative blood was started pending results of the lab test to determine George's blood type. The blood bank was alerted because of the certainty that the patient's devastating chest wound would require many more units of blood. George was barely alive, his blood pressure far too low to perfuse his organs. His left lung had collapsed, and he had a "sucking wound" of the chest, meaning the negative pressure in his chest cavity was lost because of the hole in his chest wall, preventing what was left of his lung from inflating.

The team went about its work with steady, practiced precision, following the steps needed to increase his blood volume, get oxygen into his system, assess the damage to his heart and lungs, and decide what surgical steps might be needed to stabilize him enough to have a chance to survive. It was too early to think about what survival might look like, given the chance of brain damage from lack of oxygen, stroke, or any of a number of other possible bad offshoots of suffering an internal explosion.

His clothes were cut off in the immediate moments of treatment. A wire and small microphone were found inside his belt buckle. The wire was taped to his belly with flesh-colored adhesive tape. It ran around his back, across his buttocks, ending at his anus.

"My God! This man is wearing a wire!" a nurse called out. "Do you want me to pull it out of his rectum?"

"NO!" said the surgeon. "Way too much vagal stimulation, his heart can't take it. We've got a cop here, everybody! I want the hospital administrator here right now. Don't touch that thing, and keep his belt here. No one says anything about this! Go!"

Mr. Martello arrived, was told about the wire and probability of having a device in his rectum. He knew immediately that the county District Attorney had to be notified, and when the device was removed, it had to remain with the victim, never out of sight of the surgeon, its chain of possession carefully documented.

Though no one said it out loud, thinking the victim was a policeman, and not the criminal he had been labeled when he first arrived, had a subtle, animating effect on the team. Everyone was thinking the same thing—we can't lose this one.

Howard Fyne, the San Mateo District Attorney, was immediately notified; ironically, just as he was first hearing about the attack on Judge Preston from the sheriff's office. He immediately sent two assistants to the hospital to retrieve whatever the device might be, adding that they were not to let anyone else— sheriff's people or county police—touch it. The assistants arrived at the hospital about twenty minutes later, took possession of the pants and belt with part of the wire attached, then stationed themselves outside the operating area to wait for the surgeon to remove whatever was on the other end of the wire. They did not discuss why they were there with the county police officers.

Meanwhile, George Laine was still alive. His blood pressure, while up slightly, was still dangerously low. The sucking wound had been temporarily closed, and chest tubes had been inserted to remove blood still leaking into the chest. A tube had been inserted through his trachea to provide artificial breathing, heavily saturated with oxygen. A thoracic surgeon had arrived, felt that Laine's heart was probably not severely damaged, but almost certainly the protective sac surrounding the heart had been torn. They prepared to move Laine to an upstairs OR so they could open his chest, either when he gained enough ground to tolerate it, or he would die without one last heroic effort. The DA's men followed the group.

Mr. Martello also fielded a call from Captain Henderson, head of DAPO in San Francisco, who explained that George Laine was a "Violated Parolee," thus a prisoner of the state, and his division would be in charge of guarding him until he was well enough to be sent back to San Quentin. Mr. Martello was warned that no one other than hospital personnel could to be allowed anywhere near him. Captain Henderson appreciated Mr. Martello's cooperation. Mr. Martello didn't say anything about the DA's involvement, reasoning that his troops would be there before Henderson's.

Let them fight it out, he thought. *And I'll have to be damn careful what I say to Mrs. Preston, too. What a mess!*

Chapter 40

"Tony? Tony who? You know George? How?"

"I know him well. But please, no last names. Let me talk, and if you get a call from anyone, take it; I'll call you back."

"Who are you? Are you the one who got George into the wedding? Are you the one who sent George to my husband's house? How could you do that?!"

"Just listen to me, Constance. George is a dear friend of mine. We met in prison when I was young and stupid. My time with George, the talks we had, the books we read, it helped me survive in there. When I got out, I was able to take charge of my life in a way I never imagined before. I owe the life I have now to George.

"So, to answer your question: Yes, I did help George, some of it very reluctantly. In fact, I didn't want him to go to the wedding at all. And, I *begged* him not to confront Alfred. I knew it would turn out badly, at least from my—from our—point of view. But George was insistent; he would have found a way to do it with or without me. It's hard to explain, but..."

"No, I get it, Tony. It's all coming back in a huge memory wave... Please—tell me what you can. I promise to listen."

Over the next twenty minutes, Tony told Constance what he knew about George, starting with the shock of learning a scant six weeks before that he was out of prison and living in the Tenderloin. He said the reason he even knew he was paroled was because "sources" told him there was a guy just out of San Quentin that somebody high up the ladder was trying to get sent back.

"You can't imagine the shock when I heard the guy was George Laine."

He told her about their meeting, what an amazing moment it was to see his friend again, free and outside of prison. He explained he only knew George as a fellow inmate, and that in all their years together, George had never mentioned his crime or anything about his life before incarceration.

"Most inmates can't shut up about their conviction, what a raw deal they got, but not George. He never seemed bitter about what had happened to him. Even the part about his nine years on death row..."

"Nine years! Alone for nine years, Tony!"

"I know it, but somehow he figured out how to focus only on what was right in front of him and accept what he couldn't control. He never said it like that, but that's how it seemed to me...

"But let me get back to our meeting. When he got out, he was in a state of shock. It may sound hard to believe, but the idea of parole never entered his mind. His life was there, in prison. A half a century of isolation narrowed his life down to one endless, unchanging routine. There was no hint of it ever changing, and he didn't waste a minute thinking otherwise. He didn't see it coming. He was a wreck at first, but being George, he pulled himself together and tried to figure out how to survive in a world he no longer knew.

"And before you ask, in all the time he was locked up, he never knew you were married to Alfred. When he was released, the warden gave him some old records, stuff he had no idea about before. That's when he found out you had married Alfred, someone George said wasn't trustworthy—an opportunist. At that point, he had no idea where you were, or if you were even still with him. But it didn't matter; he was determined to leave it alone.

"I brought up the rumors about someone wanting to put him back in San Q. He told me he couldn't tell if someone was after him or if it was just a holdover of prison paranoia. It helped him to know he wasn't misreading the situation. When we talked about who might have it in for him, I brought up his crime—

whatever it was—I didn't know any details—thinking maybe someone from the past could have a grudge. He didn't think so. For whatever reason, I just blurted out that whatever his crime was, I didn't think he was guilty of anything. He was really uncomfortable about it, but he finally said I was right.

"Of course, I asked if he had any idea who could have done it, and if that person could still be out there. Again, he didn't see it. When we got into it, he said that in the past, he had even wondered if Alfred could have somehow been involved. But he had long ago dismissed the idea. He thought Alfred had to be an academic, probably a retired lawyer somewhere. Whoever was behind the pressure was obviously a powerful figure, more likely someone related to an inmate he had crossed in the past.

"When I asked him what Alfred's last name was and he said, 'Preston,' I started to sweat. And when I told him what his wife's first name was, it all came out... It was a terrible moment for George. But even if it was true, he said, he wasn't going to change anything he was doing, and he certainly had no intention of trying to contact you."

"Oh, Tony, I can't imagine how badly both of you felt. I'm shaking right now. Is that all there was?"

"Yes, at that point. There was no plan. I gave George my phone number, and he went back to what he was doing. Just in the last few days, I learned George spent a lot of time at the library learning to use the internet. Once he had that, he couldn't resist looking for you. Whatever he thought about Alfred, he was happy to see you again. He wasn't at all tempted to try to contact you. It was a huge relief for him to see pictures of you and Rebecca, knowing that what he had done on death row and beyond had possibly made a real difference for you and Rebecca. That was enough, more than he could have ever dreamed possible."

"You can't imagine how much this means to me, Tony. Like George, I never dreamed I would have anything approaching closure with him. Even if he doesn't make it now, I have that gift. Thank you. And by the way, I never for one second imagined that George was guilty of anything. He was framed, Tony. Framed!"

"That's the scariest part. But you know that takes us even a step deeper. We have to talk about Alfred. Can I go on?"

"Yes," she said quietly, almost in a whisper.

"George was in a lot of distress when he found out you had married Alfred. He understood it, knowing the state you were in at the time that he was sent up. But he still had a lot of doubt about Alfred's motives—then and now. And to be brutally frank, the more all of this unfolded, the more he suspected that Alfred had a hand in trying to get him revoked."

"Why?! Was he afraid George would come looking for me, mess up our life, and maybe let Rebecca find out Alfred isn't her real father? That had to be it, right? Tell me that's it, Tony."

Tony was silent for a few moments, started to speak but Constance broke in. "Holy God, Tony, you don't...you're not saying George thinks Alfred had something to do with Julia's—that's the name of the girl who was killed—with Julia's death? Does he think Alfred is covering for someone? After all, Alfred was there throughout that hideous time. But Alfred's father was his lawyer. Surely if Alfred knew something, he would have told his father, right? And that could have saved..."

Suddenly, Constance was silent. Tony waited.

"Listen, Constance, don't take this past what we know. I have more to tell you, but not now. You need to know that if George survives, and nothing else gets in the way, he will almost certainly be sent back to San Quentin. It's the quickest way to isolate him. You'll have to be ready for that. But there's a possibility other facts could emerge that could change everything. I'm working on that part now. Please don't ask me about it. You can help George most right now by helping Rebecca. She's going to need all your attention. Let me work in the background. I'll be back in touch as this plays out."

"Wait a minute, please, Tony! I have so many questions!"

"All right, but quickly. We can talk more later."

"Please, Tony, I just have to get this straight. You're telling me that George spent all those years in prison not knowing anything about me at all, right? And it wasn't until he was paroled that he found out I had married Alfred? That's all he knew the first time you saw him?"

"That's right. He didn't know anything else. He thought Alfred was a lawyer, and you were probably living a quiet life in some college town. He was rattled, but everything that was happening to him made him anxious. He was dealing with it like he always did—think it through, don't let it control you. So, he saw the good side for you, and just wanted to leave it at that, no matter what he thought about Alfred.

"When we put it all together the first time I saw him, he still didn't believe it, especially the part about Alfred being a big-deal judge. All the rest of it came out later when he learned how to get around the internet. He didn't want to think about it, but it was more than he could hold back. That's when he started to fill in the blanks and realized it was Alfred who was pulling the strings. Like you, he wanted to believe it was just about using his muscle to keep himself secure. Logically, it's understandable Alfred would worry about him showing up and exploding his happy life. But as the pressure got more intense, George began to think there was more to it. Then there was an event that tipped over the whole thing."

"The murder of the girl in his boarding house, right? RIGHT?"

"Yes. So you heard about that. Well, George expected something, and when it happened, they damn near caught him. If that hadn't happened, I think he would have let me send him far away from here. But killing that girl and planting evidence pointing to him really jolted him, and when he saw your daughter's wedding notice, he snapped. He couldn't play dead and protect you from that knowledge any longer. He realized you would have to be told. Actually, what he said was, you'd be furious if you found out he didn't trust you to know. He hated the idea of putting that pressure on you; it ate at him. He finally made up his mind that not only did you have to know, but he also had to confront Alfred. He didn't tell me what he planned to say, and he seemed oblivious to the possible consequences for himself. I couldn't stop him, Constance, so I did the best I could to give him a chance to make it work. You know the rest."

"Thank you, Tony. I will be careful. Please call me again, will you?"

"I will."

Constance sat on Rebecca's front porch swing, her feelings of rage and confusion gradually starting to give way to long-suppressed memories of George, Rebecca, and the time before their dream became a nightmare. Feelings of anger and remorse were still there, but she began to sense a tinge of hope.

The rattle of her phone jarred her out of her reverie.

"Mom, it's me. I'm calling from the hotel. We're leaving for the airport. We've got a three-thirty flight; it gets in before five."

"Good. Give me a call when you land."

"Look, Mom, I have to tell you—I called Dad. He's in terrible shape. That maniac attacked him, Mom! He tried to kill Dad! Why aren't you with him? He needs you NOW! He said you won't come home! What the hell is the matter with you?! If you don't go home, I'm going to send Philip to take care of Erik, and I'm going home to be with Dad. He needs me! He needs both of us!"

"Listen to me, Rebecca. I want you to come here before you do anything else. Your first obligation is to Erik, not to either of your parents. He'll be home around six, and he'll immediately know there's been a major disruption. There's no pretending, Rebecca. You know Erik will want to know what's happening, and I won't dodge it. Whatever your father is dealing with can wait until you see us. It's your choice, of course, but this is one time I really hope you'll listen to me. It's not about choosing sides in some stupid family spat; it's way beyond that. But either way, at least call me when you get in."

A few minutes later, she reached Mr. Martello who reported that George was at that point still alive, still in the ER, still in critical condition. She thanked him, got a bottle of water, and returned to the porch swing to think.

Chapter 41

ROBERT MADE HIS WAY THROUGH midday traffic, arriving at the DAPO building at 1:30. Tomaras was in her office, protected by her secretary, Mrs. Timms, who insisted she was entirely capable of delivering anything he might have to give her boss. Robert asked, with all the deferential urgency he could muster, if she would at least tell Miss Tomaras that he had an urgent communication from Leroy Fortune. Sensing the annoying man would not give in, she called Tomaras, told her the situation, and while staring at Robert, asked what she wanted her to do. Apparently, Tomaras said she had no idea who Leroy Fortune was, and for him leave the damn package and get out. A smug smile dawned as Mrs. Timms hung up the phone and, with exaggerated slowness, delivered the message.

Robert was weighing his options when the door to Tomaras's office opened.

"'Leroy Fortune,' you say? Yes, sorry, didn't recognize the name at first. I'll take it. Thank you, Mr., ahh?"

"You're welcome," Robert said and quickly left.

Tomaras was in a foul mood, still recoiling from an earlier call from her boss telling her he was taking over the Laine case. When she asked why, he said that Laine had just attacked a judge, "damn near killed him," and he was sick and tired of her "pussyfooting around" with such a dangerous criminal. End of call. She immediately called Dalton, but he wasn't in the building; his secretary had no idea where he was and would only say she would relay the message when she heard from him. Tomaras slammed the phone down knowing perfectly well she wasn't going to hear from Edward Dalton any time soon.

She opened the package from "Leroy Fortune" and started to read. About thirty minutes later, she called the San Mateo District Attorney's office to say she had vital information about the George Laine case and would be delivering it personally.

The crash team delivered George Laine straight into the operating room just before three o'clock. His blood pressure was again disappearing, and it was clear that no matter the risk, they had to open his chest to stop the bleeding. As soon as they started to work, a nurse eased the condom-covered device out of Laine's rectum. She put it in an emesis pan and took it to the two men waiting in the hall.

"Do you want me to take it out of the condom? It's pretty nasty..."

Yes, they did, as long as she was careful not to cut the wire going through the knot tied in end of the condom. And, yes, she could wash the condom once they had the recording device in the evidence bag. The condom and the device were placed in separate green plastic bags labeled EVIDENCE. The nurse's name and time of delivery were recorded, and the men hurried away.

The IT department at the county government building had been notified to prepare for an urgent matter in the DA's office, a job involving an unknown type of a miniature recording device. By the time the device was delivered to an upstairs conference room, two IT technicians were already in place with an array of electronics ready to play whatever might be on the device. A court reporter had been pressed into service to record what was on the mystery tape—assuming there was anything there at all—and a secretary was ready to take notes on the meeting. The participants gathered, including the DA, Howard Fyne, his two assistant DAs, both just back from the hospital, and Ronald Prentiss, Chief of Police for San Mateo County. The IT techs examined the recorder, pronouncing it a highly sophisticated device using a new digital mechanism that would require yet another audio machine to allow the group to hear whatever might be recorded.

While that was being set up, Aella Tomaras arrived with the package of Laine's notes. She insisted on being included in the meeting, saying she was certainly the only one who actually knew George Laine, and as his probation officer, she had a proprietary interest in the case. Chief Prentiss immediately objected, saying he had been told by his men at the hospital that Captain Henderson was in charge of the Laine case, therefore she had no reason to be included. The DA overruled him.

When the recording was finally installed, the IT technicians confirmed there was audio, and they were ready to start. The DA began by listing the names and credentials of all the participants, including the IT techs, for the court reporter. He briefly stated the purpose of the meeting—to listen to a recording device retrieved from the rectum of one George Laine, alleged to have assaulted Judge Alfred Preston—going on in considerable detail about what was known at that point about the assault, ending with a request that participants help the reporter by holding their comments until the recording was finished. The room was deadly quiet when the sound was turned on.

It began with scratching noises and muffled words, all of it inaudible, followed by a loud noise to which one of the techs said, "Car door." Then more scratching noises, followed by silence, then a voice, unmistakably that of Judge Preston.

"Hello, George. I should have known you had one more trick up your sleeve."

"Holy shit," mumbled Chief Prentiss.

"Quiet, please," said the DA.

What followed was a bit unclear—there were too many miscellaneous noises to make it out—but it sounded like there was an exchange at the door of Preston's house, something about another listening device, followed by more crackling and scratching sounds. Finally, the voices again emerged, apparently because Laine was either standing dead still or was seated. The judge said something about being a hero if he shot George on the spot. Everyone in the room was quiet, straining to hear every word.

"He's holding really still," whispered one of the ITs to the group. They heard Preston say he would shoot Laine if he got "bored." Even clearer was Preston saying "Bravo" to George for figuring out he had killed Julia Penthoser. They heard George carefully lay out the evidence, not just that Alfred had killed Julia but that he also had a hand in having Kitty Marren murdered. They also heard enough to realize there was a connection between the judge and "Metzi" and "Carlos," probably policemen. "Dalton" was presumed to be Edward Dalton, head of the Victims of Crime Project in San Francisco.

When they heard Alfred say, "Soles are for shoes, George," followed by a loud report, everyone flinched. There were more scratching sounds, a brief silence, then Preston, obviously nearer the microphone, said clearly with icy sarcasm: "Nice of you to drop by, George." That was followed by more silence, then what sounded like Preston mumbling something about hands or handedness. Next, the call to 911, followed by the call to Dalton. Most of it was faint, even with the volume turned up to the maximum. Shortly after that, there was chaos as emergency people arrived and the EMTs took over. The ambulance siren could be heard through the noise, but the audio stopped abruptly later when the wire was severed in the ER.

After the recording stopped, the room was deadly quiet for a long thirty seconds.

Fyne broke the silence. "Given what we just heard, we now know Judge Preston is a liar; worse, he may also be guilty of two—maybe three—homicides. But we're obviously a long way from proving anything. The tape suggests a lot more than it actually gives us, especially when you consider that the judge is probably right in saying a recording made under these circumstances could easily be challenged. Take your pick—entrapment, words taken out of context, statements made under duress. It doesn't matter. All it takes is doubt, and he walks. Then where would we be?"

Fyne went on to remind everyone of the obvious fact that Alfred Preston was a powerful man with deep pockets and a lot of allies, while George Laine was a convicted rapist and murderer, easily painted as a madman who turned his unexpected parole into a tool for revenge.

Looking at Tomaras, he added, "And whatever he may have written in his prison diary won't have the weight of a flea's kneecap in a court of law.

"Let's break it down. The idea of successfully prosecuting Judge Preston for a murder committed over fifty years ago is absurdly remote. Maybe we can do something with the killing in the city, but that relies on a lot of other witnesses falling in line, people with a lot to lose even if they cooperate. The only realistic chance we have is to prove that the judge assaulted George Laine with intent to kill. To do that, we need to prove motive, the only thing that will dissolve some weird self-defense argument. That's where all of us need to get to work. Go at this as if the tape didn't exist, find witnesses like those cops or Dalton, catch Preston in lies, all of it. Otherwise, the judge walks, and if Laine lives, he'll rot away in San Quentin.

"So, where do we start? Let's get copies made of Laine's notes, homework for everyone. Even though it's remote, we have to put someone on the original murder and the trial. It's old, but we're going to have to learn as much as we can about it to put this puzzle together. Someone is going to have to go to Oakland first thing tomorrow morning. Any other suggestions?"

"I may have another way in," said Chief Prentiss. "I'm embarrassed to say it, but I brushed off the investigating detectives who said they thought Preston's story was bogus. Obviously, I was wrong. If forensic evidence shows he's lying, we can charge him with felony obstruction and tampering with evidence. Even if we don't get him for murder, those two felonies could put him away for the equivalent of a life sentence. At the very least, just charging him will keep him pinned down, give us time to look deeper, and maybe turn on one of the others. It means I'll have to tell the two investigating detectives about the recording; I can't keep that from them. They're very careful, though. I know they'll guard that information carefully."

"Okay, that's a start," said the DA. "What did your guys say was wrong?"

Prentiss told the group about the fancy knife, glass in the wrong place, scratches on the gun butt, and the fact Laine certainly could not have been charging Preston when he was shot with the small caliber pistol. They talked about how, exactly, they should approach the judge to minimize the chance he would clam up and throw everything he could back at them. They decided to try for a non-threatening interview, getting pushy only if they had to. If it worked, maybe the judge would contradict himself or add other details they could explore. It was thought that anything more frontal would probably force their hand before they had enough juice to hold him, go after a search warrant or more importantly—his phone.

The DA said he would call his counterpart in the city, Sam Clevenger, without bringing up the tape, to find out if his office was investigating the murder at Laine's hotel. If they weren't, and they were simply accepting the conclusion of the investigating cops, he would push them to take a harder look. He would ask what her autopsy showed, and if her body hadn't already been cremated, then he would request that she be kept on ice for now. He would also ask Clevenger to question the three men named on the recording, hopefully without having to reveal his source.

"I know who Dalton is, but who are the other two? Cops, right?"

"Yeah, cops. Dirty cops," Tomaras said. "They're in the Tenderloin where we put Laine. Dalton kept riding me about revoking Laine. Metzi and Carlos kept trying to get something on him, too. When that didn't work, they got some street muscle to try to take him out. That was a disaster. Then there was the murder at the Madrid. They were the investigating cops, the ones who said they found the dead girl's underwear in Laine's room."

"Got it," said Fyne. "By the way, how the hell did Laine get out of there? And where was he between then and today? Obviously, someone was helping him, even Preston saw that. So who is it?"

Tomaras said she had no idea, but guessed it might have been the guy who delivered the package. They agreed that was another avenue to be followed.

The discussion went on for another hour. In the end, it was decided that Captain Prentiss would get his detectives to bring Preston in for an interview, and only if he resisted, tell him it wasn't an option, and add he might want to bring a lawyer. If—as everyone expected—he still balked, they would have to up the ante and threaten to have him arrested. Hopefully, the San Francisco DA would get on board, use the hotel murder investigation as a way to pull in the two cops, and see if he could rattle them. Just how to approach Dalton was still unclear.

"What about Mrs. Preston?" one of the assistants asked. "Sounds like she removed herself, but she's in a terrible position. Do we contact her?"

"Let's think about it. Meanwhile we'll meet tomorrow, maybe late afternoon. Mrs. Tomaras, you're welcome to come back, too."

"It's Miss Tomaras, and yes, if I still have a job, I'll be back."

Laine came out of the operating room at five thirty, critical but alive. The bleeding from the anterior chest wall and left lung had been stopped, and the pericardium (the sac around the heart) had been repaired. The bullet was found embedded in the posterior chest wall. It, too, was treated with great care to preserve the chain of possession. Laine's blood pressure was up a little, relatively steady, obviating the immediate need for another transfusion. He was also showing some spontaneous movements, seen as a positive sign. Everyone agreed with the surgeon's assessment that George Laine was "one tough son-of-a-bitch."

Around the same time that George was being moved to the recovery room, Rebecca called her mother.

"Mom! We just got in! The first thing we saw when we got off the plane was all the people watching televisions showing our house, Mom! Our house! And Daddy was talking to reporters in the yard! You couldn't hear anything, but the captions were all about him being attacked by some lunatic who had already killed a woman in San Francisco! It's the guy from the wedding, Mom! He tried to kill Daddy, Mom! What is it about this you don't get?"

"What are you going to do now, Rebecca? Are you coming home?"

"We've got to get our bags. I'll call you when we get down there. But I'm going to call Daddy first."

A few minutes later, Constance received a call from District Attorney Howard Fyne. After introducing himself, he asked if he could speak to her "off the record" about what he called "the terrible situation with your husband."

"Which husband?" she answered curtly.

"Straight to the point. Well, really, about both of them, starting with George Laine. I just spoke to the hospital administrator. He said Mr. Laine just came out of surgery. He's alive and holding on. Obviously, the situation is tenuous, and they plan to do more surgery when he's strong enough."

"Thank you for that. What about the other one?"

"That's even more difficult, at least in the sense I have to be careful about what I say. But could I first ask if you have been in contact with him today? I believe you're not at your home right now."

"I am at my daughter's house in Hillsborough. I've spoken only briefly with Alfred. He called me after he shot George. I have no plan to be in further contact with him, and certainly won't be returning to Northern Woods."

"Can I ask why, Mrs. Preston?"

"Yes, you can. I do not believe George went to the house to harm Alfred. It's a very long story, one I'm not going into now. Perhaps we can talk about it sometime, but not now."

"I understand. Thank you. You've given me what I need right now. Let me add that we will conduct a thorough investigation of the incident—and beyond. In spite of what you may hear on the news, we accept nothing until it is proven with certainty. And that includes any assumptions about George Laine. I can't say any more."

A few minutes later, Rebecca called to say she had talked to her father, and that she was going to see him before coming home. She said Philip would hire a limo and come straight back. She asked her mother to assure Erik that she would be there as quickly as possible. "Obviously, I'm worried about him, too."

"It's funny, Rebecca, but I think Erik is going to do better with this than the rest of us."

After Alfred begged off from the reporters, he went in the house, poured a large glass of scotch, added two ice cubes, and sat down at his desk. His phone rang. He answered cautiously, adding a slight tremor to his voice. It was Rebecca saying she was back and wanted to see him before going home. He said that would be a "lifesaver."

Almost immediately, the phone rang again, this time the call was from Lieutenant Orlando. He apologized for interrupting His Honor, but he did a have a few of those "loose ends" he mentioned, and...

"Look, Lieutenant, I'm in no mood for loose ends right now. This will have to wait until tomorrow. Call me in the morning. Maybe I can see you here. Depends on how I feel."

"Of course, Judge, tomorrow morning would be fine, but I'd appreciate it if you'd come down to the office, let's say at ten o'clock. Would that be all right?"

"No, it won't be all right. I told you to call me tomorrow, and I'll see what I can do."

"With all respect, Judge, I must insist. We have an open investigation, and we need to take a careful look at exactly what happened. That's especially true on the off chance the intruder survives and has a different story to tell."

"Of course, he'll have a different story! Don't you know who he is, what he's done? Besides, if he survives, he's going straight back to prison where he should have been all along."

"Well, he won't go back before he talks to us. Even in prison, we can still interview him."

"His word isn't worth spit, Lieutenant."

"Perhaps, but we still need to clear up some problems with your statement."

"What the hell are you talking about, 'problems'? Are you questioning my integrity? Are you?!"

"No, sir, I'm only doing what you as an officer of the court would do if you were me in a situation as serious as this one. We need your help, we're trying to make it as easy as possible, but it must happen tomorrow morning."

"Well, it's not going to happen tomorrow morning. I'm going to call your captain and settle this right now."

"Sir, the captain told me to call you."

"What?!"

"And he said he thought you might want to bring your attorney with you. So, please, let's just get this settled. Ten o'clock. If you prefer, the officers in front of your house could bring..."

The line went dead.

Constance looked at her watch. It was just before six. *Erik should be coming home about now, she thought. Why aren't I more nervous about what I'll say to him?*

Then the phone rang again. It was Rebecca saying in a suddenly subdued voice that there had been a change in their plan. They were both coming straight home. "Dad called. Something urgent came up. He said we'd have to wait until tomorrow."

Alfred's next call went to Vince Alcon, his friend, lawyer, and sometimes confidant. Alcon's wife, Bee, answered, immediately saying how upset they both were over the news of the attack. Alfred said he was fine but needed to talk to Vince. Bee said he was at the club, probably finishing a tennis game, and—

Alfred cut her off and called the club.

"Hey! Alfred! Jesus, man, you really had a close call today. You okay?"

Alfred went straight into the "problem" he was having with Ron Prentiss and his "piss-ant detectives" who were questioning his account of the attack. Alcon immediately turned serious, especially when he heard the part about bringing an attorney to a must-have interview.

"What could it be, Alfred? Do you have any ideas?" Vince asked.

No, he didn't, unless in his upset state he might have gotten something wrong. "But who can think after something like that?"

Alcon's advice was to call the detective right back, say he would comply with the request, and yes, he would be bringing his attorney. Meanwhile, Alfred needed to sit down, very carefully review what happened while it was still fresh, and write it down, leaving nothing out. "I'll be at your house at eight o'clock in the morning. Have some coffee ready. We'll review the notes, I can see exactly where everything happened, and maybe we can do a mock interview. We'll insist they record the interview and provide us with a copy. We stick to your script, and I won't let them insinuate anything into the record we don't agree with. That ought to do it, Alfred. Get a good night's sleep. We'll deal with this, don't worry."

Erik got home at six, already aware of the news about the attack on his grandfather. He hugged his grandmother and asked how she was doing. He didn't seem overly upset, especially when he heard his mother and "New Dad," as he called Philip, would soon be back.

"The guy who went after Granddaddy, was he the man from the wedding? The one I talked to? The one with the present?"

"Yes, Erik, it was. You remember him, don't you." It was a statement, not a question.

"Yes, Grandma, I do. He didn't seem like someone who would go after Granddaddy with a knife. That's what they said on the news. I heard it coming home in Donnie's mom's car."

"He's not."

"You know him?" the boy asked calmly.

"I do, from a long, long time ago. I didn't even know he was alive until the wedding."

"They said on the radio he was a murderer and that he's been in jail, like, forever."

"That's right, since 1958."

"God! Nineteen-fifty-eight!" He paused, looked at his grandmother and half asked, half said, "You knew him before that?"

"Yes, Erik. I was married to him."

Erik sat down, thought for a moment, and said, "I kinda wondered, Grandma. I knew it had to be something like that. What was he like? I mean…you don't have to say, you know. I'm just, well, curious."

"He was a really good person, and while it might sound crazy right now, I believe he still is."

"I do too, Grandma."

Rebecca and Philip arrived home just after seven. There were hugs and awkward small talk, but the chatter quickly faded.

"There's no easy way to start this conversation, so I'll begin where I left off when I called you in Baja. The man who is said to have attacked Alfred is George Laine, the man who left the locket for you at the wedding. The reason it caused such an uproar, and why we're confronting this horror right now, is the fact I not only knew him before he went to prison…I was married to him."

"Dear God!" exclaimed Rebecca clamping her hands over her ears. "A murderer! You were married to a murderer!"

"Let me finish, Rebecca. You're going to have to hear this, but if you'll just listen, you may change your mind."

"Change my mind! Are you crazy?!"

"Please let Grandma talk, Mom."

"You shouldn't even be hearing this, Erik! Go do your homework!"

"I already know about it, Mom. Grandma and I talked before you came home. And besides, I'm the only one who actually met him. He's the one who gave me the present."

"Holy shi…God! You met him? Mom, what did you tell Erik?"

"Hold on, Rebecca," Philip said. "Erik should stay. Let your mother finish."

Rebecca put her head down and took a deep breath. "Go ahead, it can't get any worse."

"Yes, it can, but we'll survive it. Now let me…"

Rebecca snapped bolt upright, dropped her hands, and said, "Oh, no. No, no, you're not going tell me, tell me that…"

"That George Laine is your real father? Yes."

"Cool!" said Erik.

Rebecca appeared not to hear her son, fell back on the couch, stared at the ceiling, shook her head in a silent "no," but didn't speak. Constance glanced briefly at Erik. The suggestion of a smile seemed to flit across her face.

Over the next hour, she unfolded the story, everything from the time she and George met, through the murder of Julia Penthoser, the trial, conviction, and their visits on death row. She broke down when describing their last visit, and the terrible night when she thought he had been executed. Philip said in a comforting way that he could imagine how devastating that would have been, but wondered how it was possible she didn't know George was alive, or later, find out he was somehow moved off death row.

In a halting way, Constance answered, saying she found out about the court order that made it all possible when she confronted Alfred at the wedding, immediately after the shock of seeing the locket and realizing George was not only alive, but out of prison. "Alfred and his father somehow did it. They even arranged a silent divorce, so we could legally marry. Alfred told me it was all done to protect me from having to go through another night ahead of the inevitable."

"But when he wasn't executed…" Philip trailed off as he saw what the consequences of telling her would have been. "But what about George, didn't he ever try to get in touch? He could have found a way around the order, especially after he got off death row, right?"

"He did it to keep me from a devastating truth, one that would throw whatever life I had in turmoil all over again. He wouldn't do that, and I'm dead certain he didn't intend to contact me after he was released, not until just before the wedding. I can also tell you that when George came out of prison he did not know I was married to Alfred, and finding out didn't turn his head. But then everything caved in. Someone wanted him back in prison, someone with a lot to lose if George ever did try to find me. That 'someone' was Alfred Preston."

"Of course, it was, Mom!" said Rebecca standing up, suddenly energized. "He didn't want some crazy murderer ex-husband finding us! He was obviously protecting us—why can't you see that?!"

"Because there had to be more to it than that."

"Like what?!"

"I don't know, but whatever it is, it made George risk everything to confront Alfred."

"You mean kill him, don't you, Mom? Kill him for having you! Kill him for all those years in prison!"

"No. George did not try to kill him. And before you say another word, listen to me—George Laine was an innocent man, destroyed and discarded, a man who in spite of that horror, lived his life protecting me, protecting us."

"What are you saying, Mom? That Daddy had something to do with his crime? Is that what your newest crazy idea?"

"I'm not sure of anything beyond what I've said. Now you know everything, and all of us, *all of us*, are going to have to be strong and get through whatever happens. In the meantime, do what you feel you have to with Alfred, but be careful, and if you can, keep what I said in confidence."

"You mean don't tell Daddy I just found out my father is a rapist and a murderer?"

"It's out of my hands, Rebecca. Do what you will."

Chapter 42

VINCE ALCON ARRIVED AT THE house just before eight o'clock in the morning. Over coffee, Alfred reviewed his notes detailing everything that happened the day before. He also told the lawyer about his history with George, about the trial and its aftermath, everything right up to the moment George burst through the door. When he was asked how he knew so much about George, literally from the moment he was released from prison, Alfred was vague, saying he was always aware of George, and "people" in the know kept him apprised of each parole hearing, including, of course, the final, "disastrous" one that saw him released and placed in the Tenderloin.

"Details, Alfred, details. The police are going to ask the same questions. They'll want to know who your contacts are, and how you knew to literally anticipate the assault. It could read that you actually *invited* the attack, Alfred. So who alerted you? If you provide the name, it doesn't look suspicious, right?"

"Okay, it's Edward Dalton, from the Victims group. He was on the parole board. He's in the same building with Laine's PO. Once Laine was out, everyone knew. Of course, I worried. I didn't want him showing up looking for Constance, much less trying to kill me. Who wouldn't be on guard?"

Alcon agreed it made perfect sense. He asked again if there could be anything, the slightest detail that might have made the cops nervous. "There has to be something in this, something big enough to warrant telling you to have a lawyer along. Can you think of anything else?"

No, the judge could not. As they drove to the station, Alcon cautioned Alfred to stick with short answers, not answer anything he wasn't sure of, and "For Christ's sake, don't offer anything new. Take your time, and watch me, Alfred. If I take off my glasses, it means you're drifting. If I wipe them—shut the fuck up."

They arrived at almost 10:30 a.m., but Detective Orlando and Sergeant Moses didn't appear to mind the delay. They readily agreed to record the session and provide a copy for the judge. They were shown into a conference room just off the chief's office. The interview began at 10:40 a.m. with an obligatory listing of the participants and a brief statement by Detective Orlando that the judge was appearing voluntarily to help with the investigation into the break-in and assault perpetrated by one George Laine, "currently a patient in critical condition at the San Mateo Hospital."

Orlando began by asking the judge to again go over the details of the assault. Using his notes, Alfred retold the story without interruption by the detectives. When he finished, Mr. Alcon asked if there would be any more questions, to which Detective Orlando replied that, yes, he did have some questions, starting with exactly how His Honor knew that George Laine might come to his house and attack him. That took Alfred into a lengthy explanation of his past history with the assailant, his marriage to his former wife, the parole, the killing of a woman at his hotel, and Laine's subsequent appearance at his daughter's wedding.

"That was the last straw, you see. I knew when he pulled that off, it was just a matter of time until he came after me."

"Why?" asked Sargent Moses.

"I figure seeing Connie—my wife, that is—would have made him crazy, and we all know there's nothing scarier than a crazy killer."

"Okay," said Orlando, "I get it that you were worried that maybe Laine would do something, but it sounds like he was pretty cool about the wedding appearance. It's like he was needling you, maybe. But why do you say he was 'crazy,' or that he would come after you on Monday morning? You weren't worried on Sunday, right after the wedding?"

"I told you his history, the murder, prison time, all of that…"

"What else?"

"I already told you—I was aware of Laine being paroled, that he was in the city, and that he apparently killed a girl in his hotel a week before the wedding. Is that crazy enough for you?"

Alcon was wiping furiously.

"How, exactly, were you able to follow Laine so closely?"

"Look, I'm a judge, a member of the legal community; I have many contacts in law enforcement…"

"Who, specifically?"

Alfred looked at Alcon who asked if that kind of confidential information was really germane to the immediate investigation of the attack on the judge.

"It would help, Counselor."

"Look," Alfred said impatiently, "if it will help get this over with, I often hear from a good friend in the Victims of Crime Project, Edward Dalton."

"Thank you, Judge," said Orlando. "I appreciate that. Now, just a couple of other things before we stop. I'm puzzled that you didn't see Laine come up the walkway. It goes by the den window. You said, I think, that maybe he came across the lawn, right? But how would he know you were in the den, that he had to detour around your window?"

"You're the detective, Lieutenant, you tell me."

Alcon slipped off his glasses.

"Maybe he saw me through the window from the street; I don't know."

Alcon started wiping his glasses.

"Yeah, maybe, but the street is a little lower than the window. But who knows? Then there's the glass breaking, right? You heard that, grabbed your gun, and what, ran out into the hall?"

"That's right."

The glasses went back on.

"So you were facing the door from where? What I'm wondering is if you stood by the den wall or went out in the hall?"

"Into the hall."

"Right. So at that point you were facing the front door. Had he already reached in and flipped the latch? Did you see his arm? Or did he already have the lock open and was snapping the chain?"

"I don't know, really. It happened so fast. I picture him crashing through right in front of me. Why the arm thing?"

Glasses off.

"Well, when he broke the glass he had to reach in fast, get the lock open, and put his shoulder to the door. You said he stumbled, presumably because the door frame broke pretty easily. See what I mean? He had to do all of that in just a few seconds."

"So?"

Wiping started.

"So, there was a lot of glass on the floor. He had to whack the glass a couple of times to give himself room to get his arm in and twist the lock without getting cut. I didn't see blood on either shirt sleeve, so I'm guessing he didn't cut himself."

"What are you saying, Detective?" Alcon asked, wiping vigorously.

"I'm just not sure how he did it so fast, Counselor. And another thing—take a look at this photograph of the floor just inside the door," Orlando slid an 8x10 picture across the table in front of Alfred. "See anything that strikes you, Judge?"

"Hold it a minute, Detective," Alcon said. "First of all, the recording can't see the photograph. On top of that, I think you need to stop playing games and say what concerns you."

"Sorry. Getting ahead of myself. I'm showing Judge Preston a picture of the glass on the floor inside the door. Most of the glass is about a foot from the door sill, and I'm thinking it may indicate the door was open when the glass was broken. And before you ask, there was no weather strip under the door that would have broomed the glass away from the sill when the door flew open. If there was, the glass would be all over the place. But we can leave that for now. Let's move on and try to wrap this up."

"Glad you take my point, Detective," the lawyer said flatly.

"Okay, so suddenly he was in the hallway, he had the knife up, was coming at you, you back peddled into the living room, and shot him, right?"

"Yes. Are you still hung up on where he fell?"

Alcon wiped his glasses and cleared his throat.

"Yes, I am. I looked up the ballistics of that particular round. It just doesn't have the energy to stop a charging man. He almost certainly would have fallen forward."

"'Almost certainly,'" Alcon added.

"Make that 'certainly,' unless there was something else going on the judge may have left out."

Alfred shrugged.

"Then there's the problem of the scratches on the butt of the pistol, scratches suggesting it may have been the pistol butt that broke the glass. By the way, there were no scratches on the handle of the knife. And if Laine used his elbow to break the glass, his shirt would have been torn and bloody. I need to know, Judge, if you actually staged the scene and…"

Alfred jumped to his feet. "Are you accusing me of a crime, Detective?!"

"STOP!" commanded Alcon. He told Alfred to sit down, "And don't say another word. So all of this make-nice stuff was camouflage for an ambush on a distinguished juror. That may work for some petty criminals, but not with us. This interview is over. Either charge my client or we're leaving."

"There will be no charges at this point, Counselor, but our investigation will continue. We'll be in touch, and Judge, it should go without saying—you must remain available for further questioning."

Once they were back in the lawyer's car, Alcon said, "We have to sit down and go over this again, Alfred. I'm on your side, but I won't be able to help you without the complete story."

Alfred agreed. Nothing more was said as they drove back to Northern Woods.

Chapter 43

GEORGE LAINE MADE IT TO almost 3:00 a.m. before he had to be taken back to the operating room. In spite of earlier stitching, both lobes of his shredded left lung were still leaking blood, forcing the surgeon's hand—the entire lung had to be removed, a tricky procedure under the best circumstances, but way beyond perilous for someone in Laine's condition. It took nearly four hours, but around the time Alfred and his lawyer were having their first cup of coffee, George was being taken back to the recovery room.

Around the same time, Philip took Erik to school, then continued on to his office, leaving Rebecca and her mother to continue their conversation. Rebecca was contrite over her treatment of her mother the night before. She started by asking Constance to tell her about George and their relationship, the start of a three-hour talk. At the end, they hugged.

"When I went to bed last night, Mom, all I could do was ask myself how you could have kept all of this from me all these years. When Philip got up, we talked, and he asked me an awful question—when it comes to telling the hard truth, and you absolutely had to pick one over the other, who would you be more likely to believe—your mother or your father?

"He said, 'It's not an abstraction,' that soon I would have to decide, and I'd better not make a bad mistake.'"

"Is that what changed your mind about me?"

"That and Erik. I heard what he said when you told me George Laine is my real father. He acted like it was good news. I kept asking myself, how can he act like that? What does he know that I don't? I remember him saying he met George, just for a couple of minutes, but somehow he came away with a good feeling about him. Erik is not easily fooled. I can't ignore that."

She stared out the window briefly, turned back, and said, "I've got to ask you, Mom—in all the years that you've been with Dad, did you ever doubt him? Did you ever get the feeling there was something, maybe, really wrong?"

"I've asked myself that question a hundred times over the last few days, Rebecca. The short answer is no. When George was convicted and we went through that nightmare, I had absolutely no support anywhere, not from my family or his. George's dad was dead, his mom was sick, my parents were far away and disabled. Our former friends evaporated. I was trying to work, care for you, and somehow keep myself sane. Alfred and his parents were a godsend. His mother was a genuinely caring person, and they offered comfort and literally the only support I had. George never cared for Alfred, thought he was an empty vessel, but over time he seemed to soften, and I came to believe he really did love us. Was it a show? I don't think so. But now I wonder if I had it backwards. Maybe I was actually the one giving him something he needed to get a foothold in the world. He was never the man George was, but George was gone, and I put everything I could into making our new life work.

"Looking back, sure, there were plenty of rough spots in Alfred's thinking, but I walled that off. And none of it ever suggested anything as devastating as what I'm seeing now. I guess it's harder to see through one big lie than a bunch of little ones."

"Thank you, Mom. That makes a lot of sense to me. Still..." She paused, took a deep breath, and said, "Still, my brain and my emotions are on two different tracks. Part of me wants to accept what you're saying about George Laine, and part of me is aching over Dad. I just can't see him as anything but 'Daddy,' the Dad who put band aids on my scraped knees, came to my dance recitals, and was so damned protective about who I dated. I can't turn my back on him, even though I'm terrified that I'll find out something awful. We trusted him completely! What if it was all a lie?! I don't know how I'll deal with it." She stopped, wiped her tears, took a deep breath, and looked at her mother.

"But whatever I'm feeling, it can't be anything compared to what you're going through. I'm so sorry." Again they hugged, and Rebecca said, "I've got to call Dad. I dread it, but no matter what, I have to see him. I need to know what he says, how much of this he wants me to know. Beyond that...I don't know, but I'm really scared. What else is there?"

"None of us know at this point, Rebecca, and I promise you I'm not holding anything back. While you call Alfred, I'll call the hospital. I haven't checked since early this morning."

"Do you think he'll make it, Mom? Does he have a chance? It would be so awful if he got this far and died."

"Yes, it would."

Chapter 44

ALFRED AND HIS LAWYER GOT back to Northern Woods around noon. Alcon was hopping mad at Alfred for making him look like a "third rate pettifogger" in front of the two detectives. Alfred was apologetic, but clearly more focused on what the detectives may have in mind than he was about his friend's wounded pride.

"Hold on, Vince, I'll explain it to you. Just listen."

The lawyer sat with his arms folded across his chest, legs outstretched, ankles crossed, a skeptical scowl on his face, his notepad idle on a nearby chair.

"I did stage the scene, but I had a damn good reason. I shot that bastard in self-defense; it just didn't go down like I said it did…I was concerned I might not be believed if it came out that I actually let him in the house in the first place. So here's what happened."

Alfred said he certainly did think Laine might come after him, just as he told the detectives, and he was ready, literally with his pistol in his hand when Laine rang the doorbell. But Laine wasn't raging at that moment; in fact, he asked almost politely if he could come in to talk. He even promised he'd leave as soon as he had his say. Alfred said he told Laine he would let him in, but he was fully prepared to use his gun if Laine made any move to attack him. He said they sat in the living room, the gun pointing at Laine, and told him to get to the point and leave. He said Laine quickly went from polite to irritable to angry. He was suddenly livid with the judge for "taking my wife away from me" and wanted to know what the judge was going to do about it. When Alfred said he'd had enough, Laine jumped up, cursed him, and took a step forward. The judge said at that point, he was terrified Laine would pounce on him—they were only five feet apart—so he pulled the trigger. Laine went down, and the judge immediately realized he would have an awful time saying why he'd opened the door in the first place, so he impulsively staged the scene to make it look more like a fearsome attack.

"When he went off and looked like he was going to attack, gun or no gun, I was scared shitless, so I shot him. And I'd do it again."

Alcon thought about what he had just heard, then said with exaggerated caution, "Okay, Alfred, if that's what happened, *really* happened, then you have to call Orlando right now and tell him you want to see him as soon as possible. Then you'll have to lay it out exactly as you said, but be prepared for a lot of pushback. You know perfectly well that when people change their stories, there's a high probability they're still not telling it like it really went down."

"I know, Vince. But, listen—I'm not ready to call Orlando quite yet."

"What!"

"I'd like to see what their next move is, maybe have a chance to sniff this out. There's a good chance no one will want to take this any further, given who they're dealing with."

"Dealing with you, or dealing with Laine? Dealing with a judge or a convicted murderer?"

"Both. And if it goes any further, yes, I'll call him."

Alcon didn't like it at all. "Think about it—if Laine dies, this could become manslaughter or even murder! You're playing with fire, Alfred!"

"No proof. My word against his. *Better* if he dies, believe me."

As far as Alcon was concerned, there was nothing better about any of it; in fact, it was getting worse by the minute. He made it clear that in spite of their long friendship, ignoring his advice in a matter as serious as this would force him to bow out. He brushed aside Alfred's promise to call Orlando at the first sign of additional pressure. "Twenty-four hours, Alfred. Not a minute more. If you don't call Orlando by this time tomorrow, I'm done."

After the lawyer left, Alfred returned Rebecca's call. He got her on the first ring, was apologetic, glad to know she was all right, and hoped they could meet. Rebecca said she was uncomfortable about coming to the house, given what had just happened there, and suggested they meet at a downtown coffee shop. Alfred said he didn't want people coming up to talk to him, suggesting instead they meet by the pond in the Northern Woods Park. "That's where we used to go when you were a little girl, remember?"

Rebecca remembered, and an hour later they met, hugged, and sat down on a bench by the dam. Their conversation wound around Baja, Erik's band costume, Philip's latest writing project, and how they used to sit and watch the ducks fight over chunks of bread. Finally, Rebecca said, "We have to talk about it, Daddy."

"I know. It's complicated, honey, you see…"

Rebecca held up her hand and said, "Why didn't you and Mom ever tell me about George Laine? That he was my biological father. That he even existed at all!"

"Truthfully, sweetheart, your mom and I never talked about George Laine. He was supposed to have died, and it was far better to leave it that way. I was your father, and as far as I'm concerned, I still am."

"Mom says you never told her you knew he was alive. Why did you do that? Wasn't she strong enough to know? Didn't you owe it to her?"

Alfred repeated his claim to have been protecting her from a lifetime of anguish. "When you understand what George Laine did, you'll understand it wasn't a lie, no matter what anyone else might think."

"What if he was innocent? Mom certainly thinks he was. Maybe keeping it from her allowed the real murderer to go free. Mom says you never told her you thought he was guilty, at least not until she confronted you at my wedding. I just want the truth, goddamn it!" She abruptly stood, looked down and said, "I want to say I believe you, Daddy. With all my heart, I want to believe you. But I don't." She looked at her watch, took a deep breath, and said she had to go home to meet Erik when he came back from school. Alfred asked when he would see her again. She answered through her tears that she didn't know, hurried back to her car, and drove away. Alfred sat for a while watching the ducks squabble over an invisible scrap of food.

Back at the house, he called Dalton, asked what he was hearing, and was relieved to hear him say almost casually, "Not much." No news yet about who was helping Laine, either. He did report the happy fact that the Bitch had been fired for mishandling the Laine case. She had already cleared her desk and left the building. He added that he heard Laine was still "hanging on by a fingernail." Alfred told him to keep his ear to the ground and report anything else he might pick up.

Laine was indeed still barely alive, but there were some hopeful signs, including a steadily-rising blood pressure, increasing arterial oxygen saturation, and some spontaneous movement that could be an early sign he might regain consciousness.

Just before the DA's group met in the late afternoon, Fyne again called Constance to tell her the hospital reported Laine to be incrementally better, and asked if she had anything new to add to the situation. She thanked him, said she had no new information, but did have a request. She told Fyne about the infamous court order, asking if there was some way he could get it canceled. If not, she planned to hire an attorney and pursue it herself.

"We all know how long that could take. But you could get a hearing in a heartbeat. It could even help you in some way."

Fyne said he understood and would definitely pursue it.

At 4:00 p.m., the DA's group met. Tomaras had called to say she had been permanently sidelined, but wanted to be sure that the investigator in Oakland took a careful look at the appeals, and most especially, the original court order. "I think those are the key documents." The DA, having had a chance to read through Laine's notes, agreed, saying he had already alerted his assistant to focus on them, plus any amendments, as well as the divorce decree. He wished Tomaras well.

The session began with a report from Chief Prentiss about the interrogation of Judge Preston. Clearly, he was lying all the way, something Prentiss thought his attorney saw as well. "Let's give it a day, see what happens, and bring him in again. Frankly, I think we should arrest him before he comes up with some dodge we haven't thought of yet." Arrest or not, he thought they should also try to get access to his phone. "We could find a pattern of calls to Dalton, and from there—who knows? Maybe all the way down to the cops."

"'Fishing,' that's what the courts will call it," said Fyne. "Unless, of course, we have solid evidence Preston is lying without having to mention the recording at all." Fyne thought the case would be even stronger if the city DA, Sam Clevenger, found something in the Dalton–Preston connection.

"When I talked to Sam, he had no idea about the killing at the hotel. He heard it on the news, just assumed it was part of the crazy story about George Laine. But he's on it now. He has investigators at the hotel, and he's looking into the pathologist's report, even though it's probably too late to save the body."

Going after Metzi and Carlos was another matter altogether. At this point, there was no specific reason to pull them in; it would just put them on their guard. Getting Internal Affairs involved would be a bureaucratic disaster, especially when the police union got involved. Better to wait for Clevenger's people to frisk the Madrid and see what turned up.

There was also some concern about Laine being moved to the trauma center in the city, well away from their jurisdiction. Fyne said he had already raised the issue with Clevenger, hoping the DA would give him access to Laine when—and if—he could be interviewed. He already knew from Clevenger that there might not be much he could do to keep the DAPO people from sending Laine back for the parole violation, but he would do his best to delay it if it came to that.

The decision was made to call the judge back for another round, this time focusing on his relationship with Dalton. They could also see if Preston would give them his phone. If he put up a fight about any of it, they would have to arrest him and see if they could make an obstruction charge stick. If that happened, then access to his phone and his financial records should be relatively easy to get. Fyne would review the LA documents and file an emergency petition in the circuit court within the next two days to get rid of the old court order. "We don't want to let this go over the weekend. Pressure, gentlemen. Pressure. Someone's going to crack."

Detective Orlando called the judge at 7:00 p.m. requesting another meeting the next morning—Wednesday. The judge said he would come in. "In fact, I was about to call you to see if we could get together again." He said ten thirty should be possible, but first he had to be sure his lawyer would be available.

Preston called Vince Alcon, but Bee said he was out for the evening. "He left you a message in case you called. It says to tell you to call Sheldon Berkowitz or Gregory Miller." Alfred mumbled his thanks.

"So much for twenty-four hours, you bastard," he mumbled as he looked up the two names. He knew both men tangentially, didn't really like either one, but thought Berkowitz would be the tougher of the two. He reached him at his home, briefly explained the situation, and asked if he would be able to help. Berkowitz said he couldn't because he was due in court, but he would get one of his associates to give him a call. An hour later a woman named Harriet Brunner called, said she would be able to help, and wanted Preston to come to her office at 7:30 a.m. to prepare. He didn't argue.

The mood in Rebecca's house was considerably better than it was the night before. There were no angry words, no crying, and the references to George were all about concern. Rebecca reported seeing Alfred but didn't comment further. Constance went to bed thinking something peaceful could possibly emerge from the chaos and pain of the last five days.

Constance slept well, but it was a restless night for Alfred. As a precaution against a search warrant, he cut the knife's sheath into scraps, smashed George's wire device to flinders, and deposited both in a dumpster in a neighboring development. Still, he kept wondering what was driving the police. Why did they seem so indifferent to his lofty community status? He was convinced there was an enemy force behind it all, someone who engineered Laine's miraculous rescue at the Madrid and his appearance at the wedding. Who? Who could possibly have so much detailed knowledge of all the players, plus the resources and motivation to press such a relentless attack?

There was only one name that stood out—Dalton! He wasn't rich, but he was well fixed. "Shit, he could live out his life on just what I've given him." *He's also a do-gooder at heart. Maybe it suits his whacko sense of justice to take my money at the same time he's screwing me. Or maybe he just smells danger, knows who to call, and he's trying to get ahead of it. Or even worse—someone's gotten to him and turned the bastard on me.*

But it would be disastrous to make a mistake risking it all on a hunch. "So how do I figure it out without tipping my hand?" He fell asleep trying to imagine the perfect trap.

Early the next morning, Alfred met Harriet Brunner in her office at Berkowitz Partners LLC. Hers was a small office befitting an associate, but she had a reassuring law degree from Yale Law School on the wall, along with several honor society awards, all of it pointing to someone on the way up. She invited His Honor to sit down, immediately addressing what she knew to be his disappointment over being represented by an associate.

"Mr. Berkowitz is sorry he could not be here personally, but he had to be in court today. I will hand this off to him as soon as he is available, assuming we can't settle the matter quickly." She went on without interruption saying what she knew, then asked the judge to please go over it all right from the start. Alfred gave her an abbreviated review of the background, repeated his statement that he had shot the assailant in self-defense, told her that the police were skeptical of his account, and that it was he who had contacted Detective Orlando the night before.

"You see, I need to set the record straight. I'm ashamed to tell you this, but I was not entirely truthful with the police the first time." He explained that having let George Laine into his house, he thought it would raise doubts about his claim of self-defense, especially since he had been warned he might show up. "It could make it look like I lured him in and shot him. So I staged it."

"I don't have to tell you, Judge, you could be charged with at least two felonies without even considering some kind of manslaughter. I'm glad you called the police, and I encourage you to tell them exactly what really happened no matter how damaging you think it might be. Our best shot is to get ahead of any charges, present your mea culpa, and—here's the important part—cop to a misdemeanor charge. They might go for it, and who knows? Maybe we can even get them to drop it later. The only fly in the ointment is if they have another agenda, that they know something or suspect something you aren't even aware of. Most likely, it's related to the assailant. Or maybe someone has a grudge, knows something, and they're pulling strings we won't see until it's too late. Any ideas?"

"None. Believe me, I've thought about it, but I can't think of anyone. I mean, sure, lots of people I sent off hate me. Some of them are well placed, too. But anyone specific? No." *Except Edward Dalton,* he thought.

"Okay then, let's play it straight out. Don't wander off topic, don't offer anything you aren't asked, and if you're not sure, look at me and I'll jump in. Just follow my lead."

At police headquarters, Captain Prentiss was having a similar skull session with his two detectives. He had a new plan, one triggered by Preston's call.

"For sure, his lawyer is on him to correct his story. We can't let that happen before we charge him. If we listen to one freaking syllable, he could beg off the felonies. So you two stay out of sight, and the minute he walks in the station, we'll have a uniform arrest him, read him his rights, then as a favor, we'll clear the processing room, no handcuffs, no holding cell, polite all the way. Just process him and take him straightaway to the conference room. Then let him talk. Be really careful you don't say anything that would tip him off to the fact we have the recording. Don't forget to work on the Dalton angle. Get as much as you can, and see if he'll cough up the phone. By the time you finish, we can present it to a judge, hopefully without letting reporters know…"

"You're dreaming, Captain. There's no way to take him to court without everyone finding out."

"Maybe we could try to slip him in during lunch break, when the court is empty. We won't ask for bail. Get him out quietly. If it doesn't work, so be it."

"For sure the press will find out—and he'll use it."

"Fine. When the other players hear about it, they'll get nervous. Let that work for us."

When the judge and his lawyer entered police headquarters, they were shown into a side room where two officers were waiting. When they said the judge was under arrest and started to read his rights, he erupted over being "tricked" and demanded to see Chief Prentiss. Ms. Brunner calmed him down and advised that he say nothing more. After being processed— including fingerprints and photographs—he and his lawyer were taken to the conference room where the detectives were waiting. His lawyer protested the arrest, pointing out her client was appearing in good faith to make a statement that if they had only waited would have settled the entire matter without making it into a "three-ring circus."

Detective Orlando said the decision to arrest the judge was made because the judge's "clearly contrived" explanation of the intrusion rose to the level of "criminal intent to distort the investigation." Ms. Brunner retorted by saying that her client wanted to correct the record, and repeated her assertion the arrest was, "Unnecessary, heavy-handed, and profoundly regrettable." She hoped that once His Honor had a chance to explain, they would immediately correct their "obvious mistake."

Judge Preston was reminded that the interview was being recorded, and that because he was under arrest, anything he said could be used in evidence going forward. He was invited to continue.

The judge then told his corrected story, emphasizing that the core issue remained self-defense. "I feared for my life." He sealed his case saying that having been warned about the probability of an assault, he had every reason to assume imminent danger when Laine became enraged and began to move toward him. He concluded his statement by saying, "My mistake—the only reason we're in this room right now—was letting him through the door in the first place. Obviously, it was a stupid impulse."

The detectives didn't question the new account, but instead moved directly to the part about being informed ahead of Laine's appearance. "You told us before that Mr. Dalton of the Victims of Crime Project warned you about the possibility of an attack. Tell us about your involvement with Mr. Dalton."

"Aren't we getting off the subject, Detective? The issue is about being warned. Please stay with the specifics."

"Very well, let me sharpen the focus of my question. You have told us twice now that you were forewarned that George Laine would possibly, maybe 'probably,' try to harm you. You told us that Mr. Dalton was the one who gave you that information. So we would like to know when you were warned, and exactly what Mr. Dalton told you."

"Well, I've had a number of talks with him. He and I have worked together before, and knowing Laine's history—remember, he's seen him at parole hearings—he was naturally concerned for my well-being, especially after hearing that Laine apparently attacked and killed a woman, a prostitute, I believe, in the hotel where he was living after he was paroled. Laine escaped, disappeared, and Mr. Dalton feared he would come after me."

"How did Mr. Dalton know that it was Laine who had murdered someone?"

"He has his ear to the ground, Detective. His office is in the DAPO building. He keeps track of many criminals, Laine among them."

"By 'ear to the ground' I assume you mean police in the Tenderloin?"

"And elsewhere, yes."

Orlando was tempted to ask about Metzi and Carlos but thought better of it.

"Okay. Tell me, did Mr. Dalton know about your personal relationship with Laine before the murder at the hotel?"

"Yes, I told him. I don't recall exactly when, but I had to tell him after the murder, for sure."

"Okay, well that's something we can clear up when we talk to Mr. Dalton."

"Talk to Dalton? What does he have to do with the attack on me, and why I'm here today?"

"Well, sir, there's an assumption floating around that Laine is guilty of killing the woman in his hotel, seen as proof of just how dangerous he is. But we don't know that for sure. We don't know how or why Mr. Dalton would come to think that. You see? If Laine wasn't the killer people seem to think he is, then it changes the whole narrative about what he was doing at your house, and impinges directly on your story."

Alfred didn't say anything.

Orlando continued, "There's another thing we haven't talked about, too. How did Mr. Laine get to your house? Indeed, where has he been since he left the hotel?"

"I have no idea," Alfred said dismissively.

"Does Mr. Dalton know? Surely, you discussed that before the attack."

"Don't put words in my client's mouth, Detective. Ask your question, please."

Orlando rephrased the question. Alfred said they may have talked about it; he just didn't remember when.

"Have you talked to Mr. Dalton since the attack?"

Yes, Alfred said he had. "Maybe a couple of times."

Then Orlando popped the question: "Could we have your cell phone, Judge? It would help with the time line."

That got Ms. Brunner's attention. "Sorry, Detective, but if you're going fishing, you'd better bait your hook with a warrant."

The interview ended when they were told the court was empty and the judge could be arraigned and released quickly, "as a courtesy." On the way back to her office, Ms. Brunner puzzled aloud over both the seeming overreach of the arrest, and the focus on Edward Dalton. "They hardly bothered with your revised account of the assault. Why are they so interested in the events before the attack? It's like they've got something else on their mind, something about the attacker, not the attack." She dropped the judge by his car, promised to bring Mr. Berkowitz up to speed, saying they would be back in contact by the end of the day. She advised him to avoid the inevitable pressure to talk to the press, finishing with, "And don't talk to Mr. Dalton, either. They won't have any trouble getting your phone if they realize you were in touch with him right after the interview."

Alfred went to the Northern Woods Club to call Dalton. "Christ, Judge, I was about to call you! What the hell is going on? I just got a call from the DA asking me to come to his office to talk about the murder at the Madrid! I asked him why he wanted to talk to me, and he said he hoped I could help with what I knew about the investigating officers. That's Metzi and Carlos! I asked him how I could help with that, and he said it was because I knew a lot about Laine and that could be a big help. Big help, my ass! This is scary shit, Judge! Didn't I tell you when I first called you that it didn't make sense that those two jerkoffs got to the Madrid so fast? Didn't I? If I tell the DA that, it'll open a huge can of worms, but if I don't tell him, and they find out they were somehow involved, it comes back to bite me! Where's all this coming from?"

"That's what I was going to ask you, Dalton."

"What?! Are you saying you think I'm talking? Are you?!"

Alfred apologized, said he was rattled because he'd just been arrested for obstructing the investigation into the attack. "I overplayed the assault, but don't worry, I'll handle it. It isn't about you. The only reason they want to talk to you is to find out more about Laine. They don't know him like we do."

Far from being reassured, Dalton was apoplectic, choking, even tearful over what he saw coming. The judge told him that if everyone stuck to his story, it would work out fine. "Just keep to the basics—you were only trying to help me, an old friend, someone you respect, and you don't know anything about what happened at the Madrid. I'm sure not going to say anything about it, so there's no way in, see?" He reminded Dalton that Metzi and Carlos were hard as diamonds and wouldn't say a damn word. He also said that if Laine survived, he was going back to prison, and with nothing more than the word of a convicted murderer, the whole thing would die down. He ended by saying he was going to buy a throw-away phone, so they could stay in contact "under the radar."

Alfred went home still not entirely convinced Dalton wasn't involved. Either that, or the mystery man in the background was feeding someone information.

By Wednesday afternoon, news of the Republican takeover of the House of Representatives was replaced by the shocking news that Judge Alfred Preston, heroic survivor of a vicious attack by a rampaging murderer two days before, had been arrested for providing false information to police. Speculation over Republican plans was no match for hunger to feast on salacious details of murder and misplaced justice in San Mateo.

Judge Preston again appeared in his front yard with reporters, this time to express wounded bewilderment over being arrested, even as he was trying to work with police to provide additional information on the attack. A reporter asked what "false information" the judge might have given.

"Look, young lady, I'm seventy-five, not thirty-five. I'm damn lucky to be alive. You don't have something like this happen to you one minute, and get every detail exactly right the next." He promised a vigorous defense, quoting his lawyer's quip that the arrest was "a clumsy publicity stunt."

Constance was about to call Mr. Martello when Rebecca rushed in with the news of the arrest. Together they watched the news broadcast, including endless reruns of Alfred's front-lawn indignation, narrated by various experts speculating about what drove the police to pounce on the poor judge. Attention was again drawn to the condition of the attacker, his survival now more vital than ever. The news reported that Laine had "stabilized" to the point of having a "fifty-fifty" chance of surviving.

Mr. Martello confirmed the positive report, adding that if George continued to improve, he might be strong enough to move to the city trauma center over the weekend. Constance asked if—beyond the legalese of the official report—there was any sign he was regaining consciousness.

"I shouldn't be telling you this, Mrs. Preston, but, yes, he is floating in and out of consciousness. It's a really good sign, but please don't say anything about it to anyone."

While the news was good, it was obvious that when George was moved to the trauma center, Constance would lose her direct source of information from both Mr. Martello and the San Mateo DA. She wanted to call Mr. Fyne to press the reversal of the court order, but she held off, not wanting to let her anxiety risk irritating her vital link to George and the greater investigation. She also realized that even with reversal of the order, she would probably be blocked from any contact by state parole officials. She hoped Tony would call again; in the meantime, her only choice was to wait and see how it all played out.

Chapter 45

MR. BERKOWITZ CAME OUT SWINGING. Within twenty-four hours of the judge's arrest, he filed a request for an expedited hearing to compel the prosecution to show all the evidence they would use in their case. Citing the apparent mismatch between the severity of the charges and paucity of evidence to support those charges, the defense demanded access to all evidence, including anything related to "Possible informants or other sources not otherwise mentioned that could in any way be providing information supporting the charges against Judge Alfred Preston."

"That last part had me worried," the DA said as he read the freshly-minted document at the start of the Thursday afternoon meeting. "Berkowitz has a good nose for the unexpected. But as of an hour ago, we have some fresh meat to throw him—a good distraction from mystery informants. Clevenger's people found a witness at the Madrid who can give Laine an airtight alibi for the time of the murder. One William H. Howland, a.k.a. Cowboy, reports that because Laine thought someone might try to kill him, he spent two nights in Howland's room sleeping on the floor between the guy's bed and the wall.

"Laine couldn't possibly have slipped out, murdered the woman, and returned without Howland waking up. He was with Laine when the noise started in the morning, and at the woman's door a few minutes after the body was discovered. At almost the same time, cops started arriving, trying to keep people from leaving the hotel. Laine got out by pulling the fire alarm, triggering the sprinklers, and pushing past the cops in the panic that followed. So we can prove Laine didn't kill the girl, and get this—the cops who said they found her underwear in Laine's room were Metzi Arino and Carlos Zópilo!

"Oh, and did I forget to tell you? The coroner's report says the woman was not raped. Now Clevenger has reason to bring in the cops, and Dalton."

Fyne reminded the group they had to act quickly, before the hearing. They agreed to meet again Friday morning to get all their evidence together, and prepare their strategy for a showdown with Berkowitz. With Laine no longer a suspect in the murder, assuming he survived, his account of the encounter might factor in as well. With the weekend looming, he and Clevenger decided to wait until Monday to question Dalton and the cops. It would also allow more time to see if Laine regained consciousness. Meanwhile, Fyne put an assistant on preparing a petition to void the court order. With all of the information assembled, including a report from the DA sent to Oakland, the group would have plenty of weekend homework.

For Constance and her family, the weekend was endless and confining. Philip did all the shopping, answered the phone, and fended off reporters who found their way to the Upton home. Erik missed school on Friday, slipped out, and spent the weekend with a friend. It seemed impossible to turn on the television without hearing a rehash of the Alfred Preston arrest story. Public sentiment was solidly behind the judge. Swelling the angry chorus, various interest groups were weighing in with their perspective. The tough-on-crime crowd howled about the porous justice system. Death penalty people made Laine their poster boy. The few who dared support the police, or urged restraint until the case was heard in court, were drowned out by the others.

On Monday morning, Metzi and Carlos were questioned by the DA about the death of Kitty Marren and the events that followed. They weren't accused of anything, but the questions were sharp, especially about how they got to the Madrid so quickly, why they focused on searching Laine's room, where they found the underwear, and why they instantly connected it to Laine.

Even though they were questioned separately, their answers matched exactly. They were getting ready to go on shift when they got a call about a body at the Madrid. It was only a few minutes away from the station. Everyone in the department knew about Laine, nothing unusual about that. He had already been involved in an assault and a possible drug deal. Of course they looked in his room; they looked in lots of rooms. The underwear was on his chair, couldn't miss it. He set off the fire alarms and split. Who wouldn't think he looked guilty?

Dead end.

Edward Dalton wasn't very helpful, either. Of course, he knew the judge. Of course, the judge was right to worry about Laine. At first, he thought it was just about a killer getting released, but later—can't remember exactly when—the judge told him about being married to Laine's wife. Of course, he assumed the cops were right about Laine killing Marren. It fit the old crime; after all, he knew all those details from his work on the parole board. Of course, he warned the judge to watch out, who wouldn't? No, he had no idea who could be helping Laine—he'd love to know himself. No, he wouldn't give anyone his phone—certainly not without legal advice.

Another dead end.

Chapter 46

MIDDAY MONDAY, PHILIP ANSWERED THE phone for what seemed like the two hundredth time in the past four-and-a-half days. He had a standard rap—after hearing the caller was another reporter, he politely but firmly said the family had no comment to make and would appreciate having their privacy respected, goodbye.

"Hello, this is Tony. Can I speak to Constance, please?"

"Tony? Tony who?" he said preparing to hang up.

"Don't!" exclaimed Constance, grabbing the phone. "Tony! Thank God! I've been worried you wouldn't call."

"I didn't want to intrude unless I had something important to tell you. I know this has been the week from hell for you and your family. Can I ask how it's going?"

"Yes, of course. You're the key to it for me—for us, really. Because of all the craziness, we've been staying out of sight here at the house. Erik was with friends, went to school with them today. He'll come back tonight if things quiet down. Rebecca's husband, Phil, has been keeping the press away. That's given the three of us time to try to make some sense of it all. In many ways, it's been harder for Rebecca than it has for me, especially with the news of Alfred's arrest.

"For me, though, hearing that George is better has made a big difference. I've also had a call from the DA; nothing specific, he was careful with his words, but I got a strong sense he isn't buying the idea George tried to kill Alfred. Not like the press this morning," she added.

"Attacking the police always sells papers. You can expect more, brace yourself. Back to Rebecca, how is she handling it?"

"She's really struggling, Tony. She wants to believe me, but her world is upside down right now, so we're taking this very carefully. But you said you had something to tell me, please. I hope it's something positive."

"It is. I hope we can keep this between us for now—I don't want my sources to think I talked to anyone. I know you'll want to say something to Rebecca, and it's your call, but I hope you'll hold on just a little longer."

"Don't worry, Tony."

"Okay. Well, my sources tell me the DA's people—not the San Francisco cops—were all over the Madrid investigating the murder of Kitty Marren. They turned up someone who's given George an alibi for the time the girl was killed. The cops in the Tenderloin are in an uproar over the investigation because the DA just questioned a couple of them about their account of what happened. Sounds like fallout from something the prosecutor has, maybe solid evidence to question the judge's version of the attack. They may have more than that, I don't know; that crowd is really tight with their information. But at this point, it looks like there's a better than even chance the charges will hold, and they'll be able to proceed to trial. That doesn't change anything for George, at least not right away, but it should put a dent in Alfred's armor. By the way, the hearing is Friday, do you plan to go? It will be excruciating…"

"Yes, I am going. I've talked about it with Rebecca, and she's with me; we really have no choice. Is there anything else I should know?"

"No, not right now. As I said, the DA and the prosecutor aren't talking. There certainly is other evidence out there; I just don't know what it is. I'll call again when I have something." In fact, Tony did not know if the recording had survived, and if so, what role it might have in the upcoming hearing. *We'll find out Friday,* he thought.

Constance thanked Tony and hung up convinced that no matter how painful the hearing would be, it would finally free everything from a lifetime in the shadows.

Chapter 47

THE HEARING WAS SET FOR Friday, November 12. By the middle of the week, Laine was coherent enough to talk to investigators. When asked about why he had worn the wire, he said it was "insurance" but wouldn't elaborate. He denied he was trying to get Alfred to incriminate himself about anything he had done in the past or that he was planning to turn the recording over to police. He refused to say a word about who was helping him, even after being told it could prevent him from testifying against Preston. They reminded him that without his help, the judge might slip through with nothing more than a couple of misdemeanors. Laine seemed indifferent. Baffled investigators hoped his confusing statements were only the product of a drug haze. Maybe later, he would come to his senses. Asked if he wanted to see Constance, he said he would, but that wasn't his call to make. He felt he had done as much as he could, and how things played out from here was not in his hands.

Going into the hearing with only what they had from the detective's investigation made the team nervous, to say the least. Laine was going to live, but he was still in violation of his parole, and refusal to answer any questions about where he had gone, or who had helped him, meant there would be no effective way to fight his revocation. Worse, as far as Preston's trial was concerned, it made him an unreliable witness, even if somehow the recording was accepted as evidence. Dalton and the two cops had lawyered up, refusing to say anything beyond their vanilla stories about good intentions and doing their duty.

Two days before the hearing, it was clear they had to introduce the recording, hoping the judge would at least listen to it before making a decision. They also knew Berkowitz would immediately fill the air with objections. It was a no-choice risk. If it failed, Preston would take a non-fatal hit, or even possibly skate away unscratched.

During the discussion, the DA was called out of the meeting by an assistant who said a call had just come in from a woman who said she knew who killed Kitty Marren.

"I saw in the papers that Judge Preston is going to get off for shooting George Laine."

It was true that the news continued to cast a doubting eye on the case, reinforcing the solid line of people standing in vocal defense of the judge. That day, the *San Francisco Chronicle* ran an editorial describing what it saw as yet another example of the police blaming the victim to cover their own incompetence. The DA agreed that there had been a lot of bad press, but the situation wasn't hopeless, especially if the caller had some new information. And could he please have her name, and what she knew about the case?

"I know who killed Kitty Marren, and it wasn't George Laine."

The DA decided not to press the name issue, invited her to continue, perhaps starting with who did kill Kitty Marren.

"It was the cop, Carlos. He did it. He tried to get Laine, and when he couldn't do that, he killed Kitty. Laine and Kitty were close. There's no way on this earth he would hurt her."

"By 'Carlos,' I assume you mean Carlos Zópilo? How do you know it was him?"

"Because I was there. I saw it!" The caller broke down at that point. Fyne told her to take all the time she needed, and could she at least give him a first name?

After a long pause she said, "Minouche. Minouche LaHoy, and I should be arrested, too. I saw it! I didn't stop it! Kitty loved Laine. He respected her, and I let that bastard kill her and get Laine shot, and he'll go back to jail. I'm the one who should be in jail!"

The DA assured her she would not go to jail. He asked if it would help if he sent someone to get her so they could continue in the safety of his office, but Minouche refused, saying she was too afraid.

"You don't have to be afraid of me or of being arrested."

Minouche said she wasn't afraid of Fyne, or even jail. "It's my boyfriend. If he finds out I talked to you, he'll kill me." Fyne asked his name, assured her he would be picked up, and assuming he had a record, he could be held while everything got sorted out.

"That won't work. He always gets out. I have to disappear."

"If what you are telling us is true, I promise I can make that happen, too. We can hold your boyfriend as an accessory, maybe more. There is absolutely no way he will get to you. So please tell me what you saw. Don't leave anything out."

Through sobbing self-recrimination, Minouche told the story from the moment Carlos approached her and Bingo Poole on a street corner in Hunter's Point, to the dreadful moment she realized Carlos had just killed her friend. "And I took him there! I did it just as much as he did!" After another thirty minutes of intermittent cries for help and threats of hanging up, Fyne was finally able to find out where she was. He called Clevenger to make sure he wouldn't mind if Fyne sent a car to the city to pick up the potential witness. Together they decided it was actually better if Minouche went to San Mateo instead of the city. Clevenger volunteered a couple of his people in case the local cops got testy about jurisdiction. As they approached Minouche, Bingo spotted them and took off. They caught him; even better, they recovered the pistol he tossed during the chase. He was handed over to San Francisco police on a weapons charge; given his record, conviction would almost certainly mean a three-strikes life sentence.

Fyne relayed Minouche's information to Clevenger just before midnight Wednesday night. Because news of the arrest of Bingo Poole and disappearance of Minouche LaHoy could easily find its way to Carlos, Metzi, and even Dalton, they decided to detain all three immediately on accessory charges.

Early Thursday morning, with Fyne sitting in, Robert Clevenger questioned Carlos, hitting him straight out with the fact they had a witness who saw him murder Kitty Marren.

"You're finished, Carlos. We've got you for first degree murder, extortion, and planting evidence in order to incriminate George Laine. It will be a frigging miracle if you don't get the death penalty, but even if you don't, you'll be in a super-max the rest of your miserable life. How does it feel to know you'll be locked down twenty-three hours a day while Metzi, Dalton, and Judge Preston are at the beach drinking piña coladas?"

Carlos was defiant at first, but as the reality of taking the rap alone sank in, he finally asked what kind of a deal he could make. Clevenger said he couldn't promise what a trial judge would accept, but he'd reduce the murder charge to manslaughter, drop the rigging evidence charge, and condense the rest into a single charge of accepting bribes.

"The worst would be twenty-five to thirty years, but it could be twenty with the possibility of parole in sixteen or seventeen years. Beats the shit out of death row or a four-by-eight in Pelican Bay."

"I'll think about it."

"No you won't, Carlos. Your Popsicle is melting fast. If I see the stick, the deal is off. Make up your mind."

Carlos caved, made a lengthy statement, and signed it just before noon on Thursday. In it, he gave details about the money he and Metzi got from Dalton to either put George Laine back in prison or kill him. He admitted they both knew the money came from Judge Preston. He blamed Metzi for dreaming up the idea of killing Kitty Marren to incriminate Laine if Carlos couldn't tap Laine straight out.

Next, they went to Metzi, applied the same pressure they had with Carlos, but Metzi wouldn't say a word.

Against his lawyer's advice, Dalton admitted being the middle man between Judge Preston and the two cops, but vigorously denied knowing about the plan to kill Laine or Kitty Marren. He admitted that Judge Preston had been "obsessed" with getting Laine revoked or "disabled," something Dalton thought was understandable, given Laine's record and the judge's legitimate fear Laine would come after him for marrying his wife.

He signed a statement, was returned to his cell, tied a sheet around his neck, and using the guts of his ballpoint pen, wedged as much of the sheet as he could into the crack between the top of the door and the frame above, drove the ink barrel and plastic pieces into the crack as tightly as he could, stood against the door, and dropped straight down. He was found semi-conscious a few minutes later. Edema from a fractured larynx had already closed most of his windpipe, forcing EMTs to do an on-the-spot tracheotomy. He was taken under guard to San Francisco General, treated, and taken to a room two floors below George Laine.

Chapter 48

On Friday, November 12, Constance, Rebecca, and Philip approached Courtroom 8 in the San Mateo courthouse. It was one of the smallest courtrooms, seating strictly limited. A guard stopped them at the door, but when Constance told him they were members of the defendant's immediate family, they were admitted. Another guard offered them a seat in the front row immediately behind the defendant's table. They declined, saying instead they preferred to sit in the back, immediately next to the door. They were quickly seated, followed by an enormous number of reporters, lawyers, law clerks, and others involved with Alfred and the California court system over the years.

There was no jury since this was a hearing and decisions were all in the hands of the judge. Alfred sat at the defendant's table with Mr. Berkowitz and Ms. Brunner. He did not turn around as the room filled. The judge entered and sat down so quickly that the audience hardly had time to rise and be seated. The clerk announced the case. The judge smacked his gavel and told the prosecuting attorney, Ernest Helms, to proceed with his introductory remarks.

Helms began by saying that he would outline the evidence against the defendant, starting with reference to the petition filed by Mr. Berkowitz demanding the prosecution reveal everything it intended to use in support of its accusations. In particular, he said he would address what the defense termed "possible sources and other informants not otherwise mentioned."

"Obviously, Your Honor, Mr. Berkowitz is asking for two things, starting with any evidence we used *after* sharing what was already in hand—a reasonable request. We have two documents for their review. It shouldn't take more than a half-hour to read both.

"More to the point, however, the defense wants to know if there is evidence we used to build the case, but for whatever reason has not been formally declared. To put it more succinctly—are you hiding something from us that we should have a right to see?"

Berkowitz thought Helms was being suspiciously transparent, but did not object.

Helms continued, saying the prosecution hoped the court would review and accept the two new documents in evidence. In addition, the prosecution was asking the court to accept evidence that was previously known but not used to support the current charges.

"Aha!" said Berkowitz.

The judge ignored the exclamation, but asked what that evidence was and how the defense could prove it had not considered it in bringing charges against Judge Preston.

"Our case against the defendant is based firmly on forensic evidence showing the defendant lied repeatedly about the alleged attack. We don't need anything else to prove the charges. If the court accepts the two documents I just mentioned, we can add motive to the fact the judge lied. And if the court also accepts the as-yet unused evidence, the current crimes will be plainly seen in context of other, more serious crimes.

"There is no jury here, so I can ask, what 'other crimes' are you referring to?"

Then Helms dropped the bombshell, revealing the prosecution was about to bring new charges against Judge Alfred Preston, charges that included bribing law enforcement officers and conspiracy to commit murder.

There was an audible gasp in the courtroom. Alfred sat bolt upright, pushed his chair back as if he was about to leap to his feet, but stopped when Berkowitz grabbed his arm. Rebecca put her hands over her face. Philip put his arm around her shoulders. Constance stared straight ahead.

The judge held up his hand, demanded silence, looked at the prosecutor, and said, "New charges are not the same as evidence in the current case, Mr. Helms. I'm sure you realize that. So, beyond the two new documents already on the table, what is this new evidence you want to introduce?"

"Your Honor, when George Laine went to Judge Preston's house, he was wearing a recording device. That device was recovered in the emergency room after he was shot, its provenance carefully documented from the moment it was discovered. We request that you listen to the recording and render a decision about its admissibility."

While the judge tried to pound the room into submission, Alfred could be heard over the din repeatedly saying to Berkowitz, "It's bullshit!" and the lawyer telling him to keep quiet. When the room finally settled down, the judge said that assuming the prosecution had the recording and was prepared to play it, he would listen to it in his chambers with the three lawyers present. He also said his decision would be final, and the hearing would immediately resume with or without the new material.

The judge told everyone in the courtroom to remain seated, "And that goes for any reporters, too. No one leaves until I say so." The three men and Ms. Brunner retreated to the judge's chambers.

Constance, Rebecca, and Philip sat stone still. Rebecca took deep breaths to quell intense feelings of nausea, Constance tried unsuccessfully to fight back tears, and Philip simply looked lost.

In his chambers, an IT technician set up the playing device, pressed the start button, and left. The judge and lawyers listened in silence as the recording played. When it was over, the silence persisted.

"Dear God," said Berkowitz. More silence. Finally, the judge said he was inclined to allow the recording to be used in evidence as long as the defense had a copy, and it was understood that individual parts could still be challenged. Asked if he objected, Mr. Berkowitz said, simply, "I have to talk to my client, Judge.

And I would certainly reserve the right to challenge anything that wasn't really clear, or we felt amounted to entrapment."

Back in court, the judge announced that the court would accept the recording in evidence subject to an examination of its provenance. Defense also had the right to challenge specific parts of the recording. He adjourned the proceedings until the following Monday and accepted the prosecution's request that the defendant be held without bail pending the outcome of the hearing.

Judge Preston initially resisted being taken away, demanding loudly that he be allowed to talk to his lawyer. The two escorting officers ignored him, placed handcuffs on his wrists behind his back, and summarily dragged him out of the room. Sheldon Berkowitz and Harriet Brunner sat at the defendant's table staring at their hands while waiting for the room to clear.

Constance, Rebecca, and Philip were the first to leave, followed by a wave of reporters. They put their heads down, got to their car, and drove off. They only spoke to each other in fragments on the ride home, lost as they were in private worlds of pain and question marks.

Rebecca kept saying over and over, "I can't believe it, I just can't believe it! Daddy! How can it be, Mom?!"

Philip drove, every few minutes saying, "I don't know," in helpless response to his wife's confusion.

Like Philip, Constance offered random weak reassurance, her mind lost in images of George, on what he had gone through.

Alfred was taken through a long hallway to the adjacent jail where he was processed. Thirty minutes after leaving the courtroom, he sat alone in a cell dressed in an orange jumpsuit with paper slippers for shoes. His only possessions were a pen and notebook, a kit containing a towel, soap, toothbrush, small tube of toothpaste, and a pamphlet describing rules, meal times, and prisoner rights. Preston's fury had died down, replaced by a combination of dread and helplessness.

He thought about Connie and Rebecca, but their voices were fading. Even the image of Laine, usually such an energizing source of anger, couldn't displace the feeling of impenetrable gloom. *Maybe this is how people feel when they're told they have cancer,* he thought. *No, people don't hate you for having cancer, they support you, and they love you more than ever.* The sound of someone laughing seeped through the steel door. He looked at the door, at the tears rolling off the back of his hands, falling deeper down the well toward the black water below.

The press was in an uproar over the tantalizing notion there could be an actual recording of the assault on Judge Preston. With the speed of a cobra turning on its charmer, the buzz was suddenly all about clever police work possibly bringing down a lofty judge.

For Constance and Rebecca, there was no comfort in the emerging revelations about Alfred—husband, father, exemplar of virtue. Far from it—disillusionment was pushing their pain to new levels, deepening the seemingly impossible task of rebuilding trust in their own judgment. It did help to know Laine was clearly gaining ground, and while it was nearly certain he would continue to be isolated and returned to prison, there was at least some emerging reason to think even that monstrosity could be overcome. Everything beyond was a mystery.

Sheldon Berkowitz and Harriet Brunner worked late into the night trying to plan the best way forward with Alfred Preston's defense. Yes, they could challenge the recording, but if the prosecution had all the evidence they described, it would make little difference. The real problem for the two attorneys was one of honor. How could they honor their professional responsibility to advocate for their client when it was beyond obvious that he was lying to them? What about their personal integrity? Could they cooperate with the deception in either realm? Even without the recording, it was clear Preston was guilty of lying repeatedly about the supposed attack at his house. They had every reason to believe, even without the tape, that Alfred Preston and his cronies created the image of Laine as vicious killer to justify their own behavior. They knew that if a jury heard any part of the recording, they would convict the judge of at least manslaughter.

Add to all of that the inevitable evidence from financial records that would almost certainly show the judge had made payments to Dalton, and from Dalton, a pathway to Metzi Arino and Carlos Zópilo. What else could they argue? Insanity? Hardly. All of it combined meant there was simply no way for Preston to survive.

For Berkowitz and Brunner, it all came down to knowing with absolute certainty that Preston was guilty. Unless the defendant could provide some other plausible explanation for his behavior, they felt they had a moral obligation to recommend he plead his case and let them try to get the best sentencing arrangement possible. Otherwise, they would have to recommend he get new counsel.

At nine o'clock on Saturday morning, Berkowitz was seated in a small cell-like room in the jail waiting to talk with his client. He was not allowed to keep his cup of coffee, compounding the oppressive feeling of fatigue and apprehension over how he would handle his interview with the judge. After a short delay, Preston was ushered in, hands cuffed in front, and politely told to sit and remain seated during the interview. A camera mounted on the wall behind the attorney's seat allowed the meeting to be observed but not overheard.

"I know it will sound hollow to say, 'good morning,' Judge, and I want to apologize for the way the hearing ended. I had no idea it would turn out…"

"Don't worry. I don't blame you. No one saw it coming. Of course, I've been thinking about nothing else, so please, let's get right to it. What's your read on this? Be straight up with me."

"Thanks. I'll start with what I know, then what your options are."

Alfred nodded, showing none of the anger or bluster the lawyer feared he would face. Alfred's face was expressionless, his voice flat, seemingly more resigned than apprehensive.

"For starters: clearly, Mr. Helms knew he had a major problem on his hands bringing the recording into evidence. He cleverly made the point that the current charges stand even if the recording is rejected. There's little we can do with that. He also did a good job of manipulating the judge into listening to the recording. He took a chance, but it worked."

"You didn't object. You could have cut it off at that point," Alfred said matter-of-factly.

"I doubt it. To sustain the objection, the judge would almost certainly have to hear the recording first. My hope was it would sink itself; you know, most wire recordings are nearly impossible to make out. I expected the sound to be too poor to trust, so defective or vague or disjointed or something else that I could have ended it right there. The trouble is, the recording is quite clear, especially at the end when you shot Laine. You can be heard—I hate to say it—gloating after he went down. There is also some very troubling back-and-forth about the murder of Julia...umm..."

"Penthoser."

"Right, Penthoser. You basically confess to killing her, and framing George Laine for the crime. You also incriminate Dalton, Arino, and Zópilo...And it's clear you had a hand in the death of the Marren woman. I hate to say it so bluntly, Judge, but that tape is devastating."

Alfred again nodded but didn't answer. He stared at his hands, seemingly in another thought world.

Berkowitz went on. "In the beginning of the tape it sounded like you thought Laine was wearing a wire, right?"

"Yeah, I saw he was wearing a wire. I made him take it off. He obviously had a second one. I didn't think of that. Stupid of me."

"What happened to the device?"

"I destroyed it in case there was a search warrant."

"I have to ask you at this point, even though you haven't heard the recording, is there is anything you have to say about it? Any point you want to make? Something I may be missing?"

"There are parts we could challenge, but if the court accepts it in evidence, and it's as clear as you say, then, no, there's nothing I can say that anyone would understand."

"What do you mean? What are you referring to?"

"When a jury hears it, they'll see me as pure evil, someone who delights in crime. Maybe it looks that way on the outside; inside it's a completely different story."

"I'm not sure I understand."

"Well, take the part about Julia, about what happened that night. I didn't just march in and kill her for the fun of it. It sounds crazy now, but I had a really bad problem in those days, feelings that got the better of me, something I couldn't control. When we were at the end of the party, I felt really attracted to her. But what undid me was the thought she felt the same way, that she wanted me to take her home. But when George said he would take her, and she accepted, something went off inside of me. It took over. I left the party, went to her place, and waited until Laine brought her back. Then I went up to her apartment, knocked on the door, and when she opened it, just for an instant she seemed to think it was George coming back for some reason. But when she saw it was me, she got really defensive. I pushed in and told her I wanted to see her, be with her. She freaked out and started to scream. I grabbed her to shut her up, and somehow that…somehow…before I realized it, I had raped her, she was dead, and I had to get out. I took her panties, and a few other things to make it look like a burglary gone wrong. I got rid of the other stuff, but I held onto the panties. It was all an impulse; I just couldn't stop myself.

"Then the shit hit the fan—the cops were everywhere, questioning all of us. I got scared they'd find my juvenile record, so I planted the panties in George's storage locker. It was in their basement, no big secret, not even a lock on the wire door. George was the last person to see her alive, a seemingly bland guy with martial arts skill, so when the cops found the panties, they arrested George, and I got my father to defend I him."

"Did your father know the truth, that he was really defending you?"

"Yeah, he knew. He'd helped me out of a lot of other bad situations, but nothing like this. This time, he played it like he didn't know, not so much for me, really. It was for Mom. He couldn't stand knowing what it would do to her if she ever knew the truth.

"But here's the important part. I know what's coming for me, and I don't have the right to ask, but could you please keep this part to yourself? It isn't necessary for anyone to know; it won't make me any guiltier. I just want to get this over with, no digging into my motives or what's been in my head. Just 'guilty.' That's it. People can think what they like, but just let the rest of it disappear with me. It's all I ask."

"Okay, Judge, I'll make that promise, but you'll have to trust me with more of what you're talking about. I can't protect what I don't know. As long as it isn't something material, I promise not to reveal anything you tell me. I won't take notes, either. Go ahead."

"Okay, well, the truth is I was attracted to George's wife, Connie."

"Jesus, Judge!"

"Yeah, I know it sounds crazy, especially after what I just said about Julia. But it's true. And after George was locked up, I was convinced I could make her love me, too. Usually, when I was around women I found attractive I had, well, call them 'bad ideas.' But Connie was different. For some reason, I had a lot of respect for her—admiration—a woman who didn't automatically trigger thoughts I had to fight. I really did want to be her husband and Rebecca's father. I know it's sick, I get that, even then I knew it was beyond wrong, but I still did everything I could to make it happen. Dad was easy to manipulate, and Mom was crazy about Connie and Rebecca. I did everything I could to at least look like a caring person. But over time, it went from an act to something that actually felt normal. It worked, and eventually I got her to marry me.

"I thought I'd changed, that somehow Connie had an effect on me that made the rage easier to handle, that maybe it would even go away completely. I'd struggled with it ever since I was a kid, always looking at girls thinking I wanted to have them, dominate them. Sometimes I just couldn't control myself—I did terrible things. If Dad hadn't been there, I would have been in jail when I was fifteen. But with Connie, it was different. I thought she changed me. Trouble is, over time I began to see it was a lie. I hadn't really changed at all. I was just an actor playing the part of a husband, father, and judge. As long as I played my part, everything went along pretty well. She didn't have any idea what was happening inside me, and I was still able to control myself for the first time in my lousy life."

"Hold it a minute, Judge," Berkowitz said raising his hand. "A big part of me wants to tell you to shut up; this is making me sick. But I have to ask about Connie. She seems too smart to be fooled. Your 'act,' as you put it, couldn't have been good enough to hide the truth from her for very long. What am I missing?"

"Yeah, you're right. But what you can't know—or even imagine—was what the trial and whole long process of being unable to stop the execution did to her mentally. She was in perpetual shock, reduced to rubble. She could barely function. My parents and I were the only support she had. She was helpless, vulnerable, and I took advantage of it. I took a sabbatical from law school in the fall of 1959 so I could devote all my time to helping Connie."

"At the same time you and your father were making sure it happened, right?"

"Yeah, true."

"This is really hard to listen to, Judge."

"Hang on, please let me finish."

Berkowitz nodded.

"We got through the execution time, George was totally isolated, and after a couple of months, I stopped holding my breath, went back to law school knowing I had a couple of years before the stay played out, and with execution there was the slim possibility it could show up in the papers. I either had to drop Connie and get away or figure out how to get both of us away until he really was executed. I was trying to get Connie to marry me, but she still couldn't quite accept the idea of a new life somewhere. Then I caught a really lucky break.

"Back in the summer of 1958, I helped George apply for a patent on a cleaning solvent he invented. When he went to prison, he signed over all of his property to Connie, including rights to the patent on the off chance it was granted and had some value. The patent came through in the winter of 1961, and a guy from Texas Instruments who was starting a new company building mother boards offered to buy it. Connie needed money and was willing to sell it, thinking maybe she'd get a few thousand for it, something she could send to her parents back in Indiana. They were in desperate shape, and it always weighed on her that she wasn't able to help them. I told Connie I would negotiate for her, but the best I could do was 75K, a lot of money, but it hit me that if she got a lot more, maybe it would turn her thinking, free her up and see me in a brighter light. So I went to Dad, got him to add another 125K, and sold it to the guy for seventy-five grand, but told Connie she got two hundred thousand.

"It had a galvanic effect on her. She immediately saw it as a gift from George, like a message telling her to take the money and use it to help her parents. She suddenly started to imagine a new life, agreed to marry me if I would move with her and Rebecca to Indiana. Of course, I agreed. We got married, moved to Terre Haute, I took a job doing scutwork law, and Connie used her money to move her parents into a retirement home. Rebecca thrived, Connie suddenly felt she had a purpose, and we were actually quite happy. After her father died, we decided to move back to California, so I could join Dad's law firm and Rebecca could go to really good schools. It all worked perfectly. I was happy with Connie—she did her charity work, was a great mother for Rebecca, and I was able to control myself. That is until George broke out of his grave and destroyed everything."

"So it was all built on lies. You actually *bought* your wife, right? And after George was in general population, you could move home without any fear of the truth coming out, right again?"

"Yeah. I know Connie will hate me for betraying her, but I hope she'll never know what I *really* did to her, how I manipulated her into marrying me, and later, how I used her to invent Judge Preston." He stopped, lifted his cuffed hands and said, "Now look at me."

"If you'd just left him alone…"

"Yeah, but I was running on hate; plus, I wasn't going to take any chances. I got away with it before I had money and power. What was going to stop me now? George had nothing. His freedom wasn't worth ten cents. It should have been easy. What could he do to me?"

"This is a lot to digest, Judge, but I think I understand. What I hear you saying is you will plead guilty, and my job is to do the best I can with it, even though 'the best' won't be anything less than awful."

"That's right. I only ask you to keep me off death row, keep me from having to talk about any of this in open court, and get it done with as soon as you can."

With that, the interview was over. Berkowitz was reeling when he got back to his office to meet with his associate. He recounted what Preston had told him, minus the part about marrying Laine's wife and the other bizarre twists in his thinking. Together they decided to approach the prosecution with a simple deal—confession in exchange for a life sentence. Berkowitz returned to the jail and presented their recommendation to Judge Preston. He initially resisted any mention of the Penthoser murder, but under pressure, he agreed to confess to that, too—as long as no details were discussed. Berkowitz knew that including the Penthoser confession would be important from the prosecutor's point of view because it would allow a court to reverse George Laine's murder conviction. The plea agreement also accepted charges of attempted second degree murder, accessory to murder, and lying to police. Judge Preston agreed to testify against Dalton and the two policemen if necessary and waived all appeal rights.

He signed the plea document, it was notarized, and he was returned to his cell.

Chapter 49

Tony called late Saturday afternoon. "I didn't want to call you right after the hearing; you had to be reeling after learning about the recording…"

"It was awful, Tony, you can't imagine what that was like."

"Yes, I can. I saw you. You all seemed incredibly brave, especially during the time the judge was listening to the recording and people were staring at you."

"You *saw* us? You were there?!"

"Yes. A friend of mine, a reporter, got me some press credentials. I couldn't stay away. I knew George was wearing two wires, but I had no idea if either one had survived."

"That's the 'other information' you couldn't talk about?"

"Yeah. It was killing me. I wanted to say, 'But there's a recording!' but I didn't really know. My sources couldn't get anywhere near the DA and his group."

"Why, Tony? Why did George wear a recorder? I can't see George trying to get Alfred arrested—it doesn't fit."

"No. As I told you, I kept trying to get George out of the area, and he was willing as long as he first had the chance to confront Alfred. That's all he wanted—to look him in the eye and say, 'I know what you did.' That was George's sense of justice. He wanted to say it, leave, and start a new life somewhere else. The recording was his insurance against Alfred ever going after him. It was a card he wanted to hold and never play."

"Thank you, Tony, that makes complete sense to me. Tell me, when this is over, assuming George is free, do you think he'll want to be with us again? Do you have any idea? My biggest dread, now that it looks like some sort of end is near, is that George will keep thinking he still has to stay out of our life, that his mindset is so entrenched, or his emotions so ruined, that he will feel he has to live out his life in a new prison. I couldn't bear it, Tony," she said, sobbing.

"Prison has not destroyed his love for you and Rebecca. Just give it time, and I am sure—no! make that *positive*—we'll all have lunch together some Sunday afternoon. Clams with white sauce on linguine."

"Oh, God! His favorite. You *really* do know George!"

Chapter 50

MONDAY'S HEARING WAS CANCELED; NEGOTIATIONS with the prosecution were completed and presented to the court the following Wednesday. On Friday, the presiding judge announced acceptance of the deal mandating a sentence of life without the chance of parole. Judge Preston would be allowed to offer an apology but not compelled to give testimony. Formal sentencing was set for one month.

The circuit court reversed what it termed the "shameful" court order, though the ruling had no immediate effect on Laine or his isolation. Ironically, the only way Laine would be allowed a visit from Constance would be if he was back in prison. A week later, Laine was transported by ambulance back to San Quentin. Warden Thompson accompanied Laine to the prison hospital, bypassing the reception area. It was clear to everyone that his return was technical and that reversal of his confinement would be prompt, either from a court lifting his parole violation status, or outright reversal of his conviction, once Preston was formally sentenced. That process had already been initiated by the San Francisco DA. With the reversal of the court order, Laine would be allowed his first visit in just six days.

On that day, Laine was taken by wheelchair to the visiting area, not because he couldn't walk, but because he would otherwise have to be handcuffed, and the warden was determined that would not happen.

There were perhaps fifty inmates and visitors in the common area when the door opened and Laine walked in. He instantly saw Constance and walked toward her. They stood briefly looking at each other, opened their arms, and folded together, an embrace that lasted a full two minutes before they slowly separated and sat down at a small table.

"I don't know where to start, George."

"Where we left off, I think."

They talked; they hugged, all in slow motion, savoring each moment. George asked about Rebecca and Erik, and was promised a visit from both, "If we don't get you out of here first."

Finally, Constance said what she had rehearsed, the only part she dreaded asking. "Where do we go from here, George? Will you let me take you home, or is that asking too much? I simply can't imagine what must be going on in your head right now, what you are thinking about me, or what's next. I certainly don't want to crowd you. It's really selfish of me, but I have to ask."

"Yes, I accept. The last time it was you who said that, but I doubt…"

"I remember it. I've never forgotten that moment. And in all the years, I thought you were gone—forever gone—I never stopped saying it to myself."

The meeting ended as it began—with a long hug. This time, though, there would be another visit, possibly one that wouldn't end.

On Monday, December 20, 2010, Judge Alfred Preston appeared in court for sentencing. He made a brief statement of regret for his crimes, apologized to his many victims, and said he was ready to accept his punishment. Before sentencing, the judge said that while he was staggered by the enormity of the defendant's deception and the incalculable devastation caused by his crimes, he simply lacked the words to say more. "The horror you caused speaks for itself." A sentence of life in prison without chance of parole was handed down, and Preston was sent back to jail to await transport to San Quentin.

Formal sentencing triggered a series of legal moves on behalf of George Laine, starting with a request for immediate release from confinement pending formal reversal of his conviction.

On Wednesday, December 22, Warden Thompson again said goodbye to George as he boarded the bus to Stonebridge House.

Approaching the prison exit gate, the bus paused to allow an entering sheriff's car to clear the gate. As the car inched past the guard post, Laine looked down and saw Alfred Preston crumpled against the door in the back seat. As the car moved forward, he glanced up. Their eyes met for a second as the bus started to move.

The gate to Stonebridge House swung open. The bus moved around the circle, stopping at the bottom of the stairs. Mrs. Lender stood on the porch looking down as eight prisoners got out and were directed up the steps. George was the last to get off. The bus moved away as he approached the steps.

"Not this time, Mr. Laine," Mrs. Lender said pointing to a car behind the bus. "Good luck."

Rebecca got out of the back seat, opened the front door, and said, "Your ride's here, Dad."

George gave her a hug, settled into the front seat, and as he connected his seatbelt, he looked at Constance and asked, "Where are we headed?"

"Home," she said. "We're finally going home, George."

The car eased down the driveway and out the gate toward the highway.

Epilogue

Cowboy's trip to Falstaff lasted ten days. At first, he stayed in a motel, but when his money gave out, his brother and sister-in-law insisted he stay with them. Before he left, he and his brother promised they would stay in touch and never let another year go by without a visit.

The Madrid Hotel was sold, the new owners determined to erase its reputation as a dangerous crime pit. John Zwick was fired, his whorehouse closed, and all of the rooms were renovated. Even the elevator worked. Cowboy was given a room on the second floor.

It took more than a year, but María Santaella received her green card. She immediately went to work at an area health clinic serving immigrants—documented or not. At Mass every Sunday, she prayed for the man who gave her the gift of freedom, asking the Blessed Mother to give him special protection in this life and the next.

After giving testimony in Metzi Arino's trial, Minouche LaHoy left the area. Her current whereabouts are unknown.

Carlos Zópilo's confession and plea bargain were accepted by the court. He was given a thirty-year sentence for manslaughter and accepting bribes.

Metzi Arino was convicted of seven counts of conspiracy, dereliction of duty, and taking bribes. He was given twenty-six years. Two years into his sentence, he was stabbed to death during a prison riot. No one was charged.

Edward Dalton recovered from his suicide attempt, but the emergence of florid psychosis unresponsive to medication mandated transfer to the forensic unit of a state psychiatric hospital. His trial has been put on hold until he recovers sufficiently to participate in his defense. That has yet to happen.

Following Judge Preston's conviction, Captain Henderson retired. He was replaced by his deputy who immediately hired Aella Tomaras as his assistant.

Alfred Preston was admitted to a secure unit at San Quentin, one reserved for former police, some pedophiles, and others deemed too vulnerable to be housed with general population prisoners. While generally cooperative with staff, he rarely spoke, especially to other inmates. His health deteriorated rapidly, forcing permanent transfer to the prison hospital. His previously mild diabetes accelerated, kidney function deteriorated, and he suffered a series of increasingly debilitating strokes. He lost the ability walk, speak clearly, or even feed himself. He died in his sleep one year and three days after his conviction. No one claimed the body, so it was sent to the prison's contract mortuary for cremation and "disposal." After the ashes cooled down, the mortician put them in his car and, on the way home, dumped them in Draper Creek, just below the paper mill. The State of California paid Hudson and Gallant Mortuary $422 for Cremation and $134 for Disposal Services.

George and Constance moved to a small town near Scotts Valley. They see Rebecca and her family frequently, and spend a lot of time slowly walking in the Santa Cruz foothills, or simply sitting on the porch of their cottage, talking. They often have lunch with Tony and Claire. George visits Leroy regularly, and has been working with his family to press a judicial review of his conviction and sentence.

Erik is now playing third saxophone in his high school orchestra. He is trying to decide on college, and beyond that, a career either in law or music. George recommends music.

About the Author

LIKE SOMEONE GROWING UP IN a bilingual home, Philip Hirsh's formative years were divided between two worlds, one in northern New Jersey and the other in the Alleghany Mountains on the western edge of Virginia. He was educated at Phillips Academy Andover, Yale University, and Jefferson Medical College. After a residency in psychiatry at Georgetown University Hospital and two years in the U.S. Army Medical Corps, he began working in forensics with both adult and child offenders.

He used that experience to write his first book, *When Evil Isn't Enough*, a New York City crime story about psychopaths flourishing on both sides of the law. Drawing from his Appalachian memories, he wrote *Voices From the Hollow*, stories about Appalachian people, their culture, and durable values. *Voices* was a finalist in *Foreword* magazine's short story Book of the Year award in 2006. Hirsh's third book, *The Lost Tarpon*, is a collection of short stories, some bemused, some lacerating, all taking a fanciful look at just how soft conventional morality really is. *Surviving Justice* explores the possibility of measuring justice without using any of the standard tools of law enforcement or the courts. *Surviving Justice* bridges the space between physical and spiritual power, a tool like no other, useless in vengeful hands, but unstoppable when deployed in harmony with the purity of natural law.

Dr. Hirsh is retired. He and his wife live on the eastern shore of Maryland.